Scarlett Penrose

Theresa-Marie Smith

Grosvenor House
Publishing Limited

This book is published by
Grosvenor House Publishing Ltd
Link House
140 The Broadway, Tolworth, Surrey, KT6 7HT.
www.grosvenorhousepublishing.co.uk

A CIP record for this book
is available from the British Library

ISBN 978-1-83975-122-6

Prologue

Scarlett Penrose is set at a time when strangers in Looe were viewed with suspicion and mistrust. Wary Cornish locals treat newcomers as outsiders. And even though Scarlett has lived in West Looe for some while and attends Miss Clementine's academy she is still an outsider. An outsider with a secret. At the academy Scarlett has made one good friend Ruth Jago, and as she approaches the time to leave this establishment and look for employment Scarlett finds herself attracted to Ruth's older brother Jack and he with her. Will she be able to keep the past away from spoiling the future.

Introduction

In the eighteenth century Looe was a typical Cornish fishing village. With both East and West Looe reliant on smuggling to help them survive. A time when revenue officers and their informers, were hated throughout the County. And even now when you walk through the narrow streets at the dead of night, or stand looking out to sea, with rays of moonlight shining down upon Looe Island and the coast and coves nearby. You feel the past and present become one and set free your imagination. I have had this feeling and it sowed the seeds of my writing Scarlett Penrose.

Chapter 1

Fourteen young ladies from Miss Clementine's small academy in West Looe set off in pairs following the said lady down Horse Lane and onto the quay. Briskly they made their way towards the tiny church of St Nicholas, here to say their weekly prayers for the school's benefactor Sir Geoffrey Polgrove.

The last two girls, Scarlett Penrose and Ruth Jago, straggled behind arm in arm giggling as they watched Miss Clementine's straight back descending the hill. They passed Ruth's humble cottage at the bottom of the lane, and both girls gave her youngest sister a wave as she sat barefoot on the cobbles outside. To Scarlett's disappointment there was no sign of Ruth's handsome brother Jack.

Ruth was only able to attend the school because her father, Tom Jago, had saved Sir Geoffrey's life when the schooner *Tamar* floundered off Black Rock. Unfortunately, most of the men aboard had drowned. Sir Geoffrey was one of the lucky ones. Tom Jago had hauled him out of the sea and into his boat, there to lie in an undignified heap, thankful for his life.

Sir Geoffrey was a great believer in education, so the two eldest Jago children, Jack and his sister Ruth, had been schooled at Sir Geoffrey's expense as a measure of gratitude. Not that Ruth's brother had made any use of his learning, brilliant scholar though he was. Jack had left the nearby boys academy and joined the crew of a Looe lugger as soon as he was old enough, and indeed brave enough to face Sir Geoffrey's anger. Scarlett Penrose attended Miss Clementine's by annual subscription paid for by her father.

Once down on the quay it was busy, the tide was up and as many as three boats deep were tied in together alongside one another. The stone cobbled harbour was crowded. Seagulls screeched overhead as lobster pots and baskets of fish were passed hand to hand and brought ashore, there to be stacked onto all manner of carts, or carried away to the fish cellars, some to be smoked in the cluster of huts nearby. The smell of the river mingled with that of the freshly caught fish. As was usual, a group of ragtag sailors lolled about on benches outside the Jolly Sailor drinking ale, they nudged each other and watched the approaching young ladies with much appreciation.

Miss Clementine stood impatiently waiting at the bottom of the church steps, hurrying her girls along, displeased by the admiring whistles and other sounds of approval aimed at her older girls, maybe even herself. Her face flushed crimson with embarrassment at the thought. It was always a relief when she ushered the last of her young ladies into the tiny church, today was no exception.

After the service the girls were dismissed and went their separate ways, some had chaperones to meet them, but Scarlett left with Ruth and walked a short while before saying farewell in Princes Square. Reluctantly, Scarlett set off up West Looe Hill heading for the near top and 'Tamarisk' a dwelling larger than the humble cottage where Ruth lived. But not a happy place.

Today the steep hill seemed never-ending, and as Scarlett trudged on, she wished she had a home like Ruth's. The Jagos may be poor, but Ruth had a warm family, and surely no secret that lay in her heart like lead as she herself did. A secret so terrible it could never be revealed.

Scarlett wasn't sure her parents knew just how much she could remember of what happened back then; it was never ever spoken about. But she did remember, still had nightmares about the jeering crowd of villagers that had surrounded their cottage in Sennen Cove. The loud shouting and hate-filled accusations spat from their mouths was vicious and frightening. She'd stood holding onto her mother, who desperately tried to comfort her frightened child. Even friends she'd played with the day before joined in. Polly Carbis, her very best friend, had aimed rotten fruit at their windows until at last customs officers and soldiers had come to their rescue. How they knew the peril they were in she didn't know, only that they dispersed the angry mob and escorted her mother and herself on horseback away from Sennen Cove.

Her father had escaped all of that and was waiting stony-faced to greet them when the revenue cutter they were on arrived in Plymouth. Her father offered no help as they ascended the steep granite steps and were hurried along the harbour arm. Scarlett had chanced to look back, upset to see the look of loathing on the faces of men watching, an old vagrant seated on a wooden box spat in their direction, a great lump of phlegm glinted in the morning sun. Back then, she was too young to fully understand why she sensed such hatred.

Afterwards, in an isolated cottage beside the Tamar, Scarlett had lived a solitary life with her mother, her father's long absences from home a relief to both mother and daughter. Scarlett's mother had tutored her well, for she was not without learning. For a long while their lives had been untouched by further drama. But all that had ended now. Her father had been posted here to West Looe and had ordered her mother accompany him along with their daughter. No amount of protest on her mother's part would change this demand. Before they left, Scarlett had been firmly instructed day upon day that no word of what had happened at Sennen must she speak, no one must know their past beyond that they'd lived beside the Tamar.

They had settled here in West Looe, her mother a near broken woman since Elijah her father was more often home, constantly berating her with harsh words and worse. Her poor mother tried hard to hide the bruises he inflicted. Scarlett was older now, she knew the cruelty her mother suffered and would have spoken out to her father about it, but her mother would hear of no such thing, worried for her precious daughter's safety.

As Scarlett lifted the latch of Tamarisk Cottage and entered, her heart sank; her father was home. The heated conversation her parents were having abruptly stopped, and closing the door with downcast eyes Scarlett walked over and sat on the settle beside the range. Elijah gave her no manner of greeting but beckoned to his wife, they withdrew to the small room to one side of the parlour and continued to argue.

In that room set out on a large oak desk lay all the equipment for map-making but none of it was ever used. Scarlett knew her father's occupation told to all who enquired was a falsehood, a lie. Why this deceit was necessary chilled her to the bone as she remembered the hatred in the eyes of the good folks of Sennen. He was a spy for the revenue.

'There's something I don't like about them new people up the hill,' Mary Jago said to her daughter Ruth that night. 'That maid's mother keeps to herself and hardly passes the time of day with Annie Bishop she shares the well with, just a nod of the head that's all she gives old Annie and off back indoors she hurries. Buys nought from old Billy Barnes and im heaving that barrow of his up the hill an all, just for Annie and a few others further up. Walks down the hill and buys in the Harms's and them much more expensive than old Billy. I seen the husband riding off this morning with a lot of stuff strapped to his horse, map making Scarlett said he did, for I questioned her the other week, seems he works for thems that own mines. But queer folk they be so be careful, our Ruthie, keep what you says guarded till we know more about them.'

'But Scarlett seems really nice, Ma.'

'Just remember what I've told you. Be sure to mind your words.' Mary wagged her finger to add meaning to her words.

It was then Jack came in followed by his younger brother Luke, Mary told both sons the same, and went on stirring the fish stew in a black pot over the open fire.

'Don't go on, Ma, the Keeper said the same yesterday, he's watching the goings-on up at Tamarisk, he'll miss nothing,' Jack replied, rubbing the flagstone floor with his boot making sure it was level.

'Thinking she's right comely does our Jack,' Luke jested, but their mother was not amused.

'Best not be so friendly with the girl once you leave Miss Clementine's at the end of the month, Ruthie, you'll be in service and no doubt you'll not see much of her.'

Ruth remained sullenly silent. She liked Scarlett.

The next day when Scarlett walked down West Looe Hill to school, she once again felt the scrutiny of an old man who sat on a rickety wooden bench outside his cottage mending nets. There was something rather frightening about the way he watched her. He wore a battered old hat and had a long grey beard with a sunken mouth that was never without his clay pipe, what Scarlett did notice though was how alert his eyes were, today they made her shudder as she hurried past.

'Who's the old man who sits outside his cottage opposite the Jolly Sailor, he frightens me staring like he does?'

'Oh! That, that's the...' Ruth faltered remembering her mother's words. 'That's just old Oggie, he's harmless.'

She laughed, and waiting til Miss Clementine's back was turned, threw an apple core across the room at Opal Tresco, sending her and Scarlett into fits of giggles.

Later that afternoon as the girls walked down Horse Lane, unbeknown to them a man sat astride his horse near the top of Bray Hill, both horse and rider were perfectly still, hidden behind dense trees. He watched the luggers with their accompanying chorus of gulls make their way into the mouth of the river and safety of the harbour. More interestingly, his eye fixed on the schooner *Raven* which having been turned was at present moored close to the mouth of the river. Here the quay narrowed and sloped downwards until it disappeared beneath the present high tide.

From his vantage point he could see the whole of West Looe quay, and for a moment his eyes fell upon the two girls, one girl in particular caught his eye as the sun glinted on her red hair, he'd seen her last year when visiting Elijah Penrose in his hideaway on the Tamar. Tonight, he'd see Elijah again, the daughter too he hoped, a malicious grin spread across his rugged face and he watched the girl more closely, a beauty indeed, her innocence ready for the taking.

On her way home that day, Scarlett had lingered in Princes Square with Ruth, they'd been larking about with Jack and Luke. Just being near Jack Jago brought a redness to her cheeks. Jack, with his twinkling eyes and roguish manner. He'd made them both laugh as he boasted, 'Truth be told, I had to hide earlier to escape the attentions of Opal Tresco.'

'I can't believe Opal would be interested in the likes of you,' Ruth had answered, and he'd gone off with a swanky walk, turning to grin at them from time to time, Luke striding along beside him.

Reluctantly Ruth had had to go home, she had chores to do for her mother, leaving Scarlett alone, that is until Jack reappeared.

'If I'm not to be the love of Opal's life, is some other maiden going to claim my heart?' he said, softly with a mischievous grin. He took her hand and led her to the narrow lane at the back of the Jolly Sailor.

Scarlett felt her cheeks burning. He stood now, one arm on the wall so close to her she could feel his breath on her face, his eyes searched hers and Scarlett made no move to leave.

For a moment it seemed he would lean forward and kiss her, she found herself so hoping he would, and then the spell was broken. The pot boy came, noisily pushing a barrow out from the side door of the Jolly Sailor and Ruth came back and sought them out. She gave Jack a questioning look before babbling on about tangled ropes and a tear in the *Alice*'s sail. Scarlett knew Luke's ketch was his pride and joy.

'Luke sent me to fetch you, tis in a right state he is.'

Jack gave Scarlett a reluctant smile and immediately set off towards where the *Alice* was tied up further along the quay towards the bridge. Ruth gave Scarlett a wave before she ran off after her brother. Scarlett trudged up West Looe Hill feeling quite alone.

She arrived home still trying to calm her burning cheeks, unbelievably happy for Jack had so nearly kissed her! Though her happiness quickly disappeared when her mother scolded her for being late, overwrought she shouted at Scarlett, 'Your father's coming home and bringing an important guest.'

Scarlett took a deep breath. It was pitiful to watch as her mother scrubbed the table for all she was worth, fussed over the mutton stew and stirred the vegetables cooking in pots over the fire, fussing and rechecking that all was in order, and all for a cruel man who treated her as a skivvy, not a wife.

She ignored Scarlett's pleas to help her. Terrified as usual there'd be something not to her husband's liking. Something he could scold her for.

'He came home earlier, strict instructions I've got, you must eat now then go straight to your room and to stay there. And no telling anyone nothing about this, not a soul, it's none of their business and I wish it wasn't ours.'

A short while later, with little enthusiasm Scarlett ate in silence as her mother, age-worn with work, scuttled here and there tidying the sparse contents within the cottage, terrified of her overbearing husband.

Scarlett finished eating; all thought of what had gone on previously that day gone. Except for the time alone with Jack.

'I'll fetch you in more water from the well before I go up,' she told her mother and picked up the wooden pail, lifted the latch and stepped out through the narrow doorway to the side of the cottage. As usual, she noticed Annie Bishop peeking out from between the thread-like curtains of her upstairs room. She was tempted to wave but instead felt sorry for the woman who had nothing better to do. She lowered the pail down the well and hauled it back up. Suddenly cold, she shivered and hurried inside.

Indeed, it was much to Annie's annoyance that Tamarisk Cottage stood back from the lane on an angle, which meant that she could only see the front of it and the well they shared to the side. From the back of Tamarisk ran a rough track that wound uphill from the stable to emerge further up the hill. Annie could see none of this, which being nosy she thought a great pity.

The tallow candle beside Scarlett's bed had long gone out before she heard voices in the room below. The creaking floorboards in her room meant it was impossible to go to the far corner to listen beside her door. Soon she heard her mother run upstairs and sobs coming from the room across the stairs. She felt it such a pity so gentle a soul had become the wife of such a cruel man. Scarlett recognised the voice of her father's guest, remembered the brutally hard-faced man who'd visited them before, she hadn't liked him. Suddenly from the room below came the sound of a fist banging down on that scrubbed table, and the man whose name she couldn't remember raising his voice until he bellowed out at her father in rage, 'Mark my words, Elijah, you will work hereabouts, bugger the twenty-one-mile rule. And believe me I'll have the skipper and crew of the *Raven* hanged if it's the last thing I do. Rules are made to be broken.'

'But Jeanette will worry the local folk will find out I'm a traitor as they did before,' her father shouted back. 'I don't want to put her or my daughter through what happened at Sennen again.'

'Not frightened of your wife are you, never took you for a skirt hugger. I've had word, Elijah, the *Black Diamond* another notorious smuggling ship has been spotted off Fowey. I'm counting on your help to catch these villains as they bring ashore their contraband. You will obey me on this, Elijah.' The table was thumped once more. 'You will.'

Scarlett sat up in bed scarcely breathing; the man's temper frightened her. Already she felt sympathy for the free traders; instinctively she felt the grip of fear, knew the terror of the past could be repeated. The disgrace and shame would be too much to bear. Thoughts of the terrifying vengeance the villagers may have carried out if they hadn't been rescued remained with her. Would they have become tired of just throwing fruit and calling them vile names? She remembered cowering in a corner as her mother frantically barricaded them in their cottage. She wished the man downstairs had never come here. It seemed a long time before she heard the door bang behind the beastly man when, finally, he left. But even then, she couldn't sleep and saw the dawn light appearing before she did.

By morning most of the fishing boats and the schooners had sailed on the early high tide. She heard from Ruth as they walked up Horse Lane that her father and Jack had signed up as crew on the *Raven*.

Scarlett knew better than to ask were the *Raven* was destined.

'Tis better money and the *Lucy*'s skipper, old Will, he'll take um back once they're home.'

'When will they be back?' Scarlett asked, she tried not to sound overly interested, knowing all too well there were secrets this tight community kept to themselves, had seen Jack easing a flagstone back into place when she'd come calling for Ruth one morning. Now the knowledge of what she'd overheard the night before lay heavy on her heart, she felt afraid for her friends. Twas the *Raven*'s crew her father's visitor sought to have hanged. Scarlett fell silent.

On waking that morning, she'd remembered the visitor's name, it was Robert Reader and he was a riding officer. She'd been a good eavesdropper long before they'd come to West Looe, had heard his name and what he was. He may be seeking the *Raven* and the *Black Diamond,* but Scarlett realised other customs officers alongside him would be ready to snare those unaware, these coastal waters were being so intently spied upon.

Ruth noticed how quiet she'd gone and laughed. 'What's your interest in our Jack, you smitten like Opal? Can't you wait for him to be back? Best not tell Opal, she'll be fighting with you over him.'

'No, silly, I was just wondering.' Scarlet blushed.

At the top of the lane they'd caught up with Opal and some of the others dawdling along before starting the day's schooling. Opal turned around and looked at Ruth.

'Your Jack's gone then so's me brother.' She smiled at Ruth, then pulled a face at Scarlett having overheard snippets of their conversation, for she herself had more than a little liking for Jack Jago.

'Wonder if it'll be like last time, mother's hoping so, me too.'

Ruth stared open eyed at Opal and sensing she'd said too much the girl turned back round, her cheeks flaming red. Scarlett felt uncomfortable, an outsider which in truth she still was, she'd didn't blame Ruth for shutting Opal up.

Annie Bishop made her way slowly down the West Looe Hill, she bought nothing from the market, but joined Oggie seated on his bench. Oggie touched his battered hat as a greeting. 'What's up, Annie, summat must have brought you all the way down ere?'

'Something and nothing really, truth be told. You knows I'm keeping me eye on them new folks. Well last night in Tamarisk there was candles lit downstairs best part of the night, funny that. Ever so quiet it was, and well around midnight I'm sure I heard the pounding of horse's hooves galloping up the back lane. Funny time for them to have visitors.'

'Keep watching, Annie.' Oggie drew on his pipe. 'I'll send young Mark up next week to have a word with you, tell im if you sees any more funny goings-on.'

With Oggie's help, Annie slowly rose to her feet.

'You want me to walk you back up?' he asked, but Annie firmly shook her head, her independent spirit not allowing her to give in, she'd been dependant on no man thus far in life and wasn't about to start now.

Oggie watched her slowly making her way home, stopping here and there to speak to them who knew her. When she was gone from sight, he pondered on what she'd said. Word had come that dragoons had been spotted in Polruan, which only meant one thing, probably not connect to the folks up the hill, newcomers though they were. In the past, before his replacement, Robert Reader always had dragoons ready and waiting for his orders, oft times in Polruan. Was the hated riding officer back?

Across the road in the Jolly Sailor, two men were seated in a secluded alcove where a small lattice window looked across to where Oggie sat. They were also talking of Robert Reader. Five years ago, he'd been posted between Saltash and Fowey, then by the grace of God he'd been posted further down the coast and even spotted lying low in a remote inn on the road to Port Isaac on the north coast. His replacement was lazy and not averse to bribery.

'Why's the bastard back in these parts, if word he is be true? That's what bothers me,' Seb queried. For now, we'm best call off all landings til we know for sure what's happening. Send Luke round to Polperro to tell Ginger, though I reckons they'd ave had word already.'

'Best warn the *Raven* when she's spotted off the coast on her return later this month,' Nathan whispered. Giving a furtive look as Ben the new pot boy walked past. Nathan's uncle and at least six other Looe men were abroad the *Raven*.

Seb drained his tankard dry. 'The *Raven* will be well laden and easy prey for Reader's cutters if he is back. The ruthless bastard has men killed just for killing's sake, he takes few prisoners and those he does are hanged. Not on Cornish soil but across the border.'

'I know,' Ben replied. 'One of them was my cousin.'

Chapter 2

In the days following the visitor to Tamarisk nothing dramatic happened, other than it was with a sad heart Scarlett neared her last week at Miss Clementine's Academy. Her mother had been sent for and discussions held as to what Scarlett would do once she left. Something Scarlett had begun to wonder about.

The Miss Catts who lived in Prospect House, which was not quite as grand as the name suggested, had requested Miss Clementine pay them a visit as they had a position one of her girls may be suitable for.

In truth, Miss Clementine, even after she'd met with the sisters, was unable to quite fathom out the exact duties required. The Miss Catts had a niece Hester, it seemed she visited them infrequently, but now she was older when staying at Prospect House she needed a companion who could also teach the basic subjects. When the girl wasn't there the employee would help their cook conduct general duties and deal with any guests in the manner of housekeeper. It was an odd position being offered and Miss Clementine was worried that whoever she placed there would be poorly used. She had thought of Opal, but Scarlett had a much more refined manner and more likely to be able to carry off the facade of housekeeper even though she was barely sixteen. The remuneration offered by the sisters was good. And what other employment was there for a girl not brought up like most around these parts to help with the gutting or smoking of fish. Scarlett's fees had been paid by her father without need of any support. Alas coming late to her academy, the girl had no languages, so a governess's position was out of the question.

Jeanette Penrose, Scarlett's mother, seemed a meek little woman who on talking to Miss Clementine had accepted the position on her daughter's behalf straight away. Almost too quickly Miss Clementine thought. But Jeanette Penrose knew Elijah her husband was away, she could for once make a decision about this herself. His involvement with Robert Reader bothered her greatly, the twenty-one-mile rule had given her comfort here in this county with its perilous roads and jagged shoreline, beyond that what her husband did seemed a long way away. But she was sure with Robert Reader's influence, Elijah could be persuaded to ignore this rule and work closer to home inside of the twenty-one-mile rule stated by law.

The position being offered by the Catt sisters meant Scarlett would remain living at home but live in when required and this she felt would suit both herself and Scarlett. For indeed, how empty her life would be without her. Jeanette Penrose prayed Scarlett would agree with what had been settled though nothing was certain, for Scarlett had to undergo an interview with the Miss Catts before the appointment would be confirmed.

Scarlett was not too keen when told by her mother what had been discussed. Ruth was going into service with Sir Geoffrey, not as a lowly kitchen maid where most girls started, but as a junior housemaid, she was to live in at Polgrove House and accepted her lot in life without complaint.

She on the other hand had misgivings about the Miss Catts. She often walked past Prospect House and it looked dark and rather scary, she was dreading the interview and only went because Miss Clementine had reassured her the sisters seemed good people and her mother had insisted she go.

A steep path followed by steps led down from the top of Horse Lane to the harbour. Scarlett turned left when she reached the quay and walked along beside the river. Her appointment was for three o'clock. Today was a particularly dismal day with a fine drizzle of rain, the dark clouds overhead made the house seem even more drab than usual. She raised the heavy iron door knocker and paused for a few seconds before letting it drop, she waited nervously biting her lip until the door was opened by the cook herself, her apron covered in flour.

'Thems ready for you, miss, come in out of the rain.'

She led Scarlett into a gloomy room with candles already lit. In two chairs placed one each side of the mantelpiece sat the Catt sisters both dressed in black, their grey hair plaited and twirled on top of their heads in a rather odd fashion, but their faces held welcoming smiles.

The sister sitting to the left of the mantelpiece motioned Scarlett to be seated on a chair positioned directly facing both sisters. This was all very formal and nothing like

Scarlett had somehow expected. Having sat down she almost jumped with fright when the same sister spoke.

'Miss Clementine has told us you are of good character, and I think my sister Emilia will agree when I say you look the kind of girl we desire to employ. Our niece will be here shortly and there are preparations to be made. She will need a companion of sorts. Her lessons too must not be neglected. You will teach her daily in all the subjects you are capable of, it's a great pity you have no languages, and alas I feel I must warn you she can be wilful, spoilt you see by her father after the death of her mother. She—'

'You make her sound a somewhat terrible creature,' the other sister snapped breaking into her sister's rhetoric, I pray, Matilda, stop it now.'

Miss Matilda stopped in a huff looking most put out by the interruption then carried on talking. 'If we offered you the position as I described it to Miss Clementine who no doubt made clear to you what we expect, are you prepared to accept it?'

Scarlett swallowed hard; she had a great many questions she dare not ask. It seemed she had to make a decision here and now. 'I would be pleased to accept,' she answered boldly, and the sisters turned to each other and nodded their approval.

Miss Matilda stood up. The interview was at an end.

'Emilia, pull the bell for Bessie,' she instructed her sister, and almost immediately cook opened the door wearing a clean apron and Scarlett rose to leave not quite knowing whether she should curtsey or what exactly to do in this strange household.

'Show Penrose out will you, Bessie.'

Scarlett thanked the Miss Catts and followed Bessie out into the hall.

'I'll be glad when you're here,' Bessie exclaimed with genuine warmth, 'that little Missy runs rings round her doting aunts but she's a little madam, and it'll be good for me to have someone to talk to apart from Millie, not all there sometimes that girl is. I'll have her make up one of the bigger rooms in the attic for when you're living in. With the early morning rising you may want to. I overheard them talking you're to wear grey in the mornings and navy at all other times, they've a good eye, no doubt they'll place an order with Lyles's over in East Looe. All you need will be waiting for you when you start.'

Just then the sound of what surely was organ music came from somewhere in the house. Cook stifled a giggle. 'You should see your face, maid, tis a picture.' Singing now accompanied the music, it was very slightly off-key, but the hymn was sung with such vigour you could but smile.

You'll get used to it,' Cook said, opening the front door. 'Out you goes this way, just the once.' And Scarlett couldn't help but giggle as she made her way home along the harbour. It had been a most odd afternoon.

The river was running high almost level with the cobbles on the quay; a great many boats were homeward bound to unload the day's catch. Both sides of the harbour were a maze of masts. She waved to Luke in his little boat *Alice* with the one sail and set of odd oars, so small amongst the fishing boats she feared he would be crushed.

Scarlett had long guessed that Oggie was the person referred to as the Keeper, odd bits of conversation she'd overheard here and there had convinced her it had to be him. She raised her hand in greeting as she passed him sitting as usual watching all that went on, and began the walk up West Looe Hill.

Her mother stood in the doorway of Tamarisk, arms crossed, anxiously waiting. As Scarlett walked down the path, she hugged her daughter to her in a rare show of affection.

'Did you accept the position?' Jeanette asked, eager to have the matter settled in case Elijah should suddenly return.

'Yes, Mother, the Catt sisters seemed nice but rather a strange.'

'I'm sure Miss Clementine wouldn't place you somewhere she didn't think suitable,' Jeanette said trying to brighten her daughter's rather negative response, 'your friend Ruth will have it a lot harder than you, that I can promise.'

'Don't worry, Mother, I said I'll go there, and I will.'

'Tis for the best and I'm sure your father will approve,' Jeanette encouraged not knowing if he would or not. What she did know was that Robert Reader, who Elijah seemed to hold in such high esteem, had a bad reputation when it came to women, and she hadn't liked his manner, or the nasty smirk he'd given, when enquiring after her daughter the last time he was there.

The following day when they had a chance, Ruth and Scarlett sat on the granite wall opposite Miss Clementine's. Each had a tale to tell as Ruth had been up to Polgrove House earlier that morning. Ruth was giving Scarlett a detailed description of the vast kitchen at Polgrove and of the other servants she'd met that morning when suddenly she stood up, staring towards the mouth of the river.

'I've got to go,' she spluttered, and began running down Horse Lane towards home.

Scarlett followed her gaze and knew what had caused Ruth's hasty departure, a revenue boat with six oarsmen was at the river's mouth and entering the harbour. She held her breath wondering which side of the river, East or West, it was headed, saw everyone stop and watch as she did. Just before the bridge of seven arches, the revenue boat slowed, tying up on the East Looe side of the river. Scarlett felt an almost tangible sigh of relief descend upon West Looe. Felt at one with her fellow watchers.

Ruth came back up the lane holding her side with a stitch. 'Had to warn me folks, Ma already knew, Oggie too. Tommy Banks had seen the sods rowing up the coast past Hannafore Point.'

The two girls watched in silence as three vessels moored over at East Looe were searched, so too a cottage adjacent to the ramshackle smoking yards. They were too far away to properly hear the insults shouted between the revenue and gathering crowd. An old man sitting on a fish cart shook his fist at one of the revenue men who angrily raised his musket.

An order was shouted by the man who'd been seated at the helm of the revenue boat, his men quickly returned to their boat, then rowing with perfectly timed strokes, turned the boat around and made their way to the mouth of the river making south towards Plaidy.

'Good riddance,' Ruth spat, making no attempt to hide her hatred.

'I agree,' Scarlett rejoined, eager to show her support.

'Well they're not as smart as they think they are, I bet they're having a laugh at their expense now, them across the river.'

Later as the girls walked home, Ruth suddenly asked, 'We'll keep friends, won't we, Scarlett?' For Ruth realised times like these would soon be in the past.

'Of course we will.' Scarlett linked her arm through Ruth's. 'You up on the hill in Sir Geoffrey's grand house and me down with the Miss Catts, we'll surely have lots to talk about.'

When the final day came, it was with regret and sadness that Scarlett and Ruth left Miss Clementine's Academy. Each pupil leaving was presented with a blue leather-covered prayer book in a white box, with an inscription written in the finest of hand, bearing their name and marking their date of leaving. Opal's red chapped hands tightly clutched her prayer book to her ample bosom, and behind Miss Clementine's back, she poked her tongue out at Scarlett. Then as Miss Clementine stood in the entrance vestibule saying her final farewells, in a triumphant voice, Opal announced she'd been asked to come back next term and help with the little ones.

Scarlett's face reddened and Opal looked triumphant knowing Scarlett would wish she'd been offered such an opportunity. Miss Clementine watched saddened as she saw Scarlett's reaction. She sighed as Opal sniffed and wiped her nose on her sleeve, regretting her offer of employment, dismayed as Opal walked down the steps to the quay with an exaggerated swagger. Scarlett turned and smiled at Miss Clementine, she'd accepted she'd being working for the Miss Catts and that she and Opal were always to be at odds with each other. One reason being they both liked Ruth's brother Jack.

'It's all I could offer her, and I doubt she'll remain long,' Miss Clementine explained, when Opal was lost from sight. Then just as Scarlett and Ruth began to walk home, she called Scarlett back. 'If it really doesn't work out with the Miss Catts come back and see me.'

'Thank you.' Scarlett was so relieved she felt like kissing Miss Clementine's thin cheek, but shook her hand instead, then ran to catch up Ruth, at least she wasn't stuck forever at Prospect House if she truly hated it.

Luke came striding up the hill to meet them, a big grin on his face. 'There's been word the *Raven*'s been spotted making her way past Portnaire Rock, Father and Jack'll be home come tomorrow.'

Scarlett hid her excitement as the three of them walked down to the quay. The prospect of seeing Jack Jago made her heartbeat quicken. But together with the excitement came the ever-present worry that the *Raven* would be intercepted by the revenue, this dulled her excitement and filled her full of dread. She could but hope the *Raven* would sail home safe to harbour. She'd never sleep tonight however hard she prayed all would be well.

Oblivious to what his sister's friend was thinking, Luke waved them goodbye and went to help old Will unload the day's catch. Will nodded a greeting to the girls as they passed, and Charlie Tom chased them along the quay with his handcart, making them squeal with laughter.

Where the quay narrowed and wound its way round past the side of St Nicholas Church, the girls sat down on the steep granite steps leading down to the river, wide enough for them to sit side by side, and far away enough for the smell of the newly landed fish to become just a little less strong.

More boats were making their way in and Scarlett noticed Ruth waving at a young fisherman on board the *Starfish*. He blew her a kiss and Ruth giggled, blowing one back and waving till the *Starfish*'s masts disappeared in amongst the other vessels further up river. But before it did so, he'd shouted something to Ruth.

Scarlett had been paying little attention to what was happening between her friend and the young lad on the boat, her thoughts solely on the fact that Jack would be home tomorrow. She jumped when Ruth spoke to her.

'You've been lost in thought since we saw Luke, thinking of our Jack are you? Maybe Opal is right, you do like him.' Ruth nudged her friend, and smiled.

'Don't be silly. Of course, I don't,' Scarlett replied, pulling a face, and Ruth said no more about her brother. The young man Ruth had been waving at now stood across the river on the opposite quay. Ruth stood up and cast an anxious look down the quay before giving him a quick wave which he returned before walking off.

Afterwards Ruth was strangely quiet.

'What's the matter? Who's that young man who's brought a blush to your cheeks?' Scarlett asked.

'That's Sam, the love of my life; and promise me, Scarlett, you won't tell a living soul.'

'Of course not, silly.'

'I could be in deep trouble. You know the other week the housekeeper up at Polgrove sent for me cause Lyles's had got the order wrong for my morning uniform and I can't start work till I get it. Well, I met Sam Trembright, knew him from when his family lived up from our place. Well, I've met up with him whenever I can since. Nice he is, but now he lives over the other side of the river. I know Father and Jack will say I'm to have nothing to do with him. Sam just shouted to me; he'll row across tomorrow afternoon. Never thought Jack ud be home nor me old man. The tide'll start creeping in in the early afternoon, deep enough for a rowing boat to cross, but too shallow for the likes of the *Raven*. Best hope the *Raven* don't come in on the early morning high tide, if it does then I'll have to be careful. We've a secret place where I wait for Sam. I so want to see him, think I love him, Scarlett, really love him.'

'Neither Jack nor your father would be that angry, would they?' Scarlett asked in all innocence.

'They would, you've not been here long enough to know how it is here between East and West.'

The two girls sat in silence, oblivious to the noise and activity further down the quay or the rising tide creeping slowly up the steps on which they sat. Scarlett worried Ruth's meeting with Sam Trembright wouldn't go unnoticed. She would have liked to have helped her, perhaps keep a lookout for her friend. But there was no way she could for although it was to be at the beginning of the next week she started work for the Catt sisters, Millie – the only other servant she knew of employed by them apart from the cook – had been sent up to Tamarisk with a note to say she was to go to Prospect House the next afternoon. Miss Hester, the Miss Catts niece who she'd be tutoring, was paying her aunts a visit and would like to meet her. Scarlett felt intimidated by the 14-year-old already and felt the Miss Catts had organised this meeting so young Miss Hester could scrutinise her.

The rising tide and wet toes finally forced the girls to move and when they said goodbye at the bottom of Horse Lane, each had their own thoughts on tomorrow.

Scarlett woke early a little after dawn and slipped out of the cottage before her mother was awake. She felt full of excitement at the prospect of seeing Jack. Quickly she made her way down to the quay. The tide was high, the quay already bustling with noise, busy with fishermen preparing to set sail, some had already left and soon few luggers remained. There was no sign of the *Raven* so a disappointed Scarlett returned home. Did this mean her friend's meeting with her Sam would be without discovery?

Once there she helped her mother mending linen from the big house at Lanreath. Jeanette was a good seamstress, and whilst Scarlett could do some of the easier work, her mother did more intricate tasks, carefully repairing fine lace-edged bed linen and other delicate items, which the housekeeper at Lanreath gave only to her. Amos Cuddy would come down each week and collect the repaired linen and deliver more. Scarlett thought her mother looked forward to his visits for she often poured him a tankard of ale and the two would talk together. Scarlett would see her mother looking happy, laughing even, which was never the case when her father was home. Of course, if Elijah was home Amos was never invited in. Annie Bishop missed none of this for Scarlett had seen the curtain twitch more than once on the days that Amos called.

Present yourself at the kitchen door of Prospect House at 2.00 sharp the note Millie had brought up to Tamarisk had said *be sure to enter by the back gate*, with today's date written beneath. Thus having eaten no lunch for she was too nervous and with her mother's reassurance that all would be well, Scarlett set off in good time and was soon walking along Market Lane which ran behind the houses that fronted onto the quay. A few of the houses had stables, Prospect House had the largest stables, they'd been built a good while ago for the timber looked old and leaned a little to one side. It seemed the living quarters were above with one of the windows so misshapen it was boarded up. An adjacent gate had a notice which read 'Prospect House Tradespersons Entrance', Scarlett turned the handle and saw an uneven path ran down to the right of the stables. Scarlett made her way down it and knocked on the back door as instructed. Millie ushered her in.

'The young madam and her father have come early, not rung down for you yet. Bessie insists she'll take you up and show you your room herself. Why I'm not good enough to do that I don't know.'

Just then Bessie appeared. 'Good timekeeping, that's what I like. I'll take you up, show you your room. Millie, tell us quick sharp if she's summoned, follow me.' So, Scarlett followed Bessie's well-rounded figure as she struggled up the stairs until finally when they were at the top of the house, Bessie led Scarlett into what would be her attic bedroom when living in.

'Mistress's wants you dressed in your full afternoon or housekeeper's uniform, as them calls it, just for Miss Hester to see you. Why in heavens name I don't know! Uniform's laid out on the bed as you can see. Get changed and come down straight away, then I'll tell the Miss Catts you're ready for them if they haven't summoned you already, best be quick.'

Once she'd gone, Scarlett gazed about her room. It was smaller than her room at Tamarisk but not the tiny attic room Ruth had described she'd be sharing up at Polgrove. The iron bed looked sturdy and the small chest of drawers more than ample for her belongings. A bowl and water jug were set up on a washstand in the corner. Going over she peered out of the small un-curtained window, glad she could see the river with its quays each side.

She hastened to change into the new stiff uniform laid out on the bed, a knock came on the door. 'Cook says you're to hurry up.' Millie opened the door and came in, and seeing Scarlett struggling with the buttons on her dress, hurried over.

'Here let me help; don't want Bessie getting in a flap.' The younger girl finished the last of the buttons, slipped on the starched cuffs and handed Scarlett her cap. Scarlett had thought to bring a couple of her mother's hair pins just in case, and managed to gather her hair up, pinning it beneath the lacy cap with ease. Millie ran into the adjoining room and brought in a small piece of broken mirror.

Scarlett had a quick look in it and Millie clutched it to her like a precious treasure as she ran back to another attic room where she slept. Quickly both girls went downstairs to where cook was waiting.

Bessie looked her up and down. 'You'll do,' she said, then told Millie to fetch a cloth, telling Scarlett to hold her skirts high, and had Millie wipe Scarlett's rather dusty boots, which made Scarlett feel dreadful.

'Wait there,' Bessie ordered as Scarlett thanked Millie more than once for what she'd done.

'Get back to your work, Millie,' Bessie grumbled as she started up the stairs. 'Them carrots wont peel themselves.' Millie grimaced and went back to the bowl on the kitchen table and half-heartedly began to peel the carrots.

'You're to go up when they ring,' Bessie declared, huffing and puffing as she came back down again. 'Typical that is, they've had me up and down stairs asking me if you're here and so on, only to make you wait now I said you're ready. Come and sit at the table, maid, tis always a different house when that Miss Hester's here.'

Scarlett offered to help Millie, but Bessie would have none of it.

'You'm not employed here yet, just be glad to sit and do nowt.'

More than forty minutes passed before the bell summoning her rang.

'Off upstairs with you, same room as you was interviewed in, be sure to knock and wait to be told enter.' The bell jangled again with an impatience that sent Scarlett running up the stairs.

Two voices called out 'enter' when she knocked, and very nervously Scarlett did so.

The sisters were seated as before and in with them a young girl sat beside the table by the window, a tall gentleman Scarlett presumed must be her father standing at her side.

'This is Miss Marshall our niece,' Miss Matilda Catt said, and Scarlett not knowing exactly what to do nervously bobbed a curtsey at the young lady.

'Miss Hester has some questions she'd like to ask you, Penrose.'

'I quite understand.' She turned to face Hester Marshall.

'Let me see your hands, come here I want to make sure you're clean.'

Scarlett walked across the carpet towards the girl her face devoid of expression, but seething inside. More questions followed; could she dress hair, could she handle a pony and trap? She was scrutinised from head to toe by a girl who she thought to be most ill-mannered. The Catt sisters and her father stayed silent.

At the end of this distressing ordeal, she was dismissed with a snooty turn of the head by Miss Hester and a nod from her father. Scarlett felt like running downstairs and out the back door never to return. Instead, ashamedly she burst into tears and was comforted by Bessie.

'Horrid little thing she is, that Miss Hester. You ought to hear some of the things she says about my cooking. Soul destroying, she is, more than once she's had me weeping and her but a slip of girl. Tis a good thing she only visits here, don't live here.' Scarlett felt better hearing this but feared exactly what her future would be like, working here with that little tyrant.

'I'll go upstairs and take my uniform off, get my own clothes on,' she told Bessie.

'Then take yourself off home and we'll see you on Monday 6.30 sharp,' Bessie replied.

'The spoilt little madam won't be here then,' Millie chimed in.

The bell jangled on its spring once again. 'They'll be wanting afternoon tea now, off you go, maid. Millie, you help lay me the tray for upstairs.'

Once back in the attic room, Scarlett snatched the cap from her head, and was grateful to rid herself of the navy-blue dress, cuffs and apron, glad to be back in her own if rather shabby clothes. She neatly folded her uniform and lay it on the bed. Going over to the window she looked down the quay towards the entrance of the harbour, a ship was moored, her masts taller than other vessels; the *Raven* must have returned to West Looe earlier. Scarlett sped downstairs.

'See you Monday morning,' Bessie said, brushing flour off her hands as Scarlett wished her and Millie a hasty goodbye before running out through the back door, her mind spinning with the thought of only one person.

Chapter 3

As Scarlett approached the end of Market Lane, she could see there was a commotion on the quay. Even Oggie had left his bench and was standing by the Jolly Sailor watching. Scarlett ran to the edge of the crowd trying to peer over the jostling throng to see what was going on. It was noisy with hollering and shouting, she pushed through to the front and choked back a cry of dismay as she saw two men holding Ruth's father back as he yelled abuse at them and struggled to get to the young man lying battered and bleeding on the ground.

There was a disturbance in the crowd and casting aside anyone in their way, two burly men arrived and quickly helped the young man to his feet. They half carried half dragged him to where the quay narrowed and where a rowing boat was tied up. Foul insults were shouted as they helped the injured young man into the boat and began to row across the river, a woman possibly his mother began to descend the steps on the opposite quay waiting for the boat to arrive. Sam Trembright the young man Ruth had waved to was carried up onto East Looe Quay, and as Scarlett watched she began to cry.

'Don't shed no tears over that blighter from East Looe,' Oggie spat, making her jump.

'No of course I won't. Twas just a shock seeing what was happening.'

Oggie walked away and the crowd began to disperse. It was then she saw Jack. He was holding Ruth by the arm and marching her towards their cottage. Tom Jago followed, red in the face and holding his hand which obviously hurt.

Scarlett stayed where she was, then suddenly Jack looked over in her direction.

Keeping hold of his sobbing sister, he thrust her forward towards the cottage doorway and walked over. Jack was obviously as furious as his father.

'And being her friend, I suppose you knew all about just who my sister was meeting up with this afternoon?'

Scarlett stood open-mouthed not knowing what to say.

'No, she didn't,' Ruth cried, as Tom Jago bundled her through the door. 'Leave Scarlett alone.'

Scarlett stared into Jack's handsome face, he'd been gone an age and she'd waited so long to see him again, but not like this.

'I don't believe you.' His eyes searched Scarlett's face for the truth and her heart thumped under his scrutiny.

'Don't think to help her, Scarlett, she knows the rules here even if you don't.' With that, he walked away.

Scarlett stared after him, shocked to see through the open door of their cottage, Tom Jago slowly taking off his belt before slamming the door shut. She lingered on the quay feeling wretched, scared to think what punishment Ruth's father was about to inflict on her friend.

From a vantage point near Island Cottage she watched and waited but the usually open door of the

Jago's cottage remained firmly shut. In the end she had no option other than to go home, her mother would be waiting. Slowly she walked past Oggie who raised his battered hat to her as she passed.

'The maid ull know she done wrong, she'll take her punishment and twill be over with.' He coughed and spluttered, taking the clay pipe from his mouth, examining the end of it as thought it was the cause of his coughing.

'Yes, I know,' Scarlett told him, but as she climbed the hill she worried about her friend. What was happening to her now? Tears welled in her eyes together with a mixture of emotions.

At the door of Tamarisk she was dismayed to hear her father's voice, and saw through the window him pacing up and down. She lifted the latch and a warning glance from her mother told Scarlett he was in an ill mood.

Ignoring her entry into the cottage, with his voice raised so surely Annie Bishop would be able to hear him, Elijah demanded to know of his wife, 'What manner of people are these Catt sisters, Jeanette? You should have consulted me before sending Scarlett into servitude.'

Jeanette raised her head and looked him steady in the eye. 'It's a good placement, she's a companion to the Catt sisters' niece and taking on great responsibilities, isn't that right Scarlett?'

Elijah didn't wait for her to reply, but continued to shout at his wife. 'I don't think Scarlett should be employed there; send a note to that effect, now!' In temper, he banged his fist down on the table, making both women jump.

Scarlett walked over and stood beside her mother.

'Miss Clementine kindly put me forward, recommended me to them, I have already accepted, I shall not let her down nor them.' Scarlett looked defiantly at her father. 'You shall not stop me.'

Elijah glared at his wife. 'Such impudence. Is this what I've been paying for at that so-called academy? To educate my daughter to speak to me in such a fashion.'

Jeanette stepped forward. 'Let Scarlett be, you paid for her to be educated, pray let her use it.'

Elijah looked at his wife in total disbelief, it was unheard of for his placid wife to take a stance against him. It reduced him to silence. The clock on the mantle chimed the quarter hour and as it did so, Elijah snatched up his hat and gloves, swung a saddle bag over his shoulder and made to leave.

'Your take full responsibility for her, Jeanette, it'll be you I blame if this arrangement fails.' He took a money pouch from his pocket and placed it on the table; he gave Jeanette a long lingering look. Scarlett saw her mother hold his gaze and for the briefest of moments saw a flicker of the two people they once had been.

'Take care,' Jeanette said in little more than a whisper, Elijah's face took on its usual stern glare and he was gone, slamming shut the door. Neither mother nor daughter moved. A short while later they heard the hooves of his horse picking its way up the uneven lane behind the cottage, all was peaceful once again.

The first thing Scarlett wanted to do once she was dressed the next morning was to go and see Ruth and find out how she was. Scarlett had been late to bed the previous night after comforting her mother. A thunderstorm in the early hours of the morning had kept her awake, with hailstones hammering down on the rag tile roof, and the wind rattling every window frame. Unable to sleep, the scene on the quay had played over and over in her mind as she'd huddled beneath the bed clothes. She was so glad Jack was safe ashore. Her longing to see him now tinged with trepidation. She even felt a little scared of meeting him.

But once downstairs, her first task was to help her mother mop up the muddy water that had seeped under the back door during the storm. This done, Scarlett hitched up her skirt and paddled over to the well to fetch clean water so the flagstones could be scrubbed. Annie Bishop appeared in her doorway; the old soul stood pail in hand looking out across the pool of water that had formed along the path from her cottage to the well.

'Fetch us a pail, maid, I'll catch me death wading through that lot,' she called out, and Scarlett made her way through the earthy brown water to fetch hold the wooden pail. She filled it to the brim and carried it into Annie's dark parlour.

'You'm alright, maid, remember I said that.' Annie grinned a toothless smile before ushering her out.

Dark clouds still lingered overhead, the gulley that ran down the opposite side of West Looe Hill was brimming over with water. A bunch of boys were gathered a little further down by the entrance of Well Lane, they'd paused for breath exhausted from pushing two large tubs up the hill. Scarlett was shocked they'd been so bold, for it was obvious the tubs were full, and in broad daylight they were taking a risk. She was grateful her father wasn't home. One of the boys saw her watching, he nudged the others and they wasted no time setting off again up the lane.

Scarlett went upstairs and took off her skirt with its sodden hem, downstairs she opened the back door and squeezed out the water, setting the skirt out across two chairs to dry before the fire. Anxious to go out she'd wash the dirtied hem another day.

Jeanette sat at the table exhausted with all the cleaning up. Scarlett was going to tell her about the boys she'd seen earlier, but just then Amos came from Lanreath with his horse and cart. He made his way up the path, a broad smile on his face, clad in strong boots he took no notice of the water that nearly encroached above the doorstep. Jeanette greeted him warmly and gathered together the mending he was to take back to Lanreath, placing it in linen bags. He placed on the table two fresh bundles for mending and sat down watching Jeanette busy herself fetching out a jug of ale and two pewter tankards. Scarlett fetched her warmest shawl and took her leave, escaping down the hill to see if she could see Ruth. She shivered as the cold wind blew in from the harbour; the clouds above brought the promise of more rain.

She noticed that Oggie wasn't sitting outside his cottage and the quay was strangely busy for no fish were being landed. At the bottom of Horse Lane her heart sank, all seemed too quiet at the Jago's cottage; the front door was still shut tight.

Trying to control a large wheelbarrow, Ted Curnow almost ran into her.

'Why's it so busy?' she asked, taking a peek under the piece of thick canvas Ted had over the contents of the barrow. Underneath were five small tubs.

'Gotta be off, get these up home; ships gone aground off Hannafore.'

'Not one of ours?' Scarlett quickly looked along the line of masts relieved to see the *Raven* still moored up.

'No, come up the coast from somewheres, the crews abandoned her, it got a bit ill-tempered down on the beach with us locals, we saw um off, wreckers rights we ave.' With that he was gone, and wrapping her shawl tighter, Scarlett scrambled up the muddy path to Hannafore, whilst others scrambled down with their plunder. She saw Opal and her younger brother coming towards her dragging a heavy sack.

'Have you seen Ruth?' Scarlett shouted, as a sudden gust of wind snatched her words away.

Opal stopped and took a deep breath. 'No,' she wheezed, 'but the rest of the Jagos are on the beach.'

From the top of the hill, Scarlett watched the swarm of people below, engulfed now and then in spray from the pounding sea. They hung on to the rocks before struggling to clamber onto the wreck of the ship. The weather worsened, the sky darkened, and a ferocious gale whipped up the sea pounding it against the ship. So strong was the wind it caused Scarlett to stumble as she ventured closer to the cliff edge to watch. It began to rain heavily and soon she was wet through but still she tried to search out Jack. She doubted that Ruth was down there; surely not! For they were all in danger now.

Mesmerised by what was happening, Scarlett stood firm. The ship lay on her side smashed to pieces on the jagged rocks; two men soaked by the sea were sawing at her masts whilst others with long knives were stripping her of her sails. Soon the ship would be little more than a mass of wood floating in the sea, the pity was she'd nearly made it safe to harbour.

After a while, heavily laden donkeys led by exhausted men moved slowly past. Others toiled with kegs of brandy chairs and all manner of the ship's furniture. Scarlett was just about to join those going down the hill when the man beside her yelled, 'God help um.' All eyes followed his gaze along the barren cliff top, there coming over the ridge from the direction of Port Nadler bay, were red coats.

A warning cry went up from those on the cliff, a young boy ran down the hill and someone began ringing the bell of St Nicholas, alerting the good folks of West Looe that lives were in peril. The crowd on the beach fled in all directions, some discarding their spoils as they scampered from the wreck and the beach. A pistol shot was fired and along with everyone else, Scarlett ran, abandoned goods from the ship cluttering her way.

By the time she got home she could scarce breath. Soaked through, Jeanette sent her to bed listening as Scarlett told what had happened.

'Was it just the red coats?' Jeanette queried.

'I think so,' Scarlett sobbed, unable to keep her teeth from chattering. Jeanette gave her some of the rum she kept for special occasions only and piled two more blankets on her daughter's bed.

'Rest now, I'll go down later and bring you any news I can.' She feared for her daughter. It was no time to catch cold two days before she started work.

Over the next two days, Jeanette forbid Scarlett to go out, which she found most frustrating. Once just when it was getting dark, Scarlett had looked out from her bedroom window and thought she caught a glimpse of Jack leaning against the wall of Annie's cottage. With beating heart she'd quickly slipped out the front door but no one was there.

During those two days all the misgivings Scarlett had had about working at Prospect House returned. The previous week she'd stood staring at the house from a little way along the quay. She wondered who had given the house its name, for although the sun shone the place looked so dark, entombed by ivy so dense it almost crept across the windows, hiding them from view. There was no outward sign that anyone lived there, the curtains drawn almost shut. How unlike it was to the sea captain's house built closer to where she stood, for a maid had been scrubbing the doorstep and in one of the windows that was slightly open a small boy had stood looking down at her, he'd waved and unseen hands had pulled him back, and the window swiftly shut.

This morning another note had been sent up to Tamarisk from the Catt sisters. There was a change in her employers' requirements. It seemed they wanted her to live in when she commenced the position offered. A chance for her to fully appreciate what was required of her, and for them to ensure she was suitable and capable of the tasks required. This was a disappointment, but Scarlett felt determined to insist she be allowed to live out at times, once she had proved herself to them.

She hastened to pack a few items needed in a carpet bag, heartily wishing she didn't have to leave her mother here at Tamarisk alone with her father. For there would be no witness now to his ill treatment.

The thought of living in at Prospect House made her feel anxious, it was a rather strange household, her mistresses rather odd too. As a thousand worries filled her head about this, she worried too about Ruth for she was supposed to start in service today up at Polgrove. Would she be able to?

As Scarlett carried the carpet bag downstairs, above all else she felt an overwhelming desire to see Jack. She wanted to free herself of the memory she couldn't forget, the anger in his eyes that day on the quay, how enraged he'd been about Ruth's friendship with Sam Trembright, and them once good friends. How angry he'd been at her too! She wondered what Jack would do now? Would he rejoin the crew of the *Raven*, or help Will with the fishing? Once she'd begun in service and living in, she'd not likely be able just to slip out from her mistresses' house and stroll along the quay to see if he was there. Prospect House seemed like a place she'd be locked away in, but there would be half days off, her mother insisted she made sure of that. And indeed, she would.

As she waited for her mother to come home from collecting linen to be patched from the impoverished household where Mrs Potter lived further up the hill, Scarlett tried to remember some of the positive things about Prospect House. The Catt sisters didn't seem so bad, Bessie and Millie had seemed pleasant enough, did it matter too much that the house was grim or that unlike Ruth who knew what duties would be expected of her, Scarlett did not entirely know.

It was hard parting from her mother, there were tears shed by both.

'Remember you're not far away, be sure to visit me when you can,' her mother declared between sobs.

'I will, don't let my father bully you, and if he hurts you too much tell Amos; promise me,' Scarlett replied.

Jeanette reached out and hugged her daughter. 'I will, maid, don't go worrying about me.'

Wiping away her tears, Scarlett began walking down West Looe Hill, her old carpet bag clutched tight in her hand. She would pass close to the Jagos' cottage on the way to Market Lane. Ruth had been told last week she had to be up at the big house at 5.30 that morning, so if she was able, she'd be long gone by now.

The door of the Jagos' cottage was open, and Tom Jago had his lobster pots stacked up on the cobbles outside to dry. An old chair sat uneasily upon the cobbles and beside this fishing nets were piled ready for mending. But there was no sign of life within. Quickly she walked on in case Tom Jago should be watching from the window, she felt a little frightened of him now. Near the entrance to Market Lane she paused, glad to see the tall masts of the *Raven*. Pleased the ship had not set out on another voyage.

Just as Scarlett stepped into Market Lane, an arm shot out and pulled her into an alleyway. About to scream, she caught her breath then heaved a sigh of relief, for it was Jack.

'I've a message from Ruth.' He grinned, brushing tumbling black curls from his eyes. 'I'm to tell you all is well with her, what she did was wrong, and that she wishes you good luck today.'

Scarlett now quite recovered wondered if this was true. Her heart skipped a beat; Jack Jago had never seemed so handsome as he did now.

'Is she really in good spirits, your father didn't beat her half to death, did he?'

'She done wrong, deserved all she got, but mother saw to it she was able enough to start up at Polgrove, don't you worry.'

'But Jack, Sam Trembright was your friend once, doesn't that mean anything?'

'Like I said before, he doesn't live in West Looe now and that's an end to it, she'll not see him again.'

He looked deep into Scarlett's face. 'Promise me, Scarlett, you'll not encourage her to disobey what's been told her, or I can promise our dad will give her another sound thrashing.'

'It just seems...'

'Seems what?' She looked up into Jack's dark eyes, so serious and searching. Scarlett changed the subject.

'What happened with the red coats, did they catch anyone?'

'Of course not, silly, we'd all gone by the time they got down on the beach.'

He raised his hand and stroked the side of her cheek. Heart pounding, she felt herself blushing as he moved closer, eyes twinkling now, gone the serious Jack he'd been but seconds earlier.

She felt his thumb on the nape of her neck now moving gently in a circle, softly caressing her warm skin. Felt his breath on her face as he pressed her back against the wall.

'Tis such a shame, but I best let you be on your way, maid, don't want to upset those odd sisters you're to work for, but I've got something to give you for good luck.' And with that he kissed her full on the lips. It seemed to Scarlett the kiss went on for ever, then suddenly he let her go, and stepped back.

'Be off now,' he said. Then with a grin and a wave he was gone, striding back towards the quay, leaving a breathless Scarlett to hurry on to Prospect House.

Flustered, feeling all the world must be able to tell what had happened just a few moments ago, Scarlett knocked on the back door and was ushered into the kitchen by Millie.

'We're all of a rush, words just come Julian Marshall's calling on the sisters this morning. Bessie says you're to take yourself off upstairs and come straight down when you're ready, uniforms laid out as before, tis the grey you'm to put on, then wait down here till she comes back.'

Picking up a square of thick cloth, Millie lifted the copper kettle off the hook above the fire and poured boiling water into two delicately shaped silver teapots, then quickly carried the heavily laden breakfast tray upstairs. Scarlett took a deep breath, picked up her carpet bag and followed behind her.

When she was dressed and with her hair once again pinned beneath the plain cap that had been laid out, Scarlett hurried downstairs. But not before she took a quick glance out the window, somewhere further along the quay Jack would be, and she blushed just thinking of him. Longed for the next time they'd be able to meet.

Down in the kitchen she was surprised to find seated beside the fire a thickset man with ruddy cheeks and wild grey hair. 'You the new maid?' he asked gruffly, looking Scarlett up and down. 'Bit scrawny; hope you're stronger than you look. Mr high and mighty Marshall says I'm to show you how to handle the pony and trap so yous can take Miss Esther about. Must be ashamed of me or summat. Old Dolly, she ain't no pony and she can take some handling, mind of her own she got.'

'I'll manage her,' Scarlett replied a little more sharply than she meant to, for indeed when they'd lived beside the Tamar, it was Scarlett who for the last few years until they moved to West Looe had had no choice but take to handling their pony and trap herself. She had learned well from young Philip Day who'd worked for them, he'd helped with the vegetable growing and all that needed doing. Philip had made living there, in so isolated a place beside the Tamar, bearable. With the pony and trap he'd taken her and her mother out along the muddy and rutted tracks beside the river, occasionally to the nearby village market, never questioning why they didn't ask to go with him more often.

Philip had helped the previous owner of Treredden, and when Elijah had bought the place had just stayed on growing from boy to man.

Whenever he was home, Scarlett's mother always vowed to tell Elijah the isolated cottage he'd found to hide away his wife and daughter was taking its toll on them. But she'd lacked the courage. Jeanette had taught Scarlett at home, so she met scarcely anyone her own age and apart from when her father came home, the only other person she saw was Philip. When Scarlett was twelve Philip had died of a fever, even today just thinking of him brought a lump to Scarlett's throat. He'd been kind to her, kept her interested in life itself, with his tales of the Tamar and life beyond Treredden. When Elijah came home and was told Philip had died, he'd pay no one else to help around the place, too fearful of prying eyes and unwanted questions.

After much pleading he'd allowed them to keep the pony and trap and Scarlett had taught herself to manage it, having watched Philip when they'd ventured out and having always helped look after the pony. She was undaunted by the barely accessible tracks –'smugglers trails' Philip had called them. She remembered those words and with them the cold remembrance of Sennen. What her father had done, his betrayal of local men whose families they knew, this filled Scarlett with overwhelming shame.

She looked at the man before the fire and realised she'd seen him before up on Hannafore leading the two donkeys laden with ship's furniture on the day of the wrecking.

Bessie came in, all hot and in a fair bother. 'Got that damn fire in the parlour alight at last,' she exclaimed, 'Millie and me been trying to get it to take best part of an hour.' She sat down red in the face and heaved a sigh of relief.

'I'm mighty glad you're here, girl; I hate it when we've surprise visitors.' She looked at the old man. 'And don't you go thinking you're staying put and can nod off, you've work to be doing, Ivan, and take your eyes off young Scarlett if you please, be off now.' Ivan picked up the plate, thick chunks of bread glistened wet with dripping.

'You can get your own ale,' Bessie ordered, and he did, filling a battered pewter tankard up to the brim leaving very little in the jug. A wink to Scarlett and he was out the door.

'Whilst we've a moment on our own,' Bessie began, and pulled out a chair for Scarlett to sit down. 'It's best I warn you how things are with Mille. Silly girl's got it in her head you're going to try and take some of her tasks off her. I've told her you're not, you'm got enough work of your own, but I don't think she quite believes me. She does for the sisters, it's a lot for the maid but she manages well enough. Quite protective of them she is. Come from the poor house did Millie, eager to please, no doubt of that. When Anne who used to do for Miss Matilda and Miss Emilia left us, Millie took on her duties. She'll settle to having you here, but thought it best you knew.'

Scarlett smiled. 'I'm hoping we're to be friends, I'll make sure as not to upset her.'

As Scarlett rose from her seat, Millie came down to the kitchen and Bessie asked her to show Scarlett Miss Hester's room.

'A small room on the first floor's been set aside for schooling. Millie's set it up for you but it's you who must take responsibility now. Mr Julian is most eager that Miss Hester's absences from school don't quell her lively mind. Miss Clementine has agreed to supply suitable learning materials which you, Scarlett, have to collect sometime later this week.'

'Can't see why she just can't stay at school,' Millie grumbled. 'Just makes more work for us her coming and going.'

Bessie shooed them out the kitchen. 'It's not for us to questions those upstairs, get along now.' She went over to the dresser and placed newly dried crockery tidily back where it belonged. 'Little Miss Hester knows how to get her own way that's why,' she mumbled to herself.

Scarlett was surprised when Millie opened the door to the most pretty of bedrooms, furnished with exquisitely delicate furniture and hung with the finest of drapes.

'She won't want to know none of the learning like her father's ordered. But play at being a young lady and visit with her friends who live nearby. Like as not pretending you're her abigail. Spiteful and nasty; you upset her she'll go straight to the sisters and create, that's why Anne left.'

Hearing this did not make Scarlett feel in the least happy. She stayed silent as Millie showed her what chores were needed to be done, for already two trunks of clothes had been sent from Chapeldown House where the Marshall's lived. All must be crease free and hung ready for Hester to choose what to wear. The whole of the room must be cleaned before the young madam arrived, if she found things not to her liking, she had the temper of a dowager duchess, whatever one of those was. 'I'm just repeating what Anne said,' Millie sighed. And Scarlett could see that without doubt Millie was frightened of Miss Hester, and no wonder.

In a finely embroidered linen bag edged with pink ribbon in the little area off the main bedroom, which was to be Miss Hester's dressing room, was a collection of mending Anne had abandoned when she left.

'I was too frightened to touch it,' Millie declared, 'I'm no seamstress.'

Scarlett tipped the contents of the bag out onto the top of one of the trunks, thanks to her mother's teachings she could repair its contents quite easily.

'Don't worry, I can do this,' Scarlett told her. And a relieved Millie, having told Scarlett where the school room was hurried back to the kitchen leaving Scarlett alone to ponder what the days ahead would be like.

Every garment Miss Esther possessed was of the finest quality, excellent satins and silks, her bonnets were of the highest fashion. Indeed, they were as fine as any she'd seen up at Lanreath when she'd gone to the big house with her mother when extra help was needed.

Having decided to go in search of the school room, Scarlett was just about to open the door opposite the bedroom when surprisingly Ivan came upstairs.

'What you about?' he queried, and Scarlett explained she was looking for the school room. 'Ain't in there, it's here.' He opened a door further towards the back of the house and stood still as a statue whilst she entered. The unused room was so dismal Scarlett felt most disheartened. She pulled back the dark brocade drapes and surveyed the unused room, it would take an age to clear away the dust gathered on every surface and underfoot, a pile of soot sat heaped in the hearth. Housekeeper and companion Miss Clementine had said, but it would take some work to make this room presentable.

'Ivan could you—' She looked but he was gone. Millie need have no fears of Scarlett taking her work, she had plenty of her own, the problem was where to begin.

Later that morning, Millie came up to the school room and said Scarlett was to set aside the scrubbing brush and pail of water and to change into her best dark blue uniform. Thus, hastily transformed into her best uniform and housekeeper's manners, Scarlett opened the door to Mr Julian Marshall. He arrived looking very elegant indeed. Knocking on the sisters' drawing room door, she ushered the unsmiling man inside, he was clothed in the highest of fashion, but the cut of his clothes however fine, made Scarlett like him no more. She'd helped Bessie prepare a cold luncheon for the sisters and their brother-in-law, served Mr Julian's coachman some of Bessie's thick vegetable broth then helped Millie with the washing up. Already she was tired.

In the afternoon Mr Julian left and Millie served the sisters tea. Scarlett changed back into her grey uniform and spent time trying her hardest to remove some of the deepest of creases out of Miss Hester's clothes. She'd start on the school room again tomorrow.

Finally, her first day drew to a close and, exhausted, Scarlett climbed the last twisting stairs to her attic room, a tallow candle lighting her way. She looked out of the window. The river sparkled in the moonlight. She thought of Jack's kiss warm upon her lips and craved for their next meeting. 'No followers,' the sisters had told her after she'd accepted the £1.10s.0d a year they'd offered. Scarlett's face glowed, she smiled a secret smile. Was Jack to become her follower? She so hoped so.

The next few days presented little time for daydreaming. Scarlett saw little of the sisters only heard Miss Emilia thumping out hymns on her organ and at the oddest of hours. She was relieved when at last the school room looked presentable. Ivan had helped with the removal of the soot and had arranged for the chimney to be swept. The cleaning proper she'd found herself alone to do. The dust had made her eyes sore and caused her to sneeze incessantly. Millie had helped take down the drapes and beat them on the line outside, rehung they looked little better than before. Ivan, who Scarlett had begun to warm to, found suitable furniture, desks for both herself and Miss Hester to be seated at, some bookcases and an oil lamp he set upon a three legged table.

It was to Scarlett's dismay that on the Thursday afternoon as he hauled in a well-worn rug and set it down on the bare floorboards, that he blurted out when finished, 'Just so you knows, maid, Bessie been out to the back yard and sent Mary Jago's boy Jack off with a flea in his ear for hanging about by the back gate. Not that she's supposing it's anything to do with you, maid, just thought I'd tell you like.' Scarlett thanked him, face reddening under his scrutiny.

Poor Jack, she'd felt down all day after hearing this. More than ever she longed to escape from the confines of Prospect House, longing for the next day when she'd be going up to Miss Clementine's for the schoolbooks. But on the Friday, her hopes of doing this were dashed when she learnt from Bessie that Ivan had gone in her place for it was feared the schoolbooks and writing materials would be too heavy for her.

That same day Scarlett had boldly asked the sisters if she could sleep out on her half day as there were a few more items she needed to bring down and her mother had need of her. They had reluctantly agreed.

Busy though she was with preparations for Miss Hester's arrival, it seemed Sunday would never come, the long clock in the kitchen chimed the hours slowly away until she'd be free. Her half day and a night in her own bed. Prospect House felt like her prison. When it finally came, a full fifteen minutes before midday on the Sunday, she was changed into her own clothes and ready to be off, bidding Bessie and Millie goodbye. She stepped outside and closing the back door firmly behind her, Scarlett breathed a sigh of relief, she'd half hoped Jack would be there to greet her. Once out of sight of Prospect House, Scarlett lifted up her skirts and ran down Market Lane towards the quay.

The tide that ruled so many lives was out. Weaving in and out between the drying nets and lobster pots, Scarlett made her way along the quay. Abruptly she stopped, rooted to the spot just where she was, what she saw brought a lump to her throat and shattered her romantic thoughts. Jack was standing his back against an iron rail, there in front of him and very close indeed was Opal. They were talking, Opal started to laugh, Jack too, someone hollered over to them and Opal linked her arm through his and they began walking towards the Jolly Sailor. It was then as they hurried across the cobbles out the way of a wagon laden with coal that Jack turned his head and saw her. Scarlett fled, frantically running up West Looe Hill, brushing away the tears that ran down her face. She heard Jack calling her name as breathless she carried on.

Scarlett could hear he was getting closer, running faster than she could until finally he caught up with her.

'Come here,' he shouted angrily and reaching out grabbed her arm and forcefully drew her into Well Lane, hauling her along to a place where they were quite alone. 'What's the hell's the matter with you?'

Scarlett struggled trying to free herself, but she was no match for Jack's strength, his strong arms held her still, she looked away couldn't look at him so deep was her hurt.

'So you saw me with Opal, silly maid, I suppose you think something's going on between the two of us.' He put a finger under her chin and forced her look at him.

'I know you and her aren't the best of friends but I've known Opal and her brothers all me life, we were just talking. Heaven forbid I ever think of Opal like I think of you.'

Scarlett gulped looking up now into his deep hazel eyes. 'It's just you seemed so friendly I thought you'd forgotten about me, Opal's always liked you. I got jealous.'

'Oh, Scarlett, I gave up my place aboard the *Raven* to Luke. Just so I'd be about when at last you were let out that fusty old place you're in.'

Jack pulled Scarlett even closer and she leaned towards him feeling ashamed and a little silly, he enfolded her in his arms and gently brushed the side of her face with his calloused hand. Moments later he was kissing her with a passion more fierce and demanding than before. An old woman came out her cottage further up the lane, neither Jack nor Scarlett heard her tut of disapproval at the sight of such wanton behaviour.

At the top of Well Lane was a stone seat, from here you could see over all of West Looe down to the river. Jack and Scarlett sat there together as it grew towards dusk, the air held the cold chill of autumn, but it didn't matter.

Reluctantly realising her mother would wonder what had happened to her, Scarlett told Jack she had to go. 'The sisters have let me sleep out tonight,' she told him. 'I'm to be back at 6.30 tomorrow.'

'I'll be waiting down the hill to walk you back, hopefully cook won't come out and have another go,' he teased.

'Ivan told me about that.'

'He's all right is Ivan, if you need get a message to me, tell him, he'll pass it on, I know he will.' She shivered and Jack held her close, his woollen jacket rough against her cheek. As they neared the bottom of Well Lane, Scarlett stopped. 'How's Ruth?' she asked, shocked she'd entirely forgotten to ask after her friend.

'She's fine, she got a message down to us by way of one of the boot boys. Knew Ma would be worrying.'

Together they walked hand in hand just as far as not to be seen from Tamarisk or Annie Bishop's cottage. Jack gave her a long lingering kiss, one hand he slipped beneath her shawl and gently over the bodice of her dress. When they drew apart, Scarlett waved him good-bye as she ran on up to Tamarisk.

The cottage was in darkness, faint moonlight from the open shuttered window fell upon a note left for her on the table. Scarlett pulled one of the candle stubs from the bundle tied together hidden at the back of the lowest drawer in the dresser, these little gifts from Amos Cuddy mother and daughter stowed away, hidden from Elijah. Scarlett lit the candle from the embers of the dying fire and placed it in a pewter holder. The note said her mother had been sent for this very day and would be staying up at Lanreath for the next week at least. The West wing was to be opened up and she was needed there. Lanreath's mistress had sent for her and needing the work she could not refuse. She hoped all was well with Scarlett and hoped to see her soon.

The disappointment Scarlett felt when reading the note left her in tears. She ate a little bread and cheese, fetched in water from the well and sat for a while glad no bell would ring for her to hurry and obey.

A tired Scarlett carried her candle upstairs and placed it in its pewter holder. Since she'd left, her mother had put fresh linen on her bed, crisp and white the sheets were, they may be old, but they too came from Lanreath and had once been of the finest quality. How comfortable her own bed was, better than the hard mattress she slept on at Prospect House. She undressed and contentedly lay down in her own bed and blew out the candle, her thoughts a turmoil of disappointment and happiness.

Chapter 4

It was as she lay in the peaceful silence of Tamarisk that she heard it, the creaking of a floorboard on the small square landing outside her room. The creaking floorboard was familiar, it always creaked when stood upon. But tonight, she was alone. Scarlett lay completely still wondering if it was just her imagination, too frightened to sit up and look towards the door. She listened, relaxing a little when no other sound followed. She lay, eyes open, staring out into the near darkness of her room. Her frantic heartbeats gradually eased. Her breathing slowed; it was nothing.

The next sound when it came was much closer, someone was in her room, beside her bed, a shadow loomed over her, she smelt the foulest of breaths upon her face. Stale ale and the flat smell of rum. Her scream was stifled by a gloved hand pressed hard against her mouth. Terrified, Scarlett stared up into the evil face of her father's friend Robert Reader. In one movement with his free hand he stripped the bed clothes from the bed, ripping from her body the cotton bed gown, eyes glistening with lust as he gazed down at her naked body. Scarlett bit into his gloved hand, kicked and twisted frantically trying to escape, but she was no match against his strength, his hold on her far too strong, he forced her head down further into the pillow. A cruel twisted smile formed on Reader's fleshy lips as he cupped one of her breasts within his other gloved hand and squeezed hard.

'I hope that fellow I saw you with earlier hasn't had the delights of your sweet body yet, for you'll be no virgin when I've done with you.'

He let out a merciless harsh laugh, taking his eyes off her for a minute as he made to unbutton his breeches. Scarlett bit into his gloved hand once again only harder this time. It must have hurt, for the briefest of moments he lessened the pressure against her mouth and she managed to scream and free herself, desperately running towards the door only to be grasped by her hair and flung back down on the bed.

Frantically Scarlett sought to cover her naked body. She spat out at Reader in fury, 'Don't touch me, you bastard, or I'll tell my father.'

'Tell him what exactly, that you enticed me into your bedroom like a wanton whore?'

He took off his long coat, revealing two pistols lodged within his belt. He saw her gaze at them. 'You ever been pistol whipped, want to find out how it feels?' His mouth curled in a cruel sneer. 'Now are you going to give me what I want willingly, or must I take you by force?'

He leant closer to her and Scarlett like a trapped cat sprang up and clawed his face. She drew blood; Reader struck her face hard with the side of his hand. Taking off one of his gloves he wiped his cheek, blood soaked into the cuffs of his coarse linen shirt.

Enraged, he reached out and pinned Scarlett to the bed by her neck, she could scarce breathe. He leant down, his face almost upon hers, his breath made her want to retch. She felt one of his hands slowly creep down her body, caressing her where no man had been before, terrified of what was about to happened. With renewed strength, she struggled and kicked out blindly, aiming with all her strength for the place she knew would hurt him most.

Reader swore loudly and leapt back, Scarlett fled to the window that half faced Annie Bishop's, praying the busybody would be watching as usual.

'You little vixen.' In two strides he was beside her, lifting her off her feet and over his shoulder, dropping the still fiercely struggling Scarlett forcefully down on the bed, pinning her to it and straddling her with his body.

His weight took her breath away. She opened her mouth to scream but was silenced by his mouth on hers, his probing tongue filled her mouth and she gagged. Once more he was fiddling with his breeches and Scarlett closed her eyes, she felt powerless to stop what lay ahead.

Then suddenly, forcefully he was lifted off her. Stumbling blindly about he hauled up his breeches. Unsteady on his feet, Robert Reader stood as her father held him in a firm grip.

'In God's name cover yourself,' her father shouted at her, as angrily he propelled Robert Reader out of the bedroom. There was such a clatter her father must have pushed Reader down the stairs. There followed a great deal of shouting and swearing. Scarlett fetched out another nightgown and trembling got back to bed. Pulling the bedclothes up round her neck as she listened.

Finally, the back door slammed shut. After a while she heard her father's footfall upon the stair. The light of his candle flickered momentarily under her door. Scarlett held her breath.

There was a knock and the latch lifted, her father stood in the doorway. 'He didn't—' He hesitated. 'Are you as you should be?' he queried.

'Have no fear on that score. You returned home just in time.'

He ventured further into her room. 'No need to tell your mother about tonight. Don't go bothering her with what's happened.' The door closed.

He said nothing else, showed no compassion for the ordeal she'd suffered. Scarlett lay against the pillows still traumatised, long into the night she cried silent tears and it was an age before she slept. Too soon she was woken by their neighbour's cockerel, now she had to face Jack and the day that lay ahead, she couldn't tell him. Her ordeal another secret to be kept. However much Robert Reader had violated her, no knowledge that the hated riding officer had been to Tamarisk must ever be revealed.

Scarlett gathered together all she needed for the following week and hid her torn nightgown amongst it. Glad to escape a meeting with her father, she lifted the latch and slipped quietly out of Tamarisk. Her body ached from fighting off Reader, the bruises on her arms hidden by the sleeves of her dress, those on her neck for the moment hidden by the high collar of her dress, these would be less easy to hide when she wore her uniform. She felt sick remembering how she'd been mistreated, but must set aside her troubled thoughts, for with Miss Hester arriving today there would be much for her to do.

When Jack wasn't there to meet her as promised, Scarlett was overly hurt and disappointed, but she had no time to linger and wait for him. Tears formed in her eyes as she hurried on down the hill, a knot of apprehension grew also, there must be a reason for Jack not being there as promised.

It was as she passed the Jolly Sailor, the unease she felt became reality. Even before the quay came into sight, she knew something was wrong.

A crowd was gathered, they stood in huddles watching as men from the revenue whose uniform she knew only too well, were being ordered to unload the fishermen's early morning catch so their boats could be searched. The tide was high, and she could see two other revenue cutters out on the river. Two more luggers were held at anchor between them waiting to be searched also. Robert Reader stood on the deck of the *Anthony* giving out orders.

A cluster of men lined the quay's edge, Oggie among them, joining in goading the revenue. Overhead a multitude of gulls swooped and screeched, encircling the catch in carts and rough wooden boxes scattered on the quay. Scarlett stopped where she was, taking in the scene before her, she could see none of the Jagos except Mary and a group of women Scarlett recognised, they stood watching a little way off. Scarlett so wanted to go and ask Mary where Jack was but knew it would be foolish to draw attention to Mary should Robert Reader chance to see them talking. Across the river the quayside was lined with fishermen watching just as she had with Ruth that day earlier in the year. Both East and West Looe united in their hatred of the revenue.

The crowd on West Looe's quay swelled and grew into a jostling angry mob, they began to close in on the revenue and muskets were raised in response. Scarlett dare not linger and watch or she'd be late. Slowly she began to weave her way through the crowd, desperate not to be seen by Reader. The folks that watched the revenue now watched in silence, they knew Reader was a ruthless bastard who'd think nothing of getting his men to fire into the crowd. She hoped no tubs would be found hidden beneath the catch, she'd lived in West Looe long enough to know this happened.

Scarlett looked towards the quay, for the moment Robert Reader had his back to her, barking orders. Quickly Scarlett made her way towards Market Lane. Just then a cheer went up, hopefully a sign nothing had been found on the lugger being searched. She turned briefly, and in that moment locked eyes with her tormentor even though he was now a fair distance from her. She could tell by his swaggering posture, his fixed glare full of malice, that all this was his doing, his revenge, a way of showing her his power. Robert Reader was a very dangerous enemy.

Scarlett ran the rest of the way to Prospect House. *What else would that beastly man do?* She hoped Mary had told her boys to stay away from the trouble on the quay.

Opening the gate, she hurried up the back path and into the warm kitchen. Bessie in a fluster as ever told her without so much as glancing up from the range, 'Upstairs, quick as you can, wear your grey for now, once you've helped me with the sisters' breakfasts, best check for the last time that everything's right for Miss Hester; she's a madam. Will make trouble for you if she can find it.'

Once ready and with apron tied and cap fixed, Scarlett tried to force open the tiny attic window so she could look out and see further down the river towards the quay, but the window wouldn't budge. The high white collar of her grey uniform she hoped would hide the bruises on her neck, what excuse she would tell if they were seen she hadn't fathomed yet, but there was no time to dwell on this and she hurried back to the kitchen. Only now as she unfolded and placed the delicate tray clothes in place and assembled the fine china for the sisters breakfast did Scarlett tell Bessie about the revenue.

'Wonder if that's why there no sign of Ivan this morning?' Bessie mumbled under her breath and stopped what she was doing. Hurriedly she wiped her hands and went out down the back path to the stables. Millie came downstairs clearly pleased to see her back.

And Scarlett quickly explained all that was happening, and they stood together watching out the window as Bessie hurried back.

'Thought the old fool had overslept but he's not there, neither is Dolly or the wagon. He'll be waiting till the coast is clear, that's what I think, best not to worry at the moment.'

With cook and Millie busy with preparations for later in the day, Scarlett went to ensure that all was in order for Miss Hester's arrival. Millie had set the fire in the school room even though it was unlikely to be used that day, also the fire in Miss Hester's bedroom, just in case. Scarlett couldn't see anything in Miss Hester's room that she could complain about and made her way over to the window, she couldn't resist the temptation to lift the catch and open the window. Leaning out she could see the revenue boats still out on the river and hear the outraged crowd on the quay. Anger had overcome their silence.

Unfortunately for Scarlett she did not looked to her left, for then she would have seen the coach travelling over the bridge from East Looe. But she didn't see or hear it until it stopped beneath the window at the steps to Prospect House. Too late, Scarlett hastened to close the window but not before she glanced down to see Miss Hester's face looking up at her from the window of the coach.

She wasn't ready and knew she had no time to change into the appropriate dark dress she should be wearing to meet her young charge. To her dismay, Mille had already opened the front door and Mr Julian and Miss Hester were in the hall as she descended the stairs still wearing her grey uniform.

Miss Hester looked her up and down in a most disparaging manner. 'Why exactly were you gawping from the window in a most unseemly matter?'

Scarlett was given time to answer. 'My aunts will be informed of your behaviour; it was most unseemly.'

Mr Julian handed Millie his hat and cane and walked past Scarlett, ignoring her. Hester Marshall followed handing Millie her bonnet and gloves and letting the girl her untie her cloak and take it from her. She walked past Scarlett, thin lips pressed together, head held high in a haughty manner.

Millie closed the door and Scarlett red in the face sighed with relief. Millie giggled. 'I can't believe you were caught doing that, she's bound to tell on you.'

'I know,' Scarlett groaned and begged Millie not to tell Bessie.

'She'll be cross the visit's got off to a bad start.'

A short while later the bell jangled, and Millie answered its summons.

'Miss Matilda wants to see you, right away in the small drawing room,' she announced pulling a face behind Bessie's back.

At once Scarlett made her way to the dark room where Miss Emilia played the organ. Like the other rooms in Prospect House, it was dark, heavy drapes shielding it from any daylight. Miss Matilda sat in the cold room with its unlit fire, and by the flickering light of the oil lamp set on the table, Scarlett could see she looked decidedly cross.

'I'm extremely disappointed, Scarlett. Miss Hester is very vexed with you. I need some explanation as to why you were behaving like you were. I can't believe you were leaning out from the window in the manner she describes.'

'It was just that the quay is swarming with revenue, boats are being searched. I just wanted to see what was happening, that's all.'

'And why pray would any of that be of such interest to you?'

'I was worried for some folks I know, that's all.'

'West Looe men can deal with the likes of the revenue; they don't need you to be worrying. Men are no importance to you. Remember that. Apologise to Miss Hester this minute and I will try and persuade her this was an isolated misdoing on your part. Then go and change your uniform.'

Like a naughty schoolgirl, Scarlett knocked and entered the drawing room and did as Miss Martha instructed. When she'd finished, Mr Julian twitched his lips and looked towards his daughter, who sat with a most sour look upon her face.

Mr Julian's eyes then bore into Scarlett's. 'Any more such behaviour and you'll be dismissed without a character. Understand that, Penrose.' Scarlett nodded, wishing Miss Clementine had never sent her here.

Dismissed, she fled and changed her uniform then returned to the kitchen, there to burst into tears, telling Bessie and Millie of Mr Julian's threat.

'Tis a warning,' Bessie declared. 'Be careful of Hester Marshall, she's a spiteful child, hopefully one day someone will put that girl firmly in her place.'

Unfortunately, Miss Hester had cast all below stairs in disheartened spirits. And the rest of the day fared no better. The cold luncheon when served was met with no enthusiasm by those gathered in the dining room, and Tam Beckly the butcher had badly let Bessie down, for the mutton she served in the evening was undoubtedly tough. Soon after the meal was finished, Mr Julian duly left without a word of praise for Bessie, something she took very much to heart, for usually he sent word of praise for the food she'd prepared.

Exhausted and grateful the long day was nearly over, at last Miss Hester sat before the mirror in her room as Scarlett brushed her hair and plaited it ready for the young miss to go to bed. Not a word passed between them.

It was as Scarlett made her way downstairs she glanced out the narrow window on the half landing which overlooked the stables, through a chink in the sackcloth covering a grimy window set in the stables roof, she saw a faint glimmer of light. Ivan was back.

Indeed as she entered the kitchen so did he, snatching his battered hat off his head as he came in.

Millie was still upstairs getting the sisters ready for bed, so it was just the three of them in the kitchen. Scarlett couldn't fail but notice the look that passed between Ivan and Bessie, she felt there was something they thought it best spoken of in private. There was an uncomfortable silence before both of them looked at her.

'Off to your bed now, maid, you'll be busy tomorrow no doubt,' Bessie encouraged.

'Could I just ask Ivan?'

'No maid you could not; can't you see the poor man's tired?'

She turned and lifted the heavy copper kettle from its hook; Ivan winked at Scarlett and mouthed the words, 'Jack's safe.' Scarlett grinned, and bit her lip as Bessie turned round.

'I'll wish you both good night then,' she said, feeling happier than she had all day and forgetting just how tired she felt, climbed the stairs to her attic room.

The next morning when Scarlett saw Ivan in the kitchen he just nodded and said nothing more about Jack, Scarlett had expected it to be like this, she was not one of them yet, a real local to be trusted. That would probably take years.

Early in the day Miss Hester threw a tantrum. Scarlett heard her shouting at Miss Emilia, 'I don't want her. Send her away. I want a proper lady's maid, not her.' Scarlett knew Miss Hester was referring to herself and stood still listening on the lower half landing. She heard Miss Emilia reply.

'You shall resign yourself to Penrose as your maid, and you will do as I say and ring for Penrose this very minute.'

The atmosphere when she was duly summoned was decidedly frosty. Miss Emilia wasted no time in leaving Miss Hester's bedchamber. Then impatient at the speed Scarlett was taking in fastening the tiny buttons on the front of her damson morning dress, Miss Hester brushed Scarlett's hands aside and in doing so tore one of the delicate rose enamelled buttons from the bodice and burst into tears like the child she was. Scarlett patiently searched and found the button, fetched her sewing box and sewed the delicate button back in place. This caused a thawing in the relationship between the two of them, and as Miss Hester dried her tears, she actually managed to say, 'Thank you.'

After breakfast, Scarlett taught her charge from the books provided by Miss Clementine. The Ladies academy her charge attended had taught her well and she was a surprisingly knowledgeable pupil.

Mr Julian called to collect his daughter in the early afternoon, taking the sisters also in a hired carriage to meet with and old acquaintance and landowner in nearby St Martin's.

It was a relief when finally the party left. Bessie had sent Millie over to pay the drapers in East Looe who had sent someone calling at the back door twice for monies owed to them the previous week when the sisters had been out. Bessie settled herself beside the fire, where Scarlett found her sound asleep.

Taking her shawl from its peg, Scarlett couldn't resist the dire need to escape from the house and sneak out and see whether Jack was on the quay. She'd just be gone a minute. Quietly closing the door behind her, she set off down Market Lane. The fishing boats had obviously sailed on the morning's high tide, leaving a few old men behind mending nets and Oggie sitting on his seat opposite the Jolly Sailor watching. Missing nothing.

Only the *Raven* was moored up, its crew busy preparing to sail when the tide was right. Handcarts piled with provisions were gathered by the narrow gangplank resting on the quay. Scarlett shielded her eyes from the watery sun and searched its deck for Jack. She saw Luke who waved; he ran over and shouted down an open hatch for Jack. When he appeared, there were many raucous comments and whistling but Jack took no notice and was soon beside her, leading her down the narrow alley behind the Jolly Sailor.

Once there amongst the empty barrels stacked against the walls, he stopped and pulled Scarlett to him, lifting her chin and kissing her for ever so it seemed. When at last he set her free, he grinned. 'Worried about me, were you? Did Ivan pass on my message telling you I got back safe?'

'I was scared you'd be caught smuggling, I'm not daft, Jack, I know what goes on.'

'Oh! You do, do you? Well don't worry yur head about it. Sod the revenue, they'll not get me. Near caught poor old Will though, just managed to sail on to Polperro in time, he did.'

Scarlett leaned forward resting her head against Jack's course woollen coat. He grasped hold her hands and she felt his fingers entwine themselves in hers.

Someone hollered for Jack and Scarlett sighed, 'You'd best go. Besides, I've got to hurry back, Bessie's asleep by the fire, there'll be hell to play if she wakes and I'm not there.'

Jack let go of her and pushed back his fringe of black curls, ignoring whoever it was calling him and kissed her once again.

'This isn't a long voyage I'll be back Sunday week and I'll take you up the river in Luke's boat. Bout time we spent some time, quiet like, on our own. This Sunday go see our Ruthie if you can, they ain't a bad lot up there, knock on the back door and like as not they'll let you see her if she's there, Sunday's her half day too.' Scarlett wondered if she dare go even to the back door of such a grand house, but it would be good to see how Ruth was getting on.

They said a quick goodbye on the quay, shared one last kiss before Scarlett fled back to Prospect House, getting there only just in time before Bessie woke up.

Chapter 5

Scarlett had only once seen the main entrance to Polgrove Hall situated on the rutted lane leading to Polperro. It had been on one of the days she was out with Ivan showing him she was capable of handling Dolly and the dog cart.

They'd set out along the quay to the bridge dividing East and West and Ivan had told her to take the steep lane that wound its way up the hill from the end of the bridge.

It was only a short distance before they came to a high stone wall. A little way further up the hill were two stout pillars and a set of elaborate iron gates, firmly closed. Forming an arch over these was a carved stone stag. Scarlett had slowed Dolly almost to a halt as she stared at the grandeur of it all, peering through the gates to get a better look at the neat drive disappearing between an avenue of trees.

'Keep your eyes on where you're going,' Ivan had shouted at her for in that moment of lost concentration, one of the wheels had sunk into a mud filled ditch jolting Ivan from his seat. He was not happy.

Thoughts of that day filled Scarlett's mind as on the following Sunday she made her way towards the tradesman's entrance at the rear of Polgrove Hall. Millie had told her how to get there by taking a short cut up May Hill, not far from Prospect House. The Polgrove Estate was so large that most of West Looe was owned by the Polgrove family. Scarlett followed Millie's instructions. Finally, she found herself in a wider lane and ahead of her a pair of large wooden gates, beside these a smaller gate. On the wall was a brass bell which tentatively Scarlett jangled. From a little way off came the sound of another bell, then footsteps approached, a tiny wooden square in the small gate and protected by black iron bars was drawn aside, a tired looking girl much younger than herself, glared out a her through a greasy fringe.

'I've come to see Ruth Jago; it's her half day,' Scarlett stated, hoping to sound far more confident than she felt.

The wooden square was slammed across and the laurel handle on the door turned, and the door was opened. 'She's not finished her work yet, best wait in the kitchen if you want.'

Scarlett followed meekly behind the girl. The giant shadow cast by the huge house made her shiver. The girl with the greasy hair had an even dirtier apron on and as Scarlett stepped foot inside the hot cavernous kitchen, she was dully stared at by at least five girls and a small older woman she took to be the cook.

'And who pray is this you're letting in, Polly?' the hollow-eyed old woman asked, rolling pin in hand.

Someone sniggered, 'Ain't supposed to let in any old riff-raff.'

'I've a good position, I'm no riff-raff, I'm just wanting to see my friend, that's why I'm here,' Scarlett answered hotly.

'What you do then?' a sloe-eyed girl enquired.

'Bit high and mighty you seem to me,' said another.

Scarlett lifted her head high and stared back at the lot of them. 'My employment is my business, not yours.'

Ruth arrived just as Scarlett began to wonder if coming here had been a mistake. 'Scarlett,' she cried running over to hug her friend warmly. 'You met my new friends?' she asked in all innocence, and Scarlett nodded as those who'd taunted her went back to work.

'We're not allowed to take any one upstairs; wait here I won't be long.'

But Scarlett already aware of glaring eyes replied, 'I'll wait outside, don't be long.'

As she waited, Scarlett felt glad she was not working here, something she thought never to think, for truth be told she had been more than a little bit envious of Ruth's working up at the big house.

Ruth came running out and the girls linked arms, she led Scarlett along a path which led past the stables and finally ended with a stile over which they climbed into a badly neglected meadow.

'So, do you really like working here?'

'I didn't at first, I hated it. You asking because that nasty lot in the kitchen were getting at you?'

'Yes,' Scarlett replied, 'two of them in particular.'

'That a be Jilks and Weyland, take no notice, got me down them two did till I got the measure of them, having a big family I'm used to standing up for meself.'

They sat side by side on the long dry grass, woollen shawls tugged tight about them, looking down at the river leading to the sea. A chill northerly wind whipped around their ankles, just for a moment an awkward silence fell between the two girls.

'You seen our Jack?' Ruth queried, and Scarlett managed to reply as normally as she could.

'Once or twice.' Which wasn't a lie.

'I haven't, never go down to the quay, keep away from the lot of them.'

'Why?'

'Because I'm still seeing Sam Trembright; and don't you dare tell, promise me you'll not.'

'I won't tell,' Scarlett promised.

'I love him and he me,' Ruth said defiantly. 'They'll not stop us seeing each other and I'll not have him suffer the consequences if they ever find out. Having a father like mine and brothers like Jack and Luke, thick headed and obstinate, I fear for Sam, me and all.'

'Don't worry I'll never tell,' Scarlett declared, but all the same she felt guilt ridden knowing Ruth's secret and knowing she must keep it from Jack. She remembered that day when Ruth's father had beaten her for seeing Sam and the dreadful fight Jack had had with him. Indeed, it was best Jack didn't know.

'What's it like down in your place?' Ruth changed the subject much to Scarlett's relief. 'How you getting on with the two crazy sisters? Old Ivan who works there, he's a good un; Father says he'd trust that man with his life.'

'It's all right, hard work, and that young Hester Marshall who's staying a while, she can be nasty. But I do have an attic room of my own and with Millie so possessive over looking after the sisters, it's not too bad really.'

Ruth snatched at a clump of grass. 'I can tolerate it here, funny to me them lot was in the kitchen because

I didn't start in service on the lowest position. Told um, I did, how Father saved his Lordship, and old cook told um to stop, but I still have to share with one of them all the same. The one with the odd shaped eyes, wouldn't trust her one little bit. You can tell they're not Looe girls, they all come from Duloe, one of the villages Sir Geoffrey owns. Employing girls from Duloe is something his wife insists on, heaven knows why. Seen me a few times one or two of them have with Sam, so I'm thankful they're not local.'

Scarlett couldn't help but be a little bit curious. 'So when do you get to meet with Sam, surely not very often?'

'Whenever we can, he wants us to get away from Looe, start out together where there'd be no animosity, taking whatever work he can.'

'Surely, they'd all come round in the end, his folks and yours?'

'No, Scarlett, they won't. Anyhow Sam's got to know someone who drinks in The Swan, lives up Plaidy Hill, he says he can get our Sam on the *Black Diamond*. He's been on the last two voyages out of Fowey and their looking for able crew, trustworthy like, the captain's a brute but the money is unbelievable, a great deal more than our Jack's getting on the *Raven*.'

'But isn't it the *Black Diamond* the revenue are after catching?' Scarlett queried, worried for Ruth's Sam who she hardly knew.

'Who told you that?' Ruth spun round to face her friend in astonishment.

'I... can't remember,' Scarlett replied, her voice faltered. For a moment, she was afraid Ruth would pursue the matter further, realising how easy it was to forget herself, betray knowledge she shouldn't know. Only knew because of her traitor father.

'Whoever told you that's an out and out liar!' Ruth spluttered, narrowing her eyes.

'Why?'

'Cause the *Black Diamond*'s the fastest ship there is, and no old revenue sloop could catch her. Sam says her captain's more clever, got more men and boats willing to help get the goods ashore than the revenue has in the whole of Cornwall, outwit the lot of um will Captain Ferris. There I've said too much but I can trust you Scarlett, have no fear my Sam'll be alright.'

'I'm glad you've told me about Sam, it's so good to see you happy.'

'I am happy, Scarlett, love im to bits I do my Sam.' A comfortable silence settled between the two friends.

Scarlett sat looking out to sea and her thoughts turned to Jack. Next Sunday she'd be out on the river with him, just seven days till she'd see him again.

Suddenly Ruth jumped to her feet and ran to meet Sam Trembright who came lumbering across the field from the other direction. He hugged Ruth lifting her off her feet, kissing her passionately as they walked towards Scarlett.

'Good day, Scarlett.' Sam's tousled blond hair looked more untidy than the last time she'd seen him, but the look on his face as he held Ruth round the waist and kissed her once again was full of love.

'You won't go telling on us will you, Scarlett?' he begged giving her a beguiling look.

'She won't,' Ruth giggled.

'I won't tell a soul.' Scarlett smiled back at the happy couple. 'But I must be going; your time together is precious.'

She left them and walked back down into West Looe and instead of going back to Prospect House went up to Tamarisk to see her mother.

Jeanette jumped as she entered the cottage and when she turned round Scarlett could see her eyes were red and puffy from crying. The cottage smelt of tobacco, she must have just missed her father.

'What's the matter?' Scarlett ran over and put her arms around her mother, she felt Jeanette's thin shoulders shaking.

'It's nothing, maid.' She tried to smile. 'It's good to see you. Amos brought me a little tea last week, I'll make us a cup and you can tell me how you're getting on.'

But as she made the tea, her mother broke down and began to cry, there was no way she could disguise whatever was causing her sorrow, so pulling out a chair Scarlett sat her mother down and took over the tea making.

'It's something to do with Father isn't it, what's happened?'

Tea made, Scarlett sat opposite her mother, waiting as she dried her eyes.

'Your father's been here with that awful man Reader. Raised his fist to me Reader did, when I reminded him of the King's law that informers aren't to work within 22 miles of home. Poured scorn on my words, came right up close and laughed in my face and Elijah just stood by and said nothing, nothing!' She paused, red-faced with anger.

'Down in Warren Cove they are tonight with a platoon of red coats, out to catch some unlucky souls, and I know one they could catch for sure – Amos. I know he does a bit of smuggling thereabouts with others from Lanreath. What if he's caught?' Jeanette took a deep breath, and wept uncontrollably dabbing her eyes with her apron, leaving Scarlett feeling sick with worry and completely helpless.

It hadn't shocked her to hear her father had let Robert Reader treat her mother so badly, after all he'd hardly seemed outraged when catching Reader trying to rape his own daughter. She would never forgive him for that.

'And, Scarlett—' Jeanette bit her trembling lip and reached out to take hold her daughter's hand. 'There's something else what bothers me; what if Amos catches sight of Elijah and recognises him, what would that mean for us, maid? I couldn't go through what happened at Sennen again, and I don't want to move on, why should I? You and all, girl, it would be the end of your life here too.'

Scarlett swallowed hard, any chance of happiness, of falling even more in love with her handsome Jack would be over. He'd think her scum, probably come shouting at their door throwing stones like the folks in Sennen. She remembered her slip of the tongue that very afternoon. Ruth hadn't suspected anything she was sure, but she'd have to be more careful. And praise God she was very much on the side of the smugglers.

'Is there anything we can do about tonight?' Scarlett asked her mother. She stood up and walked towards the window, looked out and stared down West Looe Hill. No one must be caught tonight.

Jeanette joined her daughter by the window. 'I've got an idea, maid, something Amos and me laughed about last year, he never did find out who'd put it there. But it worked.'

Scarlett was curious to know more.

'It was just before harvest last year and dark by the time Amos climbed the steps leading to his quarters at Lanreath. By the light of his lamp, clear as day, he sees what he thought to be a bundle of sorts lying on one of the steps, only it's not a bundle just a wide stone wrapped in white linen, so as to show it up well in the dark. Amos can read, there was a message on it '*revenue offshore*.' Proper quick, Amos wasted no time in spreading the word. Mystery was, who put the warning there, he thought it must be one of the master's sons, but he never did find out. We'll do the same, maid.'

'Warn who, though?' Scarlett questioned, sceptical that this idea would work.

'That Ivan down at your place, friend of Amos, he is.'

Jeanette busied herself going out into the back yard and fetched in a suitable flattish stone, none too heavy. She got a white linen petticoat, and using Elijah's quill and ink, wrapped it round the stone and wrote a neat message. '*Revenue at Warren Cove*'.

'This is the difficult bit. Can you place this in the stables at Prospect House so Ivan will see it? You'll have to be mighty quick; you can't afford to be seen. I've an old needlework bag you can carry it down in.'

Scarlett was more than a little worried about doing this without getting caught. 'But we don't even know if Ivan can read,' she protested.

'Don't you worry, maid, he'll like as not take it in to Bessie if he can't, he'll know it's important.'

The thought of being found in the stables by Ivan terrified Scarlett. She stayed with her mother for a while longer, taking her leave at a time when usually Ivan would be taking a mug of ale with Bessie before she began preparations for dinner this evening.

Indeed, as Scarlett glanced through a gap in the back gate at Prospect House, she saw Ivan and Bessie in the kitchen deep in conversation. Feeling like a thief, she eased the stable door open and slipped inside. Taking out the linen covered stone, she placed it on a rickety wooden table beside Ivan's spare pipe. Then hurriedly opened the door just wide enough so she could creep out. Taking a deep breath, she opened the gate, neither of those supping ale glanced out through the window as she walked down the path to the kitchen door. Halfway down she panicked and looked up grateful that the stable doors where at such an angle that none of the houses backing onto Market Lane could see them.

As she entered the kitchen, Bessie looked up. 'Them's all out, thank heaven, none of um back till later, been invited out to Poltreaze with Mr Julian, bit of peace and quiet we've all got.' And Ivan nodded his head, looking at her through bleary eyes. 'Millie's upstairs getting things ready for the sisters' return. I told he to leave it for now, but she wouldn't.'

Scarlett took off her cloak and bonnet, she reached up and hung them on the high hook at the back of the door. Bessie poured more ale into Ivan's tankard and Scarlett took her leave of them, tightly clutching the old needlework bag. As she made her way upstairs, she wondered how much longer Ivan would remain in the kitchen.

Earlier when Scarlett left Tamarisk, her mother had shed more tears and was pacing the floor. Frustrating as it was, there was nothing Scarlett could do now but wait. Without knowledge of when the sisters and Miss Hester would return, she sat on the half-landing stairs leading up to the second floor, watching fretfully out of the long window, impatient beyond belief. Thankfully it was to be but minutes before she heard the kitchen door bang shut, and in the faint light cast from the window of the kitchen, saw Ivan unsteady on his feet swaying down the path. Scarlett stood on tiptoe now; what if he didn't see her warning? She held her breath hoping upon hope he would, then saw with relief just visible above the back wall, Ivan with lantern in hand set off down Market Lane. She sighed, suddenly feeling exhausted and just as she felt so the family returned, and she hastened to assist them. Mr Julian helped his aunts and daughter descend from the carriage and escorted them into the house before taking his leave.

Millie was suddenly at Scarlett's side and the evening continued as was the custom with Scarlett helping Miss Hester to bed and afterwards going down to the kitchen to fetch her charge a drink of hot milk. As she began to carry the silver dish with the hot drink upstairs, she heard the kitchen door open, felt a draft of cold air. She paused and took two steps back down the stairs.

'Whatever's the matter?' Bessie cried, and Scarlett heard Ivan gasp for breath between coughing and trying to speak.

'A drink, woman, get me a drink and I'll tell you.'

She heard Bessie pouring ale into his tankard.

'Someone, God only knows who, left me a warning, tis bad if what said is true. I only hopes we're in time to save them poor souls tonight. I've sent word for beacons to be lit up Hannafore and across on the island. Luke Jago's ran along the coast towards Warren Cove, he's lighting one there soon as he can. It seems revenue and red coats are watching Warren Cove, over forty men of ours are down there, I knows that for a fact waiting for the *James Robert* from Guernsey laden with contraband.'

She heard Bessie drawing out a chair, and careful to walk on the left-hand side of the stairs where they didn't creak, Scarlett continued up to Miss Hester. If only she could tell her mother warnings were to be lit so the run would be abandoned. This would ease her mind over Amos. Pray God the warnings were in time. At least there was hope now.

Before she went to bed when all was done, Scarlett looked out from her attic window, she said a silent prayer for those down the coast at Warren Close.

The next morning, Ivan sat as usual by the kitchen table, he looked tired and Scarlett so wished she could ask him if he'd had word all was well. The mayhem of the daily ritual of the house took place, with breakfast trays and Millie as usual determined none should help. Miss Hester had risen early and was dressed and had breakfasted long before the sisters had rung their bells. She was excited having been told by her father the previous day that a new trap was being delivered from Liskeard, one more suitable for the likes of herself than the one presently at Prospect House. Ivan knew nothing of this, not yet.

Miss Hester heard from the school room the hubbub of voices at the back of the house and flew downstairs before Scarlett could stop her. Without cloak or shawl, she ran down the path just as those delivering the new trap took their leave. They had helped Ivan place it in one of the outbuildings alongside the stables. Miss Hester rudely brushed past him to inspect it. What she saw did not please her, for the trap although much improved from the present one was still just a trap, nothing grander, even if it was of a more elegant design.

Ivan stood aside, puffing away on his pipe whilst she continued to examine it.

'I want you to take me out now, Ivan, fetch Dolly, ready her now. Do you hear? I want to go out now.'

Ivan looked at her long and hard. 'Beg pardon, miss, but it's starting to rain, you'll get soaked through, Penrose an all.'

'Are you refusing to do as I ask?'

'That I am, miss, for your own sake, you'll like as take a chill if we go now.'

'Well if that's the way of it, we'll see what my aunts say, shall we?' With that she pushed open the back gate and in an attempt to dodge the puddles already beginning to appear, lifted her skirts higher than decorum would have permitted and stomped up the path. The blue ribbons in her hair already limp from the rain.

Scarlett shook her head as she went after her charge, whilst Ivan heaved shut the outbuilding's wide doors and headed back to the stable.

The row which followed could be heard all over the house. It ended when Miss Hester flounced out of the drawing room and ran upstairs sobbing.

Scarlett was unclear quite what to do; go after her charge and risk having the young madam's anger directed upon herself, or leave Miss Hester to see out her tantrum alone. She decided unless instructed otherwise she would go to the school room and prepare some future lessons. Millie joined her and together they listened to the sisters' animated conversation which continued on.

'I blame her father,' they heard Miss Matilda say. 'Sending her to that expensive academy, she's got to learn she's born into trade not gentry, there's a difference. Just as good as them we are but there'll be no fancy carriage for her here. Whatever next? Her head's full of the kind of lives some of the very privileged girls there lead, but she's not one of them.'

'Quite right,' Miss Emilia heartily agreed. 'Come, sister, look.' Miss Emilia must have drawn aside the heavy drapes for she declared. 'And wanting Ivan to take her out in this weather. We'd best have a word with Julian, maybe he could take her up to the quarries one of these days to see where the money for her fine education comes from.'

The querulous day ended with Miss Hester throwing another tantrum as Scarlett plaited her hair for bed.

'You're hurting me, you useless girl,' she screamed, and in quickly turning round to scold her, caused the lace edging on the sleeve of her nightgown to catch upon a delicate china pot containing hair pins, it fell to the floor and broke into many pieces. Scarlett began to pick them up.

'Get out!' Miss Hester cried red-faced, and boiling with anger, Scarlett was most pleased to do so.

She went down to the kitchen and helped Millie out with the scouring of pans and the endless washing up. When all was finally finished, she fetched out the wicker mending basket Anne the maid who'd previously worked there had used. She dare not go to bed, even after Millie came down having attended the sisters. Bessie took a hot drink into her sleeping quarters and bade them goodnight. Scarlett sat repairing the frayed edge of a delicate tablecloth, Millie told her it was sometimes used if special visitors came to the kitchen for a gossip with Bessie. Miss Matilda rang down for Millie who stomped towards the stairs in a huff.

'Thought I was done for the day,' she moaned as she went up. For a precious few moments Scarlett was alone, and how precious these moments were with nothing else to do but hope all the folks from last night were safe and then wonder about the next time she'd see Jack.

Chapter 6

There was one thing about Miss Hester that Scarlett couldn't fault, which was her ability to erase from her memory anything she found distasteful the previous day. The preceding day was quite forgotten and in the morning she was her usual self and asked her aunts if Scarlett be allowed to accompany her on a short walk for, although cold, the sun was shining and it was what she wanted. The sisters, relieved to avoid any repeat of yesterday's tantrums, agreed on the one condition they kept well away from the where the quay was the busiest along by the Jolly Sailor.

'Tisn't the place for you to be,' Miss Emilia stated firmly.

'Yes, Aunt, I quite know that,' Miss Hester replied sweetly, and mid-morning accompanied by Scarlett they duly left by the front door and turned to walk towards the bridge away from the quay. Miss Hester chose not to walk over the bridge or across into the track leading to the mill but begged Scarlett they walk up the hill a little. Scarlett pleaded this was unwise but had no choice other than follow her charge as she strode on ahead up the stony track which led to a scattering of cottages. A narrow path wound its way from here to the higher end of Horse Lane. Scarlett had walked here before with Ruth.

There had been little conversation until Miss Hester suddenly declared, 'We shall be going with my father to

Moorswater Manor to visit Mr Francis Kestrel. I attend the academy with Isabella a distant relative of his, she considers me one of her closest friends. It will be good to have you in attendance as my abigail.

'Will Ivan be taking us?' Scarlett enquired.

Miss Hester looked at her shocked. 'Off course not, you ninny, Father's hired a proper carriage to take us.'

Scarlett stayed silent wondering what would be expected of her, she hoped Bessie would know. Suddenly Miss Hester sat down on the stone wall overlooking the harbour in almost the exact spot she and Ruth had sat on the day they'd seen the revenue searching the luggers moored over in East Looe.

'This is—' Scarlett was going to say as they were almost opposite Miss Clementine's academy where she'd finished her schooling. But Miss Hester had raised her chin in such a haughty manner she thought it best to say nothing.

Looking down from where they sat there was so much to see, the tide was in, the luggers were returning, the smell of fish and sound of the gulls drowned out the noise from those below.

They continued to walk on until they reached the top of the hill, here the lane wound its way down past the cottage where Ruth lived and ended up very nearly on the quay itself. Scarlett stopped and said with more insistence, 'We should go back, miss; I overheard your aunt saying she didn't want you to walk this way.'

'No, we will not turn back,' Miss Hester exclaimed, holding a handkerchief delicately to her nose for the smell of fish was becoming stronger now. She quickened her pace, very defiant upon the matter. Quickly they walked down Horse Lane past the Jagos' cottage, then on past the Jolly Sailor and onto the quay bustling with fishermen and fishwives. A quay full of hollering and jostling, cluttered from end to end with baskets full of the day's catch, swearing fishwives pushing handcarts between horse-drawn wagons that vied for space along the quay's edge. At the far end near the smoking sheds, fishermen were hanging nets out to dry whilst above them the swirling flock of gulls squawked louder than ever. Undaunted, Miss Hester stepped into this throng of activity daintily avoiding any obstacle which was in her way.

Following behind, Scarlett saw the looks and oft time sniggers Miss Hester received from some folk, but she herself was happy to be outside the confines of Prospect House and looked along the quay for one lugger she hoped to see. Then she spotted the *Lucy*. Mary Jago and another older woman were helping Jack's friend Will, Tom, Luke and two others unload the *Lucy*'s catch.

Miss Hester's progress onward was delayed a moment, for she was forced to stop when two women with a wooden cart pushed by swearing loudly nearly knocking her off her feet. As she dusted off her skirts, clearly put out, Scarlett rushed to help her with this task. As Miss Hester continued to walk on, Scarlett saw Will look up and touched his forelock, nudging Luke who did the same. Scarlett instinctively waved back and was caught doing so by Miss Hester who gave her a scathing look.

'You do not acknowledge such people; I won't have it,' she snapped, and made haste to escape from the unsavoury mass of people. She turned and walked quickly back along beside the river to the front entrance of Prospect House.

As Scarlett hurried along behind her charge, she took a chance and turned again. Will saw her and waved, he doffed his cap several times in a much-exaggerated manner, his grey hair blowing wildly in a sudden gust of wind, sensing she had got into trouble for acknowledging him before. Scarlett gave him a little wave behind her back and stifled a giggle as she hurried to catch up with Miss Hester.

In no time they were walking up the well-scrubbed steps of Prospect House. Scarlett wasn't sure Miss Hester enjoyed her walk as much as she had.

A rather subdued Miss Hester settled down when they returned and completed the schoolwork Scarlett had prepared earlier without a single protest. Later, having partaken of a light lunch and now wearing the pale green dress Scarlett had pressed so it had not a crease anywhere, she joined the sisters who had invited their friend a Mrs Gloria Potter and her granddaughter Sophie to join them for afternoon tea. For those in service at Prospect House it was a relief to have a day without a single tantrum. So far.

That night Scarlett was woken by the sound of a church bell being furiously tolled. Startled into wakefulness she reached for the tinder box on the chair beside her bed and lit her candle. Something must be most terribly wrong. She hurried over to look out the window, tried to open it but as always it stayed firmly shut. Two men with blazing torches ran past the house. Scarlett pressed her face against the leaded pane, she could see others running towards quay. Frustrated she pushed this way and that on the window hoping it would open, desperate to get a better look at what was happening.

A knock came on her door and Millie ran in, her face ashen. The candle in her hand trembled throwing strange dancing shadows about the room. 'Tis a bad omen, them tolling bells,' she cried shivering in her nightgown, her feet like Scarlett's cold upon the bare boards. 'Always bad it is, always.'

She too peered out from the unyielding window, watching as lanterns appeared held by those out on the river.

Bessie came puffing up the stairs. 'If you'm two up you'd better come down and keep me company, I've asked the sisters if they need anything, but they don't, worried like the rest of us they are. And that Miss Hester, well she's fast asleep!'

Quickly Scarlett dressed and hurried downstairs. It was icy cold in the kitchen and Millie busied herself lighting the range.

'I went in search of Ivan, but he'd already gone,' Bessie said quietly, she shook her head in despair. 'Pray God none of our men have perished out there tonight.'

'Could it be another ship blown off course, broken up on the rocks like earlier this year, could it not be?' Scarlett queried, unable to quell her feeling of panic.

Bessie answered bluntly, 'There's no storm, you saw the river, it was calm, there's no wind howling down the chimney, tis something else.'

'Can I go down to the quay?' Scarlett pleaded. 'Find out what's wrong.'

Bessie sighed, 'No, maid, Ivan'll bring us word, and besides young Miss Hester will surely wake and ring for you.'

They sat in silence, each watching the door waiting for Ivan's return. The sisters had stayed in Miss Matilda's bedroom at the front of the house, no doubt looking down from there just as anxious as those in the kitchen below.

Scarlett asked Bessie if she might go up to the drawing room so she could see if anything was happening out on the river. Given permission, once there she opened the long casement window and stepped out onto the small balcony beyond. Scarlett could see by the glow of blazing torches a crowd gathered on the quay; saw sails unfurled with luggers and sloops alike setting sail. Across the river a crowd was gathered also, men in rowing boats had taken to the river shouting to one another words Scarlett couldn't hear. She felt thankful that Jack was safe aboard the *Raven*.

A horrifying thought came to mind as Millie came and stood beside her watching the flotilla of boats disappear towards the mouth of the harbour, with an ache of foreboding one person came to mind, the hateful Robert Reader.

The church bell tolled on throughout the night, now at a slower pace, a solemn melancholy sound. The night seemed endless. Eventually as dawn began to lighten the sky the sisters rang for a breakfast tray. And Scarlett went quietly up to take another look out of the drawing room window. The tide was out now but a crowd remained on either side the quay. It was as she returned to the kitchen there came the most dreadful wail of grief. She ran down the remaining stairs, and the sisters also hearing this pitiful sound followed Scarlett down to the kitchen where Ivan stood, his arms around Bessie and Millie holding them to him. He carried on him the tang of the sea, but neither of those who clung to him had a care, Bessie burying her head in his wet coat to stifle the sound of her despair.

'What's happened, man?' Miss Emilie demanded, her voice faltering as she looked upon his grim face.

Slowly Ivan released them. 'Tis the revenue cutter *Sylvie*, mistress. Crept out from Talland bay, caught one of the Looe luggers out hooking up tubs. The hermit living across on Looe Island says it all happened so quick there was no time to light a beacon. He saw one of the poor blighters on board shot and fall overboard; the two others fled the ship, jumping into the sea as more shots were fired. Come in proper close to shore the *Sylvie* did, for the hermit says the lugger began drifting towards the rocks at Hannafore. The revenue seized the boat and by the line still attached, hooked up the remaining tubs then took her in tow.'

Ivan took a deep breath and coughed. Scarlett dreaded what he'd say next.

'Tis thought it's Will's boat, the *Lucy*.'

Scarlett put her hand to her mouth to stifle a cry.

'Oggie saw Will, young Luke Jago and Peter Chard setting sail earlier. Praise God we'll be after the bastard who's done this.'

'Is the crazy hermit sure one of them was definitely shot?' Bessie questioned between sobs. 'He's a daft old man that hermit.' Everyone in the kitchen looked to Ivan beseeching him to say no.

'He's sure, we're searching for all three of um now, I must get back, knew you'd all be wondering.' Scarlett glimpsed the burning anger that blazed behind his eyes. He nodded his head in the direction of the sisters and was gone.

'Known Will all my life, I have,' Bessie sobbed.

'So have we,' Miss Matilda stated and put a comforting hand on Bessie's shoulder.

Scarlett stood trembling, her teeth chattering as desperately she tried to hide the emotion she felt. Bessie reached out and took her hand, she knew Scarlett was a friend of Ruth Jago's and she'd not missed the tousled haired Jack Jago's appearance several times in Market Lane.

The day wore on; Miss Hester woke and had to be attended to. Mr Julian arrived, not in the least amused when his daughter prattled on about wanting a new dress and bonnet. She seemed unconcerned by the tragedy that had befallen West Looe. In the end she was banished to her room. Scarlett struggled through the day with a bad-tempered Miss Hester who she still had to attend to, more concerned about the visit to Moorswater than the fate of those on board the *Lucy*. This infuriated Scarlett who felt close to tears each time she remembered waving to Will and Luke so happily when out with Miss Hester. Will's wife Kathleen, the Jagos, the family of Peter Chard, all must be out of their minds with worry.

Then the bell stopped tolling.

Ivan returned. 'Best I tell the mistresses first then I'll come down, it won't take long.'

Bessie filled his pewter mug with ale whilst they waited and indeed it wasn't long before he came back.

'Alfie Thomas found a body in the sea, along towards Talland; it was that of his good friend Will. He'd been shot in the back, never stood a chance. Kathleen collapsed when Alfie returned to the harbour and tied up. Poor soul was on her knees hysterical as they carefully lifted Will's lifeless body ashore.'

In the kitchen there was silence. Bessie pushed the tankard of ale towards Ivan and he raised it to his lips drinking its contents down in one go. They all jumped as he slammed it down on the wooden table.

'No sign of Luke Jago or Peter Chard but if they swam ashore there's time yet for um to be found; we'm looking, searching the beaches and places they may hide if injured. Tis thought it's the same evil bastard done this who shot the two Polperro men last year. The *Black Diamond*'s enemy and ours, Robert Reader, for it's him who sails out from Fowey on the *Sylvie*.'

Ivan turned to go, stopped and looked back. 'I'm off with Tom Jago, taking a rowing boat searching along the shoreline, the poor man's frantic to find his son.'

After he left, daily life at Prospect House had to go on as usual but the day seemed longer than most. Miss Hester took to her bed early with a headache, much to Scarlett's relief, so she was in the kitchen when Ivan returned once more. He brought with him the good news that they'd found young Luke. As before he went up to tell the sisters first.

Back in the kitchen, Ivan slumped into his chair by the table, he too was tired, worn out by what had befallen his friends.

'Come on, man,' Bessie urged, 'out with it, where did you find him?'

'Twas Warren Cove; we rowed round the rocks this side of the Cove and beached the boat on the sands. Tom hollered his boy's name and Luke limped out from one of the caves, exhausted, a mass of cuts and bruises. Once we had him safely aboard he said after jumping into the sea he'd found it hard to swim against the current and get ashore, finally he was swept onto the jagged rocks at Warren and buffeted by the sea crawled across them until he was on the beach and limped into the cave. He'd stayed there frightened the revenue would come looking for him.'

Bessie surprised Scarlett and Millie then, for she went over and kissed his wrinkled brow.

'Get off, woman,' he growled but caught her hand in his. 'Away with you and fetch me a drink.' But as Bessie fussed around him his head fell forward, and his eyes began to close.

He was left to sleep in peace until the jangling of the sisters' bell woke him; for once, Millie was annoyed at having to answer it and Bessie tut tutted as its sharp sound had woken Ivan. With Ivan's tankard full of ale, Bessie began ladling into a pewter bowel a generous helping of her mutton stew with chunks of thick bread baked only hours earlier.

'Thanks, Bess,' he said, gratefully eating his first meal for a long time.

Scarlett sat mending a rip in one of Miss Matilda's finest of petticoats, impatient to learn more, and at last Ivan having eaten his fill and after Bessie had refilled his tankard several times told them more.

'Luke asked after those who'd been with him and broke down when his father told him Will was dead and Peter Chard still missing. He was in a bad way when we got back into Looe. Mary Jago was on the quay and all cheered as Tom and me helped him up the steps, but he didn't acknowledge anyone, and Tom and Mary helped him home in a sorry state.'

'Was Ruth Jago there?' Scarlett asked quietly.

'No, maid, she wasn't but word will have been sent up to Polgrove telling her her brother's safe. They've made a collection for Kathleen and tomorrow some of the men have taken it upon themselves to sail down to Fowey to ask folks there if anyone knows the fate of Will's boat, it may be auctioned off as is the case of many. Money's been collected should this be done sooner rather than later. I know Mr Julian's helped in this; they'll take the money with them just in case tis needed. A couple of the coastguards there will accept a bribe especially Adam French, he may be able to tell them something of the *Lucy*'s whereabouts.'

Alone in her room, Scarlett wondered. Was her father with Robert Reader now, was he part of what happened to Will? Fear of his involvement left Scarlett beyond herself with shame and terror, resentful that her life would once again be ruined by his profession as a spy. She hated her father almost as much as Robert Reader himself. The last thing she wanted was to be hounded out of West Looe like they had been in Sennen. And Jack? God, he would hate her.

It seemed that Sunday would never come. Throughout Saturday, Scarlett kept looking out her attic window, frustrated she couldn't tell whether the *Raven* had returned or not for so many tall-masted ships lined the quay, tied in so closely it was impossible to tell one from the another. If Jack was back would he try and see her before Sunday? Making excuses to Bessie, she looked out from the back gate more than once longing to see her tousled haired sweetheart, but he wasn't there. What she did hear twice, much to her surprise, was Mr Julian talking to Ivan in the stables. She was surprised he was there. Mr Julian had only ever used the front door of Prospect House in all the time Scarlett had worked there. She couldn't hear exactly what they were saying and hadn't lingered in fear of being caught listening.

Before she could gossip to Millie about this, Ivan had come into the kitchen and announced quite casually, whilst sipping his ale and tapping his pipe on the kitchen table, 'I've something to do for Mr Julian; tis important, I'll be away til Sunday night, back on Monday.'

'What—?' Millie went to ask, but Bessie gave her a purposeful stare.

'Tisn't for the likes of us to know,' Bessie stated and looked across the table at Ivan. Deep in thought, Ivan nodded in agreement.

Once he'd gone the only word that came from the outside world was from Florrie Starr the new laundress who came to collect the linen. Bessie was not taken with the woman, scorch marks on two of Miss Matilda's lace collars had meant she'd near been dismissed. Florrie had come into the kitchen and taking hold one of the wooden chairs had placed it near the fire, making herself at home and clearly not feeling the chill of Bessie's disapproval.

'No word of Peter Chard,' she said rubbing a chilblain on the back of her ankle, 'he must have drowned, poor man. Talk in the Jolly last night was of revenge, so my John said, and rightly so.'

Scarlett thought Florrie a friendly sort but when no offer of tea came and with Bessie ignoring her, Florrie picked up the calico linen bag and said a cheery goodbye to them all.

'How dare she?' Bessie spluttered, once she heard the gate bang shut. 'The captain's housekeeper next door may like her sort, but I don't. What's she thinking of coming in here and making herself at home? Bloody cheek.'

Scarlett made her a cup of tea and Bessie plonked herself down in her own comfortable chair by the fire. Thankfully the sisters troubled Millie for little and only Miss Hester who prattled on about the visit to Moorswater seemed untroubled.

Bessie knew in her heart that Florrie spoke the truth for Ivan's last words to her had been, 'That bastard Reader will pay, I'll kill him myself if I get the chance.'

'Be careful,' she'd begged, 'for you'm be strung up in Bodmin if you do.' But it had been in a fine temper he'd left to do Mr Julian's bidding.

On Sunday all was prepared for Tuesday's visit to Moorswater. Miss Hester's clothes had been chosen, pressed and were ready long before Scarlett took her leave of Prospect House to hurry down to the quay to where the *Raven* was safely moored up. She saw Jack before he saw her, he was leaning against an iron railing one foot raised slightly on a higher granite slab, staring down towards the mouth of the river. The tide running high, the quay strangely quiet.

As Scarlett walked towards him, she felt a powerful outburst of affection, knew he was mourning the loss of his friends, wanted so much to ease his pain but knew nothing she could do or say would help. She slipped her hand in his, he turned round, and Scarlett could see the sadness in his dark brown eyes.

He managed a weak smile. 'Come here, my lovely, I've thought of you so much.' He pulled her gently into his arms, holding her tightly to him before stepping back and reaching out to cup her face in his rough hands, kissing her softly at first and then more passionately before finally letting her go.

They stood for a moment in silence and Jack's gaze returned to the rippling water of the river. Two young boys in a tiny rowing boat were making there was across from East to West, they were laughing as the smaller boy furiously bailed out the boat to keep it afloat. They waved but Jack didn't wave back.

He sighed and shook his head. 'Two good men. Scarlett, two good men lost forever, tis indeed a bitter homecoming. Maybe if I'd been with them, I'd ave seen the bastards coming, maybe things would have been different, I don't know.'

'But you may have been killed too, please, Jack, don't blame yourself for not being there.' Scarlett bit her lip wondering if she'd said the right thing.

Jack stepped away from the quay.

'One thing's for sure I can't be here looking along the quay to where Will moored the *Lucy*, can't be reminded that he's gone, Peter too. Everything's changed now, everything. Our Luke stayed out on the quay all night waiting for the *Raven* to come in on the high tide. Wanted to be the one to tell me. God I'll never forget this day, never.' He took a deep breath and clenched his hands together. 'Come on, I'll take you somewhere away from the quay where we can be alone.'

Holding tight Scarlett's hand, he led her away, walking so fast Scarlett almost had to run to keep up with him, leading her along the quay and up the steep steps that lead to the top of Horse Lane. At the far end they had to cross the rutted track that led to Polperro. Jack picked Scarlett up, so deep were the muddy puddles. He set her down on the other side and they walked on past the mill to where the river forked left and right. Underfoot the damp autumn leaves almost pulled Scarlett's feet from under her as Jack hurried on. He knew exactly where he was taking her and turned off down a barely visible track. Grasping her hand more tightly, he began to stride through the undergrowth making his way through the tangle of trees that led down to the river.

Briefly, Scarlett caught glimpses of the river but soon these were gone, and dense trees engulfed them. Out of breath, Scarlett was relieved when Jack abruptly stopped and leaned back against a knurled old tree, he pulled her to him.

'Promise you'll never tell a living soul where I'm taking you, there's many would be cross I've brought you here.'

'I promise,' Scarlett told him. She hoped the flush creeping up her neck and now burning her cheeks didn't show.

'Not that Millie girl, none of them back at that place you work. Could cause the death of more good men if you tittle-tattle.' He looked at her in deadly earnest.

'I promise, Jack, I promise.' Scarlett meant it; never would she tell.

Satisfied, Jack led her carefully on down the steep bank.

As they neared the bottom, Scarlett saw a stone ledge up against which the river lapped. She slipped and Jack caught her, and taking her by the arm propelled her forward, leading her onto the ledge and round the solid buttress wall into the opening of a stone-built cavern. From where they stood you could no longer see the river; a labyrinth of trees hid the entrance and from above thick foliage hung down concealing this secret place. Inside were two six-oar rowing boats and a further two were pulled up on the stony floor. The sound of the lapping water echoed in the vaulted chamber. Jack led her further inside and the dank pungent smell of the place caught in Scarlett's throat.

Barrels of all sizes were stacked neatly along one wall and Scarlett could see the entrance to a tunnel.

At the far end was a makeshift bed propped up on old ships' timbers and strewn with thick rough blankets.

An old coat of coarse grey wool was roughly folded to make a pillow. Beside this was a four-legged stool, slightly lopsided on the uneven floor, on top of this a thick wax candle on a pewter dish.

'Tis best place I could think of for peace and quiet,' Jack told Scarlett leading her towards the rough bed.

'Father's gone out drinking and mother's shouting at the littluns. Luke isn't well and mother's forbidden him to leave his bed. When I left, he was tossing and turning in a fretful sleep. I can't deal with the mayhem, can't make myself believe what's happened to Will and Peter.'

He lay down on the bed, hands behind his head; straight faced he gazed upwards at the wet and glistening granite roof above them. Scarlett, disregarding the squalor of it all, lay beside him.

She laid her hand across his chest, felt his rhythmic breathing. This was the peace he wanted. After a while feeling cold, Scarlett nestled even closer, and this seemed to break into his silent world. He turned slightly and she stared into his dark eyes and then very gently he kissed her, drew her even closer to him, untying the ribbon that held her best Sunday bonnet, dashing it away, then carefully released her hairpins. Setting her red hair tumbling free.

She forgot what her mother had told her, forgot about the night Robert Reader tried to force himself on her and didn't stop Jack as he began kissing her with a fierce passion, nor when he began to undo the fastenings on her bodice.

She held her breath; all that mattered to her was now. Then just as Jack was about to set aside her unfastened bodice, abruptly he stopped, looked away and listened. The boats on the water within the cavern knocked and jarred together. Scarlett sat rigid with fright for she too heard the splashing of oars out on the river. Jack stood up; voices could be heard, but thankfully not close enough to hear what they were saying.

Scarlett could feel her heart beating, she bit her lip waiting until finally all was quiet again, the danger had passed and Jack let out a sigh of relief, he sat back down on the bed and leant over to kiss her forehead.

Deftly, Scarlett refastened her bodice for clearly the mounting passion between them had been snuffed out. Jack didn't protest and when she'd finished, he pulled her down on the bed beside him.

'Thought we'd have had to hide in the tunnel if they'd come nearer,' he teased. 'And tis mighty dark up there, you'd have been really scared.'

'No, I wouldn't have,' Scarlett protested, shivering as the dampness of the place seeped through her clothes. Jack took off his coat and placed it over her.

'Next week I'll take you up to Simon's Croft, no one goes there on a Sunday. The tide'll be right, would have taken you there today but Luke's let Johnny Starr take his boat round to Cawsand.'

'What you gonna do now Will's gone?' Scarlett asked softly, hoping he wouldn't be off on long voyages on the *Raven*.

'Well for now I'll be helping out on Jacob Sweet's old lugger. Will's funeral tis to be Tuesday, Peter's too, the whole of West Looe'll be there. Saddest day of the year it'll be, loved him like a father I did, treated me better my than me own, he did.'

Jack was silent for a moment; Scarlett could see he was choked with emotion.

'Jacob says he needs extra crew, though I think he's just taking me on out of kindness, he's seven mouths to feed at home, but I'll accept the offer; Ma could do with the money. After that well I don't rightly know.

'You won't go leaving me for months at a time will you?' Scarlett lowered her eyes and dare ask.

'Only if needs be, maid, can't make no promises.' He gave her a comforting hug, kissing her brow. 'I'll try not to. The *Raven*'s owners got a good thing going in Guernsey, goods that have been shipped over from France, fancy stuff, china, bales of cloth, tea along with the spirits. Fine prices to be paid here for the likes of these, so I'll take my share along the others and keep in with the capt'n.'

Scarlett tried to feel happy on hearing this, but somehow couldn't, it meant he'd be smuggling, she decided to change the subject.

'Tis Tuesday I'm to pose as Miss Hester's abigail, that's what accompanies fine ladies when they go visiting. Mr Julian's hired a proper carriage to drive the three of us to Moorswater Manor for the visit to one of Miss Hester's la-di-da friends from the ladies' college, and Mr Julian to talk with Mr Francis Kestrel.

Jack propped himself up on one arm, he looked at her with a strange intensity.

'Has nothing been said! I can tell you Mr Julian won't be accompanying you, if indeed he lets his stuck-up daughter go, not on Tuesday, not the day of Will's and Peter's funeral. Tis certain Mr Julian will be attending, and I knows Will's Kathleen approached him this very morning begging for his help. Tuesday he'll be at St Nicholas, mourning Will's and Peter's passing along with the rest of us. I expect his crazy sisters-in-law will be there too, undertook many a voyage on their behalf both men did. Folks from all around these parts will be there and heaven help any revenue who come within five miles of Looe.'

The concentrated look of aggression as he spoke these final words made Scarlett feel foolish that she should mention a frivolous outing on such a day. His comment about the sisters left Scarlett puzzled, but there was no time to dwell on it now. Snuggling closer to Jack, she wished she'd never mentioned the outing, for it had set Jack in a bad mood. Abruptly he sat up.

'And Moorswater?' he questioned, as if disbelieving what she'd said. 'Are you sure you're going there? Them like to keep themselves to themselves in that place. Tis often wondered if— What I'm saying, maid, is you be careful of Adrian Kestrel, he's the youngest son. Promise me, Scarlett, there's talk about him and some poor maid from West Looe that went in service up at Moorswater; tis said—' He stopped. 'What I'm, saying is keep well clear of him.'

'I shan't see any of the fine folks, will I? I'll be down in the servants' quarters and I hope they're a nicer lot then them up at Polgrove.'

'Well, Kitty Sharp is in the workhouse now on account of Mr Adrian's liking for girls with red hair, I'm serious, Scarlett.'

'I know and tis nice you care so, but you've no need to worry. I'll be safely below stairs, and no doubt Miss

Hester will keep me busy. But yes, I will take note of your warning.'

They lay together in contented silence with only the sound of the lapping water and occasional drip from the roof to disturb their thoughts.

'Will Kathleen get Will's lugger back from the revenue?' Scarlett ventured, brushing Jack's dark curls from his forehead.

'No, the bastards will have towed it into Fowey, no doubt she'll be destroyed, sawn in half she'll be like the rest of the luggers seized. It's not right, Kathleen badly needs money, she could have done with selling the boat. I don't know what she'll do now.'

When it grew dusk Jack led her back the way they'd come. 'Best get you back to Prospect House,' he said reluctantly.

When they got to the high wall near the back gate of Prospect House, Jack stopped. Scarlett went up on tip toe and kissed him. 'I can't wait until next Sunday,' she whispered, and Jack leant his body into Scarlett's, pressing her gently against the wall.

'Neither can I,' he said, as the spark of passion was lit once more. It was then Scarlett heard someone cough and glancing down the lane, there she saw Millie walking slowly towards them.

'I've got to go,' Scarlett told Jack gesturing at the approaching figure and hastily opened the back gate, knowing she must beg Millie to keep quiet on what she'd seen.

Millie, ever the one for excitement, promised not to tell and at bedtime they stood together looking down from Scarlett's window.

'Wonder if there's a dashing soul out there will take a fancy to me,' Millie sighed, 'only boy I get to see is old man Dantree's son when he delivers the vegetables and he's got a face like a poker.'

Once she'd gone, Scarlett was left unable to sleep thinking only of Jack and if Tuesday's outing would still take place.

As Jack had predicted there was a change of plan and Mr Julian would not be accompanying them to Moorswater. Miss Hester had thrown the most dreadful of tantrums when her father told her he proposed to cancel the visit. Such was the force of her temper that he had given way to her demand that she should go to visit her friend accompanied by Scarlett.

On the Tuesday morning, as the rest of the house prepared for the funerals, the hired carriage duly arrived and once the luggage was safely stowed on board, Mr Julian escorted his daughter down the steps and inside. Scarlett sat beside her mistress and they set off. She sat mesmerised as they crossed the bridge and took the lane alongside the river. After a long while they turned off down a much more rutted and unused track. The journey seemed to take an awful long time. Miss Hester looked decidedly queasy by the time the coachman slowed and expertly entered through the most impressive ornate iron gates and trotted up a long tree lined drive until finally they reached the mullioned windowed house. She felt sure Miss Hester was most pleased to have finally arrived. They were shown up to Miss Hester's room by the housekeeper and Scarlett duly helped two young maids unpacked her mistress's trunk when it was brought up. Miss Hester then kept Scarlett exceedingly busy, sometimes snapping at her as she waited on her mistress's every need. Scarlett had kept very calm knowing her young mistress must be nervous and missing her father. She was rather young to be here without him. Miss Hester was duly summoned by Miss Isabella, and Scarlett was shown to her own quarters downstairs via the backstairs.

Thankfully, the servants at Moorswater were much nicer than at Polgrove and none had challenged the fact that she was an abigail at such a young age. The house itself was rather grand and Scarlett did start to feel apprehensive, especially later when Miss Isabella's bell had rung and one of the maids had been sent to show her up to Miss Isabella's room.

Although the same age as Miss Hester, Isabella was clearly a young lady who felt superior, and Scarlett felt proud when she survived Miss Isabella's scrutiny and in no way let Miss Hester down.

Once dismissed, she hurried along trying to remember where the discreet servant's door was hidden within the panelled walls of the corridor. She heard voices, and two men in high spirits strode from one room across the corridor and into another only a little way in front of her, neither glanced in her direction. She heard the clink of glasses and the setting down of a decanter. Scarlett hesitated before walking on, then slowed her pace. Unashamedly listening once she'd heard one of the men ask of the other, 'Any news on the informer?'

'Not yet, sir, I've two of my own men up around the villages, got the locals involved in setting false stories and that sort of thing. Ambush the bastard we will for he'll take the bait one day that's for sure, they always do.'

'Tis important they're caught, Ferris. The shipwrights have finished with Charles Hilliard's sloop *Sunrising*. As soon as he can muster a crew she'll be out on the high seas, another ship for Reader to seek out.'

'Word has, sir, they've done good job on her down in Malpas, she'll carry 40 barrels in her hull with plenty of space for bales and other goods, but she'll still not be half as good as the *Black Diamond*.'

'My brother would be pleased to hear you say that. Tis hard to know what he loves more a comely lass or his beloved *Black Diamond*.'

Scarlett once more heard the clink of glasses as the two men laughed.

Her eavesdropping was cut short by a commotion coming from a room at the end of the corridor, there was much shouting and banging of doors. Scarlett gratefully recognised the long oak table almost beside her, this she remembered stood opposite the discreet servant's door.

As she reached for the door handle, a seemingly wild man, dishevelled in appearance, eyes open wide and red in the face came charging down the corridor, caught hold her hand and pulled her along behind him, pulling her completely off her feet as he ran on even faster, dragging her along the carpeted floor to the top of the main staircase then casting her aside in a heap as shouting voices pursued them. Scarlett screamed as forcefully he hauled her to her feet and as a stampede of feet approached them, pinned her against the wall covering her mouth with his, forcing his tongue in her mouth. She struggled, twisting and turning as his hands lifted and delved beneath her skirts. Her terror thankfully short lived, as seconds later he was unceremoniously dragged off her.

With flaming face, Scarlett went to run back along the corridor and seek out the safety of the servant's hall. But a strong velvet-clad arm shot out, hindering her escape.

'Just who the hell are you?' the younger and more elegantly dressed of her two rescuers barked.

Scarlett spluttered, 'I'm the abigail of Miss Hester Marshall. I was returning to the servants hall when—' To her dismay, Scarlett began to cry.

'Come with me.' The tone of the man's voice left her no option but to obey. They walked back to the room where Scarlett had heard the two men talking. He walked briskly over to the bell pull and gave it an almighty tug.

The other man was also there, not so well dressed, older and of more a rugged appearance, he firmly held her attacker, dragging him into the room. Scarlett bravely wiped away her tears.

Within minutes a maid arrived and was dispatched to summon help, shortly afterwards two large men of rough appearance came and took her assailant away, still shouting obscenities and making lurid comments directed at Scarlett.

The fearsome housekeeper Scarlett had met earlier entered the room.

'There has been an unfortunate meeting between this young woman and Mr Adrian, can you see to it she knows how these matters are conducted here.'

'As you wish, master.'

He turned to Scarlett and coldly spoke to her in a rudely dismissive manner. 'You will tell no one, not here, not your mistress or any others what has taken place, it was unfortunate but you are quite unharmed and have no recourse to say ill of my brother Adrian. Do you understand? It would be his word against yours.'

'Yes, sir,' Scarlett replied still feeling shaken by her experience.

'Go with my housekeeper, she will no doubt source you a place where you can rest away from prying eyes until you feel better.'

'Thank you, sir.'

Scarlett bobbed a curtsey and duly followed the housekeeper down the back stairs and into her private parlour, but not before she'd heard the master of Moorswater exclaim, 'Christ man, is no one safe from my brother?'

'I will say you have taken a tumble, are recovering and will be back with us shortly,' the housekeeper explained, begging Scarlett sit before a well laid but unlit fire in the chilly room. 'Not a word about what happened is to pass your lips; Francis Kestrel is not one to be crossed. If you are called to attend upon Miss Hester another maid will take your place till you are composed. Heed my words, maid, tell no one for your own good. When you're ready, go to the servant's hall. Ballard, Miss Isabella's lady's maid, will sit with you.'

Left alone, Scarlett looked around the small cluttered room, a large writing bureau took precedence over the rest of its furnishings. Little light penetrated through the dismal drapes. In one corner through a narrow door slightly ajar, Scarlett could see an iron bedstead, its brightly coloured quilt strangely at odds with the strait-laced housekeeper. Clearly from the size of the housekeeper's quarters, the master of Moorswater paid little heed to his servant's comfort.

Scarlett shivered; the unlit fire seemed to make the room icy cold. She longed to be back at Prospect House with a warm fire and shawl to wrap round her shoulders. Taking a deep breath, she stood up, fearful her assailant might burst through the door at any moment.

Not knowing quite what to do, Scarlett walked over and pulled aside one of the drapes and looked out across the extensive gardens, she thought of Jack, his warning about Adrian Kestrel and how simple her explanation of how safe and out of harm's way she'd be. Jack, she must never tell Jack. Not gossip to him about what she'd learned today however much she may long to, mustn't tell him of Captain Ferris being here or how Francis Kestrel did seemingly own the *Black Diamond*.

Remembering the well-lit fire in the servant's hall, Scarlett decided to make her way there. She walked very quickly the short distance along a flag-stoned passage, glad to reach the roaring fire and safety of others. A large archway separated this room from the kitchen, and she felt uncomfortable as those busily working glanced up. Did she imagine they gave knowing glances to each other? Did they guess something was amiss other than a fall?

Ballard came through from the kitchen and bade her sit down; she took a key from her pocket and opened a small wooden cupboard, then poured a rather generous amount of brandy into a glass and told her to drink it. Scarlett didn't argue, and together with the warmth of the fire, Scarlett did begin to feel better and managed to attend to Miss Hester when she rang a little while later. She ate with the servants, thankfully there were no awkward questions asked of her, she was an outsider made welcome, unlike her treatment at Polgrove.

Comfy though her bed was in Miss Hester's dressing room, the food exceptionally good below stairs, and although there had been no more distressing incidents during the visit, Scarlett was relieved when it was time for them to take their leave. Though it seemed Miss Hester was quite disinclined to leave for home, so too Miss Isabella to take leave of her friend, so delaying their departure by quite a significant amount of time. The carriage was brought to the front entrance and the housekeeper accompanied them from the house. A footman unfolded the carriage steps and helped both Miss Hester and her inside. Miss Isabella stood on the steps waving and Miss Hester lowered the window and waved to her friend as the coach took a slow turn and made its way down the drive. Scarlett too looked out as they departed and saw the figure of a man watching from an upstairs window and wondered which brother it was.

If she was quieter than usual, Miss Hester didn't notice for she herself talked endlessly upon the visit. Of Isabella's dressing room and her abundance of clothes, bales of exquisite satins etc. awaiting her choice on style before the dressmaker from Truro arrived.

Because they had left much later in the afternoon than they should have, dusk came quickly upon them. It slowed the journey, for although there was a full moon, the young lad sat up beside the coachman was called upon more than once to light the way with a burning torch, especially where the track proved particularly difficult.

Scarlett felt immense relief when they were once more following the lane which ran beside the river, the moon's rays dancing on the water a welcome sight. Soon they would be home.

'Why must I live in such a pitifully small house?' were Miss Hester's words as the coach came to a halt outside Prospect House. The sight of the house set her in a bad mood, and having briefly greeted her aunts, she had Scarlett running up and downstairs fetching this and that, demanding constant attention until after dinner was served, which her aunts absolutely refused she be excused from. Whilst this was taking place, Scarlett set about unpacking Miss Hester's clothes, relieved when finally she returned to her room saying she felt tired, and Scarlett was able to start her charge's preparations for bed. Miss Hester still voicing how unjust it was she live here, her protestations falling on deaf ears.

At last with Miss Hester's whining voice finally quietened, Scarlett went down to the kitchen where Bessie had kept a bowl of warm chicken broth for her and two slices of thick bread and dripping. Tea had been brewed and gratefully Scarlett accepted a cup.

'How was it?' Bessie asked. 'Been nice and quiet here with that little madam out the way.'

'It was a long journey, once there though Miss Hester was on her best behaviour. Didn't want to come home, that's for sure. Fancies herself too grand for this place.'

She paused, wondering what would be said if she told them what had befallen her with Adrian Kestrel. She knew she could never tell them. And she would never ever tell Jack. She fell silent. Both Bessie and Ivan were looking at her expecting her to say more. Scarlett took a deep breath and changed the subject.

'I saw lots of East Looe folks walking across the bridge when we left for Moorswater, seems the whole of Looe was making their way to St Nicholas.'

Ivan looked across at her with tired eyes. 'Aye, maid, packed the church was. Reverend Till gave them a good send off, done um proud. Sam Jago and Jack spoke, others too, the church was full with folks outside on the quay paying their respects, all of one mind, twas a killing sent poor Will and Peter to their graves and Robert Reader will pay, we'll have our justice.'

'But Reader is revenue, surely he's above justice?' Scarlett blurted hotly.

'That he is, maid, but not above our justice. There was one such as him years ago, me father used to tell me bout him, went by the name of Ruskin Tripper, he was shot, the bastard. Good riddance twas said then, so it will be with Reader.'

Ivan paused stroking his beard. 'Brave Kathleen held her tears for the sake of the children, but broke down, poor soul, as they carried the coffins out and placed them on the wagons. Will's waiting to take him to rest at Talland beside his father.'

'Poor Will,' Scarlett sighed, and Bessie cast her a curious glance.

'Didn't know you knew him?' she queried.

'I did, only a little in passing, you know how small this place is.'

She left the two of them sitting in silence and went up to bed before Bessie could ask more questions.

Tired, but unable to rest, Scarlett delayed blowing out the candle beside her bed. She felt an uneasy foreboding. Too well she knew the strength of feeling that ran in the blood of the Cornish when wronged. That night, when finally she slept, Scarlett dreamt of Sennen, waking up petrified, for the nightmare and reality were both entwined.

The following morning, she was down in the kitchen long before Millie, and Bessie was glad of her help in lighting the range. Millie had been up in the night with Miss Matilda for she had a chill and needed hot drinks and demanded the fire in her room be banked numerous times. Millie was worn out, too tired to make conversation she fell asleep at the table and Bessie let her be. Ivan when he was there seemed preoccupied and in a sombre mood, taking his ale out to the stables, not sitting with them as usual. The whole house was unusually quiet with no crazy organ playing, even Miss Hester finally finished her eulogy on Miss Isabella and settled in the school room without complaint.

Chapter 7

By the following Sunday once more Scarlett couldn't wait to escape the confines of Prospect House. Jack was there waiting for her on the quay. He held out his arm, sweeping her up in a deep hug. His brother Luke stood beside him.

'Make sure this brother of mine looks after my boat. Slammed her into the jetty up by Tanners Mill he has before now,' Luke joked.

Scarlett linked her arm through Jack's. 'I will,' she giggled.

'Where's you taking her then?' Luke questioned with a glint of laughter in his eyes.

'Simon's Croft, as if it's any of your business.'

'Good job Scarlett's wrapped up warm then,' Luke said knowingly, before sauntering off down the quay whistling.

Jack squeezed Scarlett's hand and kissed her briefly on the mouth, he helped her down the granite steps and onto the *Alice*. Once she was safely sat down, he cast off and took the oars, not bothering to hoist the sail, all the time keeping his eyes firmly fixed on Scarlett. A mischievous smile not quite hidden caused Scarlett to smile back at him. Slowly he manoeuvred the boat out between an array of craft until they were in the centre of the harbour and Jack's powerful arms had them heading upriver.

Soon the bridge was far behind them so too the scattering of cottages which straggled along beside the river. It became more breezy and Scarlett pulled up her hood and wrapped her cloak tight around her. Few words were spoken between them and those that were, were lost in the wind. Besides, Scarlett was quite content just to watch her Jack, so strong and handsome as he pulled on the oars.

As they neared a bend in the river, he rowed the *Alice* towards a short wooden jetty. Beyond this Scarlett saw an old boat, its timbers holed and rotten, lying on its side high up out of the water.

'Nearly there.' Jack grinned.

Scarlett so hoped the old rotting boat wasn't 'Simons Croft'. Once the *Alice* was tied up to a stout bollard, Jack climbed onto the jetty and held out his hand helping Scarlett from the boat.

'Welcome to Simons Croft,' he stated with laughter in his eyes as he watched Scarlett's look of disbelief at the old rotting boat.

'Follow me,' he said taking her hand, and led her beneath the canopy of bare branches that dipped down into the river.

There behind the old boat was a timber shack of sorts.

'Tis said old Scotty Simon didn't want to abandon his old boat so he pitched up here alongside her. Long gone he is now but tis still Simon's Croft. Wanted me and Luke to take care of the place. Come on in.'

Scarlett followed him through the stout door. Parts of the old boat had been used to form this strangely cosy place. Jack threw kindling and logs into the stone fireplace and lit the fire. As it sparked and crackled into life, he went over to the door and shot the bolt firmly in place, turned and began walking towards Scarlett who felt both fear and excitement.

'Come here,' he said softly. 'No one will interrupt us this time.'

Scarlett slipped the hood from her hair and walked towards him. Jack took her hands in his and pulled her closer, entwining her in his arms. She could feel the heat of his breath on her cheek.

'Now I'll show you how much I love you,' he whispered leading her by the hand, and she meekly following. He set aside a fine lace curtain revealing a large oak bed. Slowly, very slowly, he began to undress her, his eyes holding Scarlett's until she stood just in her shift, then gently he lifted her up laying her down on the bed and quickly began divesting himself of his clothes. Shyly Scarlett diverted her eyes as he slipped between the scratchy sheets, quite unable to stop her body responding to his passion with a wantonness of her own until his body slid over hers.

Afterwards, Scarlett felt no shame, only the desire to never leave this place. She nestled contentedly in Jack's arms and he gently kissed her until his passion was once more quelled with an eagerness that matched her own.

They lay energy spent, until Jack whispered softly, 'Twill soon be time to go, the tide will be on the turn and we'll not get downriver.'

'I don't want to go back ever,' Scarlett sighed, smiling sweetly at him.

'We must, maid, afore Bessie sends a search party out looking for you. There'll be other days just like this.'

They shared one more kiss before Scarlett reluctantly began to get dressed, picking up the pins that had fallen from her hair that lay scattered in the bed.

'There be no good time to tell you this,' Jack said, when dressed and pulling on his stout boots. 'Tis like this, Scarlett.' He paused and came to stand next to her. Scarlett sensed he was about to say something that would spoil this precious time.

'A man sent by one of the big gentleman backers inland came into the Jolly this week, late it was, was asking for men to crew a newly fitted out schooner her owner wants taken across to France and back up the Bristol Channel to Hotwells. Twas good pay he was offering. Jacob Sweets been good to me, but I know the Sweets hardly survive as it is without me to think about.'

Scarlett put her arms round his waist and laid her head against Jack's chest.

'Maid, I had no choice what with the *Raven* laid up, so I agreed to join the crew, Luke too. There's a vessel set ready to take us down to Falmouth where we'm to join the *Sunrising*.'

Scarlett froze. She had heard that name before, and remembered where. Moorswater.

'Say something,' Jack, spoke quietly kissing the top of her head.

'How long will you be gone?' Scarlett stumbled over the words and looked up, her watery eyes meeting his.

'I can't rightly say, longer than when I'm at sea on the *Raven*. I know tis ill-timed this, but the gentleman backer he's a good un and now I've lost any hope of owning the *Lucy* tis a blessing. Like a son I was to Will, him only having girls, he promised the *Lucy*'d be mine one day, that's why I'm driven to saving now. I want a lugger of me own, Scarlett, I gotta do something so I can have that, and now for our future also, that's if you'll still love me after what I've told you.'

'Of course I'll love you, but I'll be afraid. You out there on the high seas and then when you'm coming home, what with the likes of the revenue trying to hunt down the smugglers.'

'You calling me a free trader?' His eyes glinted with amusement. Scarlett hugged him so close she could feel the beat of his heart, she held on to her precious man never wanting to be parted.

'With the *Sunrising* being local owned, Looe will be her home port.' He lifted Scarlett's chin and kissed her again.

'Time to go, we're chasing the tide as it is.' With a heavy heart, Scarlett followed Jack as they left this special place, he took her hand as they walked to the jetty, it was almost dark now as he helped her on board the *Alice*. She looked up at the stars in the sky, she would always remember today. Jack stepped aboard causing Scarlett to hold tight the side, he placed the lantern he'd lit from the fire in the bow of the boat before taking the oars once again.

Chapter 8

How long ago that wonderful day seemed. Less than a week later, Jack was gone along with the other men from Looe who were joining the crew of the *Sunrising*. There had been no chance to say goodbye, no tearful parting, nothing at all. Those who'd agreed to join Hilliard's *Sunrising* as crew were roused from their beds and told to gather on the quay. Hilliard's sloop *Dovedale* had taken them away on the high tide. This Scarlett learnt from Ivan at breakfast on the Wednesday following her and Jack's visit to Simon's Croft. Jack was gone and Scarlett felt desolate and empty, not knowing when he'd return.

And now it was April. Scarlett turned her gaze away from the strolling players entertaining the noisy crowd on the quay, and instead looked longingly towards the entrance of the harbour.

Christmas at Prospect House had been a miserable time with the sisters and Miss Esther gone to stay with Mr Julian's merchant friends in Bristol, leaving Millie and her feverish chill behind. The poor girl was indeed ill, but it didn't stop her sulking, grumbling to Scarlett, unhappy at having her place with the sisters usurped by some unknown female borrowed from another family. Bessie had also taken ill and gone to her bed relieved the family were far away, whilst Ivan spent more time than was usual in the Jolly or the Fisherman's Arms across the way.

On Christmas day, Scarlett had taken Millie who was feeling a little better home with her to Tamarisk, there to spend a frosty and uneasy time sat at table with her sad eyed mother and unwelcoming father. It had not been a joyful occasion, but one Scarlett knew must be endured for the sake of her mother.

Today was a beautiful spring day and all was at peace in Prospect House. April sunshine blazed in through the kitchen window. And as the Spring Fair was a special occasion, permission had been given for any who wanted to attend. Miss Hester was to view the proceedings from Polgrove Hall from where, with Miss Lizzie Polgrove, she would look down upon the 'peasants' – a name, according to Miss Hester, Lizzie Polgrove called the likes of Scarlett who would be down on the quay.

Bessie had encouraged Scarlett to take Mille with her that afternoon for the poor girl scarce went out, and the sisters had said all could go. Ivan in the gruffness of early morning had warned them a storm was threatening but as the two girls sat on one of the rough wooden benches that formed part of a wide circle, this didn't seem possible. In the centre of the circle performers in vividly bright costumes were enacting out a comic play and drawing much laughter and hollering from those watching. The smell of roasting ox wafted its way across the crowd. Nothing could lift Scarlett's mood.

She felt apart from those enjoying the fair; she just wanted her Jack safely back home.

Suddenly these thoughts were shattered by much cheering and clapping as the players left and a fiddler accompanied by a juggler dressed in red and green strode into the centre of the circle. It was just as the fiddler struck up his first tune that briefly through a space in the crowd, Scarlett saw Ruth talking earnestly to Oggie. As she watched intently, Oggie pointed out a young man sat outside the Jolly, tankard in hand, whistling at any young maids that passed by.

'Come on.' Scarlett nudged Millie. 'Let's go over and have a look at that stall selling ribbons. Jack's sister's over there too.'

'You go on, I'm enjoying this,' Millie complained, smiling coyly at the handsome gypsy-looking young lad playing the fiddle.

'Alright, as long as you promise to stay put, don't want you disappearing on me.'

'Of course.'

Reassured, Scarlett walked through the crowd towards where Ruth sat deep in conversation with the young man Oggie had pointed to.

When Scarlett walked towards them, Ruth stood up and her companion raised his tankard to her. 'He's a lucky un, your Sam.'

Ruth's cheeks were all aglow. 'I'll tell him you said that.' Ruth giggled and waved him goodbye, linking her arm through Scarlett's.

'That's— Oh! I forget his name, but anyway he says Sam will be back any day now, the Black Diamond's been seen off the Lizard. Tis been awful, he's been gone a month.'

Scarlett's sombre mood was not uplifted by her friend's excitement. Although Ruth thought Scarlett had a liking for her brother, Scarlett had never said so much, and for shame she definitely hadn't told her about Jack taking her to Simon's Croft.

Ruth saw her friend's face and bit her lip. 'I'm sorry, you wanting our Jack home; you got more feelings for him than you'm letting on. Well, even me dad's getting restless waiting for the boys return. Asked around he has, schooner capt'ns, clipper crews, even the old barges trading coal, but nowts been seen of the *Sunrising*.'

'He'll be back, I know he will, it's just he's been gone so long.'

Ruth linked her arm through Scarlett's. 'You going up the hill to see your mother?'

'I'd better it must be over a month now since I visited. I'd best tell Millie to wait here for me.'

'I'll stay and keep an eye on Millie.' They both looked over to where the girl sat still enraptured by the fiddler. 'You go. Your mother will glad to see you.'

Scarlett trudged up the hill to Tamarisk only to find her mother wasn't home. On the way she'd passed Annie Bishop huddled inside her doorway gossiping to the old harridan of a woman who lived opposite. As she'd walked past, Scarlett distinctly heard her mother's name mentioned. She'd stopped and half turned letting them know she'd heard, they stopped talking and looked at one another, clutching their tatty old shawls tighter round them, then stared back at her with thin, disapproving lips.

The storm that Ivan predicted came with a suddenness, needles of rain hammered down, and the low rumble of thunder set all on West Looe Hill scurrying indoors. Relentless hailstones danced on the path outside Tamarisk and struck against the windowpanes. Scarlett feared Ruth in the confusion of the storm would lose sight of Millie. Bessie would be mighty cross if the girl arrived home alone. Anxious to get back, Scarlett went upstairs and took one of her mother's hand me down cloaks from Lanreath. It was one Jeanette didn't much care for, she said it was too fussy with its hood trimmed with gathered black satin, edged with lace. 'Too posh for the likes of me,' Jeanette had said.

She was in such a hurry to get back to Millie, Scarlett ran from Tamarisk, the cloak still in hand. She smiled as she ran past Annie Bishop's cottage, the gossipers were all indoors now, no doubt the two old women had seen Amos Cuddy's frequent visits to Tamarisk when fetching her mother to Lanreath and bringing her home again.

Near the bottom of the hill, she put on the cloak, too late to save her getting drenched. When she reached the quay, all was in chaos with stallholders and food vendors hastily packing everything away. Scarlett could see neither Ruth nor Millie. She looked through the window of the Jolly Sailor, the fiddler was in there, supping ale and patting the bottom of Betsy Sharp, he looked towards her and smiled, his handsome facade ruined by blackened and missing teeth.

Of course, Ruth may have taken Millie home with her but Scarlett daren't ask at Ruth's cottage, she was still conscious of the beating Tom Jago had given Ruth for befriending Sam Trembright, leaving Scarlett still a bit afraid Jack's father.

Not wanting to go home without Millie, there was one more place she'd look. Scarlett went down the narrow path beside St Nicholas's, carefully stepping between lobster pots and coils of rope. The pungent smell of the river wrapped itself around her. The boats tied up alongside the quay knocked and jarred together. Deep, uneven puddles meant rain soon penetrated her old boots and a further shower of hailstones soaked her to the skin. There seemed to be something happening further along the narrow stony beach once again revealed by the outgoing tide. Scarlett hurried on, curious to know what was happening, perhaps Ruth and Millie were there watching.

The heavy storm had made dusk come early. Scarlett could hear faint screams and shouts for help drowned out by the thunder overhead. As she quickened her pace, a shard of lightning lit up the river and she saw a lugger just inside the mouth of the harbour. It had capsized, the hull lay half exposed, and a tangle of greyish sails were being buffeted wildly about by the turbulent incoming tide. Those on board had surely been thrown into the churning waters of the river. She could see a cluster of people clutching onto the broken masts whilst those who were able to swim were being helped as they staggered ashore. A dozen or more men had waded out to help, waist deep in water. Others from East Looe had rowed across pulling people out of the river and into their boats. An exhausted girl crawled out of the river and slumped down on the shingle in a heap. Scarlett instinctively ran forward to help her, trying to haul her a little further out of the water for it still lapped round her wet skirts. The girl lay motionless; Scarlett wondered if she were dead. Around her everyone was busy, Scarlett stood hands on hips getting her own breath back wondering what to do next. Bending down she gently brushed hair away from the girl's face, the generous hood of her mother's cloak with its fancy black edging falling forward as she did so. The girl stirred and opened her eyes, then opened them even wider and screamed. The hair slipped through Scarlett's fingers, she stood up and took a step back, within seconds she was lost within the hustle of people helping those from the capsized boat. She could hear the girl screaming hysterically, a sound that followed Scarlett as she ran for home.

The girl on the beach she had recognised only too well, just as she had recognised Scarlett even after all these years. It sent a shiver to her very soul. The girl was Polly Carbis, her once best friend from Sennen whose family Scarlett's father had betrayed along with so many others from that village.

Back at Prospect House, Scarlett was relieved that for once there was no one in the kitchen, she took off the black cloak and ran upstairs. She heard Bessie talking to Miss Matilda in the drawing room and quickly hid the cloak under her mattress then flew back down to the kitchen putting her shawl round her shoulders and went down the path to the back gate.

Where the hell was Millie?

She stood for a moment trying to catch her breath, heart hammering and mind numb with disbelief trying to grasp the awful truth that Polly Carbis was here in West Looe. She lifted the latch and looked up the lane, so very grateful to see Millie running through the puddles towards her.

'Twas good, Scarlett, Ruth took me home with her, whe'm had tea and seed cake, sorry if you'm cross.'

'It's alright, just don't tell Bessie I wasn't with you all the time, promise.'

Millie nodded, pleased she wasn't in trouble with Scarlett.

By now Scarlett was soaking wet and Bessie was at the back door calling them inside, shooing them upstairs to get out of their wet clothes before they both took a chill.

Scarlett changed into her dark blue uniform, drying her hair with the coarse towel before pinning it up under her cap. She struggled to keep calm, the past couldn't come back to destroy her, surely not, it wouldn't be fair, and now her fear was tempered with anger. She wondered what was happening down on the beach, what tale was Polly telling those helping with the rescue.

She joined Millie back downstairs as Bessie worked the bellows trying to draw more warmth from the coals on the fire.

'In God's name, what stopped you two making it home here before you got drenched to the skin?' she blustered.

Scarlett looked across at Millie before replying, 'We went up to Tamarisk, twas raining real bad as we came down the hill.'

Millie's face reddened, the girl was too honest for her own good; Scarlett hoped she'd stay silent.

Thankfully Bessie seemed satisfied and the two of them stood before the now glowing fire. Scarlett couldn't stop shivering. Or was it trembling?

Bessie fetched both of them a mug of warm milk, and sitting at the table momentarily Scarlett closed her eyes as Millie excitedly described to Bessie in detail all about the Spring Fair, the fiddler, juggler and the stalls.

Scarlett's only thought was the shock she'd had at seeing Polly Carbis and the bitter hatred in her once friend's eyes. She experienced again the terrible panic she'd felt as Polly screamed the name she'd been known as in Sennen: Mary Trester. Screamed it over and over again hysterically at the top of her voice. Screaming it at her back as she'd ran off the beach through the gale-ridden rain.

Unable to sit still any longer, Scarlett went to stand, she felt icy cold and lightheaded, holding onto the table to steady herself. Quite overcome, it was all too much. Millie saw this and came over, sitting her down whilst Bessie hurried off to fetch Miss Emilia's smelling salts.

Sent to her room for an hour's rest, Scarlett felt no easing in her fear, for Polly Carbis was most likely at this very minute screaming a truth so despicably true, a truth that somehow she must evade, for the love of Jack Jago, for her very life here. What if Polly was taken seriously and they believed her when she said there was an informer's daughter here amongst them? What if folks became suspicious of who exactly it was she'd seen? Who could it have been? Scarlett paced the floor, realising she must warn her mother. Polly would easily recognise her, this was a nightmare; in one afternoon the life they'd built here in Looe, Polly Carbis could destroy. Scarlett clenched her fists, anger welling up in her now.

Millie's knock came on the door all too soon, and taking a deep breath she went back downstairs to carry out her duties. It was later that night Ivan opened the door and strode in, droplets of rain dripping from clothes and beard.

Bessie got up, pouring ale into his tankard. Ivan took his hat off and sat down shaking his head. 'Would you believe it? Some silly bastard in an old lugger not fit to put to sea in, capsized in the mouth of the harbour, and now he's telling us he wants it salvaged, silly bugger. Tides got it now, carried it off out to sea, and good riddance to it. No gratitude at all for us who saved his life and the others. Oh, no.'

He took a sup of ale. 'And if that wasn't enough, there's a young girl amongst them. Got a big bump to her forehead from when the boat capsized, no doubt. Whether that's caused it or not, but she's lost her wits, proper hysterical, keeps saying she's seen Mary. Who the hell she is I don't know, unless the maid's a Catholic or summat and she's seeing visions. Struggling with all the kindly folks that's trying to help her, proper nasty like. Janks has put the others up in the coaching stables but the girl she's locked up somewhere separate. Scratched the side of Betsy Sharp's face, bit poor Molly on the arm. Screamed the place down when Florrie Starr went in with a change of clothes for her. Kept shouting she was Mary. Old Beattie gave her a good slapping then and that shut her up.'

He paused fetching out his pipe from his pocket and tapping it on the table.

'On their way to Plymouth to board a ship for foreign parts they was, bout ten uv um. Janks says the sooner they leave the better. Ungrateful sods some of um, especially the girl.'

Scarlett listened trying to calm the inner turmoil that ran through every ounce of her being, hoping she showed none of the emotion she was feeling. From Ivan she learnt nothing further of the lugger's passengers and at last escaped to the sanctuary of her own room. Once in her nightgown she stood looking out from her attic window shivering, feeling every beat of her heart. The river shrouded in mist seemed stilled, only faint patches of moonlight managed to shine through on to the dark waters. Her teeth chattered and she trembled, despairing at the unbelievable ill fate that had led Polly Carbis here. And who, she wondered, were her travelling companions, a thought too frightening to contemplate, others may know her too. She pulled an old shawl off the bed and wrapped it tight round her shoulders but still shivered, icy cold. Looking out into the darkness Scarlett tried to gather her thoughts. Somehow, she must warn her mother Polly was here. Desperately she tried to think of an excuse urgent enough to absent her from her household duties and school room in the morning. But her mind was numb, she couldn't think of any excuse that would be believed.

In the end it was feeling bitter cold that led Scarlett to her bed, having first taken out the black cloak that was still damp, and folding it more neatly beneath her mattress.

She lay in bed unable to sleep, caught up in this waking nightmare. But she must have slept because suddenly she was woken by – what? She sat up in bed, alert, heart hammering, she could hear muffled voices. A deep voice uttered an oath in anger. Panic gripped her. Scarlett sat too frightened almost to breathe and as still as one of the marble statues they had at Lanreath, certain she'd soon hear a mob ascending the stairs, bursting open her door and dragging her from bed, exposing her as Mary Tresider, the spy's daughter from Sennen. Her secret past would be exposed, everyone would despise her, hate her, including Jack who she loved so much.

Scarlett sat, hands held together as if in prayer, trembling with anticipation. Had Polly quietened and become more believable, had she convinced them she'd seen the real Mary Tresider, had someone thought to wonder who that person was, that it was her? What would they do with her, the baying mob? No blue coats to rescue her this time. Tears ran down her cheeks and her shoulders heaved with silent sobbing; her beloved Jack would be lost forever.

She took a deep breath, wiped away her tears, swallowed hard, and listened. A man's voice urgent in tone was answered by a woman's, she heard the sound of a door being shut, then silence. No footsteps had raced up the stairs, no angry voices, nothing, she felt overwhelmed with relief. Maybe all would be well, but still her heart beat fast and still she felt no inner peace.

A sound came from the attic room next to hers and Millie's door opened, this followed by the soft pad of footsteps on bare floorboards. Scarlett tried to calm herself and after a few minutes found the courage to overcome her fears and go to find out what was happening. She slid from her bed and crept silently over to her door and opened it. Millie was standing on the half landing looking out the window. Both of them jumped as voices from somewhere in the house grew louder echoing up the stairwell.

Below in the darkness at the back of the house, movement. Men scarcely more than shadows were unloading barrels from a wagon and carrying them through the open gate and up the path to where the laundry jutted out, some even into the house itself.

Millie looked at her. 'You'm been crying?' Millie queried.

'No,' Scarlett replied, trying hard to seem her normal self.

Satisfied Millie confided, 'There must have been a run tonight, unexpected though, of that I'm sure. I've been here long enough to tell; I know the signs with the sisters. Miss Matilda gets all twitchy and Miss Emilia takes to the organ playing to calm herself.'

Scarlett peered out the window. 'I've never heard a thing before,' she whispered.

'That's cos it's usually planned, tonight must have been unexpected, no doubt something's gone wrong and goods have been brought here, nothing's prepared.'

The two of them stood watching until the men dispersed into the night. The back gate was shut and the dim glow from the skylight in Ivan's quarters was diminished.

'Only a couple of hours sleep left,' Millie said quietly. 'Best get to our beds.'

Scarlett got into bed still pondering how she could warn her mother of Polly's presence.

She woke early the next morning to the screech of gulls and Millie shaking her. 'It's time to get up we'm both overslept Bessie ull be mighty cross.' In a flurry of haste Scarlett dressed, pinning her cap on as she reached the final stair leading to the kitchen. She had no time to dwell on excuses to absent herself from Prospect House; instead she could only hope her mother was safely out at Lanreath. Scarlett knew her mother was happier away from Tamarisk for it held no happiness within its thick stone walls.

That morning Bessie was frosty towards both girls as they hurried into the kitchen, she banged about with the pots and glanced at neither of them. Her displeasure at their lateness did not lessen until mid-afternoon when Mr Julian made an unexpected visit which disrupted the household above and below stairs.

On hearing the sound of his voice, Miss Hester excitedly pushed back her chair and left the school room, quite forgetting herself and running in a most unladylike manner. Scarlett followed her, just as surprised as Miss Hester when her father, instead of going to meet his aunts, opened the door leading to the back stairs and disappeared from sight.

Miss Hester stopped and turned to Scarlett open-mouthed, eyes wide with amazement.

'That's very strange, my father has gone down to the kitchen, why would he do such a thing?'

'Perhaps he has something to say to cook,' Scarlett answered, thinking exactly the same thing.

'Can we follow him?' Miss Hester asked, taking a step forward, but Scarlett held her arm firmly.

'Best not, I'm sure he'll return soon, come back to the school room.'

With Miss Hester back at her mathematics, Scarlett absented herself for a moment and quietly ran up to the half landing at the back of the house. It was as she thought. She could see Mr Julian and Ivan standing on the path deep in conversation, with Ivan lifting his old battered hat and scratching his head as Mr Julian clearly issued forth instructions. Abruptly Mr Julian turned and opened the back gate striding out into the lane and turning right to enter the stables. Scarlett saw Ivan take a deep breath before following behind him.

So, Mr Julian is involved in smuggling as well. Scarlett smiled to herself as she went back to the school room. *Last night: that's what this visit is all about*, she thought.

It was two days later when the unexpected chance came to escape the confines of Prospect House to warn her mother.

It had been an ill-tempered day with the sisters informing Bessie they had invited the Reverend Mitchell from Plaidy and his wife to dine with them along with Mr Julian. Miss Emilia had overheard Miss Hester in the school room exclaiming how boring the reverend was, so too his milksop of a wife. Thus, Miss Emilia had stormed into the room and chastised Miss Hester, her eyes darting angrily across to Scarlett. 'Pray teach your charge better manners for she appears bereft of any, and to respect her elders, I'm ashamed of you, Hester.'

She stormed out the room leaving both Scarlett and her charge feeling duly chastised.

It was shortly after this when Scarlett had gone down to the kitchen for some hot milk for Miss Hester that Millie slipped on the newly scrubbed floor and was hobbling about in pain. Bessie, none too pleased to be having extra guests to feed, was not sympathetic.

'Someone's got to go to Pendry's for extra provisions; it'll have to be you, Scarlett. Florrie's niece is coming in, but it'll be too late by then. Oh my, whatever will happen next?'

Bessie continued to grumble frowning in disapproval at the now snivelling Millie and then at a hesitant Scarlett.

She sat Millie down at the table. 'No good weeping, there's work to be done, girl,' Bessie huffed, fetching a sharp knife, bowls and assorted vegetables for Millie to peel.

'It won't hurt you to go, Scarlett. Don't just stand there, what's the matter with you? Get a move on.'

Scarlett still didn't move, she felt petrified Polly Carbis may be down on the quay or in Princes Square. Pendry's was behind the Jolly Sailor and the weather warm so no chance of hiding beneath the confines of her old grey cloak's hood.

'No quibbling, Millie can't go can she? For goodness sake, Scarlett, hurry along now.' Bessie held out the order for Pendry's and picked up two baskets from beside the settle, she stood hands on hips, waiting as Scarlett took off her apron and cap. Even opening the back door and ushering her out. 'And be sure to hurry straight back,' her departing words.

Scarlett made her way down the path and unlatched the back gate, stepped out into Market Lane. It was as she hurried along to Pendry's that she made the decision to risk running up West Looe Hill to tell her mother about her encounter with Polly Carbis.

Glancing through the shop window, she could see there were three people waiting to be served, so quickly ran up West Looe Hill, arriving at Tamarisk quite out of breath, pushing the door open to find not her mother but her father looking up from the table. Startled by such an abrupt intrusion, he automatically reached for his musket which lay on the table.

'What the devil are you doing here, busting in like that, why aren't you about your duties?'

'Because I came to warn mother that Polly Carbis is here in Looe along with other passengers from a lugger that sank in the mouth of the harbour last week.'

'You needn't have bothered. She knows already, worrying her head silly about you she was until that stupid oddity of a man came and picked her up in his cart. She's safely out of the way at Lanreath for now. Told her straight I did, you're a house servant not likely to be out and see the likes of Polly.'

'But I did see her, I went to the Spring Fair and afterwards it was me who pulled her out the river. I had no idea who it was til I brushed her hair away from her face. She recognised me, and I her, I just fled then.'

Elijah stared at his daughter, remote and cold, his face devoid of any emotion.

'They'll be gone soon, so I've heard. Go back to Prospect House and stay out of sight.'

He stood up and pushing his chair back then leant forward resting his hands on the table. Scarlett could smell brandy on his breath. Saw his eyes narrow. 'A warning, daughter, don't get involved with the free traders. A search of West Looe will take place in respect of goods landed hereabouts this week, it will begin tomorrow, and broach no thought of your saintly employers being excluded take my word for it, th—'

The sentence hung in the air unfinished, for a sound came from within the small room her father used to keep up his pretence of map making. Scarlett took a step backwards dismayed to see Robert Reader saunter into sight and lean casually against the door frame.

'Scarlett.' Reader said her name in a measured tone, his eyes scrutinising her body to the extent, she felt bereft of any clothing. Next, he folded his arms and stared hard at her, a chilling, piercing gaze.

'Keep away from the Jagos, especially that Jack you've a liking for, or there'll be real trouble for that scruffy beggar of a lad. Understand what I'm saying.'

Scarlett's blood ran as ice for the menace in his words was clear and threatening. How the hell did he know how she felt about Jack? She turned and ran from Tamarisk. Reader's words stayed with her right down to the bottom of the hill. She knew Bessie would be furious she'd been gone so long, and was dismayed when she entered Pendry's only to find the captain's housekeeper from next door berating the man for the tough meat she'd had to serve her master the day before. On and on she went, bonnet bobbing as she remonstrated with old Pendry. In the end Scarlett stepped forward and put Bessie's order on the counter, ignoring the stare she received from the poker-faced housekeeper who finally left the shop.

Laden with the two heavy baskets, Scarlett ran back to Prospect House as quickly as she could. As she entered Market Lane, she realised running alongside her was one of Jack's younger siblings.

'Me brothers will be home come Saturday, Ma reckons, Da's friend says so.'

Scarlett slowed and for a moment put the baskets down, catching her breath and asking, 'You sure, really, really sure?'

'Yes.' The scruffy youngster with unruly hair the same as Jack's smiled.

'That's wonderful,' Scarlett exclaimed, and ran on with renewed energy entering the kitchen and placing the baskets on the table only then to feel the tension in the kitchen.

'Upstairs now, missy, Miss Matilda has asked you be sent straight up to her.' Bessie's face was flushed red, and Scarlett knew she was in trouble.

Scarlett knocked on the drawing room door, a sharp voice told her to enter. Miss Matilda rose from her chair, thin lipped and clearly displeased.

'Well, where pray were you? You were sent on an errand which should have taken a short while and were gone by cook's account the best part of 45 minutes.'

'I....' Scarlett stammered as she replied, for never had Miss Matilda been so cross with her. 'There was a long queue in Pendry's in front of me, then the housekeeper from the captain's house next door was berating Pendry endlessly about the tough joint of mutton delivered to her establishment the day before. I could but wait.'

Miss Matilda relaxed her shoulders and sat down again seemingly satisfied. 'Apologise to cook and work twice as hard for what remains of the day, our guests will be arriving close to noon, make up for being absent. Go now.'

She shooed Scarlett off with a wave of the hand, Scarlett bowed her head and gave a little curtsey. She made sure not to turn her back on her employer and seem disrespectful, grateful to feel the cold porcelain doorknob behind her and escape.

Downstairs she apologised to Bessie most sincerely and began enthusiastically peeling apples ready to put in a pie.

So busy was Scarlett throughout the rest of the day that thoughts of Jack and the warnings full of menace made by her father and Robert Reader, however frightening and cruel, were pushed aside until the vicar, his wife and Mr Julian had left having been excellently fed and kind words of appreciation received by Bessie.

Relieved all had gone well, Bessie eased herself into her chair by the fire and nodded off to sleep. For Scarlett and Millie there was no possibility of going up to bed however tired they may feel, for the sisters and Miss

Hester would be summoning their services when they retired for the night. It was just a matter of waiting until the copper bells high on the wall jangled.

Millie set out partly used candles on the table beside the oil lamp ready to be lit later, Ivan opened the back door and came in and Scarlett fetched down his tankard and filled it with ale.

'Do you want something to eat?' she asked, thinking of the cold meat in the pantry.

'Won't stop tonight. Gotta go, summat's on,' he mumbled.

Immediately Scarlett thought of Jack. 'Is it *Sunrising?*' she blurted, before thinking.

Ivan turned and gave her a funny look. 'None of your business, that what it is, miss.'

He left slamming the door shut behind him, waking Bessie.

'Why you say that?' Millie queried, but Scarlett stayed silent. Finally, the day came to an end. Scarlett helped Miss Hester to bed and Millie attended the sisters.

'Time we were all abed, upstairs you go now,' Bessie ordered when finally they returned to the kitchen. Lighting their candles from the lamp, Scarlett and Millie wearily climbed the stairs leaving Bessie easing herself up from her chair, stiff from the day's work.

Scarlett peeked from her window all seemed quiet. She lay abed tired with hands sore from washing the pots and pans, happy to have heard Jack was possibly homeward bound. She so hoped to see him Sunday. By then hopefully Janks would have sent his ungrateful visitors on their way. Alas her father and Robert Reader's threats worried her, she must keep Jack and his family safe from harm, must warn him to be extra careful without him becoming suspicious. Scarlett resolved not to do anything to upset Bessie or Miss Hester which would jeopardise her Sunday afternoon off. With these thoughts in mind she drifted off to sleep.

It was with a start she woke, a hand placed lightly over her mouth. 'Shush!' a voice she knew so well whispered in her ear.

She opened her mouth to say something but was silenced by a kiss.

'Jack.' she finally gasped when at last they parted, smiling as he slid from the bed and pulled off his clothes which carried with them the tang of the sea. He slipped into the narrow iron bed that made all sorts of noises under his extra weight and Scarlett tried hard not to giggle.

'Miss me?' Jack asked as they lay face to face, his breath warm upon her face.

'Of course I did. I love you but how on earth did you get here? I'll be thrown out if we're caught, not that I care; I love you, all that matters is you're home safe.'

'Climbed in through the pantry window, it wasn't locked.' Jack stroked her face. 'Crept up silent like a fox, but come here, maid, we've got better things to do than go worrying. I'm back that's all that matters.'

Twas a good while later that Jack slipped silently down the stairs and safely away from Prospect House whilst all inside except Scarlett still slumbered.

After Jack had gone, Scarlett must have fallen deeply asleep for she was woken by Millie shaking her awake.

'Put this on quick,' she urged, thrusting Scarlett's nightdress over her head.

The sound of heavy boots came pounding up the stair. Two dragoons thrust open the bedroom door and advanced into the room. Millie collapsed onto Scarlett's bed trembling, and Scarlett sat up holding her friend's hand, trying to comfort her as they watched what followed. The dragoons pulled open the two drawers in the table beside her bed, upturned them and scattered her few possessions onto the floor. The faded cotton curtain in one corner of the room between the chimney breast and the wall, forming a place to hang her uniform and Sunday best, was torn down, her few clothes cast onto the floor.

'You,' the larger of the dragoons said, pointing at Scarlett. 'Get out of bed, and the pair of you stand over by the window.' Scarlett and Millie did what they were told without question, and as they did so heard loud sounds of protest coming from the bedchambers below. Scarlett took a deep breath wondering what was happening as she heard raised voices and cries of distress.

Meanwhile the dragoons flung the rag rug she'd brought from Tamarisk across the room and upturned her shallow mattress tossing her sparse bedding onto the floor in a heap. Thankfully the black cloak with its distinctive hood, Scarlett had turned inside out, and this was hung by the hood beneath her Sunday best and lay discarded beneath it on the floor. After one long lingering look around the room, abruptly they left, passing on the half landing a familiar figure Scarlett knew only too well. He walked up the few remaining stairs and across the little landing with a swagger, placed both hands on the door frame and stood looking in at them with a cruel smirk of satisfaction on his face. Scarlett boldly looked back unflinchingly into the eyes of Robert Reader.

From the floor below, the sisters could be heard remonstrating loudly with Reader's men, their distress replaced by anger. Miss Matilda was even heard to swear. Robert Reader smiled. 'Your employer is not quite the gentle soul she portrays herself to be, best I teach her some good manners. Good day,' he mocked, giving Scarlett a malevolent look before leaving.

'The bastard,' she said out loud as he disappeared from sight. Doors banged downstairs, someone screamed. Prospect House was clearly being ransacked from top to bottom. She prayed Jack was somewhere safe and then pulled herself together and comforted Millie who was trembling.

'Come on, get dressed, the sisters need you and Miss Hester needs me. Poor souls, they are just as frightened as we are, and heaven knows what's going on in the kitchen and how Bessie's coping.'

Hastily, Scarlett dressed and ran downstairs. Miss Hester was sitting up in bed white as a sheet, seemingly hardly able to breathe such was her state of utter fearfulness. She was mightily pleased to see Scarlett who ran over and sat on the bed beside her charge and tried to calm her.

Three dragoons with bayonets fixed searched the room, which possessed much more furniture than

Scarlett's. Cupboards and chests of drawers were thrown open, the delicate stool Miss Hester sat on before the mirror on her dressing table whilst Scarlett brushed her hair had a leg broken off and lay on its side. Finally, the small room that Miss Hester used as a dressing room then became the focus of their attention. Words were exchanged between the three as the lid was lifted on a large cedar chest and Miss Hester's finest of dresses, petticoats and undergarments were rifled through and tossed awry with lewd remarks and glances made in Miss Hester's direction.

At last they left, and Scarlett shut the door behind them. 'I'll get you dressed and after I've fixed your hair I must go downstairs and offer my help.'

'You'll do no such thing, I want my room put in order first,' Miss Hester said stubbornly.

'But your aunts are in need of me, of that I am sure.'

'You're employed here solely for my needs,' Miss Hester insisted as she got out of bed in a fine temper.

There was no contradicting her, Scarlett had seen the defiant look on her charge's face too many times before.

Having dressed Miss Hester, seen to all her needs and tidied her room and replaced all the items taken from the cedar chest, at last Scarlett declared in a voice poaching no refusal, 'I must go now and see what's happening elsewhere in the house. Sit over by the window, stay there. I'll return shortly and let you know how your aunts are coping with the upheaval, you must surely be worried for them.'

'Fine do as you wish, but pray tell Ivan I want my stool repaired by him today.'

Scarlett left the room feeling sure Miss Hester's dressing table stool would be the least of Ivan's worries.

The door to the drawing room was open and Miss Matilda was sitting in her chair still as could be whilst all around her was chaos. The room, usually so dismal and dark, was stark and exposed with light, the heavy drapes having been torn wide apart. The dragoons who had searched Miss Hester's room were down here now searching and disturbing everything, casting all asunder as tapestries and books were removed and walls tapped. The dark blue carpet loosely rolled to one side.

'Go down and stay with Bessie. Millie, I have sent out on a mission. I take it my niece has had your attention and has been told to stay where she is?'

'Yes, Miss Matilda, that is how it is, I'll go below stairs to Bessie now.'

Just then Miss Emilia struck up an old hymn on the organ in the adjoining room. It boomed out so suddenly the dragoons reached for their pistols. Miss Emilia began to sing loudly at the same time 'Blessed Feasts of Blessed Martyrs'. Scarlett remembered the hymn well from the days when she lived by the Tamar and went to the little church beside the river.

'Go along now,' Miss Matilda insisted.

'Shut that din up,' one of the dragoons shouted as Scarlett retreated and made her way downstairs.

Bessie was sitting in her chair, red-faced and exhausted, but watching through the window two dragoons in the area outside.

'They've been through here and left this mess for us to clear up, my quarters too.' She struggled up, not taking her eyes off the dragoons. To Scarlett's surprise, she set two tankards of ale on a small wooden tray, and waited.

As the dragoons made their way towards the laundry, tugging open the door, she bade Scarlett take the tray out to them.

'Distract them, flirt with them if you must, but the least time they spend poking about out there the better.'

Scarlett didn't hesitate, for she saw the wariness in Bessie's eyes. She opened the back door and ventured over towards them.

'I've been asked if you'd like some ale,' she said, in a voice as saucy as she could muster.

Both emerged from the laundry and accepted the ale. 'What you do here then?' one of them asked, leaning against the wall.

'Just look after a rather spoilt child,' Scarlett replied with a broad smile.

'So, a lowly servant, with more work to do now.'

'Indeed, so don't go causing a muddle in the laundry for it's me who'll have to put it to rights.' She smiled, hiding the contempt she felt.

'Wouldn't like you to get all hot and in a bother, now would we?' the smaller of the two said winking at the other. 'Now, if you'll just—'

'You, out here and help search the stables,' Robert Reader's voice bellowed from the back gate and they left, slamming the tankards down on the tray, running down the path and leaving the laundry door wide open.

Through the open gate Scarlett saw Ivan holding steady an obviously frightened Dolly, who kept lifting her head and shifting back and forth, her hooves echoing on the cobbles. Casting a look of loathing in the direction of Robert Reader, Scarlett went back down the path to the kitchen.

She begged Bessie for carrots to feed Dolly in an effort to comfort the poor frightened animal, and handed them to Ivan, lingering for a moment to look with dismay at the turmoil the dragoons were creating as the contents of the stables were strewn asunder out into the lane, including Miss Hester's highly expensive cart, just dragged out with the old wagon and other umpteen items. Now, with fixed bayonets, the piles of straw inside the stables were being probed and tossed aside as they progressed onwards. Robert Reader stood in the doorway issuing orders. Sending men stomping into Ivan's sanctuary hence to commence a search there. Scarlett turned and ran down the path.

Bessie was trying her best to straighten the kitchen and Scarlett helped drag the settle back into place and move the table and chairs to the centre of the room. The pantry had been searched and a pile of spoilt food littered the floor. Mr Pendry's promised best leg of mutton lay scattered amongst broken stoneware that had held jams and other preserves, potatoes and vegetables were scattered everywhere for one of the devils had swept everything from the shelves, quite unnecessarily.

Bessie looked in and sighed with disgust. 'Leave that for now, Scarlett. Best go and see what's needed to do for them upstairs.' She retreated into her own quarters wiping away a tear with the edge of her apron.

'Do you need my help yourself?' Scarlet called seeing how upset she was.

'No, maid, I'll manage, upstairs with you.' And Scarlett reluctantly did as she was bidden. She wondered where on earth Millie had been sent.

Miss Emilia was still playing the organ and singing, thumping out wrong notes more frequently as time progressed.

In the drawing room under the watchful eye of Miss Matilda, Scarlett rolled out the carpet and pulled the drapes almost together across the windows, plunging the room once more into semi-darkness, then heaved furniture back in place as best she could. Miss Matilda straightened the tapestries and even helped Scarlett replace the leather-bound books carelessly thrown to the floor by the dragoons.

'Millie will help us with our rooms when she returns,' she told Scarlett whilst replacing the oil lamp back in its proper place and straightening the ornaments on the mantelpiece.

'Go down and help Bessie prepare what she can for us, but first go upstairs and look in on Miss Hester, tell her to stay where she is, then look out where your least likely to be seen and tell me if the dragoons have finished with us yet.'

It was as she left the drawing room Scarlett realised that Miss Emilie had stopped playing the organ. As she passed the now silent room, Scarlett peeked through the crack in the partly opened door. There to her amazement she saw Miss Emilia kneeling down by the side of the organ, deftly retrieving through an open side panel a handful of thin, wide books, just like the ledgers Scarlett had seen in the land agents room at Lanreath. She crept past and quickly went up to Miss Hester's, shocked by what she'd just seen.

Miss Hester was thankfully asleep curled up on her bed, nothing it seemed would disturb her spoilt and selfish life. After she closed the door, Scarlett went up to the half landing and looked out of the window where she could see the dragoons were still in the lane and still searching the stables. From the floor below she heard an angry Miss Matilda remonstrating with her sister.

'You silly fool, what are you doing? Put them back immediately, are you trying to give us over—' Scarlett made sure they could hear her coming and Miss Matilda stopped talking. Scarlett waited briefly where she was and looked over the balustrades, she saw both sisters coming out from the room where Miss Emilia had been playing the organ, then quickly make their way to the drawing room.

When she knocked on the drawing room door, it was to find both sisters sat either side of the dying fire looking quite composed. 'They're still searching the stables,' she reported. 'I will look a little later and tell you when they've gone. Can I bring you something?' she asked in a surprisingly calm voice, and as ordered went downstairs to bring the sisters tea.

Bessie hot and flustered welcomed Scarlet's help. 'Heaven knows where Miss Matilda has sent Millie,' she sighed, handing Scarlett the kettle to fill from the pump in the back yard.

'Draw the back gate open, maid, then we'm can see when the bastards have gone.' It had been an exhausting day.

By nightfall the dragoons had searched the whole of West Looe and had left. Millie returned and when asked where she'd been, said the sisters had sworn her to secrecy. Bessie and Scarlett alike were far too tired to pry.

Chapter 9

Once the journey to Penhallen had begun, Scarlett let her mind wander back to her last meeting with Jack.

'I know that place,' Jack had said. A roguish grin on his face when she'd told him that someday soon she was having to escort her charge to Penhallen a house in Polperro. What she couldn't tell Jack was that after Moorswater, she had no wish to accompany Miss Hester anywhere ever again.

'That's Charles Penhallen's place,' Jack had stated, 'his establishment may seem all respectable, but smuggling's Charlie Penhallen's main source of income, best not tell his stuck-up daughter that though.'

Scarlett had been shocked. Was there no one hereabouts not involved in smuggling?

Jack spoke in such a matter of fact manner that Scarlett had just smiled and told him she'd no wish to be away visiting.

Earlier she'd chided him, 'I was worried about you when the dragoons raided us.'

'I too was worried about you,' he replied. 'I was safely hidden away from prying eyes til they were gone, you'd no need to worry.'

Those precious moments together had been a lovely, lying together in the long grass up at Hannafore, the sky above them a canopy of blue. Jack told her not to dwell on when the *Sunrising* would sail again. 'The sooner she sails the sooner I'll be back. That's how Ma looks at it when me da sails.' And for the rest of that day she'd put such thoughts out of her mind, for she wished such days would never end.

But it had and now she was lost in her own thoughts as the carriage jolted along on its seemingly endless journey towards Polperro, she looked away from her complaining charge and stared out the window a secret smile on her lips. For she knew Jack had a plan.

The beastly visit to Penhallen had been arranged by Mr Julian ten days after the search of West Looe. Miss Hester had thrown the most almighty of tantrums when he'd further informed her she would be accompanying Maria Penhallen back to the Academy for Young Ladies in Truro after the visit. And no amount of tantrums or tears would change his mind on the matter.

A disappointed Scarlett had slipped quietly away from outside the drawing room door where she'd been eavesdropping, her eyes full of tears.

As Jack walked her home from Hannafore that previous Sunday, seeing how upset Scarlett was because the *Sunrising* might sail before she returned, he told her, 'There's time a plenty before the *Sunrising* sails for me to pay Penhallen House a visit to see my sweetheart, I'll know when you leave,' he'd soothed. And looked at her with eyes that danced with mischief, but she could tell he was deadly serious.

'Father's sister was in service at Penhallen House. Many a times when the old master was away Luke and me would make our way along the cliffs and sneak into the kitchen and be treated to beef broth and thickly cut bread.'

Propped up on one arm and kissing her now and then with a smile on his face, Jack had regaled her how as boys they'd escaped to explore the rest of the hollow empty house. Scolded by the few maids left behind and the occasional manservant, sometimes they'd been chased down the long, arched passageway which divided the main house from that where the servants slept. Jack had laughed as he described how the old master wouldn't have his servants sleeping under the same roof as himself, had all the servants locked out of the main house when the master retired for the night. The panelled door at the end of the passage locked, the servants' quarters divided into male and female, the door was opened at an unearthly hour in the morning so the under maids could begin their chores.

'So, Scarlett, this isn't the last time you'll see me before I set sail.'

'But you won't know where I am,' she'd protested.

'I knows where the maids' quarters be, light a candle, put it in the window. I'll find you.'

A deep rut in the track jolted Scarlett out of her thoughts. Miss Hester was holding tight the strap which hung down beside the window. 'Will this journey ever be over?' she protested.

'We're nearly there,' Scarlett tried to assure her, but in truth she had no idea how much further they had to travel.

'What do you know of where we are to stay?' she asked thinking to take her charge's mind off the journey.

'Only that the hateful Maria's father owns more acreage in this part of Cornwall than any other, forever boasting to us other girls, she is. She's the most spiteful and hideous person I can think of. Why my father has arranged this visit I have no idea. Maria Penhallen is an out and out bore.'

Scarlett wondered if Maria Penhallen knew her father was engaged in the smuggling trade. Jack had become less secretive about his involvement in smuggling and vowed one day he'd take her out in the *Alice* to check that tubs lowered overboard for safe keeping hadn't drifted too far away. She so hoped a chance to do this would come soon, but how she'd get out of Prospect House at night for such an adventure, she couldn't fathom.

Miss Hester's voice grew desperate, breaking into her thoughts. 'We shall never get there; I pray I will have to beg the coachman to stop, I truly feel most indisposed,' Miss Hester wailed.

Scarlett looked at her charge and was horrified to see she had turned the palest of colour. 'We are almost there; you will feel much better when we alight at Penhallen.'

By the time they reached their destination, Scarlett herself felt fatigued and a little queasy. Alighting into the fresh air Scarlett stood with Miss Hester, both relieved to be released from the confines of the coach.

Penhallen was indeed a very impressive house, perched high on the steep hillside above the harbour of Polperro. The fresh sea breeze was welcome, and Scarlett took a deep breath then stared down at the harbour entrance in disbelief. A top sailed schooner lay anchored offshore, it could only be one ship, the *Black Diamond*. She was the only top sailed schooner in these parts, it's what set her apart from the others. Ivan had told her this. A boat had been lowered and two men were being rowed ashore. It was too far away to distinguish their features but already Scarlett knew who they were – Francis Kestrel and his odious brother Adrian, who'd so manhandled her at Moorswater.

For the moment though there was no time to dwell on this, Scarlett turned and saw that a very tall woman, stylishly dressed in a plum coloured dress, was walking down the gravel path to greet them. She seemed an unlikely person to be the housekeeper at Penhallen, but she introduced herself as Grace Reynolds the housekeeper. Scarlett thought the Catt sisters would think her most unsuitable, there would be no position for such as her at Prospect House. Mr Julian and another gentleman came out from within the house walking quickly down the path.

'The bore's father,' Miss Hester whispered, in a voice so low the housekeeper couldn't hear.

'You made good time. Come let's go inside,' Mr Julian exclaimed, 'Maria's waiting for you there, is she not Charles?'

Miss Hester took her father's arm and Scarlett dutifully followed the others up the path. She stole several quick glances back towards the sea. The ship in full sail was now makings good progress westward and would soon be out of sight.

Once inside the house, Scarlett took Miss Hester's cloak, gloves and bonnet whilst pleasantries were being exchanged in the hall. The housekeeper with just the trace of a smile bade Scarlet follow her up to Miss Hester's room. At the top of the elegant staircase two young boys were caught dragging Miss Hester's heavy travelling boxes along the corridor and received a telling off by Mrs Reynolds in such colourful language it made

Scarlett blush. Hastily they grabbed hold the rope straps and carried them in the proper manner.

'There's a small room adjoining the main bedroom with a trundle bed where you can sleep to be of service to your mistress at all times. I'll send a maid to help you unpack, she'll tell you what time we dine in the servants' hall below stairs.'

Mrs Reynolds opened the door to Miss Hester's room and looked around the room nodding with satisfaction. 'I think your mistress will be very pleased with this room,' she said brightly and withdrew leaving Scarlett on her own as the boys brought in the rest of Miss Hester's boxes. When they'd gone, she sank down and sat on the bed in total misery. She wouldn't see Jack if the *Sunrising* sailed before she returned after all. He'd see no candle to tell him where she was, for she was stuck here away from the servants' quarters, and although fearful of such a daring escapade, the disappointment she felt was overwhelming. Close to tears she sat and gazed at the mound of belongings that needed unpacking. This, on top of the unwelcome suspicion that Adrian Kestrel was possibly at this moment being rowed ashore to stay here as a guest. Scarlett couldn't remember when she was quite so miserable.

The maid sent to help Scarlett was Maudie. With her help all was unpacked quite quickly. Two dresses needing pressing Maudie gathered up to take below stairs.

'We eat in the servants' hall at 6.00 there's a door to the back stairs just along from here beside the painting of the old general. Don't be late; Mrs Reynolds is a right stickler for time.'

She was about to open the door when Scarlett asked, 'Are there other guest staying here besides my mistress and her father?'

'Indeed, there's a whole house full, we'll be rushed off our feet.'

Scarlett walked over to the window and stared out to sea. Below in the small harbour she could see fishing luggers all tied in together against the quay, a mass of folk busy with the newly caught catch.

The quietness within the room was broken by the pushing open of the door and Miss Hester flouncing in, flinging herself down on the bed exclaiming, 'I hate it here. I shall beg Papa to take me home this very night.'

'I doubt he'll do that,' Scarlett replied. 'What's happened?'

'She's a show-off, that's what. I hate her at school, now I'm stuck here whilst she prattles on about how many fine ships her father owns, not forgetting the four-master *Carrisabell* at this moment rounding Cape Horn.'

Scarlett handed her charge a handkerchief and let Miss Hester snivel into it. Lacking her usual patience, she went into the adjoining room and drew out the trundle bed. The realisation she wouldn't see Jack before he left weighed heavily in her heart. It had seemed such a crazy scheme, what with him knowing the house and all that, but it was to no avail now she'd be sleeping here. Feeling totally miserable, in temper she threw a feather pillow into place then unfolded the scratchy ivory coloured blankets. A gust of wind caused the window to rattle in its frame, already there was a chill in the air. Her mood for once matching that of her charge.

As she began to unpack her meagre belongings and hang up her spare dark blue uniform and cap, Miss Hester miffed at being left alone called out for her. 'I don't want you to sleep in there, Maria will say you're my nursemaid or something, make out I need a nanny. Tell the other girls at the Academy.'

She rang the bell pull and Maudie duly arrived and was dispatched to inform Mrs Reynolds that Scarlett needed to be found a room in the servants' quarters. Given her status, she would not be expected to share.

Scarlett was surprised by such thoughtfulness on Miss Hester's part.

'You will of course be on call at all times, Penrose,' she snapped, pouting and as childish as ever.

Scarlett busied herself, then sat listening to Miss Hester's whining with much greater patience, for now she knew there was a chance she'd see Jack after all. The old trepidation at Jack's daring plan still made her a little fearful, gripped her stomach with excitement and sent her heart racing, all this far outweighed any fear that they'd be caught.

Miss Hester decided to take a nap, so Scarlett made her way along the corridor and found the discreet door to the back stairs. How different this bare staircase and rough flaking walls from the plushness of the main house. Scarlett asked a young maid where the servants' hall was and made her way there.

The servants' hall was gloomy, little light came in from four long windows, two at each end of the room. A long pine table, already laid, filled the centre of the room. No sky was visible from the windows just wild grasses blowing on the cliff face. Mrs Reynolds was standing at the far end. As she walked towards her, Scarlett was shocked to see that part of the wall behind Mrs Reynolds was glistening and wet.

'It's where this part of the house is built literally into the cliff, hence a fire burns here all year round and the place smells of damp,' Mrs Reynolds stated in a matter of fact voice, and for a moment Scarlett saw her composure falter. Behind her, Scarlett could hear the chatter of others coming into the room.

'What exactly is your position at Prospect House?' Mrs Reynolds enquired, tilting her head to one side. 'For I must know where to sit you.'

'I'm Miss Hester's companion, governess and also take the duties of housekeeper if required,' Scarlett replied boldly. 'We are a small establishment in West Looe. Mr Julian's sisters are my employees.'

'Come, you'd best sit here then.' Mrs Reynolds motioned. 'You'll be with others much as yourself, although most of them are much older and from larger households. Take care not to be intimidated,' her parting words.

A fine meal was served of poultry with a good array of vegetables, fruit jelly followed. Apart from the chatter coming from the lower end of the table there was little conversation between Scarlett and her fellow strangers at table. Leaving Scarlett in no doubt they rather looked down at this young woman seated amongst them.

Having helped Miss Hester complete her lengthy preparations for the evening, Scarlett collected her belongings and Maudie led her along the corridor at the bottom of the back stairs to the sleeping quarters. There she was shown into a small, barely furnished room. Just a narrow iron bed, table and candle holder. Four large hooks protruded from the wall, and a shabby curtain sagged against the window.

'Tis'nt too bad in ere, three of us share further along, tis colder there, cause we'm more exposed to the cliff edge. Wenna'll give you a knock in the morning, your charge has her own bell to be answered to in the kitchen, so best be in the servants' hall early to hear it through the hatch.'

'Thank you.' Scarlett smiled, not daring to think of Jack's presence in this very room.

From somewhere close by, Maudie's name was hollered, and the girl ran off leaving Scarlett alone. It was now as she placed her belongings on the bed, Scarlett noticed the catch on the leaded light window and the deep stone sill where she could place her candle.

When Miss Hester rang for her at the end of the evening, she was still grumbling right up until she got into bed. Scarlett listened to it all, thankful when the task of preparing her charge for bed was almost complete. Finally, she brushed and braided Miss Hester's hair as in a raised voice Miss Hester complained about everything, from the dress she wore to the few jewels she'd been allowed to bring with her. Maria Penhallen had of course been dressed in the most gorgeous of dresses, she'd felt a lesser person, it was a disgrace, on and on she went until Scarlett had a headache. It was a joy to blow out Miss Hester's candle.

Scarlett could now escape below stairs, candle holder in hand. One candle was a quarter spent so she'd taken a spare new one from the room she was to have slept in, just in case. With no difficulty she set off along the long passage at the bottom of the backstairs and found her room. Suddenly the thought of Jack being here seemed so real. She undressed and put on her calico nightdress, poured cold water from the enamel jug into the china bowl and washed. She drew the curtain only a little and placed the candle to the right of the sill as Jack had told her to.

She lay in bed and watched as the candle slowly burnt lower and lower. Would Jack be here tonight? She wouldn't put it past him. In the end, exhausted by the long day and unable to stay awake, Scarlett fell asleep, woken by the brush of another's lips upon hers.

'Move over,' Jack whispered in her ear. Scarlett's heart missed a beat. He'd already shed most of his clothes and slid into the creaking bed beside her. Taking her in his arms he kissed her as if they'd been parted for years. 'Off with this, maid,' he whispered softly, and tugged at the nightgown, gently lifting it up and over her head.

Now the bed groaned under his shifting weight. 'Do you think this bed'll survive our lovemaking?' he teased.

'I don't care,' Scarlett giggled, and Jack hesitated no longer, she was his once again.

It was afterwards as they lay wrapped in each other's arms that a sound came from the other side of the door and they sprung apart. Jack slipped from the bed and silently put on his clothes; Scarlett sat up clutching the blankets to her. For a little while all was quiet. Going over to the bed, Jack retrieved Scarlett's nightgown and she raised her arms as he slipped it over her. She shivered, her teeth chattering with fear. Jack crept over and put his ear to the door. It was then the small brass doorknob with the dent to one side began to turn. He stepped back behind the door motioning to Scarlett to lie down.

Very slowly the door began to open, a figure moved forward towards the bed. A hand reached out but before they could pull back the covers, Jack raised his fist and punched the intruder firmly on the side of the head. The man fell, falling heavily against the end of the iron bedstead then sprawling face down, hitting his head with a crack on the flagstone floor.

Jack closed the door. He went over and sat on the bed; Scarlett clung to him, trembling uncontrollably.

Gently he set Scarlett from him and picked up the candle holder. Going to the end of the bed he bent down to see who the intruder was. The man was still formally dressed in evening attire, the wig he wore was askew and Jack was not surprised when he saw the coppery coloured hair of Adrian Kestrel beneath. He turned Kestrel's head to one side and put his hand down in front his mouth, hoping to feel a breath upon it. There was. The man was just unconscious.

'That's Adrian Kestrel,' Scarlett said softly.

'Indeed it is, the bastard,' Jack swore, then returned to sit beside her and shook his sore hand to alleviate the pain. The candle spluttered, its life nearly spent, and easing herself from the bed Scarlett fetched the spare one she'd brought downstairs with her. She lit it, blowing out the one about to expire, and carefully once again stepped over the prone man on the floor.

'Are you sure he's not dead?' she queried.

'Have no fear, he's not dead, and believe me that's a good thing.'

'What's going to happen now?' Scarlett whimpered, recoiling further up the bed.

Jack took the freshly lit candle and set it down on the floor. He looked up at her. 'There's not too much blood.' He tore a strip off his shirt, wiped the blood from the wound and moved Kestrel's unconscious body slightly so he was able to wipe clean the flagstone floor. He stood up and paced the room.

'Jack, I'm so scared.' A tearful Scarlett reached out and grasped his hand.

'Don't worry, maid, I've decided what's to be done and I need your help, so be brave, Scarlett, come over here and hold the candle.'

In one swift movement, he lifted Adrian Kestrel over his shoulder and quietly opened the door and listened. Silence.

'Come on,' he whispered. Barefoot with Scarlett beside him, Jack walked, almost ran, along the passage and out into long corridor connecting the servants sleeping quarters and the main house, thankfully times had changed and the doors separating the two were no longer locked. Jack paused only once to reposition Kestrel's heavy body and take a deep breath before setting off again. Now they were in the main house.

It was dark and deathly quiet. When they came to the first pair of double doors, Scarlett ran ahead and opened them. The candlelight showed it to be a library, Jack made his way over to the ornate marble fireplace surrounded by a copper fender. He eased Adrian Kestrel down and lay his head next to the fender. He tore a strip of linen from his shirt and dipped it in the wound, smearing it across the fender, then checked once more that Kestrel was breathing. Glancing round, he saw on a side table glasses and a decanter set out on a silver tray. Walking over, Jack removed the glass stopper and took a sniff.

'Brandy.' He took a glass and poured out good measure, took the glass and placed it in Adrian Kestrel's hand. The contents spilt out over Kestrel's fine satin waistcoat and elaborately tied cravat. Jack then emptied the contents of the decanter completely, soaking Adrian Kestrel's fine clothes and the thick floor coverings around him. For a moment, both he and Scarlett stood looking down at the unconscious man.

'Come, my love, we must waste no time.' Taking Scarlett by the hand, Jack led her across the room and through the open doors, closing them softly, then together they ran silently back to the safety of Scarlett's room.

Jack shut the door and held Scarlett tight in his arms.

'What if he remembers when he wakes?'

'He won't remember, it happened too quickly,' Jack replied sharply. Then smoothing Scarlett's hair said gently, 'I doubt he'll even remember about coming to the servants' sleeping quarters, let alone recall out of all the rooms along this passage which door he went to. Besides, he'd been drinking heavily, I could smell it on him.'

Scarlett clung to Jack so tightly she could hear his heart beating. Smelt the smell of the sea on his jacket. Releasing her briefly he took the candle and went over to the spot where Kestrel had fallen, there was no sign of blood on the flags, he took a good look round the room, nothing.

Jack came back and sat on the bed, he looked at Scarlett with a seriousness she'd had never seen before and it scared her. 'Listen to me, maid, this is important. No one must find out what happened here tonight. Promise me you will tell no one, not even my sister Ruth when next you meet. If we're found out it could have the most dire of consequences. The Kestrel's are powerful men round these parts. I'd find myself in Bodmin, hanged for attempted murder, or transported if lucky, you too.'

Scarlett shuddered at his words. Cold fear reached into her bones.

'The most import thing is, when you hear tittle-tattle below stairs of Kestrel being found in the library, you must show no reaction different than the others sharing this gossip. Probably you'll learn whether Kestrel's gained consciousness, but ask no questions, go about your tasks as usual, try and keep out of the way.'

'I shan't ever tell a soul,' Scarlett promised. 'Heaven knows what he'd have done to me if you hadn't been here. Sheer hatred of the man will see me through.'

The faint light of dawn began to seep through the window.

'I must go, my sweet, or I'll miss the high tide, alas the *Sunrising* is sailing today. I don't want her to sail without me, there'll be the devil to pay if that happens.'

Scarlett nestled closer to him. Jack took a deep breath. 'I hate to go and leave you like this.' He gently set her away from him. 'Be brave, my darling maid, promise me you'll be brave. Have no fear, for sure that bastard won't remember, he won't, but what can he say if he did? That he went creeping round the servants' sleeping quarters in the middle of the night, his purpose to ravish some poor soul in her sleep? I'll be back before two months are out. Keep safe, Scarlett. Just think, in only a few days' time you too will be leaving Porthallen. Just try and forget this ever happened, and remember above all else, I love you.'

'I love you too.' Scarlett gripped Jack as though to never let him go, in the end he had to peel her embrace from him. He fetched his boots and old woollen socks, sat on the bed and put them on. The candle spluttered dying as Jack cupped Scarlett's face in his hands, kissing her one last time before deftly opening the window and disappearing into the night.

As Maudie had told her, early the next morning Wenna came knocking on Scarlett's door waking her with a start. She sat up in bed half asleep, half recalling the horror that had happened the night before, and shivered.

'I've heard you,' she called out, and the girl passed on to wake another soul.

Scarlett eased herself from the bed, and went straight to the window, she gazed out across the sea. Jack could be somewhere out there already, the *Sunrising* in full sail making her way, where? She suddenly realised Jack hadn't told her where they were headed. Her feet felt icy cold on the flagstone floor and in near darkness she crossed the room and poured from the jug the small amount of water remaining into the bowl and splashed its cold contents on her face, wiping it away with the thin towel hanging by a loop on a peg close by.

Scarlett remembered Jack's words of warning as she began to dress. Once more she searched for any sign that Kestrel had been in her room, there was nothing, but knew she would look again when the chance came. With haste she put on her uniform and pinned her hair up under a fresh cap, opened the door and made her way to the servants' dining hall. Just as she entered the sound of a clanging bell pulled in a much demanding manner sounded over and over again. Scarlett look up at the row of bells with their porcelain plaques beneath naming their place of summons. She wasn't surprised to see the word library. And felt a numbing fear.

'Someone, anyone, go and stop that incessant noise, will you?' Cook ordered. 'Tilda, upstairs this instant and find out what's going on.'

A plump girl with greasy locks ran past Scarlett. Minutes later she was back knocking frantically on the housekeeper's quarters. An irritable Mrs Reynolds opened the door. The various members of staff gathered round the long table having breakfast unashamedly stopped to listen to what was being said.

Mrs Reynolds was far from pleased at being disturbed by the hysterical maid outside her door, unlike the lower servants she usually rose a little later.

'Tis Lizzy, Mrs Reynolds,' Tilda sobbed. 'She went to open the shutters in the library and found a man lying in front the fireplace. Dead, he looked. Lizzy screamed so much the master himself burst in and told her to be quiet. He looked at the gent, prodded him with his foot and said the gent weren't dead and to stop her blabbering. Fled to her room has Lizzy.'

Just then several bells began to jig on their springs demanding they be answered. Groans and oaths were uttered from those who must abandon their breakfast.

Mrs Reynolds unimpressed by the slowness with which her staff were responding snapped at them, 'Get about your work, you lazy lot. Tilda, you wait here, and do stop sniffling.' Quickly she made herself presentable and Tilda followed her upstairs.

Scarlett sat alone except for Maudie, her mistress like Miss Hester slept on. From the kitchen came the sound of pots and pans, mixed with a scurry of activity, for cook and those helping her knew those upstairs would be demanding breakfast much earlier than was usual. The household would be roused if this was some important gent been found. Scarlett felt quite unable to eat but remembering Jack's words, forced a little bread down, none must know of the anxiety that filled the pit of her stomach.

'That old Squire from Talland's due at noon,' Maudie said brightly, spooning honey onto a slice of bread. 'Last to arrive he is for this ere meeting that's happening, thought we'd have a peaceful morning at least, but not now.'

Scarlett was about to answer when another bell jangled, it was Maudie's mistress.

'Must be something going on for her ladyship to be up this early,' Maudie grumbled. And still clutching her piece of bread went off upstairs. As she left, two elderly sour-faced lady's maids belonging to other guests at Polhallen came in, sitting together at the other end of the table well away from Scarlett.

It came as a relief when Miss Hester finally rang for her, and as Scarlett made her way up the backstairs, she passed Maudie hurrying down. Maudie paused excitedly telling her, 'I just seen um carrying the gent what Lizzy found. It's the younger Kestrel brother, master's in a foul mood, shouting he had no right go poking about in his library, helping himself to brandy, said one decanter's empty and the stopper's lost. I glimpsed Tilda on her hands and knees searching for it. Heard Master threatening poor Edwin with dismissal saying he should have locked the decanters away.'

'Poor Edwin,' Scarlett said, feeling more than a little guilty. She hadn't met him but couldn't help but feel for him.

'Tis a laugh is our Edwin, let's hope he don't let him go. Master were having a right go at Francis Kestrel, telling im his brother were a bloody disgrace.'

Just then they heard the click of a door and Mrs Reynolds appeared hastening both on their way.

Miss Hester, oblivious to any of the turmoil happening so close by, was her usual demanding self, pettish and quite undecided which dress she should wear and equally quarrelsome over just how her hair should be styled.

When all was finished, the pale blue coloured dress with wide lace-edged sleeves selected and finally satisfied with how she looked, Miss Hester quipped, 'Miss Penhallen is arranging a walk so we may take tea with her aunt, her carriage will be available to convey us home, you may be needed to accompany us. I shall inform you later.' She rose from the stool and left a tired Scarlett dismayed at the prospect of yet another change of clothes for Miss Hester, and of the walk to Miss Maria's aunts. Perhaps it wouldn't happen, what with the discovery of Adrian Kestrel in the library.

With care, Scarlett tidied away the two cast-off dresses whilst two under maids came in and attended to Miss Hester's bed, changing the linen and plumping up the pillows. On Miss Hester's favourite pale blue dress, the hem had come down a little, probably caught by the heel of a shoe. Scarlett fetched out the sewing box and picked out a matching silk cotton, she sat on the window seat and paused a moment looking out to sea. She knew Jack would be thinking of her, wondering what was happening at Penhallen. Then with small even stitches she began to mend the hem, thrusting the needle into the material, knowing she wouldn't let Jack down.

This short time alone with her thoughts was all too brief. Miss Hester returned accompanied by Maria

Penhallen, who announced importantly, 'We are to walk along the coast to my aunts, my governess will accompany us, you will not be required.'

She looked at Miss Hester then at Scarlett, 'Well tell her, Hester,' she exclaimed. 'You are her mistress.'

'You may take the rest of the day off, Penrose, that is until we return. Make sure to find something useful to keep yourself occupied.'

'Yes, Miss Hester,' Scarlett replied greatly relieved, the implied slight intended by Miss Penhallen totally welcome, for indeed, thank heaven for the governess.

From the press she drew out Miss Hester's dark damask cloak with its lining of matching silk, her white gloves and stylish bonnet newly delivered to Prospect House from Truro.

Scarlett sighed with relief as the door closed behind them, it was then she saw that Miss Hester had left behind her gloves. As she would at Prospect House, she went after her charge and found herself running down the main staircase, utterly dismayed to see Mrs Reynolds standing beside the wide entrance doors. The housekeeper looked up at her with an expression of such horror that it halted her instantly. Scarlett felt like a schoolgirl and her face reddened. Mrs Reynolds, having seen the gloves in Scarlett's hands, imparted this information to Miss Hester standing but a little way off, she too stopped and looked up at her. With as much dignity as she could muster, Scarlett walked down the remaining stairs to hand the gloves to her.

'Thank you, Penrose.' Miss Hester sighed heavily, as though exasperated by Scarlett's lack of etiquette. The two girls turned to leave accompanied by the snooty faced governess when they were forced to retreat back inside the hall. A portly man elegantly dressed in a dark blue frock coat, black knee breeches, yellow silk waistcoat, and boots that shone most brightly, strode through the open doors.

'Squire,' Mrs Reynolds said curtseying.

'Ah! I see I'm a little earlier than expected. Be so kind as to tell your master I'm here, will you?' He turned to gaze rather too boldly at Miss Penhallen. 'Maria, you look lovely, turning into a real beauty to be sure.'

Charles Penhallen strode quickly across the hall. Taking the squire's arm, he led him firmly away from his daughter saying in a cordial manner, 'Come this way, squire, the others are gathered already, so no need to waste time, we can begin the business in hand.'

As the two men walked down the corridor, Mrs Reynolds turned to Scarlett. 'What on earth were you thinking of running down the main staircase indeed? Some establishment you come from to behave in such a manner.'

'I'm sorry.' Scarlett bowed her head and when she looked up Mrs Reynolds signalled her dismissal. She made to walk back up the stairs she'd so recently descended but Mrs Reynolds clicked her tongue.

'Follow me,' she insisted and hurried Scarlett along holding tight her elbow, then opened a discreet door and ushered her down a set of stone stairs that led straight to the kitchen. 'Know your place in future, miss,' she chided, 'there's plenty of work for idle hands down here. More visitors are expected, and the physician's been called for the young gent Lizzy found. You can help Lizzy if it's not beneath you, she's still upset about this morning and little wonder.'

Scarlett found Lizzy setting out tankards in a room adjoining the kitchen. 'Mrs Reynolds sent me to help you, what can I do?' she asked. And a startled Lizzy turned to look at her pale faced and puffy eyed.

'Sorry,' Scarlett apologised. 'I thought you heard me come in.'

'No, I didn't, I'm a bit jumpy. Not got over the sight of that gent I thought were dead. Keep seeing him in me mind. There ain't much to do here now until these here men from the villages arrive, got to listen out for um knocking on the kitchen door. I've been told to show them in here, give them ale then when all eight have arrived, Mrs Reynolds is to inform master.'

Lizzy took a handkerchief from her pocket and blew her nose. 'Cook's just been informed these men are to be given a meal before they leave, so I'm gonna help Wenna, there's more vegetables need peeling. Cook could do with an extra pair of hands, she's proper put out with all the extra work on top of the guests already here. Mutton them having so she's said, and nothing fancy with it.'

'Who are these men that's coming?' Scarlett asked intrigued.

'Don't know, ask Maudie, she knows about everything,' Lizzy replied, and a faint smile formed on her lips.

It was hot in the kitchen, huge copper pans bubbled away emitting clouds of steam. Lizzy handed her a white apron with broad bib to protect her grey uniform. She joined Wenna and Lizzy peeling the extra vegetables now needed and listened to cooks endless grumblings. About the men soon to be expected, Scarlett learnt no more. And all the time fear gripped the pit of her stomach. Had Adrian Kestrel woken, and what did he remember?

After the vegetable preparations were finished, with Wenna she scrubbed clean the huge pine table. Scarlett looked through the hatch into the servants' dining hall impatient to see Maudie. Surely Maudie would have some gossip.

Just then a loud rapping came on the kitchen door. Scarlett walked over, lifted the latch and opened it. A huddle of men stood outside, their clothes like the men themselves were none too clean, a rough bunch they were. Lizzy stepped forward and looked down at their boots. 'There'll be no traipsing of mud in ere making work for the likes of me,' she complained, stern faced. The men began stamping their feet loosening the mud from worn boots before using the boot scraper set in the wall. When Lizzy was finally satisfied, she stepped aside and let them in. Each snatched the cap off his head as they entered, staring about, unused to being in such a fine place as Penhallen even if it was just the kitchen.

'Come on, follow me,' Lizzy ordered, she seemed to have perked up a bit, her mind taken off the events of earlier in the morning. The men shuffled after her and sat where they were told, silently supping the ale she poured, heads bowed. The last man, younger than the rest, tall with wild curly blonde hair and very handsome to the eye, turned and winked at Scarlett as he passed by, making her smile, making her forget her worries just for a moment.

The other three visitors arrived shortly after and joined those sat round the table. When they thought no one could hear them the men engaged in conversation, their voices so low they were scarcely more than a whisper.

Curious to know why they were here, Scarlett lingered just beyond the door, trying to hear what was being said, but she couldn't quite hear.

Suddenly Mrs Reynolds swept down the stone stairs with an air of superiority. 'The physician's arrived, I'm needed and for how long I don't know. You, Scarlett, show the men up these stairs to where the master and his other guests are gathered.'

'But shouldn't Lizzy?' Scarlett questioned.

'You do it,' Lizzy said coming to stand beside her. 'Taint never been up there showing folks in and the like. Don't want to neither. Men's all ere, Mrs Reynolds.'

'Scarlett, get that apron off, take them up these stairs and down the corridor to the room at the far end. Knock, wait for master to give word, then show them in. If I'm not here, master will ring when they're dismissed, go up and bring um back down, but be sure to tell cook beforehand.'

'Yes, Mrs Reynolds.'

Just then cook yelled for Lizzy, who gladly hurried off to the kitchen, and Mrs Reynolds promptly turned and went back upstairs leaving Scarlett to remove her apron fold it up and leave it in the servants' hall.

As she entered the room where the men were seated, their conversation fell silent.

'Follow me,' Scarlett stated in her most confident Prospect House voice.

'Aye, miss, that we will,' the younger of the men teased, grinning at the others, it was he who'd winked at her earlier. Scarlett led them upstairs and along the corridor, knocking on the door, waiting to be bid entry before opening it and standing aside whilst the straggly line of men who'd followed her walked past.

Some of the visitors assembled in the room Scarlett hadn't seen before, but the squire, the most flamboyantly dressed of them all, stood one arm resting on the mantelpiece, whilst Mr Julian and Francis Kestrel were seated along with the others. In the short while she stood there, Scarlett saw that on an oval table a large map was spread out, held in place at the corners by four leather-bound books.

'Come in, come in,' Charles Penhallen shouted at the men impatiently and gestured them forward. You, whoever you are, where's Mrs Reynold's?'

'With the physician, sir,' Scarlett replied.

'Well, come quick, girl, when I ring the bell. Shoo now, leave us and no eavesdropping, you hear what I'm saying, maid?'

'Yes, sir.' Scarlett bobbed a curtsey then turned and withdrew. She closed the door, so tempted to stay and eavesdrop. Just what, she wondered, was being discussed in that room, between such different men? But she dare not linger. As she walked just a short distance along the corridor, Scarlett heard the door open, she turned to see it closing, someone was making sure she wasn't eavesdropping.

As Scarlett went back to the servants' hall in search of Maudie, she remembered exactly what brought gentry and local men together, but surely a meeting such as this here today was most unusual.

She found Maudie sitting in the dining hall consoling a young man who must be Edwin. 'Master won't dismiss you. You knows he's got a temper. Threatened to dismiss me last week. Let's hope that Kestrel gent wakes up and apologies for his behaviour. Tis all his fault.'

Scarlett sat listening consumed with guilt. Edwin seemed such a nice young man. Wenna came in with a tray bearing bowls of soup and a plate of thickly sliced bread. 'Cook says you'm might as well eat now, as them fellows as like be down shortly.' Scarlett hoped the soup would quell her nervous stomach and was thankful that no bell rang to summons her while she ate.

An older manservant came to join them. 'Mrs Reynolds is just showing the physician out,' he informed them. 'Young mister upstairs has woken, miserable sods shouting and bawling, causing havoc. Mrs Reynolds sent me to fetch his brother to quieten him.'

Scarlett was just thankful Adrian Kestrel wasn't dead.

'But listen here,' the older man continued, 'before I knocked on the door to get Mr Francis, I just happened to hear a bit of the conversation from inside, heard the squire imself talking summat bout a reward, couldn't hear ow much. Someone raised their voice and said the drat informer's life would soon be theirs. Went a bit quiet then it did, and I knocked on the door. Funny thing happened then, master himself opened it. Shocked I was. T'others was all huddled by the table, looked round at me narrow-eyed like, as if I was spying on um or something.'

'They weren't far wrong there then,' Maudie laughed. 'Had the old ear to the door then, Mr Buller.'

'Well, you may laugh but it pays to know what's going on. Listen up I met the squire's man Whithers in the Talland Arms last week. Told me his master was spitting blood over losing the *Rubyanne*, reckons some bloody informer tipped off the revenue. They had men hidden, waiting on the beach for the landing. Well laden were the *Rubyanne* with tobacco and rum, all was going to plan. Sea were a bit rough but not too bad. Suddenly our lads were surrounded by revenue and one of their damn schooners come close in and shots were fired. Summat must have happened because the *Rubyanne* started to take on water, then mighty quick down she goes, cargo lost along with three of the squire's best men, including young Samuel, who we all knows as being squire's bastard son by Molly Perrin. Fond of that lad he was.'

'I knew Samuel, he was a gentle soul,' Maudie sighed. 'Little wonder then squire's furious. What happened to those on the beach?'

Scarlett felt lightheaded, upset and distressed by Mr Buller's story. Men had died and an awful thought stole into her mind, she prayed it wasn't true, but could it be her father was the informer.

'Well the tub men scattered, some had to fight for their lives, thankfully they outnumbered the bloody revenue. Withers said the squire told him he was going to put an end to this run of bad luck, once and for all.'

'Right now, there's a matter closer to home needs your help, Mr Buller,' said Maudie in a determined voice.

'I've heard already, leave it to me, Edwin, you're be going nowhere.'

Mrs Reynolds return meant their conversation was abruptly abandoned. There was a jangle of bells, suddenly it seemed everyone was needed.

'Penrose, go up and fetch the men down,' Mrs Reynolds ordered. 'Maudie, tell cook will you, lay the table and get Lizzy to refill the jugs of ale. Edwin, go up to Mr Adrian's room, stay in case he wakes. Mr Buller, about your business if you please.'

Scarlett still reeling from Mr Buller's story, went upstairs with a heavy heart. She knocked once again at the door, waited, entering when Charles Penhallen bade her do so. Most of those in the room were now standing, the meeting it seemed had gone well, the squire shaking hands with the local men as they made to leave. Scarlett led them down the back stairs. Then she helped Lizzy refill their mugs with ale. Wenna served them mutton, potatoes and vegetables then they were left on their own. Scarlett heard laughter and the clink of ale mugs, someone proclaimed in a low voice, 'A toast to the squire, bless him,' then slowly, and purposefully the door was shut.

In the absence of Mrs Reynolds, Scarlett took herself off to Miss Hester's room and sat on the window seat, knees drawn up. She sighed for everything looked so peaceful, the sea dark blue against a cloudless sky. A trail of heron gulls followed behind a lugger making its way into the harbour. It seemed unbelievable that only this morning Jack had climbed out her window in the servants' quarters.

Restless, Scarlett began to pack away some of Miss Hester's clothes ready for tomorrow's departure. As she picked up discarded pink ribbons from a small table besides the window, she saw the local men wandering down the narrow drive and past the front of the house. As they came closer, she reached out and opened the window, hoping to hear snippets of conversation.

'We'll get um with the wreckers light,' one of them rasped, and coughed into a large handkerchief.

'Flush the bastards out be best,' said another.

Then the young man who had winked at her earlier declared, 'Reckon we could draw their sloop onto the rocks if the night were dark enough. No shortage of folks willing to help us and we'm happy to share the reward with them. Somehow the revenue know when the landings are taking place. This must be stopped. I'll hang the bastard informant meself.'

Scarlett reached to open the window a little further, it grated iron upon iron and they looked up staring straight at Scarlett. Mortified, Scarlett stared back, then raised her hand and waved. One of them took off his cap and bowed to her whilst another blew her a kiss. Scarlett closed the window and sat on Miss Hester's bed. Heart pounding.

Later the sound of wheels upon the gravel drive heralded the arrival back of Miss Maria and Miss Hester. Scarlett watched as they alighted from the enclosed carriage followed by the governess.

Nervous about returning to the academy, Miss Hester was at her most demanding. Nothing Scarlett could do was right, her hair was brushed, pinned and unpinned, restyled three times before she was happy. Four different dresses were laced then unlaced, countless pairs of velvet slippers put on and cast aside. A tired Scarlett all but lost her patience, relieved when Miss Hester flounced out leaving scattered clothing and slippers for Scarlett to pack away.

Charles Penhallen had arranged the coach to take them to the academy would be at the front entrance at 10.00am. So, it was to be an early start for the young ladies. A subdued Miss Hester was quieter than usual when she returned upstairs to her room. Scarlett quickly prepared her for bed. Reassuring her that her boxes would be sent on their way to the academy the very next day. She would not be left bereft of any clothes.

'I beg you, Penrose, tell my aunts I am most unhappy, ask them to persuade Papa to let me return to Prospect House,' Miss Hester sobbed once in bed. Scarlett was surprised to see tears running down her charge's cheeks. Scarlett could not envisage herself talking thus to the Catt sisters, but she nodded her head in agreement and handed Miss Hester a lace-edged handkerchief. Finally, with Miss Hester asleep, Scarlett slipped downstairs to seek out any gossip as to how Adrian Kestrel fared.

Maudie was sat at the table with Lizzy. She greeted Scarlett cheerfully, 'Tis alright, our Edwin's staying. Mr Buller had a word with master.'

'That's good,' Scarlett replied, as she sat down. Her terrible guilt over Edwin and the decanter, could be set aside now.

'Edwin's right pleased; thought he were on his way with no papers.'

'How's the gent who caused the trouble?' Scarlett asked in an even tone.

'He's been sleeping it off, Edwin was ordered to rouse him again an hour ago.' Lizzy giggled. 'Wet the bed the gent had. Proper baby, moaning his head hurt, demanded a mirror and almost choked when he saw his swollen face and black eye. Threw a proper tantrum.' Lizzy paused, revelling in her knowledge of what was happening above stairs.

'Go on,' Scarlett begged.

Giving her audience a conspiratorial look, Lizzy said almost in a whisper, 'I were there, saw him hit out at his brother. Mr Buller and Edwin were trying to calm him. Nearly knocked his brother off his feet he did. Bellowing at everyone and in the foulest of language, won't eat anything cook's sent up, demanding Edwin fetch him a brandy. Mr Francis is really angry. Edwin heard him apologising to the master saying the reputation of Moorswater had been sullied by the stupidity of his brother.'

Scarlett tarried a while longer then wished them goodnight and went back to her room. She undressed, put on her nightgown and climbed into bed. So Kestrel had woken and seemingly for the moment remembered nothing. Now she had a little peace. But however hard she tried her mind replayed the events of the previous night, until she slept tired beyond tired.

In the morning a subdued Miss Hester made ready to leave, she insisted Scarlett accompany her to the carriage. It was clear that none of the excitement Miss Maria was feeling at their return to the Academy for Young Ladies was shared by Miss Hester.

Just before the carriage departed, she leant from the window. 'Scarlett, remember please, get my aunts to persuade Papa to let me return to Prospect House.'

'I will.'

'You may go now, Penrose.' Mr Julian ordered in a harsh voice. And to Scarlett's dismay she realised he was now standing directly behind her. 'Ivan will be here before noon to collect you.'

Red-faced, Scarlett walked back towards the house as others crowded round the coach to see the young ladies on their way.

Miss Hester's room seemed so very empty. Going into the small room adjacent to it, Scarlett began to pack away the blanket and coverlet still on the trundle bed she hadn't used. Two under maids came and stripped Miss Hester's bed and went off busy about their duties, leaving the door of the main bedroom wide open.

As she placed the thin pillow on top of the pile of bedding and bent to pick it up, Scarlett had the feeling she was being watched and turned to look beyond her own doorway to that of Miss Hester's. Standing there in his nightshirt, with hair in total disarray, head bent downwards towards his chest and looking up at her from under drooping eyelids stood Adrian Kestrel. Scarlett froze, hardly daring to breathe. For a moment their eyes locked, his piercing and evil. Clearly, he wasn't in his right mind, and Scarlett, terrified, realised there was no way she could escape. In a panic, she decided perhaps it would be best to ignore him so turned back to finish what she was doing, finally placing the trundle bed back to where it belonged, out of sight. The sound of a creaking floorboard made her jump and turn once again. Adrian Kestrel stood in the doorway of the room where she was. He looked quite mad, his eyes bloodshot and bulging from their sockets. He took a step forward and raised his right arm leaning forward to touch her breast. Scarlett backed away and screamed at the top of her voice. There came the sound of running footsteps and Mr Francis and Edwin came into the room each taking a firm hold of Kestrel.

'So sorry,' Mr Francis uttered, briefly looking back as with Edwin he hauled his brother from the room.

'We've been searching for him everywhere,' Edwin ventured to say. She saw him give Adrian Kestrel a look of pure loathing before they were gone, and Scarlett was left to recover. She sank down onto Miss Hester's bed still shaking from her encounter, not shedding a single tear until a short while later Maudie came rushing in to comfort her. Edwin must have told her what had happened.

Not until she was sat in the servants' dining hall did Scarlett feel safe. She said a reluctant goodbye to Maudie who'd shown her such kindness. Unfortunately, once they were downstairs, Mrs Reynolds sent Maudie about her duties not letting her sit for even a moment with Scarlett though she knew full well what had transpired upstairs. A while later Tilda and Edwin came in and wished her a safe journey home. The hands on the long case clock beside the dresser barely seemed to move.

'Please come soon, Ivan,' Scarlett prayed, for she longed to be gone from Penhallen. Most of the other house guests had left, leaving behind their servants who also waited for transport to convey them back from whence they came. Scarlett sat apart from them; she had no desire for conversation.

As midday approached only Scarlett and the two old sour-faced lady's maids who she'd first encountered at table that first evening remained. They occupied the only seats from where you could glimpse the yard beyond the kitchen so enabling you to see who was arriving.

Thus, Scarlett didn't see Ivan bring Miss Hester's elaborately carved dog cart to a halt, or hear his knock on the door.

'Your man's here for you,' Wenna came in and announced cheerfully, sensing Scarlett's relief. She held the door open as Scarlett picked up her carpet bag and hurried towards the door.

'Goodbye, Wenna,' Scarlett said smiling at the girl whose round face brightened before she hurried back to the steaming kitchen. At last, Scarlett stepped out into the fresh air and saw Ivan who took her bag and helped her up into the dog cart.

'Where's Dolly?' she asked.

'Borrowed one of the captain's horses, poor old Dolly, it be too far for her.' His familiar weather-beaten face broke into a smile. 'Seems yu'm been gone an age, maid.'

'So it seems to me, horrible place this.' She drew the hood of her cloak up as a fine mizzle of rain blew in from the sea.

With a shake of the reins they were on their way.

'What them two gawping at?' Ivan asked. And Scarlett turned her head to look.

'Oh them! Two sour old biddies, they be,' she answered, looking directly at the black clothed figures staring out at them, probably full of disdain at her mode of transport. As they passed close by, Scarlett did the unthinkable and poked out her tongue. Their mouths dropped open with shock, each looked at the other in sheer horror, then they quickly withdrew out of sight. Scarlett relished the moment and suppressed a giggle, whatever would her employers have thought.

'You alright?' Ivan asked as they came to the end of the drive and turned onto the rutted track leading to Looe.

'I am now your here to take me home,' she laughed.

The rain grew steadily worse until Ivan stopped. 'Best you sit up front with me I've an old piece of sailcloth will keep off the worst of it. Tis a long ways home, let's hope it don't rain all the way, we'll be proper wet through if it does.'

But Scarlett knew nothing further of the journey until Ivan woke her with the words, 'Wake up, maid, we'm nearly home.' The rain had stopped, she had fallen asleep her head resting on Ivan's shoulder, and they were descending West Looe Hill. She looked at Tamarisk as they passed by, it showed no sign of life within its cob walls. She knew on Sunday afternoon she must see her mother. She had until then to wrestle with her conscience. Just how much to tell her, if indeed anything, about the new and very determined effort by the smugglers to catch informers. Should she tell, and what if her mother told her father? Surely she wouldn't, surely not, that was too outrageous to even contemplate. But what if she said something in an unguarded moment?

With chattering teeth, a weary Scarlett followed Ivan up the path and into the warmth of Bessie's kitchen. How good it felt to be back at Prospect House. Already Scarlett had made the decision not to tell.

Chapter 10

During the four weeks since Scarlett's return from Penhallen, the sisters made sure she would be far from idle whilst her charge was absent. Indeed, Scarlett felt more tired with the household duties she'd been given than when teaching Miss Hester, however many tantrums she had to endure.

Although tired she couldn't sleep, wondering how much Adrian Kestrel had remembered, frustrated she could learn nothing of his situation. Mr Julian visited his aunts on several occasions, closeted with them in the drawing room. She had collected the tea tray on a few of these visits, but their conversation always ceased when she entered the room.

The day after she'd returned Bessie had remarked, 'You'm quiet, not said much about where you'm been or anything.'

'Nothing much to tell. Didn't like the place,' Scarlett had replied. 'I did get to know some of those in service, they were nice. And of course, Miss Hester put on airs and graces making out she were as good as Maria Penhallen but she weren't of course.'

'Twas quiet here with the two of you gone,' Millie sighed, 'I'm glad um back.'

Scarlett remained tight lipped about the visit and no more was said on the subject.

She had gone up to Tamarisk on the first Sunday afternoon off. Determined not to tell her mother about the vendetta held by the smugglers and gentry to find those who informed on them to the revenue. Best she didn't know. Jack would be back soon, and she knew in her heart she was on the side of the free traders.

Tamarisk was deserted, its door locked with no iron key hidden in the porch as was usual. Somewhat relieved her mother wasn't there, Scarlett walked back down the path and two gossiping women a little further up the hill shouted to her that her mother had been collected by the man in the cart that came for her from Lanreath.

Scarlett nodded her thanks and set off back down to the quay, deciding when nearly there to climb the steps leading to the servants' entrance of Polgrove Hall to see whether it was Ruth's Sunday off. She rang the bell beside the high wooden gate, and it was Ruth herself who slid back the wooden square behind the iron grill.

'Scarlett.' She opened the door and slipped outside.

'Is it your afternoon off?' Scarlett asked, hoping it was for she could do with her friend's company.

'No, tis beastly here, mistress dismissed two maids she found trying on her jewellery one day when she came back early. So, we've had no time off as punishment, and we never did anything.'

Ruth opened the gate and lowered her voice a little. 'Anyways, I hear from my little sister you and our Jack have got pretty close. You'm been up to Simon's Croft; believe me that's an honour.'

'Has he taken many girls there then?' Scarlett queried, feeling jealous to the core.

'None that I know of,' Ruth replied, seemingly telling the truth. 'You and my brother walking out together then?'

'May be.' Scarlett grinned. 'And how about you and Sam Trembright?'

'Love my Sam to bits, I do, twas a worry, thought I may lose him when the *Black Diamond* sailed back with fever aboard. Them in charge wouldn't let her berth in Fowey, had her anchored a fair distance offshore. Eight men died and my Sam were awful ill, but he survived. Saw him last week before he sailed off again, Ireland he be gone to this time. Saving we are till the time comes we can leave here for good.' She took hold Scarlett's hand. 'Promise you won't tell our Jack, nowt's changed, Father and the rest of them's all set against my Sam.'

'Don't worry I'll say nothing, I promise,' Scarlett reassured her friend, just as a harassed voice called out, 'Ruth, mistress has rang for you twice.'

'You'd best go,' Scarlett groaned, and turning walked back down the steps and towards the quay. She was grateful to be out of the confines of Prospect House. Weary of the dark rooms with their half-drawn drapes. Tired of her endless days filled with household chores and sore chapped hands. Miss Hester had enlivened the place and despite her headstrong ways, she missed her and the satisfaction she felt when preparing lessons, that was what she enjoyed.

She sat on a low granite wall at the end of the quay nearest to Market Lane, oblivious to other folk this Sunday afternoon. She looked through the maze of masts and listened as the boats bumped together wood on wood, heard their stout ropes pulled tight straining against their moorings. Slowly the incoming tide was creeping into the harbour and with it, gathering clouds, the sky darkened, it was now late in the afternoon but still she resisted returning to Prospect House.

Ever since her return from Penhallen, Miss Emilia had played the organ almost daily, the sound of the thumping hymns something she'd grown to dislike. In the past with the school room door shut at least she couldn't hear the sound quite so much as she did now when brushing down the stairs or polishing the endless balustrades. Her longing to look at the ledgers hidden in the side panel of the organ had not abated but had gone unfulfilled, no chance had presented itself for her to take a peek at them. But her curiosity remained.

Only the thought that Jack would be home soon lightened her gloomy mood. Finally she could delay no longer, it was time to return home.

Chapter 11

Two days later, Ivan came into the kitchen a little while after supper. Can I borrow Scarlett?' he asked Bessie. 'I need her to hold Dolly still whilst I take a look at one of her hooves.'

'Of course.' Bessie nodded and gestured over to Scarlett, who stood up eager to escape the boredom she felt that evening. She followed Ivan down to the stable and waited whilst he heaved open one of the sturdy doors. On the wooden steps leading up to the loft stood an oil lamp, its wick burnt low and emitting little light. Dolly was safely secured in her stall. Scarlett looked at Ivan expecting him to tell her what he wanted her to do, but he remained silent. It was then she saw a familiar figure emerge from the shadows and ran with joy into Jack's open arms.

'A few minutes you've got, that's all,' Ivan said, moving deftly past the lamp on the stair and going up to his living quarters.

'Thank you, Ivan,' Scarlett called after him, and he raised his hand in recognition.

Enfolded in Jack's arms, Scarlett clung to him as though her life depended on their closeness. Finally, she set him free. 'You're back a week early!' she exclaimed as Jack led her over to where Ivan stored bales of hay.

He pulled her down next to him and lay propped up on one elbow.

'Thought you'd be pleased to see me,' he teased, kissing the tip of her nose. 'The *Sunrising* suffered gale damage to her sails on the return voyage. Capt'n brought her in straight to harbour, a decision much debated amongst us crew for we'd had no time to unload. Folks busy down there now though, Capt'ns put the word out, all will be done with soon. But enough of that. I've thought only of one thing these past weeks, was all well at Penhallen after I left?'

Scarlett looked up at his face, gone was his mischievous smile, he was deadly serious now and waiting for an answer.

'Twas fine. They all thought he'd fallen drunk and hit his head on the fender. Charles Polgrove was furious and so was Mr Francis. Physician was called next morning. He stayed unconscious for quite a while. Even after he woke, I heard he was far from himself. Saw him just before I was about to leave. Standing staring at me he was, watching as I packed up the trundle bed, blanket, pillow and other bits in the little room next to Miss Hester's. Came across, reached out to touch me but I backed away and screamed, his brother and Edwin one of the manservants ran in and hauled him away.'

'The bastard.' Jack sat up and brushed back his unruly locks, a nerve quivered in his cheek. Scarlett had seen this once before when they'd been talking about Ruth's friendship with Sam Trembright and he'd been truly angry. 'So, it seems he's no memory of that night.'

'He hadn't when I left.'

'So, if he saw you packing in that room, he'll think you were always there, not know you were ever sleeping in the servants' quarters. For that we must be thankful.'

He pulled Scarlett down, so she was lying beside him. 'Precious maid, don't think about what happened, tis over.' Jack kissed her ear as both lay contentedly entwined together. One of Jack's hands crept up to her bodice, his breath hot against her cheek, and Scarlett would willingly have surrendered to his demands, for he'd aroused such passion in her that no kiss could surely quell. The spell was broken when floorboards creaked overhead. Reluctantly they drew apart and stood up, hastily brushing hay from their clothes and hair, Scarlett suppressing a giggle as Ivan made his way downstairs.

'Hope Dolly ain't seen nothing she shouldn't ave,' he teased, holding up the lamp indicating Scarlett should be getting back to Bessie.

'See you Sunday on the quay,' Jack said softly and grinned, giving Scarlett a parting kiss as Ivan opened the door.

***

On the following Sunday Miss Matilda spilt a cup of her precious tea, and as Millie was down in the kitchen baking a special cake for Miss Emilia's birthday, this meant that much to her dismay, Scarlett had to scrub clean the carpet on which the china cup lay broken, then clear away the silver tray and brew the sisters a fresh pot of tea.

Having to do all this delayed Scarlett leaving Prospect House and she ran along Market Lane, cross at being made late. There was no sign of Jack, but outside the Jolly Sailor a group of men were gathered, she could see one man standing in the centre of them, his voice raised as he spoke, and from those around him he received murmurs of agreement. Scarlett recognised him immediately, for he was as spirited in manner as he had been the last time she'd seen him. He was the tall young man with the mass of curly blonde hair who'd winked at her and looked up at the window when she'd opened it at Penhallow. From where she stood, she was unable to hear what he was saying, but the group were in accord with whatever it was, for they became noisier and more vocal with sounds of appreciation. It was then she saw Jack and Luke standing side by side with their father. Like the rest of the crowd gathered, they were totally immersed in what was being said. She felt it best that for the moment she stay where she was. Best leave the men to whatever it was.

Suddenly everything changed, a young lad no more than twelve or thirteen ran past her and on towards the Jolly Sailor pointing, shouting and waving his arms in warning. Scarlett looked towards the entrance of the harbour, and there rowing soundlessly into the mouth of the river were three black revenue boats each with four sets of oars, heading for West Looe quay.

The men outside the Jolly Sailor scattered. She watched Jack, Luke and some of the others run up the gangplank and board the *Sunrising*.

She hid behind a heavy fishing net strung out between two wooden poles, and watched as Robert Reader ascended an iron ladder onto the quay, waiting impatiently as his men came ashore. All was silent, only the gulls screeched, the place was deserted. Scarlett dare not move.

Robert Reader ordered his men along the quay stepping aside as they went aboard the *Sunrising*. A stomach churning feeling of pure terror came over Scarlett, she felt physically sick. What was it Jack had said that night in the stable? Something about damaged sails and the crew questioning the captain's decision to bring her in, how they'd not had time to unload. But he said something else after that, something reassuring. She took a sharp intake of breath, hoping the *Sunrising* was rid of her contraband.

There came the sound of fierce fighting, oaths shouted, a clash of steel upon steel. Scarlett took a chance and looked out from behind the net. From somewhere on board a shot was fired and then another. Scarlett threaded her hands through the net and held it tight.

She saw those who'd at first deserted the quay come back, a great bawling mass of them, including many women. She saw Mary Jago striding across the quay shaking her fist at Reader's men. A hush fell as six of the crew were roughly prodded down the gangplank, Jack amongst them. Robert Reader stood watching as they were chained and shackled together. The crowd grew increasingly angry; men were fighting with the revenue on the quay now.

Scarlett held her breath and withdrew behind the fishing net once more, she prayed those searching the ship would be disappointed and discover nothing.

She heard Reader shouting further orders. Those on the quay were still angrily jeering and shouting in protest at what was happening. Scarlett peeped out once more. Two bloodied revenue men lay on the ground. She saw Robert Reader fire a shot over the heads of the crowd as a warning.

At last those searching the ship returned to the quay. They had found not a thing. Reader ordered his men to unshackle those on the quay, then pursued by a rowdy jeering mob, Robert Reader and his men were gone as quickly as they'd come, rowing out towards the entrance of the harbour as those on the quay loudly cheered their departure. Once the revenue boats had disappeared round the headland, Hannah Reeve the fearsome landlady of the Jolly Sailor rolled out a barrel of ale and her husband and several others carried out wooden trays full of tankards, setting them down on the bench outside. A gesture appreciated by all.

Scarlett felt the fear slowly leave her, knew Jack was safe for now. She saw him emerging from the crowd walking towards her holding out his arms, into which she ran. He lifted her up and twirled her round. 'Come on, we've much to celebrate, we defeated the bastards,' Jack said laughing and led her into the midst of the crowd once more gathered round the speaker.

'Who is he?' Scarlett queried.

'Harry Shaw,' Jack replied, as they jostled their way forward until they were now at the front of the crowd.

'What's this all about, why is he here?' Scarlett whispered.

'Listen, maid, and you'll find out.'

Someone shouted out a question and Harry replied, 'Because there is no other way, we must join together with those like ourselves, together we must flush out informants being paid for their treachery. Treachery that costs good Cornish lives.'

Jack let go of Scarlett's hand and stepped forward to stand beside Harry. 'We must do something. Together is our only chance. We cannot forfeit our livelihoods because some evil bastard takes the king's money.'

'Well said,' Harry congratulated Jack heartily, and the crowd cheered with great enthusiasm. Now others stepped forward, each voicing his agreement that something must be done to stop the revenue.

As he came and stood back beside her, the passion with which Jack had spoken made Scarlett feel so proud, at the same time guilty to the core that her father was one of these men of whom they spoke, totally horrified and disgusted at her father's betrayal of men such as these. For a moment she felt lightheaded and swayed, resting her head on Jack's shoulder. Caught up in the moment, he didn't notice. But Scarlett was totally traumatised with the thought. What if her father was caught, recognised and linked to herself? She wished he wasn't the man he was, and that he'd never visited Tamarisk.

The crowd listened on whilst Scarlett sought to think, over the years they'd lived in West Looe, just who had seen her father. Who could recognise him and betray her now if he were caught? Annie Bishop came to mind at once, and the old biddies that lived across from them.

Unaware of the turmoil Scarlett was going through, Jack tucked her arm through his.

'This is what it needs, all along the coast an army of ordinary folk looking out for each other, sharing any suspicions they have, so we become the spies.'

Scarlett nodded her agreement, and held on to Jack as though doing so would protect her from the fear she felt inside.

'I saw Harry when I was at Penhallen,' she stated, hoping her voice sounded confident and quite normal. 'He was with some other men ushered in to meet with the gentry.'

Her words were drowned out by rowdy cheering as Harry Shaw brought the meeting to an end. Jack raised his arms above his head and began clapping as did others around them, and Scarlett caught up in the atmosphere that Harry created, clapped also, only more discreetly.

A group gathered round Harry congratulating him, and it was when these dispersed, he looked over to where Jack and Scarlett stood. Scarlett knew immediately that Harry had recognised her, he began walking over towards them.

'Good words you spoke Jack and with a passion felt by everyone here. Have no doubt we'll succeed in our endeavours.'

He turned his attention to Scarlett who felt herself blushing and hated herself for it. 'I've seen you before somewhere,' he said, a questioning tone in his voice, and Scarlett looked up into piercing blue eyes.

'I was at Penhallen House, I showed you into the room where the gentry were.' She remembered how he'd winked at her when he'd first arrived. 'And afterwards you looked up as I opened a window just as you were passing beneath it.'

'Yes, I remember now. How come you were there? I thought briefly you may have been eavesdropping on us. Always suspicious I am.'

'My mistress had gone out with Maria Penhallen and her governess, so for a moment I had time to myself and opened the window for some fresh air.

'So, who exactly is your mistress?'

It was Jack who responded. 'Scarlett's in service at Prospect House, she was there with her mistress Miss Hester Marshall.'

'Ah! Mr Julian's daughter. Well a pleasure to meet you, Miss Scarlett.' Harry grinned, then flashed a beguiling smile, and Scarlett was glad her interrogation was over. 'Keep safe, Jack, we'll speak again soon. I must be off, got someone to see up in Watergate.' And with that, Harry was gone.

Jack took Scarlett by the hand and led her through the crowd which was now dispersing in all directions. They began to climb up to Hannafore Point, Scarlett trying hard to set her fears aside.

'Time I had you all to myself, away from prying eyes,' he teased, leading her away from the rough path at the top of the cliffs, to where they would be alone. Staying there until it was time for Scarlett to go home.

Chapter 12

On the following Monday morning, and quite unexpected by those below stairs, Mr Julian took his aunts to Liskeard. Scarlett, having closed the front door behind them, went upstairs and watched from the dining room window until the coach crossed the bridge and was safely out of sight. Then upon impulse, she tugged open the heavy drapes and lifted the latch on the deep windows flinging them open and letting light and fresh air into the fusty room. She did the same in the darkened morning room, only here she could step out onto the balcony and gaze along the quay. Without Miss Hester the daily drudgery was never ending. If only she could fling open the front door, escape and run wildly along the quay in search of Jack.

Scarlett looked along the quay to where the *Sunrising* was moored and smiled. Jack had promised to take her to Simon's Croft next Sunday. She could see his handsome face, feel his dark eyes scrutinising her, the smouldering heat of his passion. Her Jack who made her feel entirely alive, and also guilt ridden about her father. Deep in thought she stood, arms crossed looking down the river, loose strands of hair blowing in the wind. Abruptly her moment of solitude ended when Millie called up for her. Bessie wanted help with filling the coal scuttles.

The seemingly endless morning was alleviated a little before noon by the hand delivery of a small white envelope with a delicate lace-like detail upon its outer edges. In a fine hand it was addressed to Miss Matilda and Miss Emilia Marshall. The liveried servant resplendent in blue and gold uniform had sent poor Millie's heart all of a flutter for she had been late in sweeping down the front steps when he arrived. Scarlett had taken the envelope from his outstretched hand and placed it on the small silver salver in the hallway. For the rest of the day Millie's encounter with the handsome young man was all she would talk about endlessly. Until Bessie had had enough and sent her out to the laundry with some delicates to wash.

Each time Scarlett passed through the hallway she couldn't help but look at the salver and wonder who had sent the delicate envelope and what its contents were. And, of course, once Millie was back working in the kitchen she was as inquisitive as ever.

'I'd best go up and take a look meself,' Bessie grumbled, 'otherwise you two are going to send me mad with your idle chatter.'

Scarlett and Millie followed her upstairs to the hallway.

'Looks to me like a wedding invitation,' Bessie stated in a matter of fact voice. 'Seen something like it before when old Lord whatshisname from Duloe got wed.' She turned it over, peering at the tiny red seal on the back. 'Don't recognise it, some I knows that correspond with the sisters regularly.' She replaced the envelope. 'Enough of this talking, best get on there's carrots that won't peel themselves.'

Scarlett sighed and begrudgingly followed her downstairs, wondering how Bessie knew so much about the sisters' correspondence.

The sisters and Mr Julian returned later than expected accompanied by Mr Francis Kestrel.

When Scarlett answered the door, Mr Francis exclaimed, 'Ah! I see it's arrived,' looking to where the envelope lay waiting to be opened.

'Bring it through to us, will you, Penrose?' Miss Matilda ordered. And Scarlett took the silver salver through having left it a moment or two for the sisters to settle.

Scarlett repeated to those downstairs what Mr Francis had said, but they were mighty busy. 'I don't know the likes of it,' Bessie fumed. 'First they're late, then they bring a guest home.' Scarlett and Millie exchanged glances as Bessie fussed about, most put out, worried the delicious leg of lamb she'd so painstakingly roasted would be spoiled and the crust on the apple pie gone hard.

Once the second and main course had been served and appreciated by all, and the tension in the kitchen depleted, Scarlett busied herself whipping the cream ready for Millie to take up.

'Glad it's Mr Francis not Adrian Kestrel that's come here,' Scarlett remarked, holding the bowl under her arm and whisking briskly. 'Rat poison's too good for the likes of him.'

Millie gave a sly smile. 'Last time when Mr Adrian came ere, I thought him more handsome than his brother,' she stated, and Bessie gave her tap on the wrist with a damp cloth.

'Get on with what you're supposed to be doing and don't go daydreaming about some toff who wouldn't give you the time of day.'

Just then the bell rang. 'I'll help clear the table with you,' Scarlett offered. 'I wonder what's going on up there. The way he said it, I wonder if that posh invitation means Mr Francis himself is getting wed?'

'I don't care who's getting wed, all I hope is that Mr Julian and Mr Kestrel don't tarry long,' Millie sighed.

Together they went upstairs. Outside the dining room door, they unashamedly eavesdropped, straining to hear the conversation within the room.

'But Skurren knows too much to be left there,' Mr Francis was saying.

'But why us? What can we do that you can't?'

'It's obvious, Aunt,' Mr Julian interceded impatiently. 'They'll let—'

But the sentence went unfinished as the scraping back of a chair sent Scarlett and Millie scurrying back to the stairs leading downstairs, only to noisily reappear as the door opened and Mr Julian looked out.

Later as they jested about what had happened, Bessie, over-tired and bad tempered gave both a telling off. 'It's nowt to do with you what goes on with them upstairs and you'll be out of here might quick if you'm caught with yer ears to the door,' she grumbled, and shaking her head with disapproval took herself off to bed.

After the final dishes were cleared away, an unrepentant Scarlett and Millie sat and waited until they would be called upon again. Scarlett wondered who Skudden was while Millie crossed her arms on the table in front of her and rested her head on them, eyes closed.

Exhausted, both hoped the evening would soon end so they could go to bed.

Finally, the bell jangled, and Scarlett went upstairs. Mr Frances was taking his leave of the sisters, so was Mr Julian. Scarlett saw both to the door, her last task to hand them their walking canes and hats. This must have been a prearranged time for Mr Frances' coach, its lamps casting a yellow light into the gloomy night, was waiting at the front of Prospect House. A plainly dressed servant in sober black opened the door and lowered the steps so they could enter. The coachman wasted no time and they were gone into the night.

By the time Scarlett entered the house, Millie had cleared away and was helping the sisters prepare for bed.

Later in the week it was announced the sisters would be away visiting for two, possibly three, days and hasty preparations were made for their departure.

On the morning they left, Scarlett shut the front door of Prospect House behind them and leant against it with relief. Both sisters had been in a complete flap when Mr Julian arrived to escort them to Bodmin, so Millie overheard mention, over an hour earlier than expected. Scarlett took a deep breath and started to make her way downstairs. Halfway down she paused. In the kitchen she could hear Bessie chiding Millie because the girl thought herself hard done by as she hadn't accompanied the sisters to Bodmin.

'Good enough for um when their ome ere,' Millie was saying.

'Stop that silly talk right now,' Bessie chided, and Scarlett ventured a little further down the staircase.

She heard the back door open and Ivan come in dragging his chair back and tapping his pipe on the table. 'What's up with the two of you?' he queried.

'Nothing,' they replied in unison.

Scarlett heard the cupboard door open and imagined Bessie pouring Ivan his ale.

'Drink up, man, tis a bit of peace and quiet we have here for a couple of days. Bodmin them's off to, so Millie says. Never known them to go there before but tis a rest for us, you tarry a while, Ivan, and whilst you're here tell all, for I seen you talking to that boy they have working for um next door. What's the Capt'ns new cook like? Her that's come all the way from Plymouth. Like there's no one good enough for him in these parts,' she huffed, and waited for his reply, whilst Millie joined in for good measure.

'Mighty fine and fancy hat she had on, I seen that with my own eyes, dark blue it was with the most enormous feather.'

With a smile on her face, Scarlett retreated upstairs. Now, she thought, was the time to take a peek at those books hidden in the organ's hidden panel. Feeling more than a little guilty, she quietly entered the music room, and kneeling on the floor removed the panel, shocked to find the space inside was empty.

'Mr Julian's taken them.' Scarlett jumped to her feet, heart thumping, red-faced at being caught snooping by Millie.

'How did you know about the books in there?' Scarlett asked shakily.

'Have done for a long while,' Millie replied with the hint of a smirk on her face, pleased to feel for once she knew more than Scarlett. 'First time was when I hit the panel by accident with the broom. Sprung open it did. The spring's been broken for over a year now, don't know what happened. But how come you found the hidden panel and why's you looking now?'

'By accident like you,' Scarlett answered, not wanting to admit to watching Miss Emilia through the crack in the door.

'You'm not a spy or anything are you?' Millie joked, and Scarlett felt her cheeks redden even more.

'Of course not, don't be daft. It's just I was curious and with the sisters away thought I'd take a look, see what's in um.'

The knot of tension in Scarlett's stomach faded slightly as Millie smiled and walked across the room to join her.

'Well I can tell you that; five rows of names and numbers. Haven't got much reading me but first column were ship's names. I know that as I recognised some me dad sails on, second row were names, middle two I don't know, and the last row were numbers with squiggles by them. Mr Julian and his sisters have other interests apart from his quarry, if you take my meaning.'

Scarlett nodded and smiled pretending she fully understood the implications. Clearly, Millie having been in service here longer than herself knew far more about the goings on at Prospect House. 'Well it's nowt to do with the likes of us,' she responded, and deftly replaced the panel and made her way out of the music room along with Millie. Just then Bessie called up the stairs.

'Scarlett, there's someone here to see you.'

Amos Cuddy was standing by the gate at the end of the path. He looked terribly agitated and Scarlett just knew it must be something to do with her mother. He stepped forward to meet her and Scarlett noticed clenched fists.

'Jeanette's taken a beating, can you get away, maid? She needs tending to, and best be you, she's abed and in a bad way.'

Scarlett felt the anger rise within her, for she knew only too well who had inflicted such cruelty. 'I'll come now. Bessie'll not say no.'

Seconds later she was sat beside Amos as he set off on the short journey to Tamarisk. As he brought the cart to a halt outside the cottage, he took Scarlett's hands in his. 'Prepare yourself, maid, tis a bad way she in, shocking a man can teat his wife so, I'd like to kill him with me own hands.'

On impulse, Scarlet gave his weather-beaten cheek a kiss.

'Look after her for me. I gotta be on my way, or master'll be after me.'

'I will, Amos, I promise.' Scarlett jumped down from the cart and ran up the path towards the front door of Tamarisk.

Pushing open the door she quickly went up to her mother's room. The still form lying on the bed, her face bruised purple and swollen, slowly opened her eyes. Fear replaced with relief at seeing Scarlett who put her arms round her mother's thin shoulders.

'When did he do this to you?' she demanded.

'Yesterday,' Jeanette whispered.

Scarlett saw that her mother's lips were dry and cracked. 'I'll fetch you some water.'

She ran downstairs and took a pewter jug out to the well, filling it to the rim, then poured a good measure into a glass. Jeanette drank it with relish before lying back against her pillows exhausted.

Going back downstairs, Scarlett fetched a bowl and filled it with water, placing it on the unsteady table beside her mother's bed. She found a clean nightgown, wash-cloth and towel and began to wash away the blood where her father's violence had torn her mother's skin. Now she saw the other deep purple bruises on her mother's body and the long tear in the bloodied nightgown. Close to tears, Scarlett cleaned the wounds and replaced the nightgown with one that was crisp and fresh.

Jeanette struggled to sit up and took another sip of water.

'What happened?' Scarlett tentatively asked. Watching as a tear rolled down her mother's cheek.

'Amos brought me home to gather some things, said he'd be back for me today. Luckily, he never came in, had to get back, head groom needed him for something. They were both here Elijah and Robert Reader. Taunted me about Amos, they did, said disgusting, lurid things. Both of them was drunk almost to a stupor. Ordered I made a meal for them, and I did from the chicken and vegetables I'd been given by Lanreath's cook. And all the time they were poking fun at me and making spiteful comments. Reader asked after you, taunted me saying he needed someone to warm his bed, thought you'd make a comely bed companion.'

Jeanette took a deep breath. 'Over my dead body, I shouted at him. He just sneered and spat across the kitchen at me, laughing. "She's mine if I want her. Isn't that right, Elijah?" And your father slumped in his chair said nothing. Pleased I was you were safely down in Prospect House. Soon as I could I left them downstairs still drinking, filling up their tankards from a small barrel Reader brought in and set down on the table.'

Jeanette began to sob, and Scarlett sat on the bed and cried with her.

'Twas when your father came upstairs and demanded his rights that I got this beating, not wanting the drunken wretch pawing at me. He'd demanded I strip naked, when I refused, he tore the nightgown off me like a crazed animal, and used me as he wanted.'

Scarlett held her mother tight, she remembered only too well that dreadful night when Robert Reader had come to her room and tried to force himself on her.

Over in the corner of the room a fire had already been set in the tiny grate. Getting up, Scarlett took the tinder box down from the nearby shelf and lit the fire with a taper, holding it there until the fire took, the gentle yellow flames somehow brought the room alive.

'Had you better go, maid, don't want you getting in any trouble over me?' Jeanette queried.

Scarlett reassured her, 'Don't worry, the sisters are away to Bodmin so there's no hurry for me to return just yet.'

Jeanette coughed, and winced with pain. 'I'm glad you can stay awhile. Cook gave me some broth to bring home with me yesterday, it's in the covered pan. Share it with me.'

Scarlett went downstairs and busied herself rattling out the embers, she fetched in kindling, filled the coal pail and lit the fire, hanging the pot containing the broth from a hook above the fire to heat. As the fire crackled and spluttered into life, she washed the discarded tankards, mopped up the table where ale had been spilt and then scrubbed it clean. The barrel she had to leave where it was. Stirring the pot, finally it came to the boil and she ladled it into two bowls and placed them on a wooden tray with two spoons. There was no bread. Only crumbs remained on the table.

Mother and daughter sat in the bedroom, the lentil broth from Lanreath's kitchen was good.

'Will you be safe here once I've gone? What if Father and Reader return?'

'I don't think they will. Heard them talking about meeting someone called Rousse,' Jeanette responded. 'And Reader, he'd gone before Elijah came upstairs. I heard the door slam, and Elijah left my bed and went soon after he'd finished with me.' She reached out and placed her hand on Scarlett's arm. 'Promise me you'll take care, Scarlett, and that young man you've taken a fancy to an all. Elijah and Reader are hereabouts for a reason. God help any poor souls they catch smuggling.'

Scarlett felt like a guilty schoolgirl, and her face reddened.

Jeanette smiled. 'Yes I know all about Jack. Amos and Ivan are like two old gossiping women. Meet up in the Fisherman's Arms off and on.'

The next day, word arrived at Prospect House that the sisters would not be returning for another four days. Whilst they were away, Bessie was happy for Scarlett to be spared from her duties for a short while each day to be with her mother who she'd been told had fallen down the stairs.

Two days later with her mother much improved, Scarlett had taken time on her way back to dally on the quay where the *Sunrising* was moored with the hope of seeing Jack. It was Luke who saw her and climbed down from the rigging to tell her Jack had gone fishing with Jacob Sweet, and that the *Sunrising* would be sailing earlier than expected.

He saw Scarlett's expression change to one of dismay. He wasn't to know how she'd been looking forward to some time alone with Jack at Simon's Croft.

'Twon't be a long voyage,' he said trying to lessen her disappointment. 'Just Guernsey. If you're feeling brave and want to see Jack, get away tonight and join us, there's a little task Jack and me have got to do for Harry.'

The thought of seeing Jack made Scarlett cast caution aside. Readily she agreed to meet them at the far end of the quay. 'Wear a warm cloak,' were Luke's departing words as he made his way back up the gangplank, and an excited Scarlett made her way home.

Bessie had long gone to bed when Scarlett sneaked out wearing the thick black cloak with its hood's gathered edge, last worn the night she'd heaved Polly Carbis from the river. Thank goodness Janks, whoever he was, had seen that lot on their way. Jack was leaning against the wall outside the back gate, he stepped out from the shadows giving her a fright. Fearing she would cry out, he placed his hand across her mouth before replacing it with a passionate kiss. Scarlett wound her arms around him, and both were loath to let this precious moment go. Finally, Jack pulled away.

'Come on. Luke's waiting for us in the boat. Twas a good idea of his, you coming with us.'

With care, Scarlett took to the iron ladder and stepped down into the *Alice*. The dark waters of the river matched the darkness of the sky. The moon hidden behind a leaden sky. Jack took up the oars, Luke untied the boat and took up the second set of oars. Silently the *Alice* slipped away from the quay out into the middle of the river. The only sound now was the pit pat of the oars on the almost still water. A long grappling hook lay on the bottom of the boat.

Feeling cold, Scarlett pulled her cloak tight round her as they left the protection of the harbour and headed out into the open sea.

'Tis only just off Plaidy we're going,' Jack reassured her, heaving on the oars. Waves now broke over the bow of the *Alice* and Scarlett held tight the seat beneath her as the boat was now tossed about on the sea.

'Once we spot the marker, we'll be off home. We've to make sure one hundred small barrels, strung together and sunk three weeks ago are still in place.'

Scarlett began to feel a little queasy as well as extremely cold. Perhaps her decision to join them tonight was a mistake. But as she looked at Jack, admiring his strength, these thoughts were quickly disregarded.

With the marker not found, Luke took up the grappling hook and began dragging it below the water, finally it caught. Lighting a shuttered lantern from a tinderbox, Jack lifted the shutters and signalled for only a brief second, but a light shone out from the shore in reply.

Scarlett felt suddenly frightened.

Jack and Luke pulled hard on the oars and set the *Alice* on a course for home. The rise and fall of the boat meant that spray from the sea showered its occupants. The gusting wind grew stronger and the sea more turbulent. Spray drenched Scarlett's cloak penetrating through to her very skin. She could taste the salty sea spray on her lips. Water began to collect in the bottom of the boat, seeping into her boots.

'Don't worry, we'll soon be back,' Jack shouted to her, his words hardly recognisable as they were swallowed up by the wind. In a short while both brothers began to tire as they battled against the heaving sea.

There was a moment's lull in the wind and Luke shouted to Jack, 'Where did this storm come from? Tis s'pose to be set fair.'

As they ploughed onwards, with one hand Scarlett gripped tight the bench seat beneath her, with the other she held tight the hood of her cloak, but a sudden gust of wind tore it from her head and tugged at the pins holding her hair, they loosened, setting her hair free to blow wildly about.

'Nearly there,' Jack spluttered trying to catch his breath.

But by now Scarlett felt far too ill to reply. Finally, they entered the mouth of the river and approached the safety of the harbour. As they drew closer, Scarlett was comforted by the faint glow of candlelight coming from a scattering of cottage windows.

Suddenly a bright light shone out sending a shimmering glow across the dark river. Jack and Luke stopped rowing. Scarlett sensed their fear.

'Oggie's warning us some bastard's about. We'll make for Hannafore,' Jack ordered.

Taking up the oars they altered direction with Jack and Luke rowing hard, making once again for the rough waters of the open sea. Swiftly they passed the headland on their right and turned towards Hannafore's treacherous rocky beach. But under Jack's direction the brothers managed to steer the *Alice* past two large boulders and onto a tiny area of sand.

'Hold tight,' Jack yelled as they beached the boat with a tremendous jolt. For a moment they sat in silence, all was deadly still. Luke stowed away the oars then Jack helped a shivering Scarlett from the boat. He took off his jacket and wrapped it round her.

'Twasn't meant to be like this,' he whispered, gently kissing her forehead.

'I know,' Scarlett replied, through trembling lips.

'Don't worry, I'll get you home safe,' Jack vowed as Luke came and stood beside them. He bent down holding on to the side of the boat to get his breath. In that instant, a wave smashed against the stern of the boat and it moved forward catching the side of Luke's foot. His yelp of pain was silenced by Jack's hand.

For a moment, Jack left Scarlett and secured the boat with a rope he fetched from the *Alice*, tying it to a shaft of rock close by.

'Lean on me,' he told Luke and led them to where a section of cliff overhung the beach. The three of them huddled together, too wet to mind the damp sand beneath them.

'It's best we stay here a while,' Luke insisted, struggling to take off his boot, then rubbing his foot to ease the pain. 'It's too dangerous to go anywhere near the harbour.'

'I know, we'll have to wait it out awhile. Then I'll take a look,' Jack answered. He rubbed Scarlett's hands, nestling her close to him, trying to stop her shivering.

For a long while they waited, feeling ever colder, until Jack declared, 'I'll clamber round the rocks and take a look. All seems quiet. Take care of Scarlett for me,' he instructed Luke.

He returned after a short while. 'No light's showing now but that means nothing. Revenue have seized it before now, and punished Oggie for lighting it. That's when they could find him of course.'

He helped Scarlett to her feet. 'I think I'll try and get you home. It's too dangerous for you to clamber round the rocks on the headland, we'll climb up onto the path along the top of the cliff and creep down towards the quay. The bracken will keep us hidden.'

'I'll wait here,' Luke interrupted. 'Sneak back to the *Sunrising* later, I will, my foot will slow me down.'

'You sure?' Jack queried, and Luke nodded.

'Tis best.'

Scarlett bent down and put her arms around Luke, she hugged him, and he squeezed her hand. 'Take care,' he whispered.

It was a steep climb but finally they were on the rugged cliff path with Jack now leading the way downwards ever closer to the quay. When they got to St Nicholas Church, Jack drew Scarlett into the shadows and looked out past the Jolly Sailor, across the square to the entrance of Market Lane.

Did it seem too quiet?

'I think we'll walk round behind the Jolly not along the quay,' he said softly, and taking Scarlett by the hand led her out from the shadows.

What happened next was so sudden they had no time to run. Robert Reader and two revenue officers appeared as if from nowhere and stood in front of them.

'So it was you, out there in the boat,' Reader spat.

One of the officers took hold of Jack who refused to let go Scarlett's hand. Reader prized their hands apart and took a firm hold of Scarlett. Jack protested fiercely and fought to free himself, but the two officers, large brutes of men, held him firmly in their iron grasp.

Reader barked the order out, 'Bind his hands and feet.'

Scarlett screamed twisting and kicking, struggling to escape from Reader's grasp. Somehow Jack managed to fight his way free and reached out to grab Scarlett's hand. Reader turned on him. With his clenched fist he aimed a blow to Jack's forehead with such force it sent Jack stumbling backwards towards the edge of the quay, and he fell between the harbour wall and the wooden hull of a large brigantine, its mooring ropes creaking as they strained to hold her steady. There was a thud, a cry, and then silence.

The two officers ran over and searched the narrow gap between harbour wall and ship's hull to see if they could see Jack in the river. Whilst their backs were turned, Reader snatched hold of Scarlett's hair forcing her head backwards. He put his mouth to her ear. The warm stench of his breath made her feel sick. 'What a pity. I shan't have the pleasure of telling your young man what your father is. Not want to know you then, will he? Leave you for the likes of me to help myself to,' he mocked.

The officers came back. 'Any sign of him?' Reader asked.

'No, sir.'

Reader roughly pushed Scarlett towards the two men. 'Hold the bitch tight, let's see what her employers make of tonight's escapade.'

Scarlett was beyond caring what they thought, she was too worried about Jack. Had Reader killed him, had he survived? As she was dragged with brutal force along the quay by the officers, the tips of her sodden boots scuffed against the cobbles, for they walked so fast she couldn't keep up. Her wet skirts and petticoats clung to her like a tight shroud, and all the time she kept struggling to look back to where Jack had fallen from the quay, and she saw nothing.

A sudden shove forced her to look forward. She saw Oggie's overturned bench and an officer standing outside his cottage, saw more standing back, half hidden in the shadows.

When they reached Prospect House, Robert Reader straightened his tricorn hat and ran up the front steps, pulling heavily and repeatedly on the handle of the bell chain.

Shortly afterwards, Millie barely opened the door an inch and peered out. Reader kicked the door with his boot, and a frightened Millie standing barefoot in her nightgown with candle in hand quickly withdrew back into the hall, startled as the door flew open. Her eyes were wide with horror as she gazed upon her dishevelled friend.

Reader shouted at her, 'Get this person's mistress here now.'

But before Millie could answer, a voice loud and strong came from the stairs leading down to the hall, 'I am her mistress, and I command your brutes unhand her this minute.'

Reader looked upwards, as did Scarlett, absolutely shocked to see standing on the stair holding a brass candelabra and looking like two apparitions, their white nightgowns covered by fine silk dressings gowns flounced and trimmed in the finest lace, stood Miss Hester and Maria Penhallen. When had they returned? What had been said about her absence from the house?

'Her mistress is who I asked for. I presume that is not you, young lady,' Reader snapped back at her.

'Oh, but I am,' Miss Hester replied in a voice as crisp as ice.

Reader's men released their hold of Scarlett and purposefully propelled her forward, so she fell at the foot of the stairs in a heap. Reader went to step into the hall, but Miss Hester stopped him. 'No, sir, you are not invited into this house. Thank you for bringing Penfold back to us. I bid you goodnight. Millie, the door.'

Scarlett watched as a red-faced Robert Reader, taken completely by surprise, stepped back, spluttering and fuming with rage as the door was closed in his face.

The two young women watched as slowly Scarlett stood up.

'There must be no disturbing Bessie, for she would most certainly report you to my aunts and you would be dismissed without character. Whatever you've been up to we shall talk about it in the morning.'

Miss Penhallen suddenly giggled, 'Oh! But you do look a fright,' and the two of them scampered upstairs like the schoolgirls they were.

Millie took a candle from the hall table and lit it from her own, handing it to Scarlett. 'You'm lucky. You'd be dismissed if the Miss Catts were home.'

Scarlett followed her upstairs. 'When Miss Hester and her friend arrived, what was said about me not being here?' Scarlett questioned, suddenly so tired she could barely climb the last stairs.

'Like I says, you'm lucky. Late it was, Bessie had gone to bed, had a drop too much port what with the sisters being away. I told Miss Hester you were visiting your mother, called to her urgent like.'

Scarlett went to ask more but Millie shook her head and yawned. 'Tell me what you been up to in the morning,' she sighed, 'them pair of girls coming home has caused me a lot of work.'

Tired though she was, the first thing Scarlett tried to do was open her temperamental attic window so she could lean out and look down the quay, but the window refused to open however much pressure she applied. She struggled out of her sodden clothes and unfastened her wet boots. With chattering teeth, she put on her night-gown and got into bed. Finally, she blew out the candle and huddled beneath the bedclothes, shivering and alone with the fear Jack may not have survived.

It was a weary, painfully aching Scarlett who lit her candle and slowly dressed the next morning, thankful for her spare grey uniform but still having to wear her damp boots as she made her way down to the kitchen.

'Glad you're up and me not having to do everything meself,' Millie moaned half-heartedly, hanging the copper kettle on the hook over the fire.

'Went in to draw the young ladies' curtains but both of them in no hurry to leave their beds, and Bessie a little late on rising. Come on, out with it, tell me all about last night.'

Scarlett pulled out a chair and sat opposite Millie at the table. Millie's mouth gaped open as Scarlett told her what had happened, and the poor girl shed her own tears at what fate had befallen Jack. So deep were they in conversation that when Ivan tapped on the back door, they both jumped in fright.

Scarlett got up and unbolted the door. Snatching off his hat as he stepped inside, Ivan asked, 'Where's Bessie?'

'Like the rest of us in this house, all over the place with the sisters away and not knowing exactly when they'll be back,' Scarlett replied.

He motioned the two of them to sit down and did so himself. 'And that's not all is it, missy? Got yourself in a bit of trouble. I've heard from Oggie some of what took place last night. I'm not surprised you look proper awful, maid, you'm lucky the young un's came home, and the mistresses away. But I have some good news for you. Tis on good account I've heard Jack's safe.'

Scarlett stifled a cry of joy, and Ivan put his finger to his lips.

'Shush. Best not set Bessie a wondering what's being said out here.' Ivan's big hand reached out and held Scarlett's. 'He's badly bruised and suffered a nasty knock on the head, sent his little sister to tell me he was alright. Knew I'd tell you.'

Scarlett got up, ran round the table and hugged Ivan, holding the great bear of a man tightly as tears of joy ran down her cheeks. Millie too wiped away a tear with the corner of her apron. Twas then they heard sounds of movement coming from Bessie's quarters. Her door opened and she peered out at the three of them.

'And what may I ask is all this? Have Miss Hester and her friend had their breakfast trays taken up? And where's Ivan's tea, his bread and dripping? Lazybones the pair of you,' she remonstrated, 'I don't know what this house is coming to.'

When Millie explained that the young ladies upstairs were loath to leave their beds, Bessie shook her head in disbelief. 'There'd be none of this lying abed if the Miss Catts were here,' she huffed. 'Never known such goings on.'

Scarlett and Millie stood up as Bessie bustled about slicing bread freshly baked the day before and spreading it with thick dripping. She placed it on a plate in front of Ivan who ate it rather too quickly. Bessie took out the key to the tea caddy, and once his tea was poured, Ivan took himself off to the stables, he'd not dally with Bessie in her present mood.

A while later the drawing room bell jangled on its spring and Millie dutifully went upstairs. She came down shaking her head with disbelief.

'Them two's sitting in the drawing room, bold as brass, still in their night attire and dressing gowns. They're in the Miss Catts' chairs on either side of the fireplace, wants their breakfast trays taken up and extra bacon, if you please. Miss Hester told me to send you up, Scarlett. Good luck, she's in a proper haughty mood.'

A short-tempered Bessie told Millie to get on with the breakfasts.

Scarlett felt her heart beating as she went upstairs. She stood outside the drawing room door, took a deep breath knocked and entered. Indeed, the sight of Miss Hester and Maria Penhallen so brazenly sitting in the Miss Catt's chairs came as quite a shock.

'Step forward, tell us what happened and make it so compelling that I would be doing you a disservice should I tell my aunts,' Miss Hester demanded.

Scarlett began to recount what had happened the previous night, but not the truth of the matter. She told them with a remorseful look on her face, she'd just slipped out to go and see if her friend Ruth in service up at Polgrove Hall was at home, sometimes she had a night off in the week if her mistress needed her the entire weekend. This was utter nonsense of course.

'You know my aunts' strict rules on their employees having followers, it wasn't some young man you were going to see, was it?' Miss Hester narrowed her eyes and looked intently at Scarlett.

'No, most definitely not,' she replied, feeling her face redden.

'But why were you wet through? It wasn't raining last night,' Maria asked suspiciously.

'Ruth was at home, we went down to the quay, thinking it would be fun to sit in her brother's boat. We went down the steps where it was tied up, stepping into it not seeing that it had taken on water, quickly we went to get out and I slipped and got wet.'

'But how come you were dragged home by the revenue looking like a drowned rat?' Miss Maria persisted.

'When we got back onto the quay, suddenly they surrounded us, heaven knows what they thought we'd been up to, we were proper frightened. They'd been drinking, made foul remarks about us. Ruth's father had come looking for her and they let her go. Robert Reader seemed to know I worked here, so they marched me along the quay like I was a thief or something.'

To her dismay, Scarlett began to sob.

'Oh pray, stop snivelling,' Miss Hester implored, clearly bored now of the whole business.

'I know I was wrong going to see Ruth, but don't often get the chance to, we was best friends at Miss Clementine's. Please, Miss Hester, I beg you not to tell your aunts.'

Clearly there was nothing else to tell. The two girls looked at each other. Maria Penhallen raised her hand to her mouth to cover a yawn.

'Who knew those below stairs led such an adventurous life,' Miss Hester said spitefully.

'I have a grand idea,' Maria Penhallen said softly, smiling across to her friend and casting a sly glance in Scarlett's direction.

A knock on the door interrupted whatever it was Miss Penhallen thought to say. Millie entered carrying one of the breakfast trays, when she left to fetch the other, Miss Hester sniped, 'You may go now; I'll ring when I've decided what's to be done with you. Get back to your work.'

Scarlett retreated and closed the door behind her, she leant against it, fearful what was to happen next.

It was after the breakfast trays had been collected that Scarlett was called to the drawing room again. Miss Penhallen was standing by the window and didn't bother to turn as she entered. 'I have decided not to tell my aunts of your behaviour,' Miss Hester told Scarlett. 'There is a condition to this, which you will absolutely have to obey.' Briefly she paused. 'As you know, young ladies of our status are not allowed a lot of freedom and there are times both Miss Penhallen and myself would like to do things and go places not permitted by our elders or the servants in our attendance. You, Penfold, could be useful for you could turn a blind eye, allow us a little more freedom than Miss Penhallen's governess, my father or my aunts demand of you. T'would be as though we were unchaperoned.' She stopped and Maria Penhallen turned round.

'Penfold, you have no alternative than to agree otherwise we shall feel morally obliged to tell your mistress's aunts of your escapade.'

'But what kind of places do you want to go? Would it be dangerous? You're in my charge; I would be blamed should anything happen to you.'

'That's just it, we don't know yet.' Miss Penhallen giggled. 'It's just that you would be useful should a circumstance occur.'

Scarlett straightened her apron. 'I have no choice but to agree,' she replied.

'Say thank you,' Miss Penhallen prompted.

'Thank you, miss,' Scarlett said meekly, and gave a curtsey to them both.

'You're dismissed, send Millie to help us dress,' Miss Hester demanded crisply.

As Scarlett made her way downstairs, she sighed with relief. No mention of the previous evening would be made to the sisters. What would become of her in the future she was beyond caring. She took over the peeling of the potatoes and sent Millie on her way. Jack was safe, and at this moment that was all that mattered.

Later that morning word came from Penhallen that Miss Maria would be expected to return home the next day. A carriage would be sent at noon. Having handed Miss Maria the neat handwritten note on stiff card, the expected tantrum followed, complete with the stamping of feet. Scarlett slipped away leaving Miss Hester to quell her friend's dismay.

After lunch all had quietened and the two girls went into Miss Emilia's music room to practise their dance steps for a forthcoming wedding.

'Is it a friend of your father's?' Scarlett dare ask, for Miss Hester was clearly excited.

'Mr Francis Kestrel,' she answered without reserve. Speculation below stairs had been right all along. It was Mr Francis who was getting wed.

They requested refreshment and it was as she brought this up to them, she had chance to listen at the half open door. Scarlett heard Miss Maria say with much delight, 'I wager I'll get the handsome Adrian Kestrel to dance with me before you can.'

'It will be me, wait and see,' Miss Hester trilled, and they both giggled. 'Oh, Adrian, who will you dance with first?' they chorused bursting into fits of laughter.

Scarlett stormed into the room, before she could stop herself the words were out, 'Stay away from that man, he's no good.'

Miss Hester and Miss Maria looked at her aghast. Scarlett walked across the room to set the tray down on the table when Maria Penhallen came and stood directly in front of her.

'And who pray are you to judge your betters? Your opinion on anything matters not one jot. You are a servant, a nobody. Get out before we think twice about the agreement we made with you earlier.' These final words she shouted loudly before stepping aside.

Scarlett set the tray down. 'I apologise, I shouldn't have said what I did.' She backed away from the table and hurried from the room, red-faced and holding back the tears she was determined they shouldn't see.

Chapter 13

The extra work involved the next morning, with the preparation for Miss Maria's departure, mattered not to Scarlett who would be glad when the troublesome girl, a bad influence on Miss Hester, had taken herself off home.

Scarlett's spirits were further lifted when Ivan managed to tell her that he had seen Jack, and all was going well with his recovery. She longed for Sunday when she could escape this place and see him.

By mid-morning all was in readiness for Miss Maria's departure. Scarlett had hoped to have as little contact with her as possible, but the wretched girl left a pair of lace gloves in her bedroom and Scarlett dutifully returned these to her in the drawing room. She had just handed over the gloves when the sound of faint drumming could be heard.

Curious as to what was happening, the two girls rose and looked from one window whilst Scarlett stole a glance from the other. Approaching West Looe from across the bridge were six men easily recognised as revenue by their uniform. The man in front had a drum which he beat in a steady rhythm. One man led a horse, across its back was draped the body of a man. As they drew nearer and turned to pass beneath the windows of Prospect House, Scarlett took a step back and stifled a cry of dismay, for she recognised the head of blond curls and the pale blue coat the dead man wore. The body was that of Jack's friend Harry Shaw, who she'd met on the quay so recently, a young man full of life, rallying the crowd to oppose the ruthless persecution of the free traders.

Suddenly Miss Maria exclaimed, 'Surely that man they've got tied to the horse's back was one of the local men my father asked to Penhallen after the sinking of the *Rubyanne*. I saw him but briefly when they were leaving, I think he was one of them. I must tell my father of this when I get home, he must have known him. I wonder what his name was.'

'His name was Harry Shaw. Indeed, he was at Penhallen. He was a good man, miss,' Scarlett stated boldly.

Scarlett didn't look at either of the young ladies who now craned their necks to follow the sad procession along the quay. She withdrew, and in the kitchen, away from the outside world, kept her emotions under control. With a heavy heart she carried out her duties, wondering how Jack would cope with the loss of his friend.

Eventually Miss Maria departed, with lackeys heaving her trunks downstairs, followed by much hugging, kissing and wiping away of tears. Scarlett was relieved she was gone. Miss Hester retreated to her room and slowly the rest of the day passed. That evening there was no sign of Ivan, who Scarlett had hoped may bring some news of what had followed once the procession reached the quay. She endured a sleepless night tossing and turning, unable to rid her mind of the sight of Harry on the quay, the cheering crowd gathered round him. She shed many a tear that night at his killing.

Early the next morning, just as Millie had finished the dusting, the sisters returned home. Scarlett saw Ivan along with the young lad who worked next door for the captain unloading their trunks and numerous carpet bags, but there came no chance to speak with him. When at last the house had settled, Scarlett passed the drawing room and overheard the sisters discussing Harry, they mentioned him by name. Ivan must have told them.

'To shoot a man in the back is despicable,' Miss Matilda exclaimed. 'Folks will seek retribution. Let's pray it leads to no further bloodshed.'

'Apparently the fellow with young Harry at the time of the shooting got away. He saw with his own eyes twas Robert Reader himself who did the deed.'

Scarlett hurried on her way, hands clenched in anger, and holding an even greater loathing for Robert Reader than she already had, if that were possible.

Down in the kitchen Millie, who was always keen to share anything overheard purely for the moments importance it gave her, was telling Bessie the gossip she'd heard earlier when replacing the flowers on the hall table.

'Get on with it, girl,' Bessie urged, fed up of waiting. 'What have you heard?'

'Seems by their talk the sisters have successfully secured Skullen's release from Bodmin. The danger's past.'

'Who's Skullen and what danger?' Bessie grumbled, hoping to hear something more interesting.

'I don't know, tis just what I heard,' Millie retorted taking Bessie's and Scarlett's lack of curiosity out on the bread she was kneading.

The drawing room bell jangled, and Bessie wiped her hands and put on a fresh apron. The sisters would no doubt want to discuss the day's menus.

No sooner was Bessie out of sight than Scarlett saw movement outside the window, the kitchen door opened, and Ivan beckoned her outside. He drew her a little way down the path and Scarlett shivered, for her linen dress was no protection on this cold and windy day. His face was solemn, and he looked intently at her.

'I'll say this quick, maid, cos Bessie won't be long. Mary Jago been to see me. Her Jack's determined to take Harry's place as decoy for the run Monday night. Tis too dangerous and Mary's beside herself with worry, she can't talk him out of it. He says it's something he must do, his duty.'

Scarlett listened realising the enormity of what Jack intended to do. Knew the dangers of such a task. He himself had told her so. Told her how many times Harry had only just escaped being caught.

'Mary asked me to have a word with him, and I have,' Ivan said, shaking his head. 'But the stubborn bugger won't listen. Needs his father here but no one knows when he'll be home. Though I reckon even Tom wouldn't be able to talk sense into him. Tis up to you, maid, if you'm two meeting up on Sunday like I knows you do. For heaven's sake, girl, persuade him not to do it. He's still in terrible agony from his injuries, Scarlett, he's in no fit state to do anything. Could barely move from his bed yesterday.'

Scarlett rested one hand on Ivan's arm and he in turn clasped a calloused hand over it.

'Don't worry I'll do my best. But you know what he's like. Even though tis dangerous, no doubt Jack sees it as a way of respecting his friend, but he has to be stopped.' Scarlett looked up into Ivan's worried face. 'With all my heart, I'll try to dissuade him.'

Ivan unclasped her and stepped back to look through the kitchen window checking for Bessie's return before continuing. 'Jack's such a daft bugger, he don't know the lie of the land round Portnadler Bay, proven places to hide like Harry did. Besides, there's others with more knowledge than Jack who have come forward offering to be decoy but he'll have none of it. I know Mary'll be grateful to you, she knows there's summat between you two. I'm sorry, Scarlett, to burden this on you. But perhaps he will listen to you.'

'I'll do my very best.'

'You'm better be going in now,' Ivan insisted, and opened the back door. Scarlett obeyed, just as Bessie's footsteps could be heard at the top of the stairs. At the same time the bell rope outside the front door was vigorously tugged to and fro. Scarlett let Bessie pass first then hurried to answer it. Standing on the doorstep were too local dignitaries who Scarlett recognised as living in one of the big houses at the top of West Looe Hill.

More work for them below stairs.

For the rest of that never-ending week, life at Prospect House became more hectic. Firstly, there was a spate of visitors and then the wedding of Francis Kestrel seemed to take precedence over all else. Uncertainty over the health of the bride's father meant a flurry of activity to ensure all dressmaking and other wedding attire, both for the sisters and Miss Hester, would be ready should the wedding be brought forward. And, of course, black funeral attire had to be freshly pressed and new ribbons attached to the sister's bonnets.

Mr Julian and the sisters attended the funeral at the little church in Talland Bay. Ivan went and so did most folks. Scarlett wished she could have been there to comfort Jack; thankful he had his mother to support him. Ivan, when he returned, was quiet and spoke only briefly to Bessie. His sombre manner broached no questions from those below stairs that day, nor the days following.

Scarlett's worries over Jack did in no way lessen, and Sunday when it dawned could not have come soon enough. Released from the confines of Prospect House, Scarlett ran down to the quay, she felt the warmth of the sun on her face and smelt the sea air for the first time since that fateful night.

She was disappointed when she reached the quay to see that Jack wasn't alone. As he took her in his arms, she felt him wince with pain, saw when he released her, his handsome face was badly bruised, and he had a nasty gnash on his forehead. He looked tired and worn, the dancing sparkle gone from his eyes.

'I'm sorry about Harry,' she said, and saw the pain the mention of his friend's name caused.'

'I know you are, maid.' Jack bent and kissed her forehead. 'I know.'

'He was a good un,' his companion stated, removing his hat from his head.

'Dan Tovey here's going to row us up to Simon's Croft. Don't want to admit it but my ribs are too bruised for me to do it.'

Scarlett still looked a little disappointed.

'Have no fear, maid, he'll not tarry there with us, will you Dan?'

Dan's face lit up in a toothy grin. 'Nope, you've got the young lady all to yourself til I comes an rows you back.'

Scarlett couldn't help but smile and Jack helped her down into Dan's boat.

As Dan rowed past Prospect House, Jack sat closest to the quay, and Scarlett raised up her hood. As usual the drapes at the windows of Prospect House were drawn close together, removing almost entirely the likelihood of being seen, but you couldn't take chances.

There was little conversation as they were rowed upriver, Scarlett pushed back the hood of her cloak and rested her head against Jack's shoulder. She enjoyed the feeling of solitude as the river became enclosed on either side by thickly wooded banks. Only bird song broke the silence. When they reached the old hulk that was Simon's Croft, Dan tied up and helped Scarlett from the boat. Jack declined his offer of help.

They watched as he rowed away, Jack studying the tide deciding how long it would be before Dan returned. Then he led her through the door and into their sanctuary.

Taking Scarlett in his arms he kissed her with a strength of passion that made Scarlett so happy tears escaped her eyes.

'Tis the thought of you that's kept me going. Felt so down I have, with the loss of Harry. He was my best friend going way back to when we were boys. Handsome Harry the girls used to call him. Salt of the earth. One of the best, and a true and faithful friend.'

Jack looked stricken with emotion. Scarlett went to comfort him but he turned away.

'First thing I must do is light the fire, for its devilish cold in here,' he blurted and began busily loading logs into the fireplace.

Once lit the fire spluttered into life and Jack led her over to the bed. 'Luke's been staying here, well he was up to when we went checking on the tubs, so the beds aired, any ways we'm soon warm it up. Lie with me, Scarlett, for I'm sore in need of comfort.'

After they had lain entwined together not talking or lovemaking just at peace with one another, Jack sat up and pulled his shirt over his head. Scarlett gasped at the deep purple and black bruises on his back and down his left side.

'Don't fuss, maid, tis nothing that won't stop me making love to you.'

'If that what's you want, then I am yours, my love,' Scarlett whispered, unfastening her bodice. Clearly Jack's bruised body hurt, so too the pain in his ribs, but he overcame the pain and it made little difference to their lovemaking. A contented Scarlett lay beside him snuggled in as close as she could without hurting him. Suddenly Jack sat up then scrambled into his clothes.

'I've no right to feel so happy with Harry dead,' he groaned. 'I can't believe the bastards killed him.' He sat back down on the bed and Scarlett quickly dressed and sat beside him.

'You were his friend. He'd want you to be happy,' she soothed, and for a while they stayed as they were, Scarlett knowing Harry's death was something it would take Jack a long time to overcome.

She began to feel cold, tried her hardest not to shiver but in the end she did, and that broke the spell of contented silence. 'Don't want you catching a chill now do we?' He smiled. And got up to put more logs on the fire.

'Was yesterday as horrible for you as I imagine?' Scarlett enquired softly.

'By far the worst day of my life,' Jack replied, looking directly at her. 'The pain of it will never go away. Watching as Harry was buried in Talland churchyard fair broke my heart. Twas folks there from West and East Looe united in grief, tis not often both sides of the river come together but they did for Harry. His parents had to be helped to the graveside, both were beyond themselves with grief. Sam Trembright who knew Harry as well as I did, we stood together, acknowledging each other for the first time since that day we fought on the quay.'

'Surely that's a good thing.'

'I don't know about that,' Jack declared harshly. 'He's no friend of mine now.'

'How come Sam knew Harry?' Scarlett queried as he came and sat beside her once more.

A sombre Jack replied, 'When we was all younger, the Trembrights and Shaws lived next door to each other. Harry was a bit older than us but that didn't make no difference. Then the Shaws went to live with Harry's grandfather at Talland, but Sam, Luke and me still kept friends with Harry, walking over the cliffs to climb the rocks together or go rowing round to Portnadler Bay. When he was older, Harry'd come back to West Looe, he used to sail on the old quarry ships for your Mr Julian, then on the schooners owned by Charles Penhallen.

'So you do know Portnadler Bay quite well then?' Scarlett asked and saw Jack's eyes narrow.

'Who bin telling you bout what I'm doing? That Ivan I suppose, I'll be having words with him.'

'Your mother's worried about you, she asked Ivan to try and persuade you not to take Harry's part as decoy in tomorrow's run. Ivan having no success in turn has asked me, don't do it, Jack, you'm not well enough.'

'I don't need anyone telling me what I can and can't do. Stop worrying, I can look after myself, Ivan don't know how much time I spent at Nadler nor how well I knows it. Come, let's sit by the fire and we'll say no more about tomorrow.'

Scarlett did as she was told. In silence they watched the flames dancing on the logs, with Jack occasionally reaching forward to throw on more wood, wincing in pain as he did so. Scarlett was heartbroken not knowing how to end the ill feeling between them. Finally, Jack let the fire die down. Scarlett fetched her cloak for now it grew cold. She was glad at last to hear Dan calling for them. Jack stood up and took Scarlett by the hand helping her up.

'It'll be alright, maid, I promise you, it will.'

As Dan rowed them back down the river, the only sound to be heard was Dan's intake of breath as he heaved on the oars, and the splash they made slicing through the water. Jack put his arm round Scarlett's shoulders, and she turned towards him, hoping for a reassuring look or even a kiss, but Jack was staring straight ahead, deep in thought.

When they reached the quay, Dan stood and took hold the thick piece of rope hanging down from an iron ring embedded in the quay. He held his boat steady and offered Scarlett his other hand to help her from the boat. As she made her way up the stone steps, Jack lingered behind talking to Dan, their voices so low Scarlett couldn't hear what they were saying.

No sooner had Jack followed her up the steps and onto they quay than someone shouted, 'Jack, come here.' This lone voice was immediately followed by others.

'I'll be back,' Jack shouted to a group of men outside the Jolly Sailor, he then hustled Scarlett along the quay and into Market Lane much too quickly for her liking, as if he wanted done with her.

'You can leave me here; I can see myself home. Get back to your friends,' Scarlett snapped, upset at such treatment. She pulled her cloak tight round her and hurried on ahead of him, quickening her pace. Jack also began to walk faster, keeping alongside her.

'Don't be like this. There are plans being made for tomorrow, I must go back.'

'Fine, well, I hope all goes well, don't try to be a hero; Harry's dead, nothing you do can bring him back.'

She glanced at Jack and could see how this comment had angered him, the nerve on the side of his face twitched and his lips were held firm together, how she wished she could take her words back.

He caught hold of her arm. 'This is the biggest run of the season; we'll make good money and I'll be more than happy to take my share. If you'm ever to become my wife, Scarlett, you'll have to stop worrying, for you will have years ahead of you just like this.' With that he kissed her hard on the lips. Then held her from him at arm's length. 'So, let me go with your blessing.'

'Jack, I—'

The stable door scraped open and Ivan glared out at them. Scarlett watched in dismay as Jack nodded to Ivan and walked quickly away.

'One of these days you'll be caught, the sisters will see you,' Ivan warned her. 'You'm be out, you know that.'

'I know,' Scarlett replied her mind elsewhere. Wondering if she should run after Jack, but he was gone from sight by now. Angry she'd not been able to finish her sentence and truly make it up with him.

Ivan opened the back gate and Scarlett walked down the path, she recalled Jack's words. 'If you'm ever to become my wife.' She felt a blush come to her cheeks and happiness fill her heart. Had he really said that?

As Scarlett opened the kitchen door these thoughts were abruptly set aside. Bessie and Millie were having words. Something that rarely happened quite so ferociously. Ivan stepped into the kitchen and the bickering stopped. 'What's going on here?' He looked to Bessie then Millie for an explanation.

Bessie all hot in the face looked at Millie. 'Well, now's your chance, ask him, go on tell Ivan what you'm been blabbering on to me about, seeing how it concerns him.'

Millie remained silent, looking down at the floor, her face crimson.

'Go on, your head was full of silly nonsense before they came in.'

Ivan crossed his arms and looked at Millie, not unkindly. Scarlett, not wishing to be part of whatever had gone on between them, took off her cloak, hung it up on the back door and busied herself putting on a freshly laundered apron.

'Out with it, Millie, either you tell me, or I'll get Bessie to,' Ivan coaxed.

Millie sniffed and looked shamefaced at Ivan. 'It was just that, well, when I brought your ale over yesterday and this morning, I thought I heard a noise, like someone were up in your quarters when you was talking to me.'

Ivan's eyes crinkled into a smile. 'Saucy madam. Thought I had a lady friend up there did you?'

'No.' Millie vigorously shook her head.

Hands on hips, Bessie pursed her lips. 'Oh yes you did. Even told me who you thought it was, the new servant girl from the captain's house. Said she'd seen her leaning out of their back gate looking towards the stables, like she was waiting for you.'

Ivan pulled out a chair and slowly sat down. 'No maid, I'm sorry to say twas all in your imagination. I've no fancy woman or anyone else. What you heard is easily explained, the skylight must have been open, things blown over or something, there's only me and old Dolly out there.

'But I...'

Bessie gave Millie a looked that silenced her in an instant. 'Apologise to Ivan,' she snapped.

'I'm sorry, Ivan,' Millie whispered, before bursting into tears.

Miss Hester's bell rang, and Scarlett left them to answer it. As she turned at the bottom of the stairs, she caught a look pass between Ivan and Bessie, there was something oddly strange about it.

On entering Miss Hester's room all thoughts of Jack and the row below stairs were quickly dismissed, replaced by Miss Hester whining on about how she wanted a French dressmaker not Miss Smith to make her dress for the upcoming wedding. She paced the floor red-faced with temper. Mr Julian it seemed had dismissed her wishes, and not only that, he'd been talking to her aunts, putting a stop to any extravagant purchases she may wish to make. Her list of grievances went on all evening until finally Miss Hester was safely in bed and the candle blown out.

A tired Scarlett was left to eat a cold supper of mutton and bread alone, for by the time she came down

Bessie had taken to her bed and Millie was busy with the sisters. Scarlett hoped the ill feeling between the two was over, and gratefully lit her candle and set off for her own bed.

Thoughts of how she wished Jack had not walked away as he did caused her to toss and turn, but in the end she fell asleep. Only to be awakened a short while later by a tapping on her door. Opening her eyes, she saw Millie slipping into her room and padding barefoot across to her bed, setting her pewter candle holder down on the bedside table.

Scarlett eased herself up shielding her eyes from the light of the candle.

'What is it? I'm too tired, go to bed.'

'I can't, I must tell you first without cook hearing. I did hear noises above the stable and it weren't nothing to do with wind blowing anything over.'

'I don't care, its none of our business.' Scarlett stifled a yawn.

'Tis to me, don't like to be made out daft in the head,' Millie grumbled, picking up her candle holder and retreating.

By midday the next morning, the ill feeling between Bessie and Millie was all but forgotten, those below stairs caught up in the flurry of activity caused by the arrival of Miss Smith the dressmaker, summoned for the final fitting of the sisters and Miss Hester's wedding outfits. Scarlett stood waiting to help Miss Hester into her dress and was mortified at how rude her charge was to Miss Smith.

'It's hideous, take it away. I shall be a laughing stock,' she shouted at the poor woman before snatching the offending garment out of Miss Smith's hands. 'It's dowdy beyond belief. Take it and yourself out of my sight.' She flung the dress across the room to Miss Smith and flounced inelegantly over to her bed and sat down in a sulk.

Scarlett felt mortified at her charge, her caustic comments led to poor Miss Smith running from Miss Hester's room in tears, heading straight in the direction of the drawing room to tell the sisters. Scarlett also escaped going down to answer the loud knocking on the front door. She opened it to find the milliner on the doorstep surrounded by boxes. Scarlett held the door open and, removing his hat as he did so, the milliner stepped into the hall, followed by his assistant. A door slammed on the floor above. Scarlett hesitated but decided it best she bade the two gentlemen follow her upstairs to the small room next to the drawing room. Halfway up the stairs she was embarrassed to hear a loud and colourful exchange of words between Miss Emilia and Miss Hester. Miss Emilia admonishing her niece for her rude behaviour to Miss Smith. The portly middle-aged man looked up the stairs, clearly uncertain whether to follow Scarlett and interrupt the participants of such a fierce altercation.

With Scarlett and Millie so busy, Bessie had sent word by the butcher's delivery boy to Florrie, and one of her many daughters had come to help in the kitchen. Scarlett, desperate to see Ivan so he could send word to Jack telling him she was sorry for the manner they'd parted the day before, found any excuse she could to go down to the kitchen, but each time Scarlett was there, Ivan wasn't. Which was really infuriating.

Word was sent down and Millie instructed to take Miss Smith a tray of cold luncheon up to the school room where she ate alone. Scarlett saw her through the open door, and thought her a very sad figure of spinsterhood, and so undeserving of Miss Hester's venom.

The milliner went to his home for an hour whilst the sisters had their lunch. Afterwards, when those below stairs thought they could sigh with relief that even Miss Hester had been placated with the promise of a new dress more to her liking, extra work was created when Mr Julian arrived unexpectedly bringing with him a young lady who he introduced to his sisters-in-law for the first time. Immediately, Millie excitedly speculated on who she was.

Bessie's patience was at its limit. 'Quiet! We've more than enough to be doing without you gossiping, get on with the lemon syllabub and not another word.'

Scarlett slipped out and filled a pail from the well in the yard, but however much she hoped to see him, Ivan never appeared. She peeped out the back gate and looked down Market Lane, neither was there any sign of Jack.

Dusk fell and a moonless night descended over West Looe. Scarlett was not in the least surprised when Ivan didn't appear as usual for supper. Bessie made no comment about his absence, leaving Scarlett to think she must know what was happening tonight.

When all were abed, and the daily toil of Prospect House was finished, Scarlett went up to her room. Standing by her window, she looked out into this the darkest of nights, she could but hope that Jack would come home unhurt, and whatever he planned to do to draw the revenue's attention away from those waiting on the beach and cliffs further along the coast would lead to the goods coming ashore unheeded.

Deep in thought, she went to bed thinking of that last time she'd seen Jack, so cross they'd had words but thrilled he'd mentioned her becoming his wife, even if at the same time telling her she couldn't change him. In her heart she knew Jack was born to this way of life, and she must accept it, knowing that forever she'd worry for his safety and for the others out there on nights such as these. Silently, she prayed for their safe return.

When there was no sign of Ivan the next morning, Scarlett began to worry.

She questioned Bessie as to where he was. 'No need to worry your pretty head about Ivan,' Bessie exclaimed sharply whilst vigorously beating egg whites in a small enamel bowl. 'Him be alright. Now out in the yard, missy, and draw me more water, and keep yur mind busy on other things.'

Having filled the copper kettle with water, Scarlett hung it over the fire. She began peeling the carrots, watching through the window for any sign of Ivan. Sure now that Bessie knew he was involved in the run last night, probably the sisters did too, not Miss Hester though, but Mr Julian, he no doubt had his part to play in lasts night's activities. She wasn't the innocent young girl who'd first come to work here anymore. Finding where the sisters hid their ledgers had taught her, they too weren't all they seemed.

Scarlett spent the rest of the day with a knot in her stomach, worrying about Jack, and still there was no sign of Ivan. Florrie's daughter came again to help out as Scarlett and Millie were busy packing for the sisters and Miss Hester's departure to Moorswater Manor. The wedding of Francis Kestrel had been brought forward. Miss Smith duly returned looking more timid than ever, she had stayed up all night altering the dress Miss Hester was to wear to the wedding, and thankfully now it was just about acceptable with the removal of the overly fussy lace trim replaced by a narrow white braided border.

Chapter 14

Even the next day, there was still no sign of Jack or Ivan. Scarlett was sure if Jack was back in West Looe, he would have tried to see her. Now with all the preparations for the departure to Moorswater complete, Scarlett stood at the top of the steps watching Mr Julian help his aunts into the awaiting carriage. Neither Bessie nor the sisters seemed in any way concerned by Ivan's absence. It was Scarlett's belief they all knew just where he was. It was a closed subject. As the coachman folded up the steps of the carriage and climbed up, settling himself on the bench seat and taking up the reins in preparation for the journey ahead, another much smaller coach approached the house, and Scarlett withdrew and called downstairs to Millie.

'Come on, there'll be hell to play if them upstairs get there long before us and they've no one at their beck and call.'

Millie came and stood beside Scarlett as their few belongings were fastened on the back of the coach by a scowling coachman.

'Don't dawdle, you two,' he shouted impatiently, then looked them up and down noting their uniforms. 'Don't the likes of you usually leave by the back door?'

Scarlett retorted. 'Well we'm not today, and you'm being paid so just get on with taking us to Moorswater.'

She ushered Millie aboard and entered herself. Just as she went to shut the door, Bessie came huffing and puffing down the steps, holding out a folded piece of paper.

'This just been left for you. Some man knocked on the kitchen door and handed it me, said I'm to make sure you know it's urgent like.'

'What was he like?'

'Ordinary, nothing special, had a felt hat on. Think he came here once before.'

'I know who that is, thank you, Bessie.'

Scarlett sat down and began to unfold the rather scruffy note. The coach lurched forward, nearly throwing her from the seat. 'The bastard,' Scarlett declared angrily, holding tight the leather loop beside her and putting the note into her pocket.

'Bet Bessie's glad we'm all gone,' Millie sighed, shuffling round on the worn leather seat to get herself comfortable. 'Good this is,' she exclaimed, excitedly looking out the window as the coach made its way across the bridge.

Scarlett pulled the note from her pocket and unfolded it. The writing was large and very uneven. It read. *Your mother needs you, go to her when you can. Amos.*

Curious, Scarlett read the words over and over again, she knew something must be very wrong for Amos to come here to Prospect House. She hoped her father hadn't hurt her mother in the manner he had last time. If only she'd been there to see him, asked what was wrong, she could have told him they were going away and wouldn't be back til late Monday. Whatever would her mother and Amos think when she didn't visit Sunday?

Her frustration increased the further they drew away from West Looe. Millie prattled on and Scarlett nodded from time to time in agreement as expected. In all truth her thoughts were far away, this on top of her worry about Jack and Ivan. What was wrong at Tamarisk? Could it be something to do with the hated Robert Reader? She felt a chill of fear, but instantly knew it couldn't be, her mother would never have disclosed to Amos she knew Reader. Scarlett felt helpless. Whatever was wrong, she couldn't help to put it to rights until she returned home after the wedding.

The coach drew up outside the servants' quarters at Moorswater. The coachman unstrapped their belongings and dropped them on the ground, spitting as if in contempt as he turned the horses around and left.

Immediately there were duties to be done. Millie was summoned by the sisters and Scarlett by Miss Hester.

Just as she had on previous visits elsewhere, Miss Hester complained about the room she'd been given. 'I don't like it in here, I should have been given a room closer to Elizabeth Polgrove, Lizzy as she wants to be known now; Elizabeth, Lizzy, she's forever changing her mind about what we should call her, I've no patience with it. Maria's room is almost next to hers. I feel slighted, it's unforgivable.' Her charge groaned bitterly on as Scarlett began setting out combs and other toiletries on the dressing table.

'This is a very pretty room, I'm sure there was no slight intended.' Scarlett tried to reassure her. Unconvinced, Miss Hester lay on her bed in the pretty, delicately decorated room, a mix of gentle pastel colours, and watched ill-humoured through the open door of the adjoining dressing room as Scarlett went about unpacking her charge's trunks and hanging up her clothes;

Scarlett anxious they shouldn't get badly creased leading to more work.

'Is there a truckle bed for you in there?' Miss Hester asked, jolting Scarlett's memory back to their visit at Penhallen and the nightmare she and Jack had been so lucky to escape from. She shivered at the thought.

'Yes, there is.'

Miss Hester rang the bell beside the bed and ordered a glass of water.

The morning of the wedding dawned, lukewarm porridge and doughy bread was an unwelcome breakfast at 6.00 in the morning. All Scarlett wanted was to be on her way home and find a way she could visit her mother.

For once Miss Hester was in the best of moods with no tantrums as Scarlett prepared her for Mr Francis's wedding ceremony. It was Miss Maria who burst in in a great measure of distress just as Scarlett began brushing Miss Hester's hair.

'Mother says I can't wear my hair up and I am so distraught,' Maria sobbed throwing herself on Miss Hester's bed. 'If I can't, you can't either.'

Scarlett looked at Miss Hester's reflection in the mirror and realised she hadn't inquired about the etiquette that should be followed regarding this. 'Shall I go and ask your aunts?' she murmured, trying not to let Miss Maria overhear.

'No, don't bother them, it's alright, continue to brush out my hair and I shall wear it loose under my hat like Miss Penhallen.'

Somewhat mollified by this, Maria Penhallen stomped off back to her room and a while later with a feeling of much pleasure, Scarlett saw her charge, who looking truly lovely in her delicate blue dress trimmed with the most exquisite of white lace and hat of matching colours, go down to join her father and aunts waiting for her in the drawing room. Miss Hester may not come from the highest of society, but she looked equal to any today. Both Miss Smith and the milliner had succeeded in their duties.

Scarlett went down and joined the rest of the servants gathered at a vantage point where they could see the groom leave to walk the short distance to the small church on the Moorswater estate. Beside him his hateful brother Adrian. Later as she sat drinking tea in the servants' quarters, she learned that Millie had found herself a beau.

Girls from the local village had been brought in to help with the wedding breakfast, hence the kitchen was bustling with organised chaos, and for just a short while those such as Scarlett could but wait for their mistresses to return.

Amidst the flurry of activity, Scarlett could plainly hear Millie's giggle, followed shortly afterwards by a scolding voice. Scarlett turned her head just in time to see Millie being marched out of the boot room by a furious elderly butler. She came scurrying over to Scarlett.

'Beastly man, just cause I was talking to Boots, well Sid his real name is. Says I look a real treat, Sid did. Try and see him again, I will, when that old stick of a bloke int about. What you'm looking so miserable about anyway?'

'Just got worries of my own.' Scarlett gave her a weak smile. 'Tis nothing I can share.' Millie nudged Scarlett as Boots came out of a small room off the servants' hall, he looked across and gave Millie a broad grin. Scarlett looked at her companion and smiled, drawn momentarily away from fears for her mother, and of Jack, also the dread that before she escaped back home, she'd have the misfortune to cross paths with Adrian Kestrel.

'Near as andsome as your Jack, is Sid.'

'No, indeed he's not,' Scarlett berated and relaxed, and for a while forgot her troubles.

In the servants' quarters they ate a miserly lunch of cold meat and bread and butter before the wedding party returned. The rest of the day passed without incident. Miss Hester's happy mood thankfully continuing throughout, and later Scarlett joined the others once again as they crowded round to seek a view of the happy couple as they departed for their honeymoon. The day had passed. When finally Miss Hester was in bed, it meant only tomorrow morning to be endured before they were to go home at midday.

In the morning Scarlett overheard Miss Maria giggling with Miss Hester, the girls stopped their conversation the moment Scarlett entered the bedroom. Together the girls left, still giggling and Scarlett retreated quickly down to the servants' quarters where she would wait to be called if needed. The guests that had stayed overnight were now gathered in the drawing room, so Millie informed her. Miss Matilda had requested a handkerchief be brought to her earlier, this is how she knew.

Several times the bell set below the brass sign declaring Drawing Room jumped nimbly on its spring, one of the housemaids would quickly go up in answer, but thankfully there was no request for Scarlett.

Would it be imprudent to start packing? Scarlett thought not, for within three hours they would be gone from here, and Adrian Kestrel would be safely out of the way entertaining the guests in the drawing room. Whilst Millie mooned about trying to catch sight of Boots, Scarlett slipped away and began folding some of the clothes and packing away toiletries that surely wouldn't be needed. Then Millie appeared out of breath saying that Miss Hester was to accompany other guests going on a stroll around the lake and was in need of her gloves and the hat which matched her cream muslin dress.

Scarlett hurried downstairs with the required items, raised her hand then paused before knocking on the door, knowing Adrian Kestrel would most likely be there. Another maid came running bringing similar items for her mistress, she pushed past Scarlett and knocked lightly on the door and entered, leaving it wide open behind her.

They were all there, the gentry, in the opulently furnished drawing room, its pale green walls covered with portraits of all sizes. The long floor-length windows framed in the most expensive damson brocade and within the room an array of young girls like Miss Hester were seated prettily, together with older women and one or two matriarchs dressed in black. The men stood idly around, some wore powdered wigs ridiculously white, others like Mr Julian wore their own hair, young or old they were richly dressed, most in stylishly cut frock coats and tightly fitting breeches, clothes like the ones she'd seen being pressed at Lanreath. One or two, like Charles Penhallen, were red cheeked and a little unsteady on their feet, perhaps after drinking too many goodly measures of brandy.

For a moment, Scarlett hesitated to enter for Adrian Kestrel was there standing with his back to her beside a small table in front of a window, there was no mistaking it was him. He poured himself a drink from a cut glass decanter. Scarlett watched as he replaced the stopper and reached for the glass.

Miss Hester looked towards the door as if put out by the time she was taking, likewise Miss Maria and others all waiting for such as herself to sally forth in answer to their bidding. Scarlett had never seen such a gathering of the moneyed upper crust of society together in one room, so lavishly dressed and seated in such splendour. Deep down she felt the stirrings of resentment, so these were the people who Miss Hester so longed to be associated with, be equal with, well she could keep them.

She handed Miss Hester the gloves and delicate hat which she impatiently pinned on herself, then without glancing in the direction of Adrian Kestrel, Scarlett made for the door anxious to be gone.

'You,' a stern voice called out. Scarlett stopped and turned. One of the matriarchs had lifted her stick and was pointing it in her direction.

'Put some more coal on the fire, and take away this tea tray it's making the place look untidy.'

Scarlett retraced her steps and picked up the brass coal tongs, she began placing coal on the back of the fire. In the background she could hear the chatter from those in the room, heard Miss Hester's companions discussing their servants.

'It's always best to keep them close by. We never know when we'll need them,' Maria Penhallen enthused, speaking it seemed to a rather plain young woman seated next to Miss Hester, for Scarlett didn't recognise the voice that meekly responded.

'I do so agree,' Miss Hester joined in.' Her voice far more refined than usual.

Lizzy Polgrove joined the conversation, 'When I'm away I always make sure there's a room or such adjoining mine should I need anything during the night.'

Scarlett replaced the tongs and stood up, she reached down to pick up the tea tray, it was large and made of heavy wood with silver handles, laden with a large china teapot, milk jug, sugar bowl and used cups and saucers.

'There was one night when last I visited Penhallen when I didn't have Penrose close by, she was in the servants' quarters and I so did miss her,' Miss Hester declared.

At that precise moment there was a lull in the general hubbub of conversation in the room. Scarlett held her breath and turned to leave. Somewhere across the room she heard a glass being slammed down heavily. As she moved towards the door, she made the mistake of taking the quickest of glances in the direction of Adrian Kestrel. His eyes bore into hers, his face dark with anger. Without doubt, he knew! Balancing the tray on her left arm, Scarlett opened the door and quickly made for the backstairs, knowing full well soon afterwards someone else had left the room.

When she reached the entrance to the back stairs, Scarlett once more balanced the tray and eased the door open with her toe. No sooner had she begun to descend the stairs than she heard the same door flung open. Footsteps thundered down towards her, a hand reached down and seized her shoulder. The material around the neck of her uniform ripped. Adrian Kestrel forced her forwards onto a small half landing. He took hold of her arm and spun her round. Scarlett clung onto the wooden tray, it acted as a barrier now between the two of them.

He towered over her and leant forwards; his sweaty face drew close to hers. Scarlett tried to take a step back but couldn't.

'I know it was you in the servants' quarters that night. Give me the name of the bastard that hit me.' His brandy-soaked breath was hot on her face.

'I know not what you mean, sir. Don't knows nothing, lots of maids sleep in them quarters.'

'But I feel it in my bones it was your room I entered, saw the look of guilt on your face just now. His name, missy, his name.'

With one hand he gripped her throat, with the other he cupped her face and squeezed it hard.

'Think the Miss Catts will approve of your whoring?' He thrust her head back and pressed his thumb hard against her throat. Scarlett kicked out and struggled to get free. Adrian Kestrel held her still, his forceful grip tightened.

'I believed it too at first, that I'd got drunk, fallen and hit my head, had disgraced my brother and myself, but then my memory of the night began to clear.'

Scarlett tried to turn her face away. He wouldn't let her; his voice was low almost at a whisper.

'Vaguely I sensed someone young within that room when I opened the door. I caught just a shadowy glimpse of her before being struck. On a later visit to Penhallen, I questioned the housekeeper. Stupid woman dare preach to me that no men are allowed in that quarter. Stated none of the younger maids of visiting gentry usually slept there, they were with their mistresses, but of course you were only there that one night. Weren't you?'

Scarlett fought for breath as his rant continued, his lip curling in an ugly sneer. She felt strangely lightheaded, his voice receding ever further away.

'I applaud Miss Hester for divulging so innocently you'd been sleeping in the servants' quarters during that visit. And you for the guilty look on your face when you knew I'd rumbled your secret. You left me for dead, now you and your lover will pay. His name.'

Scarlett felt herself growing weaker. She shook her head. Managed to choke out the word, 'No.'

'The bastard will hang at Bodmin Gaol, and I'll make sure you see the deed done.' Kestrel's eyes glinted with glee. 'You'll not live much longer than him. His name now or you'll follow him to the gallows. If you tell me his name, maybe I'll ask for clemency for you, transportation instead. So, one last time, what is his name? You're nothing but a common servant with no morals, an accomplice out to kill one of the gentry, such as I. It will be easy to get the noose round your neck too. I'll ask you one more time, his name.'

The stairs lit by candles in sconces on the wall began to fade. Scarlett began to lose consciousness. She slipped downwards against the wall and Kestrel hauled her up by the throat. Irrationally, Scarlett still clung onto the tray, thinking how much of her wages it would take should she have to pay for the breakages as at Prospect House.

Roughly, Kestrel having first squeezed her throat even harder released his grip, hoping the thought of the gallows would loosen her tongue. Instead, Scarlett bit him on the hand. Enraged, he took hold of her face again and viciously slapped it with the back of his left hand. A strangled cry escaped her lips, and somewhere far away came the unmistakeable sound of footsteps on the stair. Scarlett heard a sharp intake of breath. Kestrel thrust her away from him. A housemaid climbed the stairs towards them. He leant forward and spat in Scarlett's face then retreated upstairs leaving a trembling Scarlett struggling to breathe, and wiping his spit from her face. The maidservant took the tray. Placed it down on the landing and held a trembling Scarlett in her arms.

'That bastard, at it again, is he?' she declared angrily.

A voice called up the stairs. 'Annie, Dr Trevane's ringing his bell over and over, you up there gossiping?'

'No, Mrs Furley.' Annie led Scarlett down the stairs. 'Tis Mr Adrian, he—'

Briskly the plump grey-haired housekeeper shooed them through the kitchen and opened the door to her parlour. 'Leave her with me, go and answer Trevane's bell before it drives us all quite mad. When you're done come back here, and no mentioning any of this mind.'

Annie gave Scarlett a last hug and opened the door, momentarily letting in the familiar sounds and smell of the busy kitchen. After she'd shut the door, Mrs Furley looked at Scarlett, not unkindly.

'Here.' She gestured over to a worn leather armchair beside the fire. 'Sit down and I'll take a look at the marks on your face and neck, bathe them and see what we can do to disguise them. Annie will repair the tear in your dress. We've a little time, for tis good your mistress is walking out with the others.'

As Scarlett made her way over to the chair, she looked in the mirror hanging over the fireplace, saw the red marks on her face and neck and swayed, feeling quite overcome.

The housekeeper, not wanting a fainting maid on her hands, left Scarlett once she was seated and came back with a cup of tea. As Scarlett fought back tears and drank the very last drop, Mrs Furley brought from the kitchen a small pewter bowl filled with warm water and a piece of cloth and began bathing Scarlett's cheek and throat. This done she fetched from a cupboard on the wall a glass pot of salve.

'Now, Penrose, that's your name is it?' she queried, and Scarlett nodded.

'How far did he go, are you as you were?'

'I am,' Scarlett croaked out the words, realising she'd have to pretend this was no more than Adrian Kestrel trying to get his way with another of the maids.

Gently the housekeeper applied the salve to Scarlett's throat. 'Take this, keep it, put it in your pocket. We'll have to come up with some story as to why your neck's so red. The smarting on your cheek will hopefully go down. But for now, some good advice. Don't go making a fuss, or running to your mistress's aunts. If you make allegations about Mr Adrian it will end with you being dismissed. The gentry are above reproach.'

'I won't tell.' Scarlett looked down at the floor and fought back tears.

Mrs Furley brought her another cup of tea. Satisfied she'd keep the matter quiet.

'The other maid from your household is busy chattering to Boots. I'd have stopped it by now, but it's keeping her busy and not enquiring after you. Stay here and wait till Annie comes back, she's a good little seamstress, she'll do a good repair on your dress. Keep bathing your cheek, the colour will lessen, I'm sure.'

Scarlett nodded her thanks, for it still hurt to speak. She lay back and closed her eyes, still badly shaken by what had happened. She was half asleep when Annie came to her.

'Them upstairs who went on the walk are down by the lake, sent Dr Trevane's younger son back to request a picnic basket be taken down to the Lodge, bloody cheek. Cook's in a right state, all the guests were supposed to be gone by noon. Now she's got to prepare a picnic for them, and lunch for those who remain upstairs. But enough of them, how are you feeling? Mr A, as we call him, is a right bastard, we'm all glad when he goes off to sea, we're safe then.'

'I'm glad I'm not in service here,' Scarlett rasped.

Annie fetched over a round wicker basket and having selected the items she wanted began to repair the rip in Scarlett's dress. 'Certain parts of the house we only do in pairs. Mr A has a manservant, thank heaven, he lingers about and keeps an eye out for us.'

When Annie had finished, Scarlett stood up and took another look in the mirror, her throat and face were still very red, then she ran her fingers over where the rip in her uniform had been, Annie was indeed a good seamstress.

'Its good work you've done, I can hardly see it where it was, thank you.'

'We'm best come up with a story as to how you got them red marks or questions will be asked,' Annie stated, standing back and taking a good look at them. 'At least the colour has lessened a little on your cheek, thank goodness.'

Just then Mrs Furley returned, inspected Annie's work and nodded her approval.

'We'm thinking what to say as how she got them marks,' Annie exclaimed.

The housekeeper stood back studying Scarlett. 'Tis best I think if we say you were running up the backstairs and Annie was coming down with a tray, and caught you with the edge of it, twas nasty but you'm alright now.'

It was agreed that that sounded as if it could have happened. Scarlett slowly stood up. 'I'd best be getting on with Miss Hester's packing, else they'll be back.'

'Annie will go with you; she'll stay with you til you'm on your way.'

'Thank you, Mrs Furley.'

Together with Annie, Scarlett made her way up to Miss Hester's room and with her help all was soon folded and packed away ready for their departure. Back down in the servants' quarters, Scarlett ignored the various stares that came her way, nothing was easily kept quiet down here. She told Millie the story agreed upon which she accepted it without question. Annie fetched her a helping of rabbit pie and two stout slices of bread. After this, Scarlett helped in with the others, rushed off their feet, now having to serve up food to the numerous disgruntled coachmen and servants waiting to make their departure. They were not a happy bunch.

By the time all in their party were ready to leave, Scarlett knew every mark upon the clock face in the servants' quarters. Eventually once their employers had departed, Scarlett and Millie's carpet bags and other belongings were loaded onto the back of the same hired coach in which they'd arrived, with the same surly coachman. Because Mrs Furley the housekeeper was watching this time, with an undisguised scowl, he'd opened the door and lowered the steps for them, once they were seated, he'd folded them back. As he closed the door, Scarlett could smell ale on his breathe.

'Safe journey,' Annie called as they set off and Mrs Furley acknowledged Scarlett with a nod of the head, then turned and went inside.

As she did so, Boots emerged from behind a nearby corner and Millie with tears in her eyes waved him goodbye.

As the coach left the Moorswater Estate and swayed left to right as its wheels stumbled into the many ruts in the lane, Scarlett put her hand in her pocket, curling her fingers round the small pot of salve and Amos's note. For once Millie was quiet, and Scarlett glad of it. Now her thoughts could return to Jack. She prayed Ivan would be home when they returned, he'd know about her Jack. As for her mother, something must be very wrong at Tamarisk.

After a while, Scarlett reached forward and pulled the leather tab below the small window in the coach's rattling door. She lowered it a little and smelt the fresh pungent smell of the river. Through the trees the river glistened, the tide was up, and Scarlett smiled, they were nearly home.

Outside Prospect House the quay was empty and seeing no one was about, the coachman brought the horses to an unnecessarily abrupt halt. But someone was watching from the window beside the front door. Ivan stormed out and angrily berated him before helping Scarlett and Millie alight. He gathered their belongings, picking them up from the ground where they'd been dropped unceremoniously and ushered the two of them inside.

As Millie took herself off downstairs Ivan took Scarlett's arm. 'Don't go fretting about Jack, he got back safe.' Scarlett felt such relief she wanted to hug him and possibly would have had Mr Julian not appeared and ordered Ivan to follow him along to the loading yard.

Instinctively, Scarlett had put her hand up to shield from sight the marks on her neck, but she wasn't quick enough, and Ivan brushed her hand aside. 'What's this?' he demanded.

Scarlett told him the agreed story.

Ivan shook his head. 'Think I was born yesterday?'

'Come on, man,' Mr Julian called impatiently.

'We'll talk later, and I'll want the truth. Someone did that to you, and I want to know who.' With that Ivan quickly followed Mr Julian.

Downstairs, Bessie also questioned the marks on her neck, looking highly sceptical as Scarlett explained, but there was little time to tarry on the truth of it before the duties of the household took over all else. Scarlett was summoned by Miss Hester and Millie by the sisters, Florrie's daughter a welcome sight as she slipped in the back door and put on an apron.

Much later a work weary Scarlett sat, hoping Ivan would appear for his supper before Miss Hester wanted her once again. Bessie had been called upstairs at this unusually late hour by Miss Matilda who'd earlier informed her she had a special guest coming for luncheon the next day, and Millie was attending Miss Emilia. So, Scarlett sat alone. Frustrated she went to the window and pulled back the curtain, hoping to see Ivan walking down the path. She longed to learn more about the run, and whether Ivan himself had seen Jack. Dropping the curtain, she paced the floor, glad at least for this time alone. If only she could escape and run up to Tamarisk, find out the truth behind Amos Cuddy's note, but knew she was incarcerated here until Sunday.

She waited for Ivan in vain. He was probably drinking down at the Jolly Sailor; Bessie disapproved but Ivan was his own man.

It was the next morning before Scarlett saw him, and then Bessie was always within earshot. After finishing his bread and dripping, Ivan announced as though making a general statement, that a fair few luggers were due in on the afternoons high tide, including Jacob Sweets. As he said the name, he looked directly at Scarlett, who took this to mean Jack was with him.

As he was drinking the last of his tea a knock came on the kitchen door and Millie, just coming downstairs, hastened to answer it.

'Tis Ivan I must see,' Scarlett heard a voice rasp, and immediately Ivan went to the door.

'What you doing here?' he growled, and pulled a lanky scruffily dressed boy inside.

'Oggie sent me; DeSalles is on the quay asking questions bout her.' He nodded in the direction of Scarlett. 'Has she got a follower and the likes. Wanting a name, he is. Got four red coats with him.'

'What utter nonsense,' Bessie snorted, hands on hips. 'A follower indeed. As if. Her knows the rules.'

Ivan ignored her. 'Tell Oggie I'm on my way.' The lad tipped his cap at Bessie and went off leaving a glum and clearly troubled Ivan.

He looked at Scarlett. 'He ain't wasted no time has he, maid. You don't leave this house under any circumstance.'

'I'll make sure of that,' Bessie tutted. 'What exactly are you on about, man?'

'Taint nothing for you to worry yur head about.' A curt nod, and with that, Ivan was gone out the door.

'You sure you ain't been up to nothing?' Bessie glared at Scarlett who shrugged her shoulders and tried to portray innocence.

'Course not,' she said in a confident voice.

'Well get busy, you two. There's work to be done.'

Scarlett and Millie, knowing what Bessie was like in a bad mood scuttled off without complaint.

It was indeed a demanding day; Bessie took an early night. When Ivan came in late for supper, Millie, knowing something was going on she didn't know about, was as nosey as ever and wanted to find out what it was. It took more than a little persuasion to leave them alone.

When finally she'd flounced off upstairs. Scarlett asked, 'Who's this DeSalles? You'm looked proper worried when you heard the name.'

'And rightly so, he's the overseer for the Kestrels, and far more besides. Right nasty bastard. With Mr Frances away on his honeymoon, it seems Adrian Kestrel's got him to do a bit of snooping as to whom you'm be seen with. He's wanting a name. That's what he told Oggie. "Poor bastard that be, if you'm looking for him," Oggie had replied. And DeSalles had spat, "Poor dead bastard indeed".'

Ivan sat opposite Scarlett. 'The truth, maid. What's been going on?'

Scarlett flushed red with embarrassment and felt she had no alternative but to but to tell Ivan the whole truth about what had happened at Penhallen. He looked shocked, then so angry for a moment he was rendered utterly speechless. Getting up, he walked to and fro shaking his head as finally Scarlett choked out how

Adrian Kestrel had attacked her, causing the marks on her neck.

Ivan stopped and stared hard at her. 'I knew you and Jack had taken a liking to each other but not that it had gone so far. I'm ashamed of the pair of you. Ashamed I am. Tom will strap Jack if he finds out, the sisters will dismiss you, and God only knows what will happen to Jack if DeSalles finds him. You are both in serious trouble, best hope there's no traitors hereabouts. Shouldn't be, but money can loosen tongues. Well, least I know what it's all about, and I ain't happy, Scarlett, far from it. I'll tell Oggie tis Jack DeSalles' is after, there's nowt more he needs to know. Disappointed I am in the pair of you. Anyhows, I'll get a boat out to warn Jacob not to come in. Best he make for Polperro.' With that Ivan snatched up his hat and was gone.

***

In the days following her confession to Ivan, Scarlett had never felt more miserable. It seemed the easy friendship she'd enjoyed with him was beyond repair. Towards Bessie and Millie his manner was as always, but his eyes never met Scarlett's. She knew he was angry, mightily disappointed at her and Jack's behaviour, had thought better of them than act with such recklessness at Penhallen. She wondered what he'd say to Jack, or if he'd seen him since Adrian Kestrel had sent DeSalles to West Looe. She dare not ask him like she could have in the past. At supper on Friday, a moment came when Millie was called away by the ringing of Miss Matilda's bell and Bessie's back was turned. Scarlett pulled Amos

Cuddy's note from her pocket and slid it across the table. Ivan glanced at it and slid it back.

'I shall go up to see my mother on Sunday,' Scarlett announced as Bessie eased herself down in her chair beside the fire.

'Tis an age since I saw her last,' Scarlett stated in a matter of fact voice, her eyes challenging Ivan's, who looked directly at her for the first time.

Ivan leaned across the table. 'Best you not. There's red coats making themselves at home on the quay, drinking at the Jolly Sailor, ignoring the chilly atmosphere their unwelcome presence brings, besides tis too dangerous. They'd like a young maid like you to have a bit of fun with.'

'Ivan!' Bessie exclaimed, 'I don't like your manner. Talking to Scarlett like she's some trollop, whatever's got into you, man?'

'I'd not wish to offend such a good a maid as she, that's for sure,' Ivan replied in a slow even voice.

'I should think not,' Bessie quipped and turned the conversation to more mundane gossip, like how the captain next door had purchased a sundial, above all things.

After another sleepless night and because of Ivan's attitude towards her, on Saturday Scarlett did her utmost to absent herself when Ivan came to the kitchen for his meals. Thus, Miss Emilia found her dusting in the dining room having herself just received a note stating that Mr Julian's old nanny Miss Dorrey had taken to her bed unwell.

'You, Penrose, go down at once and tell cook to prepare a basket of food to be taken up to Miss Dorrey. The poor soul is all on her own. Take it yourself,

Penrose, you'm better at conversation than young Millie. Stay with her a while, I won't visit her myself in case it's something catching.'

Scarlett nodded and immediately went downstairs and told cook.

'Well I ope it's nowt catching. Keep well away from her,' Bessie moaned as with little enthusiasm she set about filling a basket with bread, butter, tea, seed cake, ham, eggs and lots more besides.

'I know how that old biddy reports stuff back to them upstairs, so best keep her happy.'

Thankful that it had begun to drizzle, Scarlett put on her cloak and pulled up the hood. Miss Dorrey lived halfway up Well Lane and Scarlett set off with the heavy basket. The tide was up and the quay busy, the air thick with the smell of fish hastily loaded onto handcarts, fishwives were trudging back and forth with baskets on their backs, to begin filleting and salting. Wagons full of granite rumbled past her, heading to be loaded onto Mr Julian's old brigs.

Quickly Scarlett made her way out of Market Lane and walked towards the beginning of West Looe Hill. Oggie was seated on his bench as usual, he tipped his hat as she passed. He seemed to have acquired a scruffy old grey dog who lay beside him, its head resting on his lap. Through one of the small windows of the Jolly Sailor, Scarlett spied a glimpse of a red and hurried on past. As she neared Well Lane, she could see Tamarisk. Before she'd left Prospect House, she'd decided that after delivering the basket to Miss Dorrey she'd pay her mother a visit and find out what had made Amos write that note.

Halfway up Well Lane, Scarlett stopped to catch her breath. Millie had warned her Miss Dorrey was a stern old girl. She'd soon find out if this were true.

'Wouldn't let her look after a child of mine,' Millie'd stated, and Bessie hadn't disagreed with her. An apprehensive Scarlett knocked on the door of Bay Cottage, the smallest in a row of shabby cottages climbing up the steep lane. She lifted the latch and went inside, placed the basket on the table, then ventured up the narrow winding stairs to Miss Dorrey's heavily beamed bedchamber.

The poor old soul, as Miss Emilia had called her, was sat up in bed, a frilly lace bedcap almost obscuring her face. She looked towards Scarlett with a fierce stare.

'Miss Emilia has sent me with a basket for you, there's—' Scarlett began, but wasn't allowed to finish.

'What's in it then, quickly, girl, tell me.'

Scarlett began to recite the baskets contents.

'Is that all. I'd have expected more. Fetch me a cup of tea and slice of Bessie's seed cake if you please, and be quick about it.' Miss Dorrey raised her hand and shooed her away.

Scarlett was glad someone had lit a fire, making it easy for her to heat the water in the nearby pail. She had just set the tea tray and cut a large slice of cake when the vicar and his wife arrived. Mightily relieved, she laid out another two teacups, filled the teapot and cut more cake, thankful the ungrateful old woman had company so she was able to leave. She wouldn't tell Miss Emilia about the vicar and his wife calling.

Having packed the other things away, Scarlett asked Miss Dorrey if there was anything else she needed.

'A trifle more generous basket from my past employers wouldn't go amiss, gave that family the best years of my life, I did,' she groaned, shaking her head from side to side, setting the lace cap on her head all of a quiver. 'Now get off with you, I have all the company I need,' and she gave a toothless smile to the vicar.

Scarlett picked up the empty basket and almost ran from the cottage. At the bottom of Well Lane she peered out to make sure no strangers, or red coats were about, then ran up the hill and across to Tamarisk, annoyed that Annie Bishop's curtain twitched as she did so. Did that woman ever miss anything?

The front door of Tamarisk was bolted shut. Scarlett knocked and saw her mother's pale face peek from the window.

Once the bolts were drawn back and the door opened, Scarlett found herself clasped tight in her mother's embrace. As they parted, a tear ran down Jeanette's face. 'I've longed to see you, maid, so much to tell. You're here now, that's all that matters.'

'I got the note just as I was leaving to accompany Miss Hester to Moorswater, I haven't had a chance to come here since we got back, I was going to come tomorrow. What's happened?' Scarlett looked down at the flagstone floor, bewildered at the bundles of belongings stacked neatly inside the door.

'I've to be out by next week. Don't look so worried, I'm going to live in at Lanreath, the mistress's taken pity on me. Now sit, maid, I hope you've time for a cup of tea; highest quality tea bound for the poshest of houses, Amos brought it me.'

Scarlett pulled Amos's note from her pocket. 'Why was he so worried he wrote me this?'

Her mother pulled out a chair and sat down. 'He came here and found me in an awful state, I couldn't tell him why, he was worried for I couldn't stop crying. Bless the man, that's why he wrote you. And that's before what's happened since.'

Scarlett saw how fragile and ill her mother looked, felt glad she taken the chance to come here.

'Firstly tell me, missy, why did some man come calling yesterday, horrible long pale face he had, and piercing cold blue eyes, two redcoats he brought with him, demanded to come inside, wanted to know if you had a follower and the likes. Told him I scarce sees you and know nothing, warned me t'would be bad for me if I were lying. Why was he here?'

It was harder to explain why DeSalles had come calling on her mother than it had been to Ivan. The tea quite forgotten as Scarlett stumbled through the woeful tale, watching her mother's expression tell of her disbelief, disapproval and concern.

'And what if they find this Jack, I've heard mention of the Kestrel family, them powerful gentry, if they catch him, they'll hang him, and heaven forbid. You'm too.' Scarlett's mother put her hands to her face and sobbed. 'Whatever possessed you?'

'I love Jack. He was sailing away for heaven knows how long, he just wanted to see me, he knew his way round Penhallen and took a chance for us to be together before he sailed. What happened with Adrian Kestrel, it were an accident. Besides, God only knows what Kestrel would have done to me if Jack hadn't been there. Jack hit him because he was intruding into my room in the servants' quarters to ill use me, he deserved to be hit, but we never thought it would take the horrid man so long to recover, thought he'd just come to and think he'd been drinking. Besides, them's all loyal here in West Looe, none ull tell on a Jago.'

'And you'm sure of that are you?' Ivan's words had been much the same. 'Besides, if they don't find out who he is and you carry on as before, Jack'll get you with child. You'll be turned out, and you know the mistress at Lanreath expects the highest of morals in her household, t'would be impossible for me to take you in. T'would be the workhouse, Scarlett. For your own sake, I forbid you see him again. Promise me you'll not put yourself in danger and see this lad, t'would be foolhardy to do so. I know only too well it will be hard for you to accept this is how it must be, for there was someone I loved very much once.'

Jeanette began to weep. 'Tis all too much.'

Scarlett got up and put her arms round her mother's heaving shoulders and made her a promise she knew she wouldn't keep. Sitting back down, she pointed to Amos's note. Her mother took a deep breath. 'How long you got?' Jeanette asked, wiping away tears from her face.

'Time enough for you to tell me what's going on.'

'Amos don't know this, but Reader came here the night of the run, badly injured he was, been shot in the arm, threatened to tell everyone I'm married to an informer if I don't help him. He were in a mighty rage. His right arm was tore apart by a deep wound, the skin badly inflamed, he told me he'd dug the bullet out with a knife. I bathed the wound, put salve on it and bandaged it up. Already there were signs of a fever showing on his brow. After I was done and he'd drunk your father's best brandy, with a sneer of satisfaction he came up real close and told me Elijah had deserted him during the gun battle and fled off down the coast, most likely gone to his mistress in Charlestown. He watched my reaction with a look of triumph. "Ah! You didn't know about her did you?" Then getting up, unsteady on his feet, off he goes.'

'Did you know of this woman in Charlestown?' Scarlett asked and her mother shook her head.

'No, maid. I did not.'

The next night your father came here and I confronted him, he denied this other woman but I know him too well, could tell it twas true, told him to bugger off and go back to his fancy piece. If that's what you want, he says, and gathered up some of his belongings and left without a word. Two days later, Reader comes back, wants the wound redressed, stinking it was, and him red-faced with a high fever. For sure I'm thinking he'll lose the arm.'

Jeanette paused and Scarlett reached across and grasped her mother's hands.

'I done my best, then he says he's going back to Falmouth leaving Adam French as riding officer in these parts. I'm to tell Elijah his services are no longer required. I tells him I don't expect Elijah back. He tells me then the rent's paid til the last day of this quarter then I must be out. That's next week.'

It upset Scarlett more that her mother was moving away than that her father had deserted them.

'Amos is looking after me,' Jeanette reassured her. 'Tis you I'm worried about.'

'Adrian Kestrel will never have proof of who hit him,' Scarlett stated boldly. 'Never.'

'But them in high places don't always need proof, maid, that's what I'm afeard of.'

'There's one thing does worry me,' Scarlett confided. 'A long while ago I fancy Annie Bishop saw Jack hanging around waiting for me after I'd visited here. Do you think she'd tell?'

A slow smile spread across her mother's face. 'No, maid, she'll not tittle-tattle to the likes of them. One of them old gossips across the way told me that Annie, when she was much the age you are, had a follower, young handsome lad by the name of Alfred Sellens. Him and two others were ambushed by the revenue at Watergate, caught with a cartload of brandy tubs bound for Duloe. Shot her Alfred in the back and left him dead in the lane along with two other men from Looe. Never looked at anyone else did Annie. So she won't go telling.'

'Who'd have thought that. Just a nosey old spinster, tis all I thought of her,' Scarlett replied, unable to imagine Annie ever being young.

Jeanette shrugged her shoulders. 'I'm sure tis true, them gossips were young same time as her. Anyways, Scarlett, will you come and visit on Sunday? Twill no doubt be a long time afore we see each other again.'

Scarlett was torn, she so badly wanted to see Jack but couldn't fathom out how that could come about with Kestrel's men watching. How much did they know about her? She was surprised they hadn't called at Prospect House, no doubt thinking she'd be on her guard if they did. Sunday would be the last time she'd visit Tamarisk, visit her mother here, the cottage that had been her home.

'Of course I will.' Scarlett put on a brave smile. 'Though I'd better be off now before Bessie grumbles.' She saw tears in her mother's eyes and gave her a reassuring hug.

'Don't worry, I'll be fine, and careful, and you'm best off without Father, I know that. You deserve some happiness; I know how cruel and unkind he was to you.'

Picking up the basket, Scarlett left and walked quickly down the hill. As she passed the Jolly Sailor, a man in a long brown cloak was standing under the wooden canopy at the entrance. Scarlett looked straight ahead as she hurried by, she knew he was watching her, could feel his eyes boring into her back.

As she walked the rest of the way back to Prospect House, Scarlett kept looking back to see if she was being followed. She saw no one. Just this once, she was relieved to be home. As she entered the kitchen, Millie was topping off an apple pie and told her Ivan had been called upon to accompany Mr Julian to Truro and that they wouldn't be returning until late on Monday. Bessie watched her with a hint of suspicion.

'You'm been gone a long time. Hope that old biddy appreciated what was given her.' Scarlett hurriedly put on her apron and said nothing.

With Ivan gone the tension at mealtimes eased. Scarlett was quieter than usual; all she could wish was by some miracle, tomorrow she'd see Jack.

Of course, the next morning Miss Hester went down with a chill. Scarlett couldn't believe it. Being fussed over was something her charge greatly enjoyed, and short on patience, Scarlett had in the end to apologise and give Miss Hester a dramatic account of how her mother was going in service at Lanreath, was in a completely emotional state about leaving her home, and would be distraught if she didn't get to see her daughter before she left the next day.

'Millie has kindly offered to look after you. Please, Miss Hester, can I have my afternoon off?'

'I suppose so,' Miss Hester replied reluctantly, but bring me up one of Bessie's herbal possets first, then you can go, for they send me to sleep and I'll not need you.'

Scarlett was so relieved she was almost caught by Miss Emilia running down the stairs. A short while later and with Miss Hester's posset set on the table beside her bed, Scarlett escaped Prospect House. She borrowed Millie's old grey cloak with a deep hood and kept a watchful eye out for both red coats and the stranger in the long brown cloak who she assumed to be DeSalles.

As she neared the quay, she breathed in the salty smell of the sea. At low tide on a Sunday no fish were being unloaded, no squawking birds, no shouting, the quayside inhabited by only a few. But as she walked by some looked at her in a curious manner. Passing the Jolly Sailor, she glanced inside, there was no sign of the man or any red coats. Scarlett breathed a sigh of relief. Opposite, Oggie was sat on his bench with his dog.

'Careful as you go, miss,' he said softly as she passed.

Scarlett stopped. 'I'll be careful; if you see Jack, tell him I'm at Tamarisk.'

'Think he knows that already,' Oggie answered and sucked on his pipe, leaving Scarlett very thoughtful as she walked up the hill.

Although earlier than expected, Jeanette must have been watching for her, as the front door opened as she walked up the path.

'Come in, child.' The bundle of belongings beside the door inside had grown bigger, and for a brief moment Scarlett wondered if Amos could possibly fit it all onto his cart.

Jeanette saw her daughter looking. 'Don't worry, I'm all ready to leave, but—' She stopped mid-sentence, both looked up as overhead a floorboard creaked. 'Like I told you last time, I was young once and there was someone. So, when a certain young man came calling, I told him you could meet here today.'

Scarlett opened her mouth with surprise, impatient to be off upstairs, but Jeanette put her arm out and stopped her. 'Not so much as a loosening of your bodice, do you hear, missy? Keep the image of the work-house in your mind.' She withdrew her arm and Scarlett hugged her tightly before running upstairs.

Jack was standing in the doorway of her bedroom looking roguishly handsome and much tidier than usual. He stepped forward and Scarlett ran to him. With ease, he manoeuvred them inside her bedroom and slammed the door shut with his foot.

When finally they parted Jack grinned. 'So, I take it you're pleased to see me?'

Scarlett placed her hands on his white linen shirt and felt the beat of his heart. 'Of course I am.' She lay her head against his chest. 'I love you,' she whispered.

'And I you, my sweet,' Jack replied, kissing her again, then again and again. Only releasing her when a sound came from beyond the window, halting their passion. Scarlett crept over and cautiously peeped out from behind the flimsy curtain. It was just two boys chasing one another up the hill. When she turned back, Jack was lying on the thin mattress of her bed. He patted the mattress with his hand and Scarlett, smiling happily, obeyed his command and squeezed alongside him.

'No fretting, maid. I've had a good telling from your mother on how to behave, tis surprising I'm not scared just to kiss you.' He grinned, kissing her long and hard.

Downstairs, the sound of her mother sweeping the floor and moving around was all that could be heard.

'Wasn't it dangerous, you coming here with DeSalles about?'

'No, my precious, DeSalles and his red coats don't know hereabouts like I do. Climbed over a high wall and onto the Polgrove Estate meadows, then down and across to the back of here. I admire your mother's kindness for taking the chance for us too. I'll respect her wishes.'

Scarlett snuggled up to him. 'I feel content just lying here beside you, there will be other times for love-making.'

Jack smoothed her cheek and looked hard at the bruises which still showed on her neck. Scarlett watched as his face darkened and he sat up looking down at her. 'I saw Ivan and he told me how Kestrel attacked you, him and Jacob had to hold me back for I wanted to go straight to Moorswater and kill the bastard. Now that traitor DeSalles and the red coats are here doing his bidding, the lot need shooting.'

Scarlett drew herself up to sit beside him, placing a hand on his shoulder. She could feel his temper.

'I'm bloody mad Kestrel's done this to you, frustrated I can't get my hands on him.' He swept her hair aside and stared once again at the bruises. 'The man's an animal, you are never to go to Moorswater again. Whatever your bloody employer's wishes. I knew something was wrong when Ivan was waiting for us on the quay the other day. Climbed down into the boat he did before we'd even finished tying up. Never seen him so angry. I could tell he wasn't pleased with me either. Never had a cross word, we haven't. Gone to him in the past when I've had strife with Father. Furious he was with me; said I'd badly misused you. Said he'd lost his trust in me.'

Jack shook his head, and Scarlett could tell how Ivan's words had upset him.

'In the end Oggie came over to see what was going on, he intervened and reluctantly Ivan climbed back onto the quay, and Jacob insisted I went home with him. Once there I took a lot of persuading not to go to Moorswater. Proper stern he was, gave me a right talking to, said I could ruin any future you and me might have, and that we were in bother enough.'

Scarlett felt really sad that Jack's friendship with Ivan, like her own was being destroyed by what had happened. She lay her head against Jack's shoulder. 'I think Ivan's frightened for us. I told him Kestrel never saw you, there'd be no proof twas you, but mother says them that's gentry don't need any.'

'She could be right.' Jack looked at Scarlett and smiled. 'I think Ivan's really fond of you, bit like a daughter, and I'm the scoundrel who's stolen your innocence.'

Scarlett giggled and snuggled close beside him, she ran her fingers through the tumble of black curls on the pillow beside her, brushing them back so she could see more of Jack's handsome face. 'Love you,' she whispered.

'And I you.'

It was a while later Scarlett's mother called up to her. Startled, Scarlett leapt up, tidied her hair and went downstairs.

'I hope your remembering what I said,' Jeanette remarked looking at her daughter with suspicion.

'Of course,' Scarlett replied.

Jeanette sighed. 'I've no choice but to trust you, anyways I'm off over to the biddies across the road and to Lily's next door to say my goodbyes.' She made her way towards the front door. 'There's some broth in the pot, just needs hanging on the hook a while to warm, but you'm two welcome to it. Promise you won't go until I've come back, will you.'

'I'll be here,' Scarlett told her, feeling a guilty blush warm upon her cheeks and on impulse ran over and gave her mother a hug.

Scarlett went back upstairs.

'Have I to go?' Jack asked, still lying on the bed.

'No mother's off to say her goodbyes, there's broth if we want it.'

'Come here then, you.' Scarlett obeyed and lay down beside him, then sat up and Jack rolled onto his back and began to stroke the nape of her neck.

'What's the matter, sweet.'

'Tis nothing, just mother reminding me what she said about how I could end up in the workhouse if I got with child.'

'Look at me, don't be daft. That'll never happen. I've been careful this long; besides I want to marry you. Will ask your mother proper like when all this trouble is over.'

'You're sure?'

'Of course I am.'

Scarlett slipped into his arms her face glowing with joy. 'I love you, Jack Jago.'

'And I love you, Scarlett Penrose. Tis a promise you must make though, and that is to stop worrying about me.'

'I'll try, I promise. I admit I was worried about you, how you fared the night of the run,' she told him. 'Ivan told me you got back safe, I was glad to hear that, but wanted to know more.'

Jack hitched himself up on one elbow. 'See what I mean. What do you want to know? If it's details you want, I'll tell you. Tis mundane stuff. Twas just a normal run. Well that's until the final boat was being rowed off the from beach to the waiting ship. The crew had a passenger, a man called Skurren, just released from Bodmin Gaol.'

Scarlett had heard that name before.

'Seems he'd been paid to leave these shores, short of killing him it was the best way to silence him. Somehows two of the revenue had made their way unseen along the coast. Hid amongst the rocks. They fired at the boat and Skurren fired back, I was told this by old Irish one of the tub men. It seems one of the revenue hiding amongst the rocks was hit, twas dark but Irish reckons it could have been Reader himself. Anyhows his companion never waited around; Irish heard the sound of hoofbeats right quick afterwards. Our boat got away with all unscathed.'

Scarlett felt her heart begin to thump, she shivered. Guilt rose in her like a demon of disgust. Of course, she already knew it was Reader that had been shot, and hated the dark secrets of her life Jack must never know.

Hoping her voice wouldn't falter she asked, 'How did you fare, being a decoy?'

'Oh that.' He grinned. 'That was successful, we stayed safely hidden and watched a whole troop of red coats pass by in the wrong direction.'

Scarlett's heartbeats slowed, she leaned forward and kissed Jack. 'Tis only that I love you. I worry.'

'I know.' Jack kissed her forehead.

With the broth downstairs quite forgotten, they made the most of the time they had alone. In the end it was Jack who said, 'I'd better go now, you and your mother need time alone to say your goodbyes.' He took Scarlett's hand and led her downstairs; there she pulled the curtains and lit a candle on the table.

'When shall I see you again?' she asked.

Jack wrapped her in his arms. 'As soon as it's safe, maid. Oggie told me someone in the Fisherman's Arms overheard DeSalles telling the captain of the red coats he felt badly used, sent here to find a nobody by Mr Adrian. Couldn't wait til Mr Francis got back from honeymoon so he could get back to his more important assignments. Hopefully, if that's true, then we'll see the last of him. For now, don't go fretting, but we must be careful. Say my goodbyes to your mother. We had this chance today because of her. Quench the candle and wait awhile afore you light it.' There was time for one long last kiss, then he was gone.

The cottage was still in darkness when Jeanette returned. Scarlett having sat in the settle beside the glowing fire waiting for her mother. Together they ate the broth. Each contemplating what lay ahead in the week to come.

'I like your Jack,' Jeanette told her daughter once the dishes were done and Scarlett had helped place a few more items ready by the door for Amos. 'Promise me, whilst that horrible man with the long face is about, you'll keep safely indoors out of harm's way.'

'Once I'm back at Prospect House, I'll not have a chance to be out, so don't worry about me,' Scarlett replied, sensing how anxious her mother was. 'I'm so glad you like Jack, that pleases me greatly. And give my love to Amos, I know he'll take care of you.'

They clung together each not wanting to part from the other until finally Scarlett ran down West Looe Hill with tears in her eyes.

Chapter 15

The following day, Scarlett couldn't help but wonder how things were at Tamarisk. By the time Millie took the sisters afternoon tea tray up, she thought her mother and Amos must be well on their way to Lanreath. A surge of loneliness overwhelmed her. She'd told Bessie and Millie about her mother's move and they had tried to offer her comfort. But the feeling of how much she'd miss her mother being close by stayed with her. Even Miss Hester's most childish of tantrums failed to raise any response from her.

On the following Wednesday, Scarlett was dusting in the drawing room when she saw from the window Mr Julian striding along the quay towards Prospect House. She'd paused, duster in hand and gasped, for walking beside him was her Jack.

'What is it girl?' Miss Emilia grumbled. 'Why are you gawping out the window, get on with your work, I can see the dust from here.'

'Sorry, miss,' Scarlett mumbled and got on with her work, still keeping an eye on the progress of the two men now nearing the front steps.

She heard the front door open and close, then voices coming up the stairs. Mr Julian opened the drawing room door and immediately Miss Matilda dismissed her with a flick of the hand.

Scarlett quickly made her way out of the room not daring to look at Jack, though she did feel his hand briefly touch hers in passing. Having closed the door, she hesitated, torn between eavesdropping or going on her way downstairs to the kitchen. She chose the latter, knowing if she was caught eavesdropping, she'd immediately be dismissed. Why was Jack there?

A short while later, Scarlett was so absorbed in wondering what was going on upstairs she physically jumped when the drawing room bell jangled. Millie ran up to answer it and came back to say the sisters wanted a tea tray sent up immediately. *What on earth was her Jack doing upstairs drinking tea with the sisters and Mr Julian?*

As Bessie turned away to fetch something from the cupboard. Millie mouthed the words, 'What's your Jack doing here?' Scarlett shook her head and shrugged her shoulders. An observant Bessie turned and caught the look that passed between the two, and for the second time that day Scarlett was told to get on with her work.

Millie set out the china and filled the teapot with hot water. As she replaced the copper kettle over the fire, Scarlett firmly took hold the handles each end of the tray. 'I'll take this,' she asserted and was gone up the stairs before Bessie could question it.

Having knocked, she entered the drawing room and all conversation ceased. The sisters were seated in their favourite chairs with Mr Julian and Jack standing a little way off, each dressed in such different apparel. One so immaculately smart and Jack with his mop of unruly black curls and in his usual rather untidy clothes. Scarlett couldn't tell by any of their faces or the atmosphere within the room whether Jack was in some sort of trouble or not.

A while later the bell rang again, and Millie flew up the stairs. Scarlett was so cross, she'd wanted to go, and made a face at Millie when she returned from escorting Mr Julian and Jack from the house.

'I wanted to answer the bell,' Scarlett remonstrated in a low voice, so Bessie didn't hear.

'Sorry,' Millie snapped back at her. Later tempers having cooled and when Bessie was out of the way, Millie did tell Scarlett that all seemed well between Mr Julian and Jack, and that as Jack had set off down the front steps, he had turned and given her a mischievous wink. Which of course made Millie's day. Scarlett smiled at her; all was forgiven. But still she couldn't fathom why Jack had been there.

When Bessie took her afternoon nap, Millie was ready for a bit of gossip and asked Scarlett again what was going on. It took a long time before Scarlett finally convinced her she didn't know, the two of them sat in silence then embroidering Miss Emilia's initials on new delicate lace-edged handkerchiefs. Pondering the mystery.

The rest of the week passed slowly by, each day seemingly longer than usual. Just before noon the following Sunday, Ruth knocked on the back door of Prospect House. Scarlett was surprised and pleased to see her, quickly fetching her cloak and joining her friend outside.

'Where's Jack?' she asked as they walked down the path.

'Away at sea.'

'For how long?' Scarlett asked. 'The *Sunrising*'s still moored up, I look out my window every morning. Who's he sailed with?'

'He knew you'd be disappointed, but tis for the best.'

Scarlett looked away close tears.

'Tis something happened earlier in the week, made it best he go. So, when he were asked by Nicholas Bradley himself to be part of the crew of the *Pelican* he had no choice. Best to get out of harm's way, Father told him. Tis a good ship, the *Pelican*, and its capt'n, even I've heard of him, pays his crew well, tis him who brings in all types of fripperies our betters like to own.'

Arm in arm they walked up the steps leading to the top of Horse Lane and sat together on the wall just as they'd done so many times before.

'Come on, don't look so gloomy,' Ruth coaxed. 'I'm sure you see more of Jack than I do my Sam, well leastways when the *Black Diamond*'s sailing normal. Crew can't wait for Mr Francis to return; he'll sort out what's happening. The men are restless, their money all spent and stuck here in Looe, not Fowey where their homes are. Tis lovely having Sam here, but we've a need to be saving and there's been no word from Captain Ferris as to when the *Black Diamond* will take to sea.'

Scarlett sat moodily watching two boats nearly collide with each other on the river. One had a ripped and tattered sail, which flapped madly against the mast in the wind. There was an angry exchange of words, the voices just a faint murmur carried on the wind.

'That there's a friend of Sam's.' Ruth pointed laughing at a large man waving his fist. 'He'd not want me to tell Sam about his near collision.'

'When did you see Jack?' Scarlett queried, 'and what happened earlier in the week?'

'One of the kitchen maids came and found me said my brother was come to the servants' gate. First thing he says is, I'm to tell you not to worry but he came face to face with DeSalles and two of his red coats on the quay. The red coats questioned him. It was strange, like they was really looking just for him. Right aggressive bastards they were, put the tip of a bayonet under his chin, said they had heard he'd been seen with you. That's why the next day, pressured by the captain of the *Pelican*, Jack signed on as crew.'

Scarlett sighed. 'Well, least he'll be safe at sea.'

'Love makes us vulnerable; I'd be dismissed if her Ladyship knew about Sam,' Ruth stated, looking crest-fallen.

Scarlett turned and smiled at her friend, caught up in her own world she'd forgotten others have problems too. Ruth nudged her arm. 'But would you know, Jack and Sam have spoken for the first time since they fought on the quay.'

'What!' Scarlett sat open-mouthed with shock, she clutched Ruth's arm. 'Tell me more.'

An old woman with a noisy handcart trundled past. A yapping dog at her feet.

'I never thought they'd speak again.'

Ruth shrugged her shoulders. 'Well they have.'

'The day after Jack had his confrontation with the red coats and before the *Pelican* sailed, both were on the quay when DeSalles came back. Twelve men were with him, himself all important on a huge black horse, riding down onto the quay from West Looe Hill they came, full of swagger, rifles over their shoulders. I overheard Jenna telling this to the new skivvy Walters, who I don't trust, I really don't trust. Sneaky looking, she is, always whispering, and I heard from Mary Tap one of the parlour maids that Walters fancies our Jack, seen him on the quay and outside our cottage, knows he's my brother.'

Ruth saw the look of dismay on Scarlett's face. 'Don't you worry! Our Jack's only got eyes for you.'

'I'll try not to; I know he loves me.'

'Well, I'll get on and tell you what happened next with DeSalles. Apparently, he dismounted and together with his men he began walking purposefully between the nets and handcarts towards where the *Pelican* and the *Black Diamond* were tied up. My Sam knew DeSalles was looking for your follower, it being common talk, knew Jack had been questioned. He knew the loyalty held by the West Looe men and women; he was after all a West Looe boy by birth. From the crow's nest of the *Black Diamond* he looked down on the quay and instinctively, when he spotted Jack, whistled a warning to him, same as he'd done when they were boys, and like to be in trouble. As DeSalles came closer, Sam climbed down to the deck and walked down the gang-plank, he threw a sack of provisions Jack's way, signalling him to follow him on board. By the time DeSalles ordered his men to search the *Black Diamond*, Sam had Jack safely hidden in one of the hidey holes where contraband's stored. Whether DeSalles was specifically looking for our Jack or not we don't know.'

Deep in thought, Scarlett turned away and looked towards the entrance of the harbour, Ruth did likewise and the two sat for a while each contemplating their own woes.

Scarlett slowly stood up and smoothed down her skirts, wrapping her cloak close round her in the cooling breeze. 'I'm frightened,' she admitted. 'There's something else I must ask, did Jack say anything about visiting

Prospect House? I saw him there, bold as brass taking tea with Mr Julian and the sisters, didn't half startle me I can tell you.'

Ruth giggled. 'Yes, he began to tell me about that, said you'm couldn't have look more shocked if he were a ghost. He were gabbling on twas something to do with old Isaac's, you know the ancient little man who works for your Mr Julian in the yard aside the quay. Jack was about to tell me more when the servants' gate opened and I got called in by Jenna. I can't wait to get away from Polgrove and hopefully be employed as something else, not a skivvy like I am now.' She scowled.

'Her Ladyship couldn't be bothered to walk from one side of her boudoir across to the window seat to pick up her embroidery, sent for me to do it. Besides, I'm still hated below stairs because Sir Geoffrey took me on as trainee lady's maid. They never let me forget their displeasure about that, put a few noses out of joint that did, especially po-faced Jenna.' Ruth stopped when she saw Scarlett's eyes were wet with tears.

'Tis a proper pair we are,' Scarlett sobbed into her handkerchief, 'the both of us unhappy.'

'Things will change for the better, honestly they will,' Ruth assured her.

'This is just for now; we must believe in the future.'

Soon afterwards Ruth had to leave and return to her demanding mistress. Scarlett walked with her up the steps to the servants' entrance, kissing her goodbye then slowly walked back down to the quay, it felt wonderful to be outside the confines of Prospect House. There the almost pulled-to curtains and perpetual half-light had got her down of late. And Miss Emilia had been thumping away on the organ daily, giving her a headache. As for Miss Hester she was forever going out either in the company of Lizzy Polgrove or Maria Penhallen, then grumbling about their gruesome governesses who had to chaperone them. She talked endlessly on the subject even during her lessons. It was evident to Scarlett that Miss Hester was jealous of both her friends, for no matter how hard she may try to be like them, her father was not gentry.

Twas dusk before reluctantly Scarlett returned to Prospect House, entering just as Ivan rose to leave. The tension between them was lessening a little and Ivan nodded a greeting to her as he passed.

'Tis said Mr Francis is returning tomorrow,' Millie whispered to Scarlett as she took off her cloak.

'That's no interest to Scarlett,' Bessie huffed pouring Scarlett a welcome cup of tea. 'T'wont make no difference to none here.'

Millie made a face behind Bessie's back, and Scarlett drank her tea with relish.

Each day for Scarlett was filled with the same chores and tedium as the one before. Even Sundays held no sense of approaching joy, for Scarlett had no idea how long a voyage the *Pelican* had undertaken. Each Sunday she would take herself down to the quay, knowing full well that if Jack was home, he would have got word to her, possibly through Ivan who by now had forgiven them, she hoped.

It was on a Tuesday morning as Scarlett sat with Millie polishing the silver that there was a knocking on the front door. Miss Hester herself ran downstairs to open it just as Scarlett was about to do so. There on the doorstep stood Miss Lizzy, Miss Maria and a harassed looking governess, red-faced and quite out of breath.

'It is quite impossible, I cannot walk up the uneven lane, it is all too much, you cannot go for I am in no state to accompany you.'

Miss Hester stood aside, and her friends entered the hall, the governess remained on the doorstep still berating Miss Maria in a voice so shrill Mr Julian came out of the small anti room beside the front door looking most displeased.

'But I want to go, and you must accompany us.' Miss Maria pouted then cast her eye over Scarlett. 'What do you think, Hester? This servant of yours, she looks up to the task required, can she accompany us.? But not wearing that dowdy grey uniform, surely she has something more fitting.'

Miss Hester looked at her father who, wanting peace and quiet, nodded his agreement.

'Follow my daughter up to the music room if you will, ladies, I have a letter to write and desire not to be disturbed, neither will my aunts,' he said sternly.

Miss Hester led her friends upstairs whilst Scarlett watched as the governess having been dismissed scurried away. She closed the front door then ran up to her attic room to change into her dark blue uniform, placing a little blue bonnet, which had been her mother's, on the back of her head.

Below in the music room the girls were impatiently waiting. Millie curious as to what had become of Scarlett came up from the kitchen just as they were all about to leave, surprised to see Scarlett in her change of uniform opening the front door.

After she'd ushered the girls outside, Scarlett quickly told Millie what was happening. Millie scowled knowing the whole table of silverware to be cleaned was now solely her task. She shook her head wondering what Bessie would have to say about all this.

The three young ladies linked arms and chattered away happily as they daintily walked along the cobbles in their pretty clothes and unsuitable shoes. They reached the quay where the fishermen were unloading their catch. The luggers were tied alongside one another and fish baskets were being passed across man to man onto the quay. Most took scarce notice of the girls, anxious to get their load away to the fishwives, twas here the stench of fish was strongest. Delicate handkerchiefs were now being held up against her charges' noses as they made a detour round to the very widest part of the quay.

Once past the Jolly Sailor, they had almost reached the rugged path leading up to Hannafore. In doing so they had to walk closer to the river, for the quay was narrower here. Several schooners were moored up, their ropes creaking and hulls knocking one against the another on the high tide. Scarlett searched the ships to see if by chance any bore the name *Pelican* but none did. One large ship was moored alone at the very end of the quay. Scarlett knew only too well the name of that ship.

'Come along, girls, don't dawdle, the air will be much fresher when we reach the top of the path,' Scarlett urged, wanting to quickly hurry on past the *Black Diamond* and climb up to Hannafore, but it was too late. Standing on the deck stood Adrian Kestrel. Miss Maria saw him and giggled, her friends did likewise. With a jaunty step, Adrian Kestrel made his way down the gangplank towards them.

'You mustn't talk to that man; your father and aunts would not approve,' Scarlett warned.

'Fiddle to them,' Miss Lizzy exclaimed. 'He was most charming to us when we met at Penhallen and at another ball we attended.'

Miss Hester turned and glared at Scarlett. 'Be quiet, Penrose, know your place.'

Elegantly dressed as always, Kestrel bowed to the girls. 'What a wonderful sight you make, all three of you, beauties the eye is pleased to rest on.'

'Sir, you promised when last we met you would show us around one of your ships,' Miss Maria said sweetly.

'And you would hold me to such a promise would you?' He smiled. 'Then I would be happy to offer you some refreshment aboard the *Black Diamond*. Come, follow me.'

'No, they cannot, sir. I forbid it,' Scarlett shouted at the top of her voice, and Miss Hester looked back at her red-faced with fury.

Adrian Kestrel pulled a sad face. 'Is that so,' he replied in a slow and even tone.

'Take no notice of this non-person,' Miss Maria quipped. 'We don't need a chaperone, but alas, unfortunately she will have to accompany us.'

Adrian Kestrel looked at Scarlett and gave her a malevolent smile. 'That could be very fortuitous,' he smirked.

In a very solicitous manner, he helped the three young ladies up the sloping gangplank and onto the ship, holding each with much care. He did not do so for Scarlett. Instead she carefully made her own way up. As she did so, she glanced at another ship, newly returned to the harbour. A figure stood on the bow of her deck, a coil of rope in hand ready to throw ashore. For just a moment he looked up and Scarlett could have sworn it was Jack. She looked down for a brief second as her foot faltered as she stepped onto the *Black Diamond.* When she looked again, the figure had gone, but emblazoned across the stern of the ship was the name *Pelican.*

'Take this individual below deck,' Kestrel shouted across to an unkempt member of the crew, 'she'll not be needed as I show the young ladies around.'

Scarlett opened her mouth to protest, but the man a little unsteady on his feet had already stepped forward and stood beside her.

This way,' he ordered, spitting over the side of the ship as he did so. And taking Scarlett's arm began to lead her away.

'This is all wrong, Miss Hester I beg you, tell him to let me go,' she cried out in vain and tried to hang back, twisting her head to see the girls' expressions at her being manhandled so, but they were once again enthralled with whatever Adrian Kestrel was telling them. The stairway little more than a ladder, she had to descend backwards holding tight each side. Then with a none too gentle prod to her back, she was urged forward down a narrow corridor to a small salon. It was plainly furnished in damson red with crude seating in a semi-circle of cushions on benches built into the stern of the ship, above these were four small panes of glass. A large oval table stood in the centre with a raised brass ring around the outside. None of the walls were without dark wooden cupboards. All had locks on them. The air was filled with the pungent smell of rum and tobacco. A clock struck the hour and made her jump. She sat down, and the unkempt crewman stood in the doorway, looking her up and down in a manner Scarlett found insulting.

After a what seemed an eternity the three girls, pink cheeked with excitement, came to join her accompanied by Adrian Kestrel. 'So, you can see why this is by far the most excellent of ships in this harbour or anywhere else in Cornwall for that matter,' he boasted. 'Now I just want to have a word with your maid.'

'Why ever so, sir?' Miss Maria simpered.

'Tis just a little matter, don't worry yourselves.'

Scarlett feared what was to come. She shuddered remembering his brutal cruelty, breathed deeply whilst outwardly trying to stay calm. As slowly she rose to follow him, a thump came on the deck above. 'Stay here, Mr Chater, whilst I see what that noise was.'

He came back almost at once. 'It seems we have an intruder on board, no matter, my men will find him, seek him out and punish him. Meanwhile, I have a change of plan, let me introduce you lovely ladies to a tot of rum.'

The girls all looked at Scarlett, suddenly they looked very young and vulnerable as in truth they were. Scarlett immediately retorted, 'My charges most certainly will not be partaking of rum, sir.'

'Oh! You do tend to spoil things. Come, ladies, just a little drop surely can do no harm.' He produced a key from his blue satin waistcoat and opened one of the many cupboards, exposing a small barrel, he opened the tap and poured a little of its contents into three small glasses. Handing one each to the young ladies. Suddenly the sound of a scuffle and raised voices came from above.

'Mr Chater, remain here whilst I go and find out what the devil's going on.' Chater stood on guard his back to the door frame, one arm stretched out forming a barrier.

It was now that Scarlett saw her chance to find out exactly what was going on, and catching Chater off guard, she ran beneath his arm and up on deck, horrified to see two of the crew holding a struggling Jack as Kestrel took aim and punched him in the stomach, causing Jack to double up in pain.

As Jack staggered and slowly stood up, Kestrel struck him again. 'What are you doing here?' he demanded.

'You.' He pointed to one of the crew. 'Make sure she don't go making a noise so as them on the quay can hear.' The dirty brute came and stood behind Scarlett placing his rough hand across her mouth.

'Draw in the gangplank, set the sails, we leave immediately,' he ordered.

'Tis only the three of us and the cabin boy on board, master,' one of the men exclaimed.

'You a seaman or not?' Kestrel replied. 'Do as I say.'

The brute who held Scarlett forced her over towards Adrian Kestrel. 'Do you know this man?' Kestrel shouted pointing at Jack, his face so close to Scarlett's that his saliva dripped down her face.

'No, sir, I do not.'

'Liar.' A girl emerged from behind the forward mast. Scarlett recognised her; she'd once worked in the capt'ns house next door. Her name was Joycie. She'd been dismissed for thieving. But she had seen her with Jack several times in Market Lane.

'She knows him alright, sir,' she said with glee. 'More an knows him, proper like knows him, sweethearts they be.'

'Is that so!' Adrian Kestrel exclaimed, and cast an evil look towards Jack.

'Jake Pensilva, get your harpy off my ship, then take the wheel,' Kestrel bellowed, and Joycie was dragged away protesting, tipped onto the quay face down as a furious Kestrel hauled the gangplank aboard before her feet had touched the quay.

He turned to look at Scarlett. 'Do you know her.'

'No,' Scarlett lied.

'Sweethearts, she said you be. But do I believe her or you? Take another look.' He grabbed Scarlett, telling the man who held her to go help the others set the sails. Roughly, he pushed her towards Jack. Then abruptly jerked her back.

'I do not know him,' Scarlett protested, and Kestrel turned his attention to Jack.

'I asked you once, now I'll ask again, what are you doing on my ship? Thief are you, or come for some other purpose. Seen her come on board was it?'

'Come looking to see if you'm in need of crew, that's all,' Jack replied, holding his head high and looking directly at Adrian Kestrel.

'I don't believe you. I think it was you that night at Penhallen, you were with this strumpet, it was you who viciously attacked me. Handy with your fists, are you?'

Mr Chater emerged from below deck.

'I've had to lock the young ladies in, sir. Told um twas for their own safety but they ain't too happy.' And from below deck came the sound of frantic banging and cries for help, their voices becoming ever more hysterical. Kestrel outraged shouted at the young cabin boy to get below and shut them up.

'Them's too important to leave there, best we get um off the ship, sir,' Mr Chater interceded. He took over the wheel from Jake who clambered up the rigging, relieved to hand the responsibility over to the more experienced seaman.

'Don't be insubordinate, man,' Kestrel shouted at Mr Chater. 'I couldn't care less who they bloody are. Tis what was done to me that night that's important. I'll take the wheel, tie these two to the mast, then cast off and help set the sails.'

On the quay, a bruised Joycie hobbled away, all eyes followed her, amid saucy remarks and jesting. With the tide high, none who looked upwards could see beyond the wooden hull of the *Black Diamond*.

Quickly the ship slipped her moorings, and helped by the ebbing tide, was soon passing out through the mouth of the river, buffeted by the force of a now strong south-easterly wind. The ship rolled with the swell of the sea.

And all the while Scarlett and Jack struggled to free themselves, as the *Black Diamond* went plunging on. Suddenly a powerful gust of wind caught Adrian Kestrel by surprise and tore the ship's wheel from his hands. Swearing and uttering obscenities, he sought to gain control as the wheel span this way and that, completely out of control.

Whilst he struggled with the wheel, little by little the rope that bound Jack and Scarlett to the mast began to loosen, but still neither was completely free.

The *Black Diamond* began to drift perilously close to Looe Island. Even after Mr Chater joined what crew there was, it was impossible to unfurl the sails quickly enough to steer the ship out of danger. One of the crew screamed out in agony and looking up, Scarlett saw the ropes of a large canvas sail had slipped from his grasp, tearing skin from his hands. The wind caught the heavy canvas and part of it thudded down onto the deck wrapping itself round Adrian Kestrel's feet, dragging him along with it til it stopped.

Mr Chater quickly climbed down the mast to help him, but Adrian Kestrel was out cold. Leaving him where he lay, he took the ship's wheel desperately trying to pull her round and set a course away from the rocks but with lack of sail this was impossible. The *Black Diamond* dipped and rolled wildly on with Mr Chater shouting orders.

Scarlett, numbed by fear and icy sea spray, knew if they hit the rocks around the island they could all drown, they were at the mercy of the increasingly strong winds and buffeting sea, so close to the island she could see the hermit's cave.

'We've got to get off the ship,' Jack yelled to Scarlett as her hair whipped round her face, momentarily blinding him from her sight.

'What if we can't?' she cried back.'

'We will,' Jack shouted. 'We have to.'

For a moment the squally wind lessened, and both Scarlett and Jack realised the girls cries for help had ceased. The young cabin boy appeared at the top of the stairway. Mr Chater yelled at him to help set the sails and it was as the young lad climbed the rigging that Miss Hester and her companions tentatively appeared on deck, dishevelled and sobbing. Just then the wind increased, the ship rolled, drenching the girls in sea spray. Barely able to stay on their feet, they screamed in absolute terror holding on to each other and the rail running along the side of the ship. Then very bravely, Miss Maria motioned the others to stay where they were and with her dainty shoes slipping precariously on the wet decking, edged herself closer to Scarlett. She let go of the ship's rail and made her way haphazardly over to the mast where Jack and Scarlett were bound. Quickly with nimble fingers, she freed them.

'Thank you,' Scarlett yelled as the wind increased in ferocity once more.

The bow of the *Black Diamond* dipped heavily and lurched to starboard. Bravely, Maria succeeded in getting herself safely back to join her two friends. Then all three girls screamed, absolutely terrified as they were engulfed by a huge wave.

'Hold tight,' Jack shouted across to them. He held onto both Scarlett and the rigging that had fallen down and was still attached to the mast, then as the ship righted herself, he took a chance and taking Scarlett's hand in his they managed to join the others. Another huge wave struck the *Black Diamond* and all the loose gear on deck slid wildly across the ship once more, even the coils of heavy thick rope.

'She'm heading for the rocks, Mr Chater,' one of the crew called down and quickly descended the rigging. He went over and unwrapped the sail from Adrian Kestrel's feet and propped him up unceremoniously against the side of the ship.

'Not if I can help it,' Mr Chater replied. It was then he saw that Jack and Scarlett were free.

'Leave Kestrel, take the wheel, man, try and steer us out of danger.'

He made his way over to Jack and Scarlett, unsteady on his feet as the ship continued to plunge on.

'I don't want no trouble. I got no gripe with you. As for him—' he looked over at Adrian Kestrel '—he'll come to before long. Tis best you get off the ship before he stirs, or the ship goes down. Kestrel's got his pistols on him, daren't try and take um off him in case he suddenly wakes; who knows what the mad bastard might do.'

Going back to the wheel he secured it with rope as best he could. 'Follow me, and careful does it. In the stern there's a couple of rowing boats.' He called up to his crew mate whose sore hands were now bound in dirty rags. 'Crago, all you crew. Get down on deck, she'm past saving.'

Slowly Scarlett and her charges shuffled towards the stern of the ship. Scarlett did her best to calm the girls whilst Mr Chater, Jack and the cabin boy untied one of the boats, and by ropes fastened to bow and stern, hurriedly lowered it into the turbulent sea. A rope ladder was thrown over. The young ladies recoiled in horror at the thought of climbing down into the violently bobbing boat below.

'It's quite impossible, Penrose,' Lizzy Polgrove screamed shrilly, 'I can't do it.'

'Tis a must, for nowt can save the *Black Diamond* from the rocks,' Mr Chater told her firmly, 'there be no other way.'

Miss Hester took Scarlett's hand as Mr Chater continued. 'Come on now, one by one, we'll help you; you'm not slip and fall. You, young Billy,' he called to the cabin boy, 'climb down and help steady the boat, go ashore with um take the second set of oars.'

Jack stood on the ladder and encouraged the terrified girls as they were lifted over the stern of the boat. Mr Chater held each one steady til they were safe in Jack's grasp and he helped them down the rope ladder. One by one, young Billy reached up and guided them into the boat. Scarlett watched as the boat rose and fell with the swell of the sea. She was last to be lifted up and take hold of the twisting ladder. As Jack put his arm round her waist, Mr Chater told him, 'Be sure to tell who must know what's happened here, you was helped by us crew, that this was none of our doings.'

Jack nodded. 'What about—?'

'Don't worry about us or him. He'll be more concerned about his precious ship, we'll get off her afore she hits and take the bastard with us,' he stated, turning his back on them and struggling back along the deck.

Jack heaved on the oars with all the strength he could muster and Billy, though small and very thin, proved to have more strength than could be imagined. Scarlett tried to comfort the sobbing girls. Drenched through, traumatised and with teeth chattering with cold, they clung together. The stretch of sea between them and the safety of the harbour seemed endless.

As Jack and Billy battled on towards the mouth of the river, a loud splintering sound could be heard as the hull of the *Black Diamond* scraped against the rocks. All heads turned in her direction and watched as she began to list badly. By the time they reached the mouth of the river and passed through into the safe waters of the harbour, the *Black Diamond'* s sails had dipped into the sea, and her hull come to rest on Looe island's rocky shore.

'They'll have to swim for it,' Jack spluttered, exhausted and out of breath, each pull on the oars a struggle. The girls sat huddled together clutching each other looking scared and very young.

'We'll soon be safe ashore,' Scarlett shouted across the boat, trying to reassure them.

Now they could hear the tolling bell of St Nicholas Church, the folks ashore knew something was very wrong, had seen the *Black Diamond* in distress. People began to gather on both the east and west side of the river. In West Looe the crowd ran along the quay keeping pace with the boat, watching as Jack and the cabin boy rowed on exhausted until they reached the steps leading down to the river outside Prospect House.

They stood aside as one by one Scarlett helped Miss Hester, Miss Maria and Miss Lizzy up the steep steeps, their wet skirts heavy and dragging behind them. Jack and Billy followed after securing the boat. As Jack stepped onto the quay, he reached for Scarlett and hugged her to him forgetting all protocol with the relief of getting safely back. This as the front door of Prospect House flew open and Mr Julian ran towards them, his distraught daughter falling into his arms sobbing.

'Inside now, away from these gawpers,' he barked. 'What the hell has happened?' He glanced at Jack and gave him a puzzled look of recognition.

Scarlett held tight the hands of the other two girls and followed quickly behind them. She saw Mary Jago pushing through the crowd just before Mr Julian himself slammed shut the front door. As he ushered his daughter and her friends upstairs to the drawing room, he looked back at Scarlett, Jack and Billy in the hall.

'You two.' He pointed a finger at Jack and then Billy. 'Take yourselves down to the kitchen and wait there. Tell cook you'm to be given food.' He glared at Scarlett. 'You come with us.'

The three girls soaked through with sea spray stood shivering and sobbing in the drawing room. The sisters, who had met them on the landing, tut tutted and looked at them with sheer bewilderment. Mr Julian paced back and forth in such an ill temper that for a moment he couldn't bring himself to speak. Miss Matilda pulled on the bell pull and Millie appeared wide eyed and open-mouthed as she saw the state of those present in the room.

Miss Emilia ordered, 'Get extra help in from wherever Bessie gets it and tell Ivan urgent word is to be sent requesting Miss Penhallen and Miss Polgrove's father's attend Prospect House immediately, it concerns their daughters. Tell Ivan when this is done, he is required to put more coals on the fire for we need extra heat to warm these poor bedraggled young ladies.'

Moments later, Ivan appeared. 'Words been sent ma'am; two different individuals offered their services.' He then went over to the coal scuttle and heaped more coals on the fire.

Miss Matilda looked through narrowed eyes at Scarlett. 'I should dismiss you immediately with no character. How on earth did you set out to chaperone my niece and her friends for a walk on Hannafore and bring your charges home half drowned. Pray tell us how this despicable occurrence happened. Firstly, though you will take these young ladies upstairs and provide them with suitable dry clothing. You assist with this,' she told Millie. 'Go now before they catch their deaths of cold.'

Scarlett ushered the girls upstairs to Miss Hester's room. Millie gave them towels to dry themselves with. And whilst they looked for suitable dresses in Miss Hester's dressing room, Scarlett ran upstairs and peeled off her wet dress, putting on her grey uniform and twisting her wet hair up and pinning it under her discarded white cap.

When she returned to Miss Hester's room, the girls had stopped sobbing and were attired in dry clothes. She helped Millie brush out their damp hair and neatly plait it. They were too traumatised to make any conversation.

Mr Julian called up the stairs impatient for their return to the drawing room.

'It's not fair Penrose be dismissed,' Miss Maria said, looking back at the others as they trooped downstairs.

'No, indeed it's not,' Miss Hester replied firmly, and Lizzy Polgrove nodded her head in agreement.

Mr Julian stood between the sisters chairs each side of the fire. The heat in the room was stifling. 'What the devil happened,' he demanded.

Miss Matilda looked at the girls then at Scarlett. 'You, down to the kitchen,' she snapped at Millie who was standing by the door hoping to hear more.

Mr Julian came a little closer. 'What happened?'

Chapter 16

Scarlett swallowed and spoke into the silence which had descended on the room. Miss Lizzy blew her nose softly and Miss Emilia looked at her sternly.

'We were walking past the quay when...'—she stumbled over the words—'Mr Adrian Kestrel spotted us from his ship and walked over.'

'It was all my fault,' Miss Maria blurted out, her voice raised and verging on hysterical. All eyes turned in her direction. 'He seemed so gentlemanly and nice when we've met at social functions, at Penhallen and elsewhere. He asked if I knew of his ship the *Black Diamond,* boasted about it, said one day he'd show me over it. So, we disobeyed Penrose when she tried to stop us and went ahead and joined him aboard his ship. It was moored so close to where we were.'

Mr Julian and the sisters looked at her in sheer disbelief. Miss Maria began to sob, blew her nose and quickly carried on. 'Penrose had no option other than to follow us, honestly we thought there no harm in it. But once aboard it became clear Mr Kestrel was drunk, his manner towards us changed, he tried to force us to drink rum and Penrose said we would do no such thing. He held us prisoner below deck, when we protested, he said—' her voice faltered to a whisper '—he threatened to sell us; young white virgins fetched high prices in parts of the world where he travelled.'

The Catt sisters gasped and Miss Emilia's handkerchief shook in her hand as she raised it to her mouth. Scarlett stepped forward and continued to tell what had happened.

'Tis then we heard a thump on the deck overhead, twas my friend's brother, I'd spotted him high up on the rigging of another ship just returned to harbour. He'd seen Adrian Kestrel ushering us aboard the *Black Diamond*, knew this was not where one would expect to see young ladies such as these going. He managed to jump on board, sensing something was amiss. I managed to escape and get past the crewman sent to stand by the cabin door, forcing us to stay there, and ran up on deck to see what was happening.'

'Go on,' Mr Julian encouraged.

'Before the young ladies could return on deck, Kestrel had ordered one of his men to cast off. He was very drunk. There were few crew aboard. They refused at first, saying there weren't enough crew to man the sails. Then Adrian Kestrel got knocked unconscious by a loose sail, and the *Black Diamond* began drifting towards the island.'

Miss Hester spoke then. 'We've Penrose, Jack Jago and the crew to thank that we escaped before the ship began to sink. Mr Chater, one of the crew, showed us were the rowing boat was stored that got us back home safe.'

A thunderous hammering came on the front door making Scarlett jump. She went down to open it and George Penhallen together with another austere and incredibly well-attired man pushed past her and made for the drawing room. Scarlett ran up behind them and stood just inside the door as Miss Maria's father demanded to know from Mr Julian whether his daughter's honour had been compromised by today's devilish escapade. He made no effort to comfort his daughter in the slightest.

'Penrose, you're best set to answer this question,' Mr Julian stated, loosening his cravat, uneasy at such an angry onslaught from a man he considered his friend.

'No, sir, you have no cause for concern on that matter. None of the young ladies were with Mr Kestrel on their own.'

'Come here.' George Penhallen beckoned to his tearful daughter, at first holding her at arm's length, then kissing her on her forehead. 'Dismiss the servant,' he requested loudly. Then I will hear what has happened from you, Julian, in whose care I left my daughter.'

Miss Matilda signalled Scarlett to leave with the nod of her head, and relieved to be away from the stifling heat and atmosphere within the drawing room, she practically ran down to the kitchen.

Jack was sat at the table with Billy, blankets round their shoulders, drinking tea with empty plates bearing the crumbs of eaten cake. He stood up when Scarlett appeared, after what they'd been through both wanted to hug the other, but with Bessie and Ivan seated at the table watching this was impossible. Scarlett sat down opposite Ivan. Her eyes held Jack's and he gave her a sly wink as Bessie poured her a cup of freshly brewed tea and Ivan conveniently looked the other way.

'Has any news come of those aboard the *Black Diamond*?' Scarlett asked hoping Mr Chater and the other crew were safe.

'Nothing yet, but two luggers set out to see what's become of them. Oggie's going to send word here so we knows.'

Bessie sat down and shook her head. 'Well, girl, you've certainly got yourself into a whole lot of bother now,' she exclaimed, and looked at Ivan for support. He tapped his pipe on the table and nodded in agreement. 'If you have your position by the end of today you'm be a lucky maid,' Bessie continued.

'Taint be fair though,' Millie grumbled. 'Tis always the likes of us who pay.'

'If word doesn't come soon that we'm required upstairs, then I'm taking Billy home with me, tis stupid to stay here in wet clothes for nothing. Besides mother's been up and in a right worry,' Jack groaned and tugged the blanket from his shoulders.

'In fact, I think we'll be off now. Them's not interested in the likes of us.' He reached over to Scarlett and laid his hand on her arm.

'You did good, t'would be unforgivable for you to be dismissed. Thankless bastards they'd be. Beg pardon my language, but I only speak the truth.' With that he left and young Billy followed, looking smaller and thinner than ever.

'That boy needs a good meal inside him, I don't think he's had much to eat lately. Not by the way he scoffed my lardy cake up.' She cut a slice for Scarlett and pushed the plate over to her. Only moments later the drawing room bell jangled, and Millie went up.

She came running down almost at once. 'I'm been told to fetch Jack Jago and the cabin boy,' she exclaimed.

'Twer that very posh dressed man as told me to. Didn't dare say they'd gone.'

'You stupid, stupid girl,' Bessie chided, and Ivan looked at Scarlett.

'Run and fetch um back fast as you can.'

And she did, running wildly down Market Lane, like the devil himself was behind her, but once at the end of the lane she abruptly stopped. Gasping for breath she gazed in sheer horror for marching towards Mary Jago's cottage was DeSalles accompanied by at least eight red coats. Rooted to the spot in disbelief, Scarlett saw his beady eye turn towards her. She fled back to Prospect House and forgetting all protocol ran up the stairs and entered the drawing room to summon Mr Julian.

Miss Emilia took a sharp intake of breath at Scarlett's intrusion.

'Out, you insolent girl,' Miss Matilda shouted, but Scarlett stood her ground.

'Mr Julian, please help. DeSalles and red coats are at Jack's cottage. Please come, he needs your help.'

It looked at first as though Mr Julian was going to say no, instead he asked those in the room to excuse him and strode quickly to the door. The austere man quickly followed, having first bowed his head to those present. Together the two men left, striding down the front steps and quickly along the quay, with Scarlett bold enough to leave by the front door.

A struggle was happening on the cobbles outside Mary Jago's cottage. Jack stood with his back pressed up against the wall a semi-circle of red coats holding bayonets to his chest. Mary Jago was screaming and sobbing at the same time, patrons of the Jolly Sailor come out to see what was happening. Others stayed inside fearful of the Redcoats, but brave enough to peer out at them through the windows.

DeSalles held Mary Jago by one of her wrists, she twisted and fought to free herself, she kicked out at DeSalles and brutally with his other hand he took hold her hair dragging her closer to him, then pushed her forward with such force she nearly fell.

'Hold the creature,' he ordered two of the red coats.

Mr Julian strode through the crowd and took in the scene before him. 'For God's sake, man, what do you think you're doing? This young fellow has just rescued three young ladies from being kidnapped. Tell you men to lower their bayonets this minute.'

'And who the hell are you to demand this?' DeSalles answered, sticking his chin out to show his authority. 'I'm here to arrest this scoundrel for an attack on Mr Adrian Kestrel.'

'What attack?' Scarlett watched as now the austere man stepped forward.

DeSalles hadn't seen him and turned round as he spoke, the expression on his face one of shock. He took off his hat and bowed. 'Mr Adrian Kestrel has informed me that previous to today, this fellow attacked him at Penhallen a while ago, sir. I have been seeking him out these past months.'

'At Penhallen?' They had been joined by George Penhallen himself who now stood beside Mr Julian. 'I don't think this young man has ever been on any guest list of mine,' he said in a sardonic voice. 'Pray where did this so-called attack happen?'

DeSalles' pale face took on a sickly pallor. He coughed. 'In the female servants' quarters, so I gather.'

'And what was Adrian Kestrel doing in my female servants' quarters?' George Penhallen questioned.

'I don't rightly know, sir.'

'Did he see his attacker?'

'No, sir.'

'Then why the hell are you here?'

Tis something to do with a servant girl at Prospect House.' DeSalles' eyes sought to find Scarlett in the crowd gathered round. 'Her, sir.' He pointed at Scarlett.

'How come, man?'

'I don't rightly know.'

'I would have likely attacked Adrian Kestrel myself if I'd caught him in my female servants' quarters. I've heard he has somewhat of reputation.'

Mr Julian spoke next. 'I remember there was an incident at Penhallen when Adrian Kestrel was so befuddled with drink that he was found unconscious, he'd fallen and hit his head on a copper fender, but that was nowhere near the servants' quarters.'

'Did he tell you about that?' the austere man asked of DeSalles.

'No, he did not.'

Someone whispered in Scarlett's ear. 'You know who that posh gent is?' Scarlett looked round it was the pot boy from the Jolly Sailor. 'Tis only the High Sheriff of Cornwall!'

Scarlett opened her mouth in shock. 'You sure?'

'I be certain.'

The High Sheriff dismissed the red coats and addressed DeSalles. 'This young man has no crime to answer for, but Adrian Kestrel has.'

He turned round and looked at the crowd. 'Any of you know what's happening about the rescue of them aboard the *Black Diamond*?'

A man stepped forward. 'Yes, sir. Small boat reported them all safe, a lugger'll bring them in shortly.'

He turned to DeSalles. 'On my order, arrest Adrian Kestrel immediately he comes ashore, take him and put him behind bars in the nearest gaol to where the circuit judge is travelling next. Hold him on the charge of kidnap.'

DeSalles stood stunned but immediately issued the order.

The austere man Scarlett now knew to be the High Sheriff of Cornwall turned to Jack and told him, 'Present yourself at Prospect House at noon tomorrow.'

With that, together with Mr Julian, he strode back along the quay. Leaving Jack to comfort his mother.

Scarlett entered Prospect House by the back gate. When she opened the door to the kitchen those within fell silent and stared expectantly at her, Scarlett swayed on her feet feeling lightheaded. She reached out and took hold the back of Ivan's chair to steady herself. 'Tis alright, Jack's safe, Mr Julian and the other gentleman made it so.' Everyone breathed a sigh of relief.

'Sit down, maid,' Bessie fussed, motioning Scarlett to sit in her comfy chair beside the fire. 'Tis all too much.'

Gratefully Scarlett did as she was told. 'Did you know that posh gentleman who's come here, well he's only the High Sheriff of Cornwall.'

'Indeed, we did not!' Millie's eyes lit up with excitement. 'Fancy that and me serving him tea. Though even if he is the High Sheriff, I'm glad them's all not staying on for supper.'

The drawing room bell jangled. 'Up you go, Millie,' Bessie ordered, and loving all the comings and goings Millie quickly departed.

Ivan glanced over at Scarlett. 'Them upstairs will be grateful, I've heard enough of what's taken place to know that, don't be getting despondent for they might not show it. I'm hoping Jack gets some reward, brave lad that he is, you too, maid.'

Scarlett closed her eyes. 'I don't suppose we will,' she sighed, seconds later she was asleep. Bessie left her so, until later when Miss Hester rang her bell.

On tired legs, Scarlett went up to ready her charge for bed. Still shaken by the events of today, Miss Hester was subdued. She too was tired. As Scarlett bent to snuff out her candle, Miss Hester looked up at her. 'I've done my best to see that you're not dismissed. It is my greatest hope my aunts listened to me, Father too.'

'Thank you, it's good to know you've tried.'

A thoughtful Scarlett returned to the kitchen, Bessie saw her downcast face and sent her off to bed where she tossed and turned unable to sleep.

Jack arrived the next day at a quarter to twelve, wearing his very best clothes, his unruly hair a little less untidy. He came by way of the back door thinking it for the best.

Mr Chater had called at Mary Jago's, and taken Billy with him to join the rest of the crew, homeward bound to Fowey aboard the *Jane*. Jack sat awkwardly at the table next to Scarlett, unseen by the others he held her hand tight.

'Millie go up and inform Mr Julian that Jack Jago's here,' Bessie ordered.

'Them's all up there, all three of the young misses' fathers,' Millie excitedly exclaimed when she came back down. 'Can't hear a word of what's being said though,' she grumbled and Jack laughed. Bessie gave Millie a look that silenced any more tittle tackle.

It was well past noon when the bell jangled, and Millie said that Mr Julian was ready to receive him. Jack squeezed Scarlett's hand and gave her one of his most roguish smiles as he followed Millie upstairs.

Moments later Millie was back. 'Mr Julian wants you to join them.'

They were waiting for her in the small room on the ground floor. Scarlett nervously stood beside Jack.

'You are aware, Penrose, of my aunts' strict no-followers' rule for the servants in this house?'

Scarlett nodded and he continued. 'They're not happy at your friendship with Mr Jago. From what I witnessed when you came ashore and what my aunts saw from the drawing room window, we think he is perhaps more than just your friend's brother. And grateful though they are to you both in assisting Miss Hester so bravely and the other young ladies. And the fact that all three girls pleaded that you not be dismissed, Penrose. They are concerned however about the matter. Miss Maria's and Miss Lizzy's fathers have told me there is an easy solution to the problem and discussed it with me. So, I have decided that should you marry, and Penrose you live out, then hopefully my aunts can keep you here in their employ.'

Jack went to speak, but Mr Julian put his hand up. 'I take it you do want to marry?'

'Indeed we do, but—' Jack stated and took the liberty of holding Scarlett's hand.

'Well then,' Mr Julian continued. 'Your family's cottage at the bottom of Horse Lane is far too small to accommodate you. But I do have a solution.'

He looked over to Jack. 'You know Isaac who we've been in discussion with as regards to your assisting him with his work as my bookkeeper. You know also that his eyesight is failing. He is a faithful employee and a stubborn old man who has rejected countless people I have put forward to help him. It was he who mentioned your name. Said you was a clever lad whose education had been paid for by Sir Geoffrey Polgrove in gratitude to your father. I have asked Sir Geoffrey's opinion of you, and he confirmed it was a sad day when you left your education for twas said you were the brightest pupil the school had. It's my hope we can come to an agreement. You'm clever and tis a shame to waste your schooling. Judith Isaac's sister is moving in with him because of his failing eyesight. Therefore, her cottage will become available in Princes Row. As a measure of appreciation, I intend you live in the cottage free of quarterly rent for five years, whether in my employ or not.'

Scarlett let out a cry of pure joy, and Jack was open-mouthed with surprise.

'Thank you, sir, thank you so much,' Scarlett exclaimed, hardly able to contain her self-control, whilst Jack reached forward and shook Mr Julian's hand. 'Thank you, tis very generous of you, sir.'

'Well then, we are agreed on this matter. I will inform my aunts, and obtain a special licence so you can be wed in a couple of weeks. I think this will appease them.'

'I'd marry her tomorrow were it possible,' Jack told him.

'And I him,' Scarlett replied, wanting to jump for joy.

'The family of Hester's friends talked to me yesterday of how they intend to reward you. A message will be sent down tomorrow for you to call upon Sir Geoffrey up at Polgrove. No doubt you will know soon enough what they decide. Go along now,' Mr Julian stated, dismissing the two of them with a nod of the head, then turning to look out of the window.

Millie only just managed to flee from the other side of the door as they emerged. Her footsteps on the stair clearly heard as Jack took Scarlett in his arms twirling her round kissing her over and over until the sound of a brass doorknob being turned sent them scurrying down to the kitchen.

Chapter 17

The following morning, Miss Hester was in a decidedly tetchy mood, bringing Scarlett close to tears. Then unexpectedly Miss Maria arrived and the two left for Penhallen in a splendid coach complete with a livered footman. Miss Hester's mood had lifted before they even left, for she revelled in any type of grandeur.

'Do this, do that, don't pull my hair, where's this, where's that. Fed up I am with her wants this morning,' Scarlett mimicked just as Ivan came in for his morning bread and dripping.

Millie got the strainer from the drawer and poured tea for the four of them stating irritably, 'Sisters' is busy entertaining some roguish looking old blokes from Polruan, I've just taken a tray up, not been that generous with the biscuits, didn't like the looks of um when they arrived.'

'They'll only ring down for more,' Bessie stated, with a shake of the head.

Scarlett watched as Ivan settled himself down. She pulled the note she'd written from her pocket and slid it across the table. 'Can you give this note to Oggie, I need him to give it to Amos when he comes down into Looe this week. I know he always talks with Oggie. It's a message for my mother about what's happened. I can't go marrying without them being there, even if I don't know exactly when it is, proper frustrating that is, I wish Mr Julian would tell us.'

'I'll see to it, maid, pass it on today I will. Oggie'll see Amos has it.'

Scarlett got up and went round the table and gave him a hug. And Bessie smiled, glad that harmony between the two of them was fully restored. It had taken a long time for Scarlett truly to be forgiven by Ivan for her escapade with Jack at Penhallen.

Word came later that Miss Hester was staying at Miss Maria's overnight and Scarlett glad to hear this, happily helped Bessie and Millie prepare the dinner menu which included two extra servings, for the visitors had yet to leave. When finally they did, it was long past 9 o'clock and then 10 o'clock by the time all the washing up was finished with.

With no Miss Hester to prepare for bed, Scarlett sat in the kitchen with Bessie, glad another day of chores was over. Millie had declined her help and was upstairs helping the sisters prepare for bed, she'd never lost the importance that she looked after them, and still guarded this position fiercely.

Bessie chatted on about the captain's housekeeper next door and her choice of clothes. As she nodded in agreement now and then, Scarlett happened to glance out the window. Although it was dark by the light of the half-moon, she saw the back gate swing forward and begin to open. Anxious to see who was there, Scarlett moved her chair a little for a better view. A sharp-eyed Bessie saw this and followed her gaze.

Lit by the oil lamp, Jack saw the two of them looking out, and quickly withdrew into the lane. 'It's that Jack of yours,' Bessie said exasperated. 'No doubt come to tell you what was told him up at Polgrove.'

'What's this?' Millie said excitedly as she came down the stairs. 'Tell him to come in, Scarlett, what you waiting for?'

'Whose kitchen is this, young lady?' Bessie admonished as Scarlett opened the back door and ran down to fetch him in.

There was no time for an illicit kiss because Ivan was just closing the stable door.

'Tis alright, Jack, Bessie says um to come in.' She linked her arm through his. 'Bessie's alright, you just got to get to know her,' Scarlett reassured him, pulling him along with her back inside Prospect House.

Ivan came with them. He too wondered what had been said up at Polgrove. Scarlett pulled Jack out a chair and everyone sat down round the scrubbed table.

'Well, lad, get on with it, we'm all eager to hear what Sir Geoffrey had to say,' Ivan declared. 'We may as well be told by you, saves Scarlett having to repeat it all.'

Suddenly finding himself at the centre of attention, Jack did what he always did when uncertain, and ran his fingers through his tumbling locks. He coughed, and took a deep breath.

'I was shown up to the study. After a while in comes his Lordship, tells me to sit down and offers me a drink. Didn't know what to have so declined the offer. Then he thanks me again for getting Miss Lizzy safely off the *Black Diamond*, called Adrian Kestrel a bounder and hoped the magistrate saw to it he's locked up or transported. Nothing less ull do. Sir Geoffrey poured himself a drink and sat down on a chair facing me. Felt a bit terrified, like when I was summoned to see him twice a year to hear how the tutors had reported on my progress, when he paid for my schooling cause father saved him from drowning. Tutors always reported I outshone the other students, his Lordship not knowing I hated every minute of the place. I remembered as I sat there, his dismay the day I told him I was leaving to go on the boats. That's the last time I was there.'

For a moment he paused.

'Said he'd been discussing with Sir George Penhallen how we could justly be rewarded for getting their daughters to safety. He said a thought had sprung to his friend's mind. A widow from Polperro had come up to Penhallen begging him to buy her late husband's boat. Without a penny to pay the rent and the children hungry, she feared they'd all end up in the workhouse. Sir George had known her erstwhile husband before drink took him to an early grave. Out of pity he bought the *Rose*, had her moored up on the East Looe river waiting to be sold at auction. Sir Geoffrey leant forward. "I'm going to have her taken down to Chowney's, get her rigged out with new sails, then, young Jack, she's yours. We'll pay for the work needed to make her seaworthy," he told me. I was just sat there dumbstruck, thanked him and all that, but couldn't believe what he'd said really. "I know your love of the sea," he says, "she's no good to me. Sir George and I are agreed on this."'

Jack stopped and looked at the faces round him.

'So, what are you saying, you'm been given your own boat?' Scarlett asked grabbing his arm.

'Yes, and I still can't believe it.'

'U'm some lucky bugger.' Ivan reached over and shook his hand. 'This calls for something stronger than tea, Bessie.'

Jack stood up and helped Bessie with the jug of ale. 'I was embarrassed to accept,' he murmured.

'No need for that, him and Penhallen got more bloody money than's proper,' Ivan scoffed.

'No need for swearing,' Bessie rebuked him.

'Well it's the truth.'

'Anyways, he didn't let me go afore he tells me he'd heard I was to be helping Isaac at Mr Julian's office on the quay when I was needed. Said he was glad my schooling was being useful. Said if I ever fully quit seafaring, he'll have work for me either up at the manor in the land office or at one of his newly acquired lime kilns.'

Ivan sat back in his chair. 'Did you know he's never set foot aboard a lugger or any manner of ship again after the day your father hauled him out of the water half drowned? That's the reason he'd prefer you to give up seafaring. But good on you, lad, Sir Julian and the other gents have done you proud. And I might add I reckon I knows whose boat the *Rose* was,' Ivan declared lightly tapping his pipe on the table. 'Twas old Lenny Butlers, sturdy boat she be, you'm done well there. Silly bastard took to the drink and him still a young un, fell in with a bad crowd of drinkers in Polruan.'

Jack held on to Scarlett's hand. 'Tell the truth I can't quite believe all this, a place to live, me own boat and soon a wife as well.' He grinned. 'I'll see to it Mr Chater, Billy and the others get some kind of acknowledgement for their part in our escape. I just wish Father and Luke were back here to share in my good fortune.'

'Tis any day now, lad,' Ivan reassured him, and picked up his hat from the table. 'I'd best go and settle Dolly down for the night. She'll be busy in the morning. Master Julian said I was to tell you you're to be here early tomorrow, Jack, we've much to do. Judith goes to live down at her brothers, she hasn't much to move, but there's enough we'll need to take the small wagon with us. And I'm warning you, Judith is a very fussy old spinster.'

'So tomorrow you move Judith.' Scarlett looked at the two of them round eyed. 'So, you know where the cottage is?'

'Yes, but you'm not seeing it till our wedding day and promise you'll not try and find out where it is.'

'Why?' Scarlett asked tilting her head to one side.

'Just because, that's all.' Jack laughed.

Ivan lifted the latch on the back door.

'I'd best be off too,' Jack sighed. 'What with this old bugger expecting me back here at the crack of dawn.'

'Less of the old,' Ivan retorted placing his hat firmly on his head and opening the door wide, letting in a blast of cold air. Jack bade Bessie and Millie goodnight and followed him out into the chilly night. Scarlett slipped out behind them. Ivan went on walking down the path, but Jack stopped and pulled Scarlett into his arms, kissing her with such passion she was left gasping for breath. His next kiss was more gentle, and would have lasted much longer had Bessie not knocked on the window.

'In now before you two get too carried away,' she said loudly through the glass. Jack brushed Scarlett's lips with his once more.

'I love you,' he declared as Bessie tapped the window once again.

The next day word came that Miss Hester was staying longer over at Penhallen. Scarlett busily packed a trunk full of clothes she may need, for there was no word when she would be coming home. She did this gladly for life was always better when Miss Hester and her tantrums were away.

Once the trunk had been dispatched and after the sisters had finished their dinner, Ivan came into the kitchen, but however hard Scarlett and Millie tried, Ivan would give no hint of where Judith's cottage was, only that she was moved out. Jack had gone straight into Mr Julian's office afterwards to help Isaac and was later going to seek out his newly acquired boat. For the next two days, life at Prospect House settled back into an uneasy routine.

That is until Millie back from an errand burst through the back door to say the *Sunrising* had just entered the harbour. A crowd was at this very minute gathered to greet the ship's return. Scarlett wished she could leave peeling the carrots and join them but knew that was impossible. Feeling imprisoned in Prospect House, Scarlett was quiet for the rest of the morning. Mr Julian had joined the sisters for luncheon and as Scarlett helped dry the dishes afterwards a bell jangled and when Millie answered it Mr Julian asked that Scarlett be sent up to the small room he used as his study.

A nervous Scarlett took off her apron, tucked loose strands of hair under her cap and went upstairs. She knocked and entered feeling both excited and apprehensive.

'It is all arranged that you shall marry on the 21st. I shall be taking my aunts out for the day to Duloe to visit their cousin, thus making it possible for Bessie and Millie to attend the service, and of course Ivan. I will see to it that Hannah Reeve, landlady of the Jolly Sailor, is suitably paid for a small gathering afterwards if it be your wish. My sisters-in-law will require dinner as usual later so the others must return in time to prepare for this.'

'Thank you, sir.' Scarlett bobbed a curtsey. 'Tis very kind of you.' Her mind was a whirl wondering how many days the 21st was away.

'I'll see to it Jack Jago's informed today,' Mr Julian continued, 'and my daughter asked that I give you this.'

He handed her a folded note her name clearly written in Miss Hester's hand. Scarlett put it in her pocket. 'Thank you, sir. I'll read it later.'

'One other matter. Mr Adrian Kestrel came before the court yesterday and despite his brother's plea for lenience, he has been sentenced to transportation for life. He leaves from Par with other convicts next week. No other young woman will fear him.'

'Tis good news that, sir.'

'Sir Charles Penhallen and I will travel to Par to ensure no bribery can see him walk a free man.'

'No doubt he would stoop to any means so he could stay...' Scarlett began.

'Indeed, he would. You may go now,' came a rather curt dismissal.

Scarlett curtsied and left the room, her heart sang. They had a date to get wed. Down in the kitchen, Bessie and Millie watched her descend the stairs their mouths open with anticipation.

'Tis to be the 21st. You've got leave to come to the wedding for Mr Julian's taking his sisters to Duloe. Tis only dinner they be requiring. Ivan is allowed to come as well.'

'Never in all my years of service have I known such as this. Don't go getting no airs and graces above your station, tis purely a gesture of the master's good will.' Bessie bent down to fetch bread from the bread oven and Millie grinned at Scarlett.

'Best see what I can find to wear then,' she exclaimed. 'Oh, this is so exciting. Does Jack know?'

'Mr Julian's telling him later.' Scarlett pulled Miss Hester's note from her pocket. 'He gave me this, it's from Miss Hester.'

'Well don't waste time, maid, open it up.'

She read it out. *To Penrose I give my permission for you to borrow any dresses you may deem suitable for your wedding should you so want. Together with shoes and any other items. The new dresses Miss Smith delivered recently are more suited to that of a young lady and not so girlish as many I have. I thank you and Mr Jago once more on behalf of the three charges you protected that day.* It was signed *Hester*.

'Didn't expect that,' Millie exclaimed. 'We'm be having a look before bed then, can't wait. Just shows she does have a heart after all. Makes all them tantrums worth it.' Scarlett smiled, and looked over towards Bessie who was muttering loudly for with all the amount of distraction in the kitchen the bread had burnt slightly, and she was a perfectionist.

Scarlett knew already the dress she would choose. It was a blue printed cotton with a repeating pattern of tiny roses. As Miss Smith had carefully unfolded it, Scarlett had fallen in love with it, longed to have a dress so delicate and perfect. Miss Hester on the other hand was in a sulk for the pink satin dress she liked best had been a little tight and Miss Smith had a terrible job getting her to stand still whilst she made some adjustments.

That night instead of going straight to bed, Scarlett and Millie took their candle holders and went into Miss Hester's bedroom. Millie lit the oil lamp on the small table beside the nightstand, both of them had a fit of the giggles feeling decidedly naughty as they opened Miss Hester's closet.

Millie took out several dresses to look at, but Scarlett took out the blue printed dress and lay it on the bed.

'Oh! So that's the one you like,' Millie enthused as she helped Scarlett out of her grey servant's uniform. 'It is nice. You'll look a treat,' she declared. 'But them boots won't do, will they?' Kneeling down she picked out a pair of pale blue pumps. Scarlett unlaced her boots and slipped her feet into them. Carefully she slipped on the dress. She stared at the mirror not believing how perfect the dress looked.

'One last thing, I'll be doing your hair, how about this?' She opened a drawer and poked about inside, then picked out a crystal hairclip Miss Hester wore to the recent ball in Liskeard.

'I can't wear that.' Scarlett laughed and shook her head. 'Tis too pretentious, like I'm some posh lady or something. I know what won't look too silly.' And she picked out a sprig of white flowers made of satin that Miss Hester wore clipped into her hair.

'Come here. Sit down,' Millie ordered, and without preamble picked up Miss Hester's elaborate silver hair brush and having unfastened Scarlett's tight bun, began to fashion her hair in a far better looser style, then fastened in tiny white bows of silk ribbon, passing Scarlett a mirror so she could see her creation.

'Millie, that's lovely,' she exclaimed, eyes welling with tears.

'You'm be perfect, wait til Jack sees what your wearing. Leave him speechless it will.'

The next day Ivan surprised them all by saying Mr Julian told him the small pony and trap could be used on the day of the wedding should it be needed, which sent Scarlett immediately into a frenzy of indecision. Then looking over at Bessie Ivan added, 'I seen Luke Jago early this morning, he's gone out to Lanreath, borrowed a horse from that miserable sod Nettles.' He paused, and looked towards Scarlett. 'Twas Bessie here told me to tell your mother and Amos the date you'm to be wed and where, them's to come here in the morning first before you leave for the church. Have a wedding breakfast beforehand.'

'Thank you, Bessie.' Scarlett ran over and gave her a warm hug. 'That's so thoughtful of you.'

'And afterwards we'll all walk to St Nicholas together, tis best and will be so special,' Scarlett stated, giving Bessie another hug.

'Wot you wearing?' Millie asked Ivan. Scarlett thought she saw a faint blush on his cheeks above his beard.

'Never you mind, cheeky maid,' he grunted, tapping his pipe on the table. 'I'll ask you now. Wot you wearing and you Bessie? Got to see we do Scarlett proud. Fetch out your best hats and all that.'

'Never you mind about us either, we'll not let her down,' Bessie replied, 'will we?' She looked at Millie who nodded her head in agreement.

On Sunday, Jack met Scarlett outside the back gate as usual. 'This is the last time I'll be doing this,' his greeting.

'Indeed it is,' Scarlett replied, slipping her arm through his.

'Thought we'd go up and try and have a word with Ruth, make sure she'll be able to come on the 21st. Luke was going to, but I told him we would. Ruth can ask to change her half day off and maybe have an extra hour if that old witch she works for allows. Tis her brother's wedding after all.'

'I'm not sure it's going to be that easy, tis an austere household the mistress up there runs,' Scarlett reminded him as she linked her arm through his. It was lovely to be out of Prospect House and breathing in fresh air.

They climbed up the lane to the servants' entrance at Polgrove and pulled the bell. The square of wood behind the small grill shot back and an unfamiliar face looked out. 'What do you want, who are you?' the girl with the red blotched face asked.

'I want to see my sister Ruth Jago if you please. Can you fetch her out here?'

'I could but why should I?'

'Because I'm asking you nicely, that's why.'

With that, the face vanished leaving the wooden square open. Moments later Ruth's face appeared. 'I've moments only, mistress is busy looking at material samples with her dressmaker from London. She'll soon be ringing for me.'

'Tis next Saturday we're to be wed, at 11.00 try and get your mistress to change your day off, do what you can so you can be there. Father and Luke's back home, tis a must you come.'

'I'll try my hardest, I will, I promise. If not, I'll just come anyway, what's the worst they can do?'

'You can't do that; you'll be dismissed without papers. Don't be stupid,' Jack chided.

'It won't be long before Sam and I are gone from Looe, tis all arranged up in Hotwells. His aunt's happy to have us stay with her and his uncle's got him an apprenticeship to be a proper shipwright at one of the big ship builders. Twill be a new beginning for us. I can find work up in the fine houses in Clifton.'

'But until then you need to be employed and take with you a good reference.'

'You sure you want to marry my bossy brother?' Ruth teased, as from nearby someone was anxiously calling her name. 'I'll be there and keep me blessed job somehow, don't fret.' And then she was gone.

'Family's gone to Polperro to tell my uncles and grandparents about us getting wed. Them's a lively crowd my Polperro relatives, sure to liven things up.'

'You'm have more folks there than me, but I'm happy with mother and Amos and my good friends from Prospect House.'

'Sail maker's doing a fine job. I'll be bringing her downriver soon. It's strange, me owning my own boat, like I've said before, I still can't believe it.'

'And me, we've a cottage.'

They sat on the wall at the top of Horse Lane, Jack with his arm round Scarlett, at peace with the world around them.

'Shall we go down to my cottage?' Jack whispered in her ear.

'No wouldn't be right, not with your parents out, daft it is with us being wed next week but I'd rather not.' In truth she was still a little afraid of Tom Jago.

'That's fine, come on I know where we can go.'

The quay was quiet it being Sunday, so no one saw them sneak aboard *Sunrising*, those outside the Jolly Sailor too inebriated to care anyway. Thus, they spent their last Sunday before being wed snuggled together in a single bunk, oblivious to the roll of the schooner on the river's rising tide or the sound of *Sunrising*'s wooden hull bumping against the lugger berthed alongside her.

As Jack took his leave of her back at Prospect House, he joked, 'Next time we meet twill likely be at the church.'

'I know, tis a busy week here, the sisters having visitors staying from Redruth, I know I can't escape.'

'I've said I'll sail along with Father and Luke down to Penryn with John Pearce, there's tea and sugar needs collecting from Father's friend.'

'Contraband.'

'Yes, but it'll be thrown overboard first sign of trouble, we'll be back late Thursday early Friday depending on the tide. Don't take on. They need my help.'

'I wish you hadn't told me, I'll worry now.'

'Don't, I told you because you may hear from someone or Ivan may and say something to you. So tis best you know. Twill be alright and a nice bit of money in it an all.'

Scarlett put her arms around his neck and hugged him like she'd never let him go.

'Our lives must go on as they were, my love,' he said softly when at last she let him go.

'Take care, promise me you'll take care.'

'I've a bride to come home to, of course I'll take care, you go in now and no worrying. And no telling a soul what I'm about. Definitely not Millie, she'm wouldn't mean to but I know she's often sent out on errands and might say something, you know what she's like for gossiping.'

'She wouldn't, but I won't tell a soul, I promise.'

Jack bent and kissed her one last time before opening the gate and holding it back for her to pass through. Scarlett knew she wouldn't stop worrying until he was safe home. Knew she had years of such fear ahead.

A strange week followed. The sisters' visitors arrived from Redruth. Alma and Warwick Cooper, a middle-aged couple of a quiet disposition. Apart from the extra work involved in preparing their rooms, for they demanded separate bedrooms, and the extra provisions need for their stay, they were undemanding in their requirements.

The house ran as smoothly as it always did, each morning Scarlett presented the sisters with the daily menu Bessie had written out for their approval. Bessie herself was called on only once that week to attend them personally when Miss Emilia requested a dish be served they'd enjoyed recently at the Duloe rectory, and which she wanted to describe in its finest detail to cook herself. On all the other days the menus were agreed upon and Scarlett dismissed, later to carry out her duties as housekeeper when friends of the couple arrived for afternoon tea and twice for luncheon. Never once throughout the week did the sisters make any mention of Scarlett's forthcoming wedding.

'Putting you firmly in your place,' Bessie retorted when Scarlett mention this fact.

'Never mind, maid, at least they didn't send you packing, thanks to you and Jack bringing the young ladies safe home. If they'd discovered you had a follower without that deed being done, you'd have been gone, missy. And here's something you don't know; they've said Florrie's eldest can come in and help Millie evenings with the washing up and the likes so you can get off home after the preparations for dinner are over. Also knowing that Jack is often likely to be at sea, you may stay in your present room overnight when it suits you to. So them's not that bad. Miss Hester's very precious to them and the two of you took care of her, so no grumbling.'

'When did they tell you about Clover helping?' Scarlett and Millie exclaimed both at the same time.

'When you two was busy upstairs this morning.'

'Why didn't you tell us earlier?'

'Because for once I was keeping that juicy bit of gossip to myself. Besides you two have been run off your feet all day.'

***

So between keeping those above stairs happy, Millie's constant excitement about the wedding and worrying about Jack, for Scarlett the week passed by quickly.

On Thursday the visitors left. Scarlett helped Millie strip the beds and make them up with fresh linen, for the larger room Mr Julian used when he stayed over from time to time.

The windows faced out overlooking the river. Scarlett pulled back the drapes drawn almost together as were those in the rest in the house. She wondered what the visitors thought of this odd custom here at Prospect House. As she gazed out, she realised she had no idea of even which boat her Jack had sailed on, no specific bow sprites or quirky set of the masts to identify it with.

Millie declared the coals in the grate still hot, so they left them for later and trooped downstairs to perform the rest of the day's mundane duties.

Much later when the final saucepan had been scrubbed, dried and hung on its hook, Scarlett and Millie finally sat down. Millie had a blister and took off her boots hoping neither sister would ring their bell for her, hoping for a moment's rest.

Bessie sent Scarlett to fill the kettle from the well in the yard, she came back walking slowly so not to slop water on the flagstone floor. Carefully she hung the kettle above the fire, and Bessie unlocked the tea caddy, it had been a long day and thankfully the bells stayed silent, and the three of them enjoyed their tea without being summoned.

Ivan came in joining them in their contented silence. 'Just seen your Jack,' he announced, watching the look of sheer relief light up Scarlett's face.

Chapter 18

Just hearing Ivan say those words meant that Scarlett slept well that night. When she woke the next morning, sunlight was streaming in through her window. Miss Hester's dress hanging from a hook on her bedroom door gave her a feeling of reality and how short a time it was until Saturday.

Already Bessie and Millie had their Sunday Best pressed and ready and Ivan, when asked on the Friday morning, assured the enquiring females he was quite prepared and indeed Florrie had been seen earlier delivering a parcel to him. Thus, the Friday passed in much the same way as any other only with those below stairs in a fever of excitement and anticipation.

That night Scarlett hardly slept. She was up early and the day began with a strange normality of ritual with Millie sorting out the sisters, taking up their morning breakfast, bring down the tray, the only difference being she had to assist with their preparations to leave for Duloe.

Mr Julian arrived, and Scarlett let him in. He handed her his hat and wished her well, which was nice. The sisters on the other hand said nothing as she held the door open for their departure. She watched as Mr Julian helped them into the waiting hired coach. Neither turned their head in her direction as the coachman signalled the horses to move off. 'Good riddance,'

Scarlett muttered under her breath as she closed the front door.

Everyone downstairs was pleased they were gone. Now they could concentrate on getting Scarlett and themselves ready for her big day. Scarlett decided to wait until her mother came to put on her dress unless of course it got too late, and so Bessie and Millie got ready first. As Bessie returned to the kitchen and fussed over the feather on her extremely large hat, Ivan came into the kitchen looking very tidy indeed. Florrie had done him proud.

A little after 11.00, Scarlett's mother arrived with Amos. After much hugging and welcoming Bessie sat them down with tea. Jeanette patted her daughter's arm and nodded in the direction of the stairs. 'Come on, it's time you were getting yourself ready.'

Those in the kitchen smiled to each other as Jeanette followed Scarlett upstairs. When they reached her attic room, Scarlett's mother held out a parcel. 'I've brought you this.'

Scarlett set it down on the bed and untied the ribbon, inside was a beautiful delicate white nightgown, the yoke embroidered with tiny rosebuds. Her mother must have spent many hours sewing this so finely.

'Thank you so much.' She reached out for Jeanette, who moved closer to her daughter.

'Tis my pleasure, maid. And while we have this precious time alone there's words I must say. I know you and Jack are probably more close than is proper already, so happen there's nowt you want telling on that score.' Scarlett nodded and blushed crimson. 'Tis a word of advice, serious advice about the secret past we share.'

Scarlett went over to the door and opened it, just to make sure Millie was nowhere near. She led her mother over to the window.

Jeanette took her daughter's hands in hers and took a deep breath. 'Promise me, maid, you'll never tell Jack about your father and what he did. Do not divulge his hideous past. It is our shameful secret alone. Amos, I will never tell, and yes, I feel guilty, but believe me it is for the best. Loyalty hereabouts is fiercely protective, men died because your father informed on them, and that won't ever be forgiven. Always, always remember Sennen, the good folks there found out they had a traitor in their midst and twas immediate they turned on us, would have killed your father if he'd been home. I was frightened for our lives; we were hated along with him.'

Scarlett hugged her mother close. 'I'll never tell I promise, though the guilt he was a traitor to the likes of good men like Jack and Amos weighs heavy.'

For a moment mother and daughter stood side by side looking down at the river. Scarlett passing her mother a handkerchief as she shed a tear before smiling bravely. 'He got away with being a spy because he didn't testify in court, that's how he remained obscure, out of sight, unseen by those who could recognise him. I had you to think about and no money, I couldn't leave him, cold and cruel as he was. I swear I knew not what he was when I married him.'

Scarlett's eyes fill with tears and Jeanette passed the handkerchief back to her daughter, both held each other tightly as if forever, like the secret they held within. Jeanette finally let go of her daughter. 'Tis over though, and we must enjoy our lives, he can't hurt us any more.'

The sound of footsteps on the stair made them turn.

'Come on, there's a handsome young man soon to be waiting at the altar to make you his wife,' Millie shouted out knocking on the door.

'Come in,' mother and daughter called out together. The day had really begun.

The dress was laid out ready on the bed, the shoes and the white ribbons to be placed in her hair on the bedside table. A new chapter in Scarlett's life was waiting to begin.

'You look lovely,' Jeanette exclaimed as Scarlett with Millie's help slipped on Miss Hester's delicate dress and shoes. Millie fussed, neatly pinning her hair and fastening in the tiny bows of white ribbon. Finally, she was ready, her mother and Millie looked at her with faces brimming over with affection.

'Come on, let's go down to Miss Hester's room and you can see just how gorgeous you look in her long mirror,' Millie encouraged, and the three of them went downstairs, Millie leading the way. Scarlett looked back at her mother who gave her an encouraging smile.

Scarlett couldn't quite believe it was her who looked back from the long mirror. She took a deep breath and for a moment everything seemed quite unreal. Then came the sound of laughter drifted up from the basement kitchen.

'Seems them's celebrating already,' Millie giggled, 'we'd best go down.'

In the kitchen there were gasps as Scarlett walked down the stairs. Amos stood up and walked over to take Scarlett's hand as she stepped down onto the flagstone floor.

Millie hastened to put on her best ivory straw hat and Bessie pinned on her hat complete with a neatly attached feather. Scarlett and Millie exchanged a look, knowing Bessie's favourite topic of conversation was what the housekeeper next door wore on her head.

'You ready?' Jeanette asked her daughter.

'Yes, I'm ready.' Scarlett looked around at everyone and smiled.

'Well we best be away. You sure you want to walk? I can have Miss Hester's trap ready in no time, tis no bother,' Ivan questioned.

'No, I'll walk, thank you.'

Ivan gave her a fond lingering look.

Amos held his arm out to Jeanette. 'We'll go on ahead, I'll be waiting for you at the church steps.'

Scarlett kissed her mother and gave Amos a peck on the cheek.

Jeanette patted her daughter's hand. 'Don't go being nervous, the sun's shining down on you, tis your day and Jack's.' Amos opened the door and they walked down the path.

Ivan stepped forward. 'May I have the pleasure of escorting you to your wedding?' he said and grinned.

Ivan walked her down the path, waiting as Bessie locked the back door. As they set off down Market Lane, Ivan stated, 'We should have left by the front door.'

But Scarlett shook her head. 'Wouldn't have felt proper to do that. We're alright.'

Folks along the way were all smiling and wishing her well. All knew of the wedding taking place that day. For a moment, Scarlett felt overwhelmed as she saw Amos waiting for her at the foot of the steps outside St

Nicholas Church surrounded by a crowd of well-wishers. Oggie stood a little way off, he touched his battered hat as a gesture of greeting and gave her a rare smile.

Proudly Ivan handed Scarlett over to Amos as Bessie and Millie went on inside the church. 'You look real pretty, maid,' Amos declared, a beaming smile upon his face. 'Young Jack's all done up; hardly recognised the rascal,' he quipped, making Scarlett giggle, erasing the nerves she felt inside.

At the top of the church steps they stopped and turned to the left as two of Jack's fellow crew members from the *Sunrising* opened the doors.

Scarlett held tightly on to Amos's arm as the organ began to play, so pleased he was beside her as she walked down the aisle. They were all there, the friends she'd made over the recent years. All heads turned towards her, broad smiles upon their faces. Ruth and Sam were seated behind Jack, Ruth gave a little hidden wave. Even Miss Clementine and Opal were there, seated alongside Florrie and her daughter Clover.

Standing before the alter was the Rev Stone. But the only person who mattered to Scarlett was Jack, her handsome Jack, who stood gazing down the aisle at her waiting to make her his bride. He smiled that special smile of his which showed the dimples in his cheeks, and his unruly black curls still tumbled forward however carefully tamed.

The words spoken and hymns sang seemed to go past in a haze of heightened emotion. Jack placed a slim gold band on her finger, and Scarlett looked deep in his smiling brown eyes as each said the words that would make them man and wife. The kiss that followed so loving, so passionate that the Rev Stone gave a little cough. They drew apart and the happiness Scarlett felt now that she was Jack's wife she would treasure for ever.

Then all too soon the service was over, and they were outside once more in the sunshine. Jack holding her hand tight in his as friends gathered round.

Mindful of Miss Hester's delicate dress, Scarlett went carefully down the steps, and hand in hand with Jack walked the short step across to the Jolly Sailor, thankful that Hannah Reeve had opened up a separate door to the side of the inn for them to enter. Bessie had been in a tizzy the night before, most concerned about entering such an establishment by the main door.

The money given to Hannah Reeve the landlady had been spent wisely. For the guests, long tables were set out in the centre of the tap room with a cold luncheon of roast beef and mutton. There were sweetmeats and fancies usually confined to the gentry and ale and spirits aplenty.

Luke stood up to make a speech then sat down again feeling far too nervous. Tom Jago took his place, praising his son, saying how proud the Jagos were of him, and got a rapturous applause. Tom Jago himself looked quite handsome dressed in his best.

Scarlett nestled into Jack's shoulder.

'Twas worth saving them young ladies, that's for sure, my love.'

'I wonder if they're thinking of us today?' Scarlett queried.

'No, I'm sure they're not,' Jack replied. 'Maybe your Miss Hester, she's less of a toff than the rest.'

'Tis a dress of hers I'm wearing; said I could borrow any I liked. That was kind.'

'And I'm sure it looks better in the wearing on you than it would on her.'

With the food consumed, Scarlett saw the fiddler talking with Luke and Sam. How glad she was that Sam having helped Jack hide aboard ship that day had mended the rift between the two families. There was a fluster of movement then as they asked folks to stand up and the tables and benches were moved to the sides of the tap room.

The fiddler stepped into the middle of the room and struck up a merry tune. Jack led Scarlett out to whoops of hollering and merriment. Soon they were surrounded by others dancing to the fiddler's pace. Even Bessie and Ivan joined in, which sent Scarlett and Millie into fits of giggles. Sadly, all too soon it was time for Bessie and Millie to return to Prospect House to begin preparations for the sisters' arrival home.

'Taint fair us having to leave,' Millie declared angrily, a little wobbly on her feet either through dancing and twirling round too many times or too much of the rum punch she'd been drinking.

Bessie linked her arm through Millie's and reassured Scarlett. 'She'm be all right, fresh air will sober her up if tis the punch.' Reluctantly they left saying their good-byes and were followed not long after by Scarlett's mother and Amos.

'Nights are drawing in now, we've a long way to go so I'll get back to the stables and harness the pony and trap, and we'd best be on our way.'

'I'll see to the harnessing,' Ivan said, joining them. 'I'll take a walk over with you.'

Jeanette hugged her daughter and Amos patted Jack on the back. 'All the luck in the world to ye both, only wish I was a young un again.'

It was sad seeing them leave, the wedding guests were getting louder now and the fiddler playing faster.

'Tis time I took you home,' Jack whispered, brushing his hand gently down her thigh beneath the table.

'If you say so, husband,' Scarlett replied. A blush crept up her neck for she was sure Ruth and Sam who she was seated with had overhead Jack's words, for they turned to each other and smiled knowingly.

Jack made his way to where the Jagos both young and old had gathered. He whispered in his mother's ear and Mary Jago turned to smile across at Scarlett. Once back, Jack put his arm round her and leaned forward to Ruth and Sam. 'Tis time we were gone,' he teased.

'Good man.' Sam winked at him and Ruth squeezed Scarlett's hand.

'Twill be me and Sam soon,' she said with a hint of envy.

The fiddler's tune picked up an even faster pace, and happy to leave the revellers in such high spirits, Jack and Scarlett slipped outside through the little door the pot boy had used when he'd robbed them of their first kiss, which seemed an age ago, him appearing just as the deed was to be done.

But, of course, they hadn't escaped being seen by those sitting on the benches outside the Jolly who loudly cheered as they crossed the square. Jack turned and bowed to much cheering and lewd comments. He held Scarlett's hand tight in his as he led her to the steps in the corner of the square. At the top, they followed the path as it wound round to the right and climbed upwards, it was dusk by now. Scarlett stopped for a moment and looked over towards the river and sea beyond. A salty breeze had blown in on the tide. Flickering candlelight came from the cottages clustered below. Hand in hand they walked on up the path which led them high above the rooftop of the Jagos' cottage and others on Horse Lane. Finally, it widened out and there stood three stand-alone cottages.

'Come on.' Jack quickened his pace pulling Scarlett along.

'Which one was Judith's – is ours?' Scarlett begged to know. Jack stopped.

'This one. This is our new home. Come here, my precious wife.' With ease he lifted Scarlett off her feet and into his arms. With his shoulder he pushed open the door.

In the grate embers glowed and by the light of these Scarlett thought she saw some familiar furniture from Tamarisk, but had no time to find out if this was so, as quickly Jack strode across the room. There was a narrow door in the corner with a tiny brass knob.

'Pull it open,' Jack told her.

Scarlett did so. The staircase twisted round and at the top was a single room. Against the far wall was an ornate brass bed, which seemed overly large in such a small space.

'Twas Judith's bed but all else has come from Lanreath, a gift from Amos and your mother,' Jack explained as he lay Scarlett gently on the bed, and the thick feather mattress beneath the coverlet and sheets engulfed her in its softness.

Gently Jack removed her shoes and walked round to the other side of the bed, pulling off his boots, and for a moment lay on the bed beside her.

'I love you,' he whispered, smoothing her hair.

'And I you, husband,' Scarlett giggled, before each ripped the other's clothes from their body, even Miss Hester's delicate dress was cast aside in a heap, one pearl button rolling across the floor as it was undone with such haste.

As darkness fell and a half-moon shone over West Looe, Judith's big brass bed creaked and groaned with the rhythmic passion of those who occupied it. Something that would be repeated on many a night in the days and years to come.

Lightning Source UK Ltd.
Milton Keynes UK
UKHW041048100820
367987UK00004B/1232